WORLD OF NEVEYAH

TOWER OF BONES

CONNIE J. JASPERSON

Connie J. Jasperson

ISBN-13: 978-1-68063-012-1

ISBN-10: 1-68063-012-1

Fantasy Castle © Mega11 | Dreamstime.com
Map of Neveyah © Connie J. Jasperson
Special thanks to Eagle Eye Editors

Published by Bard Books
A subsidiary of
Myrddin Publishing Group

Contact us at: www.myrddinpublishinggroup.com

This book is dedicated to Greg, with all my heart and all my love. Your support and belief in me mean more to me than mere words can possibly express.

Sherrie DeGraw, you are more than merely a sister; you are my best friend in this life. Your wise reading shapes my words.

This book wouldn't exist without the hard work and sincere efforts of Maria V. A. Johnson, Carlie M.A. Cullen, Irene Roth Luvaul, Alison DeLuca, Danielle Raver, and Mark Kenney.

This book has evolved over several incarnations, and the hundreds of hours spent combing it for errors and typos were appreciated more than you will ever know.

BOOKS BY CONNIE J. JASPERSON

WORLD OF NEVEYAH
Tower of Bones (Tower of Bones series book I)
Forbidden Road (Tower of Bones series book II)
Mountains of the Moon (forthcoming 2015)

HUW THE BARD

TALES FROM THE DREAMTIME

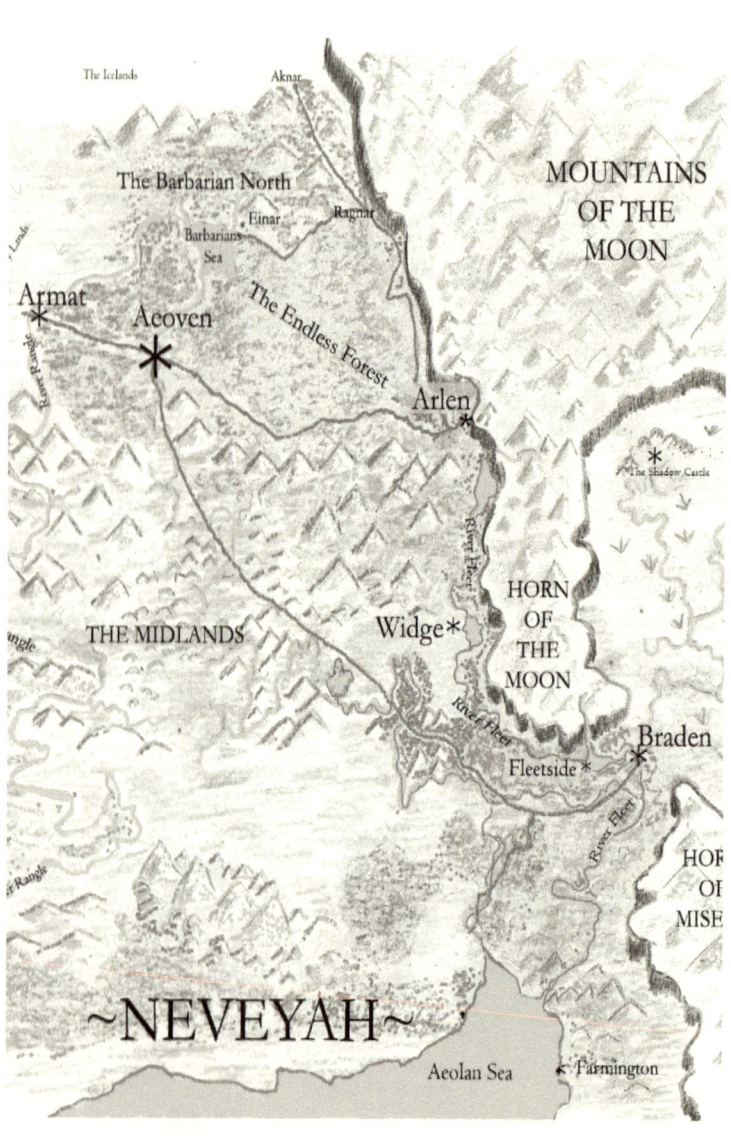

The Icelands

Aknar

The Barbarian North

MOUNTAINS
OF THE
MOON

Einar

Ragnar

Barbarians
Sea

Armat

Aeoven

The Endless Forest

River Rangle

Arlen

The Shadow Castle

River Fleet

Widge

HORN
OF
THE
MOON

THE MIDLANDS

River Fleet

Braden

Fleetside

River Fleet

HOR
OF
MISE

~NEVEYAH~

Aeolan Sea

Farmington

Chapter 1

Staggering as he landed hard, Edwin Farmer looked at his surroundings, startled and completely disoriented. "What the...! What the heck just happened?"

Nothing was familiar to him. Judging by the position of the enormous crescent moon, he thought it must be the early hours before dawn. Yet, it was midmorning only a few moments before, when he fell through the rocks and into this strange place.

"Somehow Dad knew." Edwin stood, numbly looking around, still too stunned to think clearly. "He knew this was going to happen." His low mumbles sounded out of place in the dark silence of the prairie.

It was already one of the strangest days of his life, and it had barely begun.

The day began normally enough. Right before breakfast, he loaded the cart with bushels of apples as his father asked him. He probably should have bonded and left home long before this particular morning, but he found even the girls in Markett unexciting. He'd not yet met the special girl, though he dreamed of her often.

He knew her face as well as he knew his own.

Tall and muscular from hard work on the farm, with long, sun-bleached blonde hair and frank, blue eyes, Edwin wasn't the best looking man in Markett, but something about him made women unable to look away from him.

Things began going wrong after breakfast, when Edwin rounded the corner of the sheep pen. With some chagrin, he noticed the gate was slightly ajar. Counting heads, he found one had escaped. "This is great. The sheep can escape, but I am still stuck here, rotting." Muttering to himself, he closed the gate on the rest and set out to look for the stray.

He went back into the farmhouse to tell his father and quickly made a lunch to take with him since searching could take a while. In Edwin's opinion, sheep were sometimes sly, crafty creatures, and one never knew what to expect next from them.

His father looked up. He said, "A missing sheep you say.... You do know you were not born around here, right?" Edwin nodded, wondering what direction his father was going. John Farmer wasn't a man who made idle conversation. "I left home once long ago. It started with me following a missing sheep. I found myself somewhere far away, in another world, really. This is the way it always begins in our family."

Edwin waited for his father to continue, not sure now as to what was going on. "Dad, have we received bad news?"

"No. Yes, in a way." Not acknowledging his son's bewildered scrutiny, John Farmer looked out the window, thinking. He turned back to Edwin, saying, "Look, son. There's a lot I haven't told you, and much my father didn't tell me. Please don't be too angry with me when you get to where you're going. It is simply better this way. Do you understand what I'm saying?"

Edwin nodded, completely confused. "I think so. Maybe."

John continued. "My father was right. If you have no preconceived notions, you can accomplish so much more. It's just…I was unable to finish the job, and from what I've heard lately, you won't be able to either. Just do the right thing. You will know what it is when the time comes." His father's expression changed from unhappy to resigned. "I'll be here when you return, no matter how long it takes."

He stood and hugged his surprised and perplexed son. "I knew this day was coming, but I didn't expect it so soon. Don't worry about me. I'll be fine. Take your time and do the job right. Say hello to Halee and Garran for me when you see them." John put on his hat and left for Markett with his wagonload of apples, leaving a rather stunned Edwin to find the missing sheep.

Edwin stared after his departing father. *What was Dad talking about? He actually hugged me.* Although he was having a strange morning, it made a nice change from the usual grind. He said aloud, "I'll make Dad talk to me this evening when he gets back from town."

He left the house, following the wandering trail of the sheep. It wound over every hectare of the farm, and he followed it for nearly an hour until he came to an outcropping.

The outcropping was familiar to Edwin and brought back memories. As a child, he often hid there, reading adventure stories and dreaming of doing great things. Many afternoons were spent leaning against the boulders and watching the clouds. However, that morning the old pile of boulders was a bit different.

A strange glow suffused the normally dark cleft. He stooped to see what was causing it and was grabbed, as if by invisible hands, and pulled into the glowing opening. The sensation was akin to what he assumed being sucked through a bottle's neck would be like. He didn't even have time to shout before he found himself in the center of a dark, barren prairie.

That was how Edwin found himself standing and staring about him, wondering what had just happened. His mind reeled as he realized the opening was gone. There was no way back. His outcropping was gone, and nothing was as it should be. The vast arc of the sky was dark, and unfamiliar stars shone brightly, while an immense, waning crescent moon hung high over the horizon, eerily lighting the plain spread out before him. Trying to get his breath, he gazed around, awed by the stars and the moon.

"Amazing. It's beautiful." This was no place he'd ever been before.

Edwin turned slowly to get his bearings. He stood on a vast rise in the center of a large plain. Far off in the distance, he could see what looked like a campfire. He began walking toward it, moving carefully over the rough ground. Strange shrubs and low scrubby trees materialized out of the darkness as he made his way to the distant light. The land around him was silent, as if Edwin's presence disturbed the creatures that would normally inhabit a place like this.

He felt like he'd been walking forever. His skin tingled, and the back of his neck grew itchy, as if eyes were boring into it. He jumped back in alarm as a dark shape loomed in front of him. The skeletal remains of a dead tree seemed frightening in the dark, and he looked among the sparse brush and uneven ground for a weapon. A soft crunch came from behind him, and he froze in mid-crouch before slowly turning round.

Suddenly, some sort of misshapen animal attacked him. Struggling desperately, Edwin searched for anything that could help him. His madly patting hand fell on something hard, and he grabbed the stick and attempted to drive the beast off, but the crazed creature wouldn't be diverted. Terrified, Edwin fought the wild animal with all of his strength, frantically deflecting its savage claws from his face and throat.

Nothing would deter the creature, though Edwin's stick drew blood many times. He bashed the creature in the head again and again until finally it fell to the ground, dead. With his less-than-hefty stick, it had been a close fight, leaving Edwin torn and bloodied in several places.

"That was bad," he said aloud, shuddering and fearful and feeling something running down his face. He wiped it with the back of his hand and saw a smear of blood. Gathering his courage, Edwin looked closely at the corpse and saw the gleam of metal in the light of the waning moon. Reluctantly bending closer, he found several pieces of strange money on the ground. Apparently it had fallen from the beast's clothing. The money was hexagonal, with the image of a woman on one side and that of a building on the other. Both seemed familiar to him, though he couldn't remember ever having seen money like it before.

Looking again, Edwin realized with horror his

attacker wasn't a beast exactly. He'd never seen a person like the dead creature. Its face was rat-like and its gnarled hands ended in terribly sharp claws. It was a male and wore rudimentary clothing of some sort, though it was in tatters and rags as if worn day and night for months.

I haven't been here an hour, and I've already killed someone. But he shouldn't have tried to kill me first. The poor thing must be some sort of robber, waylaying travelers. Too bad he didn't have a knife or something. I need a good weapon. But if he'd had one, it would be me lying dead on the ground. Filled with remorse, he put the money in his pocket. *I think I'll need this money more than he does, now. I'm alone in a strange world.* Edwin was as practical as anyone, perhaps more so than most, in many ways.

A horrible thought suddenly struck him, and he spoke aloud, fear cold in the pit of his stomach. "What if he's not alone?" Edwin looked around until he found a heavier stick and began walking toward the distant fire once more.

He was glad he'd found a better club, as he was attacked once more before he reached the campfire. The next creature leaped at him out of the dark, but Edwin was prepared, and this time he wasn't injured, although his clothes were torn again. Examining the corpse as well as he could in the dark, Edwin saw it was much like the first one, but thinner and more raggedly dressed. It had no money and had obviously been in many fights. He could see the poorly healed scabs and scars. The pathetic corpse stirred a sense of pity in him. The wretched creature was so desperate and died in such a horrible way.

Kill or be killed.... It's no way to live. What sort of place is this?

From a safe distance, Edwin observed the camp, worried it could be the lair of the strange creatures who'd tried to kill him.

A girl of about eighteen, clad in tight, red leather trousers and a loose linen shirt with the sleeves rolled up to her elbows, sat by the fire. She was meditating or praying. Red lacquered armor sat near at hand. She bore many tattoos of thorny red and yellow roses spiraling up both arms from wrist to neck. The tattoo of a red lightning bolt was placed on her cheek, just before her left ear, and a single rune for wisdom graced her brow. Her long, dark hair was plaited into two braids and coiled around her head like a crown. There was a fragile beauty about her, at odds with the sword in its sheath balanced across her knees.

Deciding she didn't appear to be another enemy, Edwin moved into the light of the small campfire. His clothes were torn and dirty, and he was disheveled and bloody.

The girl looked up. "You're late, farm-boy. I expected you last night."

"I'm late? I'm almost dead. If you knew I was coming, why didn't you help me?" Edwin was exhausted and angry. "Wait a minute—how did you know I was coming? And who are you?"

"My name is Aeolyn Brendsdottir. I was sent to bring you to the Temple at Aeoven. But as to why I gave you no help on your way here—if you can't defend yourself, then you're not the hero we are expecting. Others have been known to stumble through the portal. But your father will surely have told you of this and of your family's bargain with Aeos." She seemed confused by his ignorance. "This is the appointed meeting place."

Edwin didn't know what to say. "Not really," he muttered. "He's told me nothing of you or of this place." He accepted the tin cup of tea she handed him. *Why? What have I gotten myself into?*

Chapter 2

Aeolyn sat on her heels with her own cup of tea. "So, to get down to business—the Baron Stefyn D'Mal, whom, as you know, your father once fought against, stirs again. And now, we've heard he has kidnapped one who is also my dear friend. She's a healer by the name of Marya Oakheart. A quest has been called, and we're going to bring her out of Mal Evol. The Holy Father, Rall, sent me here to bring you back as his vision foretold. All will be explained to you once we arrive at the Temple at Aeoven. In the meantime, I'm to teach you the skills I have, and hope you can learn quickly. But now I must see to your wounds. This salve will help. The healers make it and add a bit of their magic to it so it works wonders."

After brusquely and efficiently tending his wounds, Aeolyn began breaking camp as the sky lightened toward dawn. Watching her, Edwin's face betrayed his confusion. Finally he asked, "Are you sure I'm the one you're waiting for? My father never told me anything about Stevin Demill. I know Dad was in an army in a foreign land, but he never talks about it, and I don't know anything about quests, other than what I've read."

His complete ignorance puzzled Aeolyn who was now unsure what to say.

Edwin was mystified too. By now, the grand notion of an adventure, which came to him at the mention of a quest, had soured in the face of his bewilderment. "I'm sorry I don't know what you're talking about. I've been on a farm since I was four, and it's all I really remember. Where are we anyway?" He looked up at the sky and the gradually lightening eastern horizon. "I do know this—we are nowhere near Markett. The sun was nearing midmorning when I fell through the rocks and ended up here. Am I still even in Ariend?"

"You're right. You're a world away from Ariend and your town of Markett. We are in Neveyah." Aeolyn tossed a bundle at him. "Get yourself geared up, farm-boy. We've a long walk ahead of us to the Temple. This place drifts further away from Armat each year, and with the rat-people infesting the area, it will be a difficult journey. We'll be at least a week on the road, perhaps longer if we keep running into the beasts. If you haven't learned something in that time, they'll have to find a better hero, I guess." Aeolyn sounded as if she didn't care one way or the other, but he could tell it was her normal manner. "Sometimes it happens, but not usually in *your* family."

Edwin looked at her for a moment, smiling. "My name is Edwin, not farm-boy, although I am a boy from a farm." He stooped and picked up the bundle, surprised at how heavy it was. He found brown lacquered armor rolled around a hand-and-a-half sword in a plain scabbard to match.

Edwin's spirits rose when he saw the sword. "I've always fancied learning to fight with one of these. I wanted to join the army, but there was no need for me. Besides, my dad says a bow is more useful on the farm." He grinned, saying, "I'm a pretty good shot, but my dad is better. Between the two of us, we win the archery competition at the county fair every year. The last two years I won in grappling, and this year I won the knife throwing contest. But that's all I know about fighting and weapons."

"Those are good skills to have, but a bow isn't useful in the sort of skirmishing you will be doing for now. It's a long-range weapon, more suited to fighting the legions of D'Mal. The rat-people give you no room to use one. They're on you before you know it. Do they not teach young people to use the sword in Markett?"

"No. Swords are expensive, even poor quality ones, which is why we're so good at archery." Edwin slowly shook his head. "Only the wealthy can afford swords and plate-armor and war-horses to carry them. Only the rich can buy a commission into the army."

Aeolyn mused over his statement. "Plate-armor is far too heavy when one must walk everywhere, though it's good you want to learn. You'll need to use a sword regularly if you intend to survive here." The implication was he might not. "Friedr will have to teach you properly, but I will start you out."

Edwin smiled and stifled a laugh at his bruised ego. Aeolyn wasn't as impressed with him as the girls in Markett, a new circumstance, but a relief nonetheless. Something about her down-to-earth sensibility reminded him of his late mother, though there was no other resemblance.

She showed him how to put on the armor, and it was a fairly good fit, but obviously not made for him. "We hoped you would be close to the size of your father. They still have his measurements in the armory. I think you're taller, but this will work well enough while we travel."

Aeolyn was a small woman, almost tiny, and her armor was obviously made specifically for her. It was tooled in red lacquer with a golden rose vine climbing the overlapping ribs of the breast and back plates, with golden suns randomly placed.

Like Aeolyn, Edwin wore his loose linen shirt under the vest and tucked into the trousers. She politely turned away while he changed into the leathers, saying, "So, Edwin, I'm bonded and have no interest in bedding anyone except my husband. I only want to set the ground rules for the trip to Aeoven, right?"

"That's good to know," Edwin replied, relief coloring his voice. He'd known from the moment he met her she wasn't the one he was waiting for, although she seemed like someone who could be a good friend. He hadn't looked forward to fending her off if she had other things on her mind than simply being his instructor and traveling companion. Aeolyn chuckled quietly; either his words or his tone had obviously amused her.

When he mentioned the trousers were too tight, she said, "They start out tight, but will fit you more comfortably soon enough. They have to be like your second skin so they can't snag or catch on anything. There must be nothing the rat-people can grab. The old-style fringed leathers with all the pockets your father's generation mostly still wears are not as good against the rats."

"I've never seen my father wear anything like these clothes," Edwin replied. "He wears cotton shirts and breeches, like everyone else."

Aeolyn shrugged, again unsure what to say.

Leather gloves, the backs of which were clad with thin lacquered steel, completed his gear. They too were a little tight.

"We'll have to burn your other clothes. They'll only weigh you down. If we don't, the feral rats will find them and stalk us all the way to Aeoven. Once you have the armor on, you'll see why the leathers must be tight. They protect you from the armor as well as being a part of your overall protection." Aeolyn also explained to him how the armor could easily be carried in four main sections, breastplate and backplate rolled around arm guards and leg guards. It was heavy, but as far as armor went, it was lighter than most and was constructed to be rolled easily, making a bundle small enough to fit into a pack. "At least your boots are perfect for walking. I was worried they wouldn't be good enough."

Aeolyn pointed him to a pack containing a bedroll, a tightly rolled cloak, and a personal kit. The kit was complete, with a razor and toothbrush along with a clean shirt and one change each of socks and underclothes. "We will mostly live off the land, so the weight of the pack should be easy enough for you to get used to." It was heavy, but not too bad.

The sword was heavy. *She carried all this how far? At least a week of travel, she said.* Edwin's respect increased dramatically. Aeolyn was obviously strong and competent.

They began walking southeast, following a faint trail through the prairie. "This road is only used by members of your family. No one else needs to as it's now in the empty lands, but Aeos won't allow it to be completely lost when it goes unused." The grass and shrubs seemed to stretch for miles in all directions around them, and the great vault of the blue sky above took Edwin's breath away. Occasional trees dotted the landscape.

"Why are these lands so empty?" Edwin asked.

"This is the far west, and most of the people of Neveyah live in the Midlands and east of our world. I don't know why this is. I heard Markett was once the furthest village to the west, but the Almighty Father shifted the veil and the town has been in the world of Ariend since the time of your great-grandfather, Liam Farmer. A few brave souls live out here, but it's dangerous, and the Temple can't protect them well. We don't have enough people for the task of protecting the Midlands as it is."

***

Over the next few days, Edwin learned a great many things about his companion. She was a battle-mage and bonded to another battle-mage named Friedr. They hadn't been bonded for long, and she missed him terribly, but their work often separated them for long periods of time. They were both journeymen and initiates of the priesthood of the Temple of Aeos in a city called Aeoven.

Edwin was surprised to discover his parents were members of the Temple clergy. He found it strange to think his father was a famous battle-mage and his mother a healer, though it made sense. She'd always dropped whatever she was doing to care for the ill. She had caught the plague by caring for the neighbors who were sick and dying.

"I want to learn more about my mother," Edwin told Aeolyn. "She died when I was young. This explains my family's devotion to the Goddess Aeos, in a country where the Almighty Father is the god of choice in many of the households. But," he added, "we always honored both deities, and my parents were sincere in their observances. Most other families in

Markett honor both."

"They are both worthy of your devotion," Aeolyn replied. "Your home now lies in the lands of the Almighty Father, though he doesn't begrudge your family's devotion to his beloved daughter Aeos. Father Rall is very clear on this."

Edwin also discovered some of why he was in Neveyah. To his surprise, Aeolyn told him his father was famous for having somehow prevented the children of Tauron, the Bull God, from conquering this world. "I've heard of Tauron, of course," Edwin replied, feeling a bit stunned. "What I've read of him isn't good. He is the renegade god and was responsible for the division of the worlds."

John Farmer had never mentioned any of this to Edwin. But then, Edwin's father was a quiet, serious man who simply got on with any task with an eye to finishing the job properly.

Aeolyn appeared surprised at Edwin's lack of knowledge in regard to his father's illustrious history. Seeing her bewilderment, he explained, "My dad would never brag about something he did. He would never talk about having been to a place like this, at least not in Markett."

John Farmer's tattoos were of a similar style to Aeolyn's, though his were mostly blue and faded. *Maybe Dad got his tattoos here,* Edwin thought to. *Another thing he never talked about.*

One thing Edwin learned immediately was that it was much harder to use a sword than the stories ever told you. Just getting it into and out of the scabbard safely was challenging. Often by the time he got it out of the scabbard, Aeolyn had already killed whatever beast had attacked them. *I'm a useless idiot,* he thought as they trudged toward a town he'd never heard of. *I'll never get the hang of this damned sword.*

"I was doing better with a club." he ruefully told Aeolyn after she killed the first creature that attacked them before he could even get the sword out of its sheath.

She laughed. "You're using your sword as gracefully as a club, so what do you expect?"

Edwin also discovered that using magic was a lot of work.

On the evening of the first day, he was amazed that she used fire-magic to make the campfire. He tried to copy what she did, finding the red energy-ropes and weaving them. To his pleasure and her great surprise, he made a little fire of his own. She leapt right on his new skill and began to teach him all she knew. Between learning how to use his sword to kill the marauding beasts and trying to understand the most basic of Aeolyn's battle-magic, he got little rest each day.

Each morning Edwin started out trying to "call" the fire to cook their breakfast. He did the same for the water for washing, letting it fill his palms and flow into the basin. Sometimes his magic worked, and sometimes it didn't. Although he could usually find the right energies, he had trouble remembering the correct weaves as there appeared to be different weaves for each task. Sometimes he could see the energies he wanted but not grasp them. Aeolyn doggedly kept at him to practice.

When he asked her why he couldn't always find the energies, she replied, "The elements are not energies, they're magic. We all must go by feel. When you have more experience, you'll always be able to sense where they are. You'll be able to tell what magic you want by its quality, and be able to use it reliably. Open yourself to the element you want. Imagine how it feels. Picture the desired result clearly, and it will come to you. Visualization is everything when trying to woo the elements."

Edwin could see them clearly when he chose to, so he couldn't understand what she was telling him. The problem was they twisted away. He tried several times to call water before he got it right. All the elements were difficult for Edwin to grasp. When they broke camp, he called earth to smother the campfire and to fill the privy hole, and he often tried several times before he got it right.

Each day, they marched as quickly as they could, and Edwin dared not lower his guard because at any time they might be ambushed. Endlessly practicing magic while walking or suddenly fighting for his life was always a struggle.

"I don't understand this," Aeolyn muttered as she cleaned her sword again. "We burned your clothes. Why are they stalking us? It's almost as if.... No. It makes no sense." When Edwin asked what she was talking about, she muttered, "There are no healers with us, so what the bloody rats are chasing us for I don't know."

Edwin's skin began feeling noticeably strange the afternoon of the third day in Neveyah, and with each passing day, it became worse, as if he were suffering from some sort of allergy. His skin felt swollen and tight, but he could see nothing wrong when he bathed. It was impossible to identify what caused the problem.

He didn't know how to explain to Aeolyn what was wrong, and so he said nothing, thinking maybe it would go away.

The first village they came to was Armat, and Aeolyn checked in at the Temple, while Edwin got settled in his room at the inn. "I had thought Abbott Cayne would authorize us to take the mail-coach to Aeoven, but he feels the rat-people won't be as bad between here and Ragat. I thought he would want to meet you but he won't have time today and we'll have to leave early tomorrow." She seemed troubled. "He's right, I'm sure. The clergy must walk whenever possible in order to remain close to those we serve."

Edwin discovered the chore of trying to have a quiet glass of ale was no different in Neveyah than in Markett.

"You're like honey to the bees," Aeolyn commented in the common room of the Wellspring Inn. "They can't leave you alone," she teased him as the spurned ladies glared at her from across the room. "What sort of charm was set on you to cause this?" It amazed her that he wanted nothing to do with these women, though he'd glanced around the room when they entered, as if looking for someone. Finally curiosity got the better of her, and she asked him why he was so standoffish to the friendly-girls.

Edwin looked at her with his startlingly honest smile and replied, "I've always known whom I will bond with. Somehow, I thought she might be here, and maybe it was why I was called to this world. But she isn't."

Aeolyn did her best to stop them bothering him, but it wasn't an easy task. There were some extremely determined friendly-girls in those rural towns. One brazen lady glared at her and told Edwin, "Leave your grumpy sister to sit alone and dance with me, pretty boy."

She finally backed off when Aeolyn laid her belt knife on the table where it would be handy and said, "My brother has no need of your companionship. Leave him be, or I'll show you grumpy."

Edwin quickly became used to his new routine. He wasn't afraid of hard work, he'd been doing it all his life. Farming was backbreaking and he was strong and muscular to begin with, but now he was sore and aching in muscles he didn't know he had. He never complained, but the strain of being in a strange place and learning a whole new way of life was beginning to get to him.

After leaving Armat, each day became a struggle for Edwin. For lack of better words, his skin felt as if it were too tight. And then there was the problem of traveling. They were only making half the time they should have been making. They spent the rest of the time fighting off packs of wild beasts, repairing damaged armor, honing blades, and tending their wounds. "I was afraid of this. We haven't even gotten as far as Ragat," Aeolyn said as she took her hammer and knocked a huge dent out of his breastplate.

Two of the ribs were buckled, and he now had another bruise to show for his efforts. Part of his instruction was how to take care of his armor. "Four days and we're barely past Armat. You blaze with chi, and they're attracted to it. Even I can feel it now, and I'm not nearly as good at sensing it as Friedr is. Once we get to Aeoven, they will give you the tattoos and the force of your chi will be much fainter. The feral rats won't hassle us so much."

Though he pressed her for clarification, Aeolyn wouldn't explain any further, saying he would learn about it in Aeoven. "I don't understand the process well myself. For your safety, I need to concentrate my attention on teaching you all I can before we get there."

Chapter 3

On the positive side, it was apparently the custom to strip the dead of anything of value, and Aeolyn split everything with him. As they knelt beside another dead rat-person after a vicious fight, she explained the coins to him. "Don't worry. This is Neveyah money. See? This is Aeos, the goddess." She turned the gold piece over and pointed to its back side, saying, "And this is the Temple. This coin is worth one hundred copper coins and ten silver coins. Someone died for them to have this money, because I've never heard of the rat-people spending it. They're never sane enough by the time we meet them. They seem to like it though, perhaps because it is shiny." Blood trickled down her cheek as she added, "I'm told the sane rat-people have their own coins, but it's different. It has a man on one side and a torch on the other."

"That's good to know, but in case you've forgotten, you're bleeding. Why don't we leave the explanations until later?" Aeolyn carried medicine, potions, and salves for pain and healing and often picked herbs as they traveled. They bandaged and treated each other's wounds as they happened, though Edwin felt something was missing. He could almost sense a healing energy just outside his vision, but if there was one, she didn't tell him, and he was too tired to ask. If he'd known the color to look for, he could have found it.

It wasn't the only thing that bothered him. Edwin struggled to put up elemental shields whenever he saw magic flying at him. Aeolyn's shields went up automatically when the creature she was facing began to call magic. "You go by the feel," she told him. "When you feel them calling water, you put up your water-shield. It is simple."

"Simple to you, my teacher, but I can't tell what they're throwing at me until it is about to set my hair on fire." After that happened, he began wearing his hair in a long braid tucked down the backplate of his armor.

After the first few days of struggling, he was able to sense the individual elements just as she told him he would, and his shields became more reliable.

"It helps you're so nervous," she told him. "You've been trying to keep the basic shield up all the time. You can raise the elemental shields much more quickly since they are already halfway built."

The main trouble was it took something called chi to maintain the shield, and he didn't have much, even though Aeolyn claimed he blazed with it. If he forgot to check all the time, it faded away, leaving him unprotected. Then he had to try to build the whole thing from scratch while dodging lightning or fire. *What a mess. At least I'm making some progress,* he thought as he trudged along.

While they camped most nights, they spent two nights at inns in the villages along the trade road. The inns were not bad, the food was good, and being able to have a hot bath was a blessing. After a small rest, they were back on the road again. At each stop, Edwin used earth-magic to dig the privy hole and fire-magic to light the campfire, and called water to bathe in. While Aeolyn cooked their meals and heated the water, he worked at lightning-magic until it was time to eat, and then he fell into an exhausted sleep. Sword practice and magic began to haunt his dreams.

Edwin was under severe stress, and with each day that passed, it was with greater and greater difficulty he was able to maintain a civil and polite exterior whenever he became tired. Somehow he managed to get by without expressing his irritation and discomfort to Aeolyn. He maintained a determinedly mild and cheerful demeanor, venting only on the rat-people who felt compelled to stalk them. *It isn't her fault. She's doing her best to teach me what I need to know. I'm being unreasonable.* He made it his top priority not to act on his impulses and spent a certain amount of time each night trying to calm himself.

His skin now felt so tight he thought it would burst, but as far as he could tell in his small shaving mirror, he didn't look any different, so he said nothing. *She'll think you're a whiner if you complain about something that can't be seen. Be quiet and get on with your job, you big baby.*

In spite of his increasing discomfort, the days passed quickly. They'd been walking for nine days, four longer than Aeolyn hoped. At long last, they walked through the gates of Wister in the early afternoon, the last village on the western trade road to Aeoven, the capitol city.

They stayed in the Lion's Share Inn, where Aeolyn told him they were only one long day's march from the Temple. "There are hot springs here and the best baths outside of Aeoven," she told him with anticipation. "After we practice, we will greatly enjoy soaking in them. At least I will."

Edwin's heart sank at the thought of more magic.

It was in Wister Edwin finally cracked under the

strain of constant training and fighting. He rebelled when she wanted him to call lightning after a long afternoon hurrying so they could be inside the gates before they closed at dusk. The inn was full, so they were sharing a room. It wasn't a problem really, but Edwin was looking forward to some privacy, something he was not going to have. He was hot, tired, and ready for a bath followed by a meal in the common room.

Of all the battle-magics, lightning was most difficult for him. Nevertheless, he made a sincere effort and was prodded and pushed until finally he snapped.

The type of lightning a novice cast was called a cat-zapper. Edwin wasn't at all good at calling them. The lightning kept twisting away, and he was frustrated at trying to call the element to him when he had so much trouble grasping it.

Abruptly, an irrational anger took hold of him. He cast a lightning charge at the rickety table between their cots, disintegrating it and leaving a charred scar on the floor, despite knowing he was supposed to aim for the small fireplace. Somehow, he turned his urge to blast Aeolyn at the unsuspecting table, though it took all his strength.

Aeolyn jumped back in surprise, her eyes wide as the table exploded. She quickly hid her shock and casually commented, "You need to adjust the spread on your aim if you're going to call a thunder-fist in our room. Next time target the fireplace."

Edwin's face turned red, and he clenched his fists in frustration. After a moment of angry silence, Edwin shouted, "What is wrong with you anyway? I can't do anything right."

"Wrong with me? I'm trying to save your life.

Learn and live, wool-headed farm-boy," she yelled back. "I didn't ask for this task, but I do it anyway." She smacked her forehead and burst out "Why did the Holy Father think I was the right one for this?"

"I'm trying to learn as fast as I can. You push me dawn to dusk, and nothing is good enough for you! Most of my questions you either can't or won't answer. If this is what I have to look forward to for the rest of this trip, I'm not going on your stupid quest. I won't do it!" Edwin felt an immense and unreasonable fury escalating in him. With his wrath came the urgent desire to blast her with every element at his command. Terrified at the sheer power of his rage, he immediately smothered it.

Instead, he forced himself to say calmly, "I'm not going to stand here and argue with you. It gets us nowhere. I'm going to sit in the common room right now and, for a change, I will enjoy the company of pleasant people who don't expect anything extraordinary out of me." He carefully shut the door despite his nearly overwhelming urge to shatter it.

Once outside in the hallway Edwin leaned against the wall, more angry and confused than he'd ever felt in his entire life. *Blessed Goddess. I wanted to kill her. No, I wanted to obliterate her instead of the table! What's wrong with me?* Edwin had never before felt such rage and was unsure what to do next. He blindly went down to the common room and was immediately assailed by an overwhelming feeling of claustrophobia. Looking around, he found a corner and attempted to hide in it. *I can't take being around the crowd in here, but where else can I go?* Desperately, he imagined a fence around himself, shielding him, and felt a little better.

As he sat in his corner, he noticed several people wearing leathers like his and Aeolyn's. One was a tall, red-bearded man in red, who stood at the bar with a small, almost fragile, dark-haired man in moss-green. They bore the prominent tattoos that seemed to have some meaning, though Edwin wasn't sure what it could be.

***

Left alone in the room, Aeolyn sat on her bed and sobbed. "Why did you send me to do this, Father Rall? I failed you and ruined him. I was never meant for this."

The rage in Edwin's eyes was astonishing, but he'd managed to bury it instead of lashing out at her as she deserved. *There's much more to him than meets the eye. He was enraged, and instead of acting on it, he simply left. Not many would have done so.* She felt tears welling again. *He has immense self-control.*

Standing before the mirror over the dresser and laying her head on her arms, she cried for a moment, feeling overwhelmed and under-equipped to deal with such an unusual student. "Friedr, I miss you so much. You would have handled him so much better than I have." She took comfort in knowing her husband was in Aeoven and only one day's hard travel away.

After washing her face and pulling herself together, Aeolyn headed to the common room. As she went down the stairs, to her great joy, two of her dearest friends were waiting for her. One of them was the person she wanted to see most in this world. She quickly looked to see if Edwin was still there and spotted him attempting to drink his well-deserved ale at a table in a corner. He appeared frustrated. As usual, Edwin was surrounded by a bevy of buxom "ladies" who obviously had plans for expanding his education in the social niceties.

Whooping with joy she took the stairs two at a time and threw her arms around Friedr and Christoph. "What are you doing here? I'm *so* glad to see you."

Christoph was a healer, slight of stature, and a dark-haired, sunny-spirited youth of twenty-one. Friedr was a huge red-haired, red-bearded warrior of twenty years, and he towered over Christoph. "We thought you might want some companionship." Christoph's joy and love of life were infectious, and the mood of a room always lightened when he entered. People often found themselves smiling for no reason at all around him.

Aeolyn pointed Edwin out to Friedr. Her student was politely denying his lap to a buxom beauty intent on sitting there. Seeing that, Friedr said, "Huh. He has a different approach, but it seems to be working rather well. How is the pretty-boy doing? Is he as good as his father?"

"He is probably better. He learns so fast I can't keep up. But, I'm a terrible teacher." Aeolyn burst into tears. Seeing Friedr and Christoph so unexpectedly caused her fears and emotions to rise to the surface again with an alarming suddenness. "Wherever we go, the women mob him. It embarrasses him something fierce." Her giggle ended on a sob. "In some ways, he is young for his age."

Friedr put his arm around her, and Christoph patted her shoulder consolingly. "You're a great teacher, little-mother," Christoph said, surreptitiously casting a spell to sooth her nerves, as much for his own peace as hers. "You've worked a miracle with him. He is strong with unfocused chi, and this is all new to him. You're doing the work of three people." He looked appraisingly at Edwin and added, "He is rather pretty for a warrior. Oh, too bad for me. He likes girls, though apparently just not *those* girls."

Aeolyn's eyes sparkled at Christoph's wry assessment of Edwin. "He's learning to fight well, and very quickly. It seems as if we fought practically every step of the way here. Something about him stirs the beasts into a frenzy, and they keep attacking. We killed three packs of feral rats today alone. He's had to learn too much, too fast." Aeolyn took a deep breath, trying to calm herself. "It's taken twice as long as it should have to come this far."

"The Holy Father told me your student is much more than we were expecting. He might even be the Hero Foretold, though if I understand the prophecies correctly, I don't think it is the right time. The Abbess and Father Rall felt you struggling, and sent us to help you. His Holiness said to tell you his faith was well-placed in you." Friedr hugged her again. "I'm here to build his sword arm, and Christoph will see to his training as a healer."

"He's a healer? How could such a thing be? I didn't know. No wonder he is buckling under the pressure. I should have known. I should have seen." Tears streaked her face again. "But he has such strong battle-magic, so I pushed and pushed. I never heard of anyone with strength in both magics."

Christoph said, "You're a dedicated teacher, and you've done well in your first teaching position. You need to trust your abilities." He smiled and squeezed her shoulder. Realizing his barriers had become fragile from both the intensity of her emotions and the pressures of the crowded common room, he bolstered them. *Fire-mages. It's all or nothing for them,* he thought, firmly telling her, "You must believe in yourself, or no one will."

"But…." Aeolyn's great weakness was her lack of self-confidence. Christoph looked helplessly at Friedr, who as usual, was already dealing with her storm of insecurity.

"No, you don't." Friedr made her look him in the eye. "You are not going to wallow in self-blame. You're just like me, with no healing magic at all, so how would you recognize it in another? I certainly can't see it, not even in Christoph, and you know how strong he is. Though," Friedr looked at Edwin with his senses wide open, "your student fairly blazes with the battle-chi. He is like a furnace. I can feel it from across the room."

Christoph looked at Edwin with his healing sight and was stunned by what he saw. "He radiates healing-chi too, and he's terribly out of balance right now. No wonder the beasts were stirred up. He offers everything they like." The healer was surprised at how much chi gathered about Edwin, despite the way Aeolyn had worked with him to keep it from building up. "He is easily the largest source of unfocused chi I've ever felt. He is very strong even at this stage. I need to get over there and bleed the excess off. He must be terribly uncomfortable."

"See? He *was* attracting them, not that he could help it," Friedr told her firmly. "The rest of the trip will be much easier. I'll be there to help, and Chris will bleed off the excess chi your student doesn't have the skill to use."

"Oh, Friedr, I missed your common sense." She squeezed his hand. "Thank you, dear one." Friedr flushed, turning nearly as red as his hair. "And thank you, Christoph. Edwin has never complained about feeling uncomfortable, and he must be going crazy. I now see why he snapped this afternoon."

Christoph looked over at Edwin, still attempting to eat his dinner with the friendly-girls hanging over him, one going so far as to feed him strawberries and wipe his mouth. Edwin's good nature and innate courtesy forced him to be polite, but he was obviously in over his head. "You know, he does seem to need a wee bit of assistance with the ladies, so I'm going to go and introduce myself to our new protégé and let you two have some time alone. You deserve it."

"Friedr can meet him in the men's baths later. You three need to bathe with soap," she replied with a sly smile, which turned into a laugh. "I want to soak for a while myself."

Christoph didn't rise to her bait. Instead, he formed a barb of his own. "I took the liberty of having your things moved to Friedr's room, and I'll bunk with the new kid," Christoph told her with his wicked grin. "I think it would be much better than having you two sneaking down the hall." Aeolyn's face reddened, but she wisely let Christoph have the last word.

"We do not have to sneak. We're bonded now," Friedr muttered, red-faced. "If they had let us bond when we wanted to, it would have been much better. *We* didn't need the trial period."

"But novices aren't allowed to bond," Aeolyn agreed. "We had to wait until I was made a journeyman."

Aeolyn and Friedr stepped out onto the wide porch and sat on the broad steps in the moonlight, holding hands. "I love you, my dear one, but yeesh. You smell like your armor, and frankly, so do I. I'm in desperate need of a nice hot bath." Aeolyn wrinkled her nose. "But just seeing you here...Friedr, I needed you so much." She laid her head against his chest, absorbing his strength, his musky scent, and all of the myriad things she missed so badly during their separation.

Friedr grinned widely and hugged her.

"And we don't have to sneak down the hall," she told her husband wickedly. "How lucky for us."

Friedr's eyes gleamed in the moonlight.

Chapter 4

Edwin looked up as the slender man in green with short, dark hair seated himself opposite. He grinned as the young man casually shooed away the flock of barmaids and friendly-girls Edwin had inadvertently accumulated.

The most determined, Rila, knew Christoph fairly well, as he often passed through the inn on Temple business. She glared at him with her hands on her hips and said, "Oh no, you don't, Christoph Berryman! Don't you even try to tell me he likes boys because he doesn't. Those tight trousers you Temple boys all wear hide nothing." Edwin choked a bit on his ale and Chris pounded on his back a few times until he got his breath. "He won't choose you over me. And when I see him, I'm telling your boyfriend you were here poaching on my territory again."

Sighing, Chris replied, "Temple business, Rila. Temple business. You're neglecting your other friends. We have matters to discuss and you're interfering." He looked at Edwin with an open, friendly smile. "You don't really mind, do you? You can tell her 'no' as much as you want to later. And we do need to talk." He cast calm and soothe on Edwin, two simple healing spells. "It's for your peace of mind that we talk now."

Edwin was blushing furiously and had a slightly frantic look about his eyes, which may have been due to the outrageous liberties some of the women were taking. He said with some embarrassment, "Thank you. I don't know those ladies, but they seem to think they know me. I'm Edwin Farmer. I see you know Aeolyn.

The young giant traveling with you must be Friedr."

"As Rila just said, my name is Christoph Berryman, and I am indeed one of Aeolyn's friends. We'll be working together fairly closely, as I am one of your instructors. But right now, you need to eat." He sat back and waited for Edwin to finish his meal. "I'll share your room tonight if you don't mind. Aeolyn and Friedr are still newlyweds." He smiled affectionately. "They've been separated for too long this time, I think."

Opening his healing sight to Edwin, Christoph began to gauge his strength. What he found was surprising, even though he'd been warned before he left Aeoven. Immediately he layered a buffer over Edwin, bleeding off much of the unfocused chi building around him. Christoph's thoughts scattered as the import of what he was seeing sank in. He now realized why he'd been chosen as one of Edwin's tutors despite the fact Dane was the better instructor for barriers and general healing. The thought struck him that Edwin would change the theory of magic as everyone knew it, and Christoph was unable to conceal his glee at working with him.

Edwin returned Christoph's smile. Unaware of the intervention, he relaxed as the massive amount of chi gathered around him was shunted harmlessly away. "She's missed him badly, and each extra day on the road has been a trial to her. I feel like I know him from all she told me about him—and you."

"Friedr will be one of your teachers, though Aeolyn will still train you in battle-magic." Christoph radiated such serenity, Edwin immediately felt his tension easing and unconsciously sat back, enjoying his company.

For the first time in days, Edwin felt calm, smiling the open and genuine smile he'd been so famous for in Markett. "She is the most thorough teacher I've ever had, but I'm afraid I haven't been a very good student," he replied awkwardly. "She's had a rough time with me since I know nothing about where I am or even why I'm suddenly here in Neveyah instead of Ariend where I should be. Also, the road here was harder and took much longer than she expected. I've tried not to let her down, but she's had to do most of the fighting. I don't really know much about swords or magic. I'm learning though. And then this evening we quarreled, but it wasn't her fault." A shadow drifted across Edwin's expression.

His body language told Christoph it was much more than a simple quarrel. Edwin was disturbed by his own reaction to it. "Unfocused chi can cause such a reaction and it can be dangerous, even deadly, especially when combined with the sort of empathy healers have. An argument can escalate out of control, with you feeding off the other person's anger, and soon your wrath grows out of control exponentially."

Christoph had Edwin's full attention now. "Yes. That's exactly what happened."

"You, especially, have a problem right now. Dual abilities are rarely seen in one person. The only other person I know of who has ever exhibited the same combination wasn't found until it was far too late to save him, and he is completely mad. Stefyn D'Mal is easily the most dangerous man in our world." Christoph's his somber expression conveyed the serious nature of his words. "Now you are in Neveyah, your empathic ability is beginning to develop at the same rate as your battle-magic. This is creating a state of nervous tension that is becoming more and more difficult for you to deal with. You were supposed to have gotten the tattoos five days ago, to help with the excess chi, and I should have begun working with you then too."

"Well, I don't know how a tattoo could help," Edwin replied, rather confused. "Yours are pretty amazing though. Aeolyn claims I need them, but she won't say why. She just keeps saying she has to push me to learn the magic as quickly as I can."

"And that is true in regard to your battle-magic, which is all Aeolyn can sense." Edwin nodded his understanding, and Christoph continued. "Tattoos done by the Temple on mages are not simply decorations. They are called augmentations and have significance both in what they depict and in their magnitude. They are the means of storing excess chi for use at a later time." Christoph held up his arms, his sleeves falling back. "Mine are for healing, along with a small ability to call water. How you will be augmented is determined by the magic the colorist who performs the ritual calls for you. It will be as the Goddess wills." He looked at Edwin closely and then asked, "But about your quarrel—why are you so disturbed, Edwin?"

"It was my fault. I really needed to rest tonight. I don't know why, but I can't bear the thought of practicing magic. It's like my skin will burst or something. It doesn't make sense, I know." Guilt rose within him, and he looked down at the table, unable to look Christoph in the eye, forcing himself to tell him what he experienced. "I'll understand if you don't want to be my teacher after I tell you what happened."

"That won't happen," Christoph said firmly. "I think I know already, but say your piece."

Numbly, Edwin confessed. "For a moment when we were quarreling I wanted to kill Aeolyn with my magic. I felt the most incredible urge to obliterate her, but instead I destroyed the table. I left the room so I wouldn't do such a terrible thing."

"But Edwin, you did *not* do it. You remained in control of yourself. Your chi is greatly out of balance, and it isn't your fault. You've been under a great deal of pressure, and there is a complication with you no one foresaw. You are a strong healer despite your ability to use battle-magic. While a few battle-mages can perform minor healings, and nearly all healers can call at least some water, so far as we know, the ability to use both magics has never before occurred with such strength as you demonstrate, except for once." Christoph's normally merry expression turned grim. "I believe I've already mentioned Stefyn D'Mal." He smiled. "Still, despite all of the stress you were under, you remained in control and didn't attack Aeolyn. You have nothing to feel ashamed of or to apologize about."

Continuing to bleed the excess chi away from Edwin, Christoph said, "The two magics war with each other. By their intrinsic natures, they must create a conflict you will have to learn how to overcome. This is one reason why I'm here. You need someone with my particular skills to guide you through this. To begin with, you and I are going to visit some of the locals tomorrow, healing small injuries and illnesses to rebalance your chi. You might spar with Friedr, but you will not do any battle-magic. We will continue on to Aeoven the day after. Are you feeling more able to be around people now?"

"Yes, actually I am," Edwin replied with some amazement. "You've been working some magic on me, but I haven't been able to pay attention as well as I would have liked today, and I didn't see what you did. Thank you for your kindness. I do feel more like meeting people now." His smile lit his face. "I'll concentrate better on watching what you show me, I promise. I just can't concentrate well tonight."

Christoph was startled by the charisma of Edwin's smile, though he was confused by his remark. He smiled back saying. "You're right. I've been bleeding off the excess chi that has built up. That's why you feel more relaxed. Tomorrow will be soon enough for you to learn what I have to teach." His smile crinkled the corners of his perpetually dancing eyes. "I think a long soak in the men's bath is in order. It also helps to rebalance one's chi. We'll meet Friedr there, per Aeolyn's firm instructions. Apparently, we all reek terribly. You'll like our Friedr, I think. I know he'll like you."

While Aeolyn enjoyed a relaxing soak in the women's spa, chatting with some of her friends who were attached to the militia and passing through Wister, the three men sat soaking in the men's hot spring where others also relaxed in various groups or singly.

Edwin was glad to meet Friedr at last. It was obvious the big warrior's heart was as big as the rest of him, and he was a *very* large man, standing easily half a head above Edwin, who was considered tall. Friedr sported a full red beard and long, curling red hair worn in a single thick braid hanging down his back past his waist. His slight northern-barbarian accent was barely noticeable unless he was upset or enthusiastic about something.

Twin dragons in black, red, yellow, and blue spiraled from the back of his left hand over his massive bicep to his shoulder. With some surprise, Edwin recognized runes for strength climbing Friedr's right arm. Chagrinned, he realized if their language was the same, then of course those runes would be as well.

Red lightning was placed on Friedr's cheek just before his right ear, and runes for wisdom and courage crossed his brow. A large rune for luck was centered in the small of his back. Thorny vines in all the elemental colors circled his right thigh, with runes for strength and luck woven throughout.

Christoph was a small man with elfin features and curling hair he kept trimmed short. He looked as if he were perpetually planning some sort of mischief. A green crescent moon on his temple cupped his left eye. Green stars were sprinkled across his forehead and cheeks and in spirals down his shoulders and both of his arms to the backs of his hands. Vines also climbed both arms and trailed down his back, circling his right thigh. Runes for wisdom and empathy were woven throughout the design. A crescent moon crossed his right palm.

"Well, you all know my story, and a boring one it is up to nine days ago," Edwin said, rather diffidently. "What's your story, Christoph?"

"Me? Not so interesting. My family lived on a farm in what is now Tauron's Mal Evol, although it wasn't part of the Bull God's territory then. It was a small village called Bryton. It is long gone now. One day when I was around five, the rain stopped falling, and the crops began to waste and die. Thorn bushes started sprouting, and nothing could stop them. By the time I was six, our village was deserted. It was nothing but a wasteland of thorns. Still my dad hung on, hoping for rain that never came. My family was the last to leave. It broke my father and grandfather's heart to leave our land. The Berryman family farmed there for six generations. My father finally moved us to Braden when I was about to turn seven." Christoph's voice took on an uncharacteristically grim note as he mentioned Braden, but it was so fleeting Edwin thought he imagined it.

"Nothing was the same there. My dad couldn't find work because the town was inundated with refugees. He did, however, discover drink, which became his sole reason for existence. My mother struggled to feed us, finally sinking to less than a friendly-girl, selling what they so freely give away, and still she seemed to have a new child every year. My father didn't notice or care. My granddad wasted away, lost in his memories and senility. I was the oldest of my siblings and felt I should do something to help support them, so I began singing in the local pub for money, gaining an apprenticeship with a bard who became my patron and who taught me the skills I would need."

Edwin was definitely picking up a feeling of emotional disturbance as Christoph told his tale. Obviously, the man felt compelled to share since he knew all about Edwin, but was reluctant to speak of it. "I went to live with my new master, traveling all over the South, singing in various pubs and common rooms. I was able to send money home to Mum regularly for my siblings, and she could stay home and care for them properly. The bard I was apprenticed to was a hard man, but it was a good enough life until I turned twelve, and my empathic talent showed itself. I lost my patron then, but was found by the Temple and my life changed for the better." Christoph's face was grim despite his attempt to keep it light. "My dad died soon after from the drink, but Mum is doing well. She raises flowers and sells them. My sibs are taken care of. The Temple aided me in helping them. See? Not so interesting a tale."

Edwin sensed Chris didn't like to speak of his childhood, and felt remorseful for having asked.

"Christoph." Friedr spoke sharply. "You didn't simply 'sing in a pub.' You were in training as a bard." Friedr looked at Edwin and took up the story. "When the healing chi started building and his empathic skills showed themselves, he went mad. His patron tried to beat the madness out of him. The pub owner saw what happened and called the constable, who arrested the patron and summoned a healer. He was twelve at the time, not unusual for healers. They usually go unnoticed until puberty. But Christoph wasn't simply singing in a pub, though he always says so. He was taught to juggle, and tumble, and tell the most astonishing tales. He plays the harp as well as any fully trained bard, and as far as singing the occasional epic quest tale goes, you should hear him when he gets going. It's never boring traveling with Christoph."

"I always wanted to learn to juggle." Edwin was interested in the skill and was more than willing to help Friedr divert Christoph from his gloom. "I never had time to figure it out though. I was too busy chasing sheep." He laughed a little at his all-too-obviously country-boy self.

Christoph immediately brightened up. "I'll gladly teach you—it's simple really. But our Friedr also has quite the story. He was on his way to becoming the chief warrior of his village of Aknar, way in the north of Neveyah. It is so far to the north it's nearly in the Icelands. All of the old warriors could see he would be a fierce fighter as he was nearly as tall then as he is now and took no abuse from anyone despite having lost his father at a young age. Then his talent began inadvertently showing itself. Fires started happening whenever he was upset or angry—it's a dead giveaway you have a budding fire-mage in the village." Christoph smiled wickedly at Friedr's discomfort.

"It's always fairly easy to find the child causing it, as they are usually nine or ten years old, and there are only so many of that age in a village at any given time. Unfortunately for Friedr, though he was older having just turned eleven, he was the only one close enough to be the source, so he suffered the consequences." Chris shook his head over the ignorance of some rural villagers. "They knocked him over the head, stuffed him in a sack, and rode three horses to death trying to drag him to Aeoven so he wouldn't burn down the whole village in a rage."

"Yes, I was a little older than the other novices, but I hid it better, so they didn't catch me as soon," Friedr said calmly. "I went back a few years ago when I first got my journeyman's pin and beat the crap out of the bastards who stuffed me in the sack, using just my fists, of course. We take vows about how we are to use our magic. Barbarian though I am, I understand vows and honor, perhaps more than some so-called civilized people do." His blue eyes were as hard as slate. Edwin suspected Friedr would be a bad enemy to have.

"They cast my family out of the village because I was a 'witch.' Such goodwill deserved some sort of reward, so I made sure they received an appropriate one. But thanks to the Temple, I've got Ma set up in a good place now. My little brother raises cattle for the Temple, and Ma rears goats. They're rich compared to the rest of our forsaken town. The elders ask my mother for permission to use the privy." He smiled with satisfaction as he finished his tale.

Edwin was shocked at how callously they'd been treated. "I don't know what to say. Though I didn't know it, my childhood was sheltered. Other than my mom dying, I never really knew sorrow, or once missed a meal, and certainly didn't appreciate it as much as I should have. I'm ashamed to admit I couldn't wait to get away from the boredom of Markett."

"There is nothing worse than a bucolic, pastoral place where nothing ever happens," Friedr agreed wholeheartedly. "Aeolyn stole her grandfather's plow horse and rode the twenty leagues from Stowe Bridge to Aeoven when she was ten. She was showing all the signs of becoming a budding fire-mage, but her parents wanted to protect her. They desperately tried to hide her from the Temple. They planned to bond her to the son of the farmer whose lands bordered theirs as soon as she was fifteen. They didn't realize what a strong and resourceful girl she was."

"They also didn't know what a dangerous thing they were doing," added Christoph. "She could have killed them all unintentionally. But she didn't. Instead she ran away to the Temple."

Friedr took up the tale again. "All Aeolyn ever dreamed of was being a mage and going on quests. She demanded they let her come to the Temple to be trained, but they refused because they felt it wasn't seemly to have a daughter who threw fire and swung a sword. One night she simply stole away, determined to go to the Temple for training." Friedr's pride in his wife's strength and determination was evident.

"Novices, like everyone else, all have to work at various tasks each day. This keeps the Temple running smoothly and idle hands busy. When she rode into the stables, it happened to be my morning to muck out the stalls. I took one look at her and knew she was the one for me. There I was, shovel in hand and smelling like a rose. This tiny, fragile little girl the size of an eight-year-old with long dark hair and big eyes jumped down off the poor old swaybacked plow horse and tossed the reins at me.

"She looked at me with this look of disapproval she has perfected and said, 'Stop gawking, you bloody idiot, and put this nag in a stall!' Her look, combined with her tone of voice, could have stopped a charging bull." Friedr was grinning like a fool and he knew it. "I never looked at another girl after that. She was always the only one for me."

Christoph rolled his eyes, "He was twelve and she was ten. How Friedr suffered for her over the years. He chased her with such determination. She led him a merry chase until *she* finally caught *him*. I learned to heal many a bloody nose he suffered for the love of Aeolyn. And he earned every one of them. He'd made it his business to decide who she walked out with, the jealous thing. She did not take kindly to his protection of her."

"Well, she had a good right fist, and she wasn't afraid to use it." Friedr laughed, and Chris and Edwin joined him.

Chapter 5

The next morning Edwin and Christoph dressed simply, as the weather was warm and they wouldn't be leaving the city. Christoph called in at the small Temple serving Wister and was given a list of patients for them to see, making the local healer happy. "We have too many patients, Chris. I'm glad you're back working with us and training a new healer."

Before they left for the first patient's home, Christoph asked Friedr to be the "patient" while he taught Edwin two important skills he had to know before he could learn to heal. The big warrior was happy enough to do it, saying, "Well, I guess he has to practice on someone. Better me than some poor, unsuspecting victim, eh?" He obediently sat, and Christoph showed Edwin how to open his healing sight.

"I didn't know what that was," Edwin said in surprise. "This is how I see the magic."

"You can see the magic?" Friedr was so shocked he stood up, looking at Edwin as if he'd gone mad.

"Only if I know it's there and what to look for," Edwin replied, surprised by Friedr's reaction, "and even then, I can't grasp it all the time."

Friedr and Christoph stared at each other with raised eyebrows, and an unspoken thought passed between them. "Well," Friedr said as he sat back down. "Well, well. Now I'm quite interested in being your first victim." He gazed at Christoph, who was as dumbfounded as he was. "Father Rall will be intrigued by this little item, I suspect."

After Christoph was sure Edwin was able to open

his healing sight, he taught him the next important step, the ability to link with other healers and follow them as they delved a patient's body. "It's like riding a sled with me. You're simply along as an observer, though later today you'll be allowed to perform small healings if you want to, and I will follow you."

With no difficulty, Edwin was able to join with Christoph and easily observed as he delved Friedr's body, scanning his internal wellbeing. As they did so, Christoph pointed out the warm, golden lights that indicated Friedr was a healthy man, saying they would be an angry red color if he were ill. "You are the healthiest barbarian in Neveyah," he pronounced as they emerged from the healing trance.

"That's because I don't drink ale to excess, which is the downfall of the bored warrior," Friedr replied piously. "Well, not too often anyway."

Christoph rolled his eyes. "If you say so, but I always wake up worse for wear after a night in the common room with you."

Friedr looked surprised he would say such a thing.

"How is your chi?" Christoph checked Edwin's levels and approved of what he saw. "Good, you will be able to keep up with me today even though you haven't been augmented yet." He looked at Edwin with his healing sight as they packed up his medical kit and prepared to depart on their rounds. "You're going to be powerful, perhaps more so than me, or even Dane. He is the strongest healer in the Temple right now. You'll meet him in Aeoven."

With each patient they saw, Edwin learned a new technique. Healing was much more tiring than battle-magic, but he found it fulfilling. "I feel like this is what

I was meant to do," he told Chris after they visited a boy who had suffered serious burns in a house fire. While the burns had been treated with little scarring, the child was unable to sleep.

Christoph had worked with the boy on getting past the trauma. Edwin had been impressed with the way he handled it. He inserted a small forgetting and a little feedback-loop that would be triggered when the boy became overwhelmed by the memory of the fire. "What you did with him is amazing," Edwin told Christoph. "The boy will be better able to get on with his life. His dreams will be normal instead of filled with nightmares."

"Loran and Dalen were able to heal his burns well, so he'll have little physical scarring, but he was terribly frightened and traumatized by the experience," replied Christoph. "One of my first patients as a journeyman was a young boy who was injured similarly, Dane's cousin Zan actually. I've had a lot of experience in working with this sort of trauma. I'll come back here in two weeks to see him again, but I think he will be able to sleep now."

When Edwin asked him why he didn't work in the infirmary anymore Christoph explained, "Something about my early experiences made me able to help people who have suffered great trauma. Healers normally have barriers we raise to prevent ourselves from being taken over by the patient we're treating. Do you recall what I've been showing you about barriers?"

Edwin nodded, and Christoph continued, "There are many things that can cause emotional trauma along with physical injury, things such as serious burns, battle stress, and rape. I treat these patients. It is especially difficult for most healers to lower their barriers enough to help with severe emotional trauma because the patient's fear can be overwhelming, and the healer must be able to stay calm in the face of the patient's terror. I work with these types of injuries."

"Why have they sent you to work with me? You must be needed much more elsewhere."

"This combination of the two magics at full and equal strength is very rare. I'm here to prevent problems and also to chronicle your progress for Abbess Halee as she can't do this herself. I have worked as a general healer and have the skills to train you. I will be going on the quest with you and the others. Marya's situation is grave. She is under terrible stress, and it's possible she may have been violated." Christoph tried to hide his worry behind a somewhat forced smile.

"I see," replied Edwin. "I never thought about the possibility. Aeolyn told me she was kidnapped." They were silent, thinking about the situation.

They arrived at the home of their next patient, and Christoph introduced Edwin to the elderly woman they would be treating for an improperly healed, broken wrist. "We're going to manipulate the bones where we can, and also relieve the muscles. Once we do this, her pain will be much less."

As the morning progressed, Christoph showed him how to alleviate their patients' suffering and heal minor wounds. "I was missing something in my life, only I never knew what. Of course, I would have eventually realized it, I think," he assured Christoph. "Of all the tasks on the farm, I enjoyed working with the animals most. My dad and I have a lot of experience treating our livestock since the animal-healer is expensive."

"Your experience in healing your livestock has given you a good base to build upon," replied Christoph. "You already have a basic understanding."

Later they rested, sitting in the common room eating freshly-baked bread with good sharp cheese and sipping purified water to regain the chi they had expended in healing. Edwin had questions—he understood they would be going on a quest to rescue a healer named Marya Oakheart, but he didn't understand the delay. "Why aren't we on the way to get her now?"

"She is a political prisoner and not in immediate danger, though it is unclear if she is being treated as a guest or a hostage. If we appear desperate to get her back, then she could be in peril. We don't have the power to meet D'Mal head-on. We have to do this so it looks like we are confused and helpless. And you still have a few things to do in Aeoven before we depart for the Shadow Castle, which will take several weeks at least."

Edwin thought about Christoph's words. "We're waiting so her captors think they have the Temple where they want them and don't see us coming for her," he said, understanding at last. "And also, I still need to work on my battle-magic. I struggle to control it. I can't even always grasp it, although I'm doing better. And then, there is the fact I need to improve my sword skills. I'm not very useful with it yet. But I always wanted to become a swordsman, and I can't wait to start training with Friedr."

"You are the only healer I have ever heard of who can wield a sword," said Christoph. "It's a conflict, you see. Healing-magic is building and preserving in the same way as battle-magic is destruction and death. A sword isn't simply for self-defense. It is for killing and maiming. The two clash strongly. The way we train in each discipline is different too. With healing, we are relaxed, allowing the student to absorb the knowledge at his own speed as a leaf absorbs the light of the sun. But battle-magic is best taught at a forced rate so the student has to stretch and develop as rapidly as possible. It is odd you have equal strength in both, but I think you will be able to deal with the conflict well enough, as long as you use healing-magic as often as you use your battle-magic. You will have to work hard to balance the use of both sorts of chi."

"What do healers use to defend themselves?" Edwin was curious. "Aeolyn is right. A bow would be completely useless against those rat-people."

"Healers have few skills in weaponry. We can use a staff, and believe me, it's a useful tool. I usually spar with Friedr, and I can stand my ground well enough to preserve my skin or cast a sleep spell." Christoph's eyes sparkled as he added, "And I can run like nobody's business."

"What he really means is he can disarm the best warrior in less time than most folks take to get their sword out of its sheath." Edwin hadn't heard Friedr approaching their table. "Our Christoph is useful in a fight, for far more than his exceptional healing skills. Once we have strengthened your sword arm, we will have you spar with him. It helps to know how to defend against any weapons you might come across. But right now, he would be leaving bruises all over your lily-white backside and then wearing himself out healing you."

Startled, Edwin agreed with the blunt assessment of his skills and managed a weak laugh. "When do we start training, you and I?" he asked Friedr, his frank smile making the friendly-girls who lined the bar staring at him swoon.

"Well, if you are rested up from your hard work healing, we can have a lesson now," Friedr replied cheerfully. He held up a bundle. "I have your armor and some practice swords here, so let's go out to the barn and exercise your soft, farm-boy muscles."

"I was afraid you would say that," replied Edwin with a grin, as he rose from his chair. "I'll do my best for you, Friedr." Soon he was geared up and facing the big man with a practice sword in his hand.

He thought he'd learned some skills in the last two weeks, but he was soon disabused of the notion. Friedr started by telling him, "Today we will begin your training in what I like to think of as the fine art of not dying at the end of some bastard's sword. Hold your weapon like this. No, see how I have my hands on the grip?" Edwin adjusted his grasp to match Friedr's. "Now the first form is the most important. It is the basis for each form and technique you will ever use. Do as I do." Friedr then began teaching Edwin the formal sword training he would need to master if he was to survive in this strange new world. "This is the stance I want you to assume, with your feet placed just so."

After they had finished and he stood trying to catch his breath, Edwin was pleased with how well he held up under Friedr's attacks, even though he had gone easy. He was bruised and sore, but managed to stay on his feet to the end of the lesson, when Friedr finally let up on him. Edwin staggered to a corner where he propped himself up and watched Friedr as he sparred with a merchant's guard who thought he could do better than the farm boy. To Edwin's surprise, the guard quickly fell, much faster than Edwin did. Then Christoph stepped in with his staff in an amazing display of skill that left Edwin breathless. Afterward, Friedr sent him off to the baths. "Christoph and I will be right behind you, or Aeolyn won't sit at the same table with us."

The next morning, they left Wister, embarking on the long day's walk to the city of Aeoven, also known as the Cathedral City. Edwin felt nervous, wondering what would happen to him when they arrived there.

Perhaps because Christoph had rebalanced Edwin's chi, they met only two small packs of rat-people on the journey. During the first skirmish, Edwin wasn't surprised to see Christoph's staff whirling and knocking his opponent off his feet, but he *was* surprised to see he didn't go in for the kill. Aeolyn immediately took care of it with her usual efficiency, in a practiced move that looked as if they had worked together many times.

"It's because of my extreme empathy," he told Edwin afterwards. "I have great support moves, but I can't bring myself to kill. The thought of killing even an animal sickens me. I'm not the only healer who can't kill even in self-defense. Probably half of the healers cannot."

The city of Aeoven was large with many shops and businesses. At the southern end of the city stood the cathedral complex housing the Temple of Aeos and the Colleges of Warcraft and Magic. As they walked, Edwin noticed small, three-sided stone shelters at the end of every street. In each one, a person sat, some reading, some doing needlework, and some obviously students working on their studies. "What are these small shelters and who are the people in them?" asked Edwin.

"They are the messengers. There is someone there at all times around the clock, seven days a week. All the people in Aeoven work for the Temple and could be called upon at a moment's notice. The messengers are crucial to the smooth running of the city and the Temple as a whole," replied Friedr. As they passed an empty shelter, he pointed down the street and said, "This is Elm Street, the weaver's street. See those large buildings down at the far end past the houses? Those house the great looms powered by the river. Someone has either sent a message or is receiving one."

As they passed Laurel Street, Friedr and Aeolyn said goodbye, stopping and letting the messenger know they were back. She made a note on her log of the time they reported in and handed them two notes. "Mail!" said Friedr happily. "Look, one is from my mum." Waving, they strode off down to their home, and Christoph and Edwin kept walking.

Christoph's bachelor quarters were located in a wing of the college solely dedicated to housing the unbonded journeyman mages. Soon they arrived at the building and checked in with the young messenger sitting at the foot of the stairs. "Hello, Kenn, I'm back. This is Edwin Farmer, a healer who will be guesting with me until he is assigned his own rooms. Could you please see if the kitchen can send us up a meal for two since we are too late for dinner?"

"Hello, Edwin." The boy's eyes were drawn to Edwin's sword. "I'm pleased to meet you. I've never seen a healer who carries a sword," replied Kenn. He was cheerful and looked about fourteen years old. "I'll do it now, Christoph. There are two letters under your door. I didn't know you'd be home tonight so I slipped them under it for you."

It was a pleasant change to spend an evening in a clean home, with a real bed and books to read. Edwin was suddenly homesick and felt guilty because he hadn't even thought of his dad or the farm in days. *I've been pretty busy,* he reminded himself. *I hope he's doing well without me. I'm sure he is. Dad is the strongest man I know.*

The kitchen staff sent two trays with hot food up for them, and soon they were seated before the fire in comfortable chairs and sipping hot chocolate. Feeling rested after having a proper bath, Edwin couldn't help but remark on the changes he had undergone in only two weeks. "Dad will never believe it when he hears what I'm doing now," he told Christoph. "I hope he's well. He's all alone now."

"Your father knows some of what is going on, I am sure, although he may be surprised to hear you are a healer. I think you are the first in your family's history born a healer. Your family all seems to bond with healers, but has always produced exceptionally strong battle-mages." Christoph stretched his feet out before the fire. "John Farmer was a famous mage, yet he came here much as you have, not knowing a thing. It seems the way of it for your family, though I don't know why. I do know he's been asked to return many times and has refused each request."

"I never knew. He never mentioned it," replied Edwin, wonder coloring his voice. "But there is apparently a lot I don't know about my father." He stared into the fire, wondering how he could have lived so closely with his parents, shared so much love and trust with them, and yet not have known a thing about their pasts. "We assume what we see about people is all there is to know until we're told differently. But he did say there was a reason for not telling me. I have to trust it was important."

Christoph nodded. "Family was always a mystery to me. I've never understood the why of things."

***

Perhaps because he was sleeping in a comfortable bed for the first time in weeks, Edwin dreamed he was standing in a wildly overgrown garden at the foot of a dark tower. He wore his brown armor, but his hair was loose, falling over his shoulders to his waist. Shadows whispered to him, begging him to follow them, but he was reluctant. They seemed like ghosts, and their whispers rustled like dry leaves in the wind. *Look for her in the Tower of Bones....*

Through a tiny window more like a grate, he saw a girl. She was thin and pale, as if she'd been ill. Brown hair in long, untidy braids hung down her back, and big brown eyes looked out of her drawn and dirty face. She seemed to have green tattoos, but he couldn't see them well. They were faded, much like his father's. She sat on a filthy, straw-covered floor, holding a book. The pages were torn out of it, and she carefully pieced it together. She sat lost in her thoughts, which from the look on her face, were grim. Mending the pages and putting them back into the book appeared to be a terribly important task. The room was dark, and he could see little of her surroundings.

Edwin had dreamt of her before, he was sure, but

she'd never been in such a dire place. She looked up, nervous and fearful. She seemed surprised when she saw him, as if she expected to see someone else. As his eyes met hers, the dream let him go, and he drifted into a more restful sleep.

Chapter 6

The next morning, Edwin and Christoph went to the dining hall for breakfast. At first, Edwin couldn't get the dream out of his mind or the girl he saw in it. He was rather quiet as they served themselves at the buffet and found a table. Christoph didn't press him, assuming he was worried about the meetings scheduled for him.

Edwin *did* have a full day ahead of him, and he soon forgot about the dream, as he was drawn into a flurry of activities.

Father Rall, a pleasant, grandfatherly man whom everyone loved and respected, stopped at their table during breakfast, chatting and sharing a cup of tea with them. Rall held the office of the Holy Seat and was the highest-ranking member of the clergy. He wore his thick white hair in a long warrior's braid exactly like Friedr's, falling well past his waist. He bore more facial augmentations than anyone Edwin had ever seen. Strong and tall despite his age, he was unmistakably still a capable swordsman with hard calluses on his hands and an alert way of moving. Whatever else he was—and Edwin suspected he was many things—Father Rall was a warrior in the fullest sense. In fact, Edwin felt he could be the strongest battle-mage in the Temple. The feeling of power the man embodied was impressive. Yet when he spoke, his voice was gentle and kindly, with a faint barbarian accent.

After they finished eating and exchanging small talk about books and interests they had in common, Rall led Edwin to his study to test him on the skills he'd learned so far. As he did so, he told Edwin more about his father. "I wish John hadn't left Neveyah, but I know why it had to be done. He did it to protect you and to let you come here with an open mind."

"But why did he tell me nothing about this place?" Edwin asked, his hurt emerging. "I was born here. I may have family here."

He felt great disappointment when Father Rall shook his head. "No, Edwin, I'm sorry. If you do, I am unaware of it, though there is a distant cousin several times removed in the town of Arlen, whom you'll likely meet on your journey. I understand how important family connections are and how isolated you have always been, but your mother's entire bloodline was lost in the fall of Mal Evol. Your father, along with Halee Randsdottir, Garran Andreson, and Pauli Oakheart, tried desperately to save them, but were too late. Pauli gave his life in that failed quest.

"Your father didn't tell you of Neveyah because your family is our secret weapon," continued Father Rall. "I quested with your grandfather, Wynn Farmer. We were close companions. He always told me his best weapon was the fact he had no preconceived notions of how things worked here. Wynn arrived even more ignorant than you, though you might not believe it. He'd never even seen a cobbled street. But he was able to make his lightning-magic work in new and amazing ways, as each member of your family is able to, simply because he didn't understand the limits as we do. We needed his ability to see new ways to use magic in our fight against the mindbender Grakken, just as we need you now. You'll read about Wynn's adventures and indeed all your family's exploits. You may be surprised to discover the history of the Temple is actually the history of your family."

Edwin sat back, plainly dumbfounded.

"So," Rall turned to his notes, "now let us see what it is about you that has Aeolyn in such a tizzy. Please light my lamp, if you will."

"Hmmm," said Father Rall as Edwin cast a small fire spell at the little lamp on his desk. "And perhaps some water? How about watering this poor plant?" He'd had the plants brought in earlier to see how Edwin would handle them.

Edwin did as he was asked and let the water flow from his palm into the soil around the rather sad-looking plant. He couldn't help but think about how sickly it appeared and how much better it would look if only it were a little healthier. Perhaps because of his thoughts, as he watered the plant, he also strengthened and healed it. He was unaware he'd done so, but the small improvement caused the Holy Father's eyes to widen fractionally.

He consulted his notes, seeing Christoph's belief Edwin could see the actual magic.

Rall stood and looked out the window, thinking about the possibilities and the impossibilities of such a thing. Finally he turned to Edwin and said, "My son, how is it you have learned so much so quickly? Your visualization skills are good, but you are nowhere near as good as your grandfather was. He was the best I ever knew. And yet, according to Aeolyn, you learned a spell for every day you have been here. My students are excellent teachers, but they're not that good. Did you know magic before you came here?"

Edwin was surprised. "There is no magic where I come from, your Holiness, none whatsoever. I simply look and see what my teachers are doing and try to copy it. Have I done something wrong?"

"No, no. You say you simply see what they are doing. When I do this, what does it look like to you?" Father Rall stood before the plant Edwin had healed and began to weave lines of brownish-green magic.

Edwin watched closely as the plant grew before his eyes and flowered. "You wove the green magic, sir. I've never seen Christoph use this sort. His is more of a deep blue-green. Yours is a brown-green."

"Ah. This is farm-magic," replied Father Rall. "It's rudimentary, something many farmers know even if their gift isn't strong enough to be trained. My true strength lies in battle-magic."

"Water," Edwin supplied. "You have mostly blue tattoos like my father. You have a large green star on the back of your left hand, and my dad has one on his shoulder. You seem to have all the colors represented, like my dad, but until I came here, I didn't know his tattoos meant anything." Father Rall nodded with a pleased smile at Edwin's perception.

"Water is indeed my strongest magic, and I have been blessed with a small ability to heal, which is why I can use the plant magics. My healing ability is minimal, limited to small cuts and minor sleep spells at best, as is your father's. Strength in water and earth enable some of us to use this plant-magic to good advantage in the farms and gardens." Father Rall stood before another plant and asked Edwin, "Can you try to replicate what you saw me do?"

Edwin closed his eyes and tried to remember. He found the brownish-green magic and tried to plait it in the way he recalled. The plant grew and budded, but it didn't flower. "I'm sorry, sir. I didn't do it right. I wasn't paying close enough attention to the weave, so I was sort of guessing."

"The weave?" Rall looked confused.

"Yes sir, the way you make the energies do what you want," Edwin replied.

"Not to worry." Rall made a note on his pad. "You did well, but it is your ability to visualize that actually makes the magic work, not weaving. Those movements have nothing to do with it, and reveal that you are preparing to call magic. Aeolyn will explain this to you, and I think you will find your attempts will improve greatly. Now what does this look like to you?" Father Rall called fire to the fireplace.

"The energies are ropes of an orange-red color," replied Edwin.

"And this?" The Holy Father called water to the pitcher on his desk.

"The ropes are made of the blue energies," was Edwin's reply.

"And this?" Father Rall called lightning, forming a ball he let go of in the fireplace.

"They are white-yellow, sir, and much more like wire than rope."

"We have, in you, another thing we have never seen before. Are you aware mages don't actually see the magic they work with?"

Edwin looked at him, taken aback by the revelation.

"We can only sense it and feel it. This is why it takes so long to learn our craft. We are blind to that which we must work with. I've never seen it, though I've always wondered what it would look like. We must visualize each element in its final form as clearly as possible when we call them. I didn't realize we actually wove energies. You see, we don't weave them physically."

Once again, Edwin was surprised. "This explains why Aeolyn didn't understand my questions," he replied, feeling rather rueful. "She kept telling me to visualize what I wanted, which I tried to do. My father always stressed visualization too. It was a habit he taught me all my childhood."

"John was preparing you to think properly for when you came here, as he was prepared by his father, Wynn. And Wynn was prepared by his father." Rall was quiet for a moment as he considered everything. "This ability to see the magic must be the result of the two disciplines combining in you with equal strength. You are the first mage, so far as I know, other than the rogue-mage, Stefyn D'Mal, to have both talents in full and equal measure. It must be the healing empathy that allows you to see elemental magic the way a healer sees into a patient. How this will manifest itself once you have been fully augmented and come into your powers will be interesting. You will spend the next six months learning what those powers are."

Edwin didn't know what to say, so he said nothing. A wave of frustration swept over him as he struggled to force down his desire to leave immediately on their quest, followed by the realization he knew absolutely nothing about magic and would be next to useless until he learned how to use it properly. However, the idea of languishing in Aeoven for months while the girl was in danger frustrated him.

Unaware of Edwin's turmoil, Father Rall said, "I

was one of your grandfather's instructors. I know you'll do well."

"I hope so," replied Edwin. "I must be the oldest novice here." His open face reddened slightly as he spoke. "All the young ones look at me strangely, and I don't blame them."

Rall laughed. "You're far too old to be a novice, you know. We won't be putting you in the novice barracks. You might as well get settled into your own rooms since you'll have several months here. We think you'll most likely leave after the winter solstice. At least, it's what the omens are looking like."

Edwin left Father Rall's study and met Christoph, Friedr, and Aeolyn in the hall as they were leaving the Abbess's study. "You're going to be my near-neighbor," said Christoph. "After you get settled in, I'll stop by your new rooms and take you down to the dining hall for lunch, and then we'll go to the infirmary."

"You're invited to dinner tonight at our house," said Aeolyn, with a sparkle in her eyes. "I have the rest of the day off to cook."

"I promise it will be the best meal you've ever eaten," added Friedr, as they went their separate ways. Still smiling, Edwin entered the abbess's reception room.

Chapter 7

Abbess Halee was an earth-mage with three tiny, green stars on her right cheek, somewhat at odds with her battle-mage augmentations. Her shirt was dyed a warm brown, and she'd embroidered the yoke and cuffs with tiny flowers. At forty-two, she remained a vibrantly attractive woman. Her deep blue eyes were warm, and her burnished coppery-brown hair was worn in a coronet like Aeolyn's. Edwin saw only a few silver threads. It gleamed in the light that came in the window of her study. Also like Aeolyn, she was physically fit and obviously able to use the sword that leaned in its worn scabbard by her desk.

Halee spent some time clarifying for Edwin exactly how clergy was structured. "Of those people who work for the Temple, only perhaps fifty are fully trained battle-mages actively working, and another forty or so are healers. Magic is in short supply since the war. We lost three-quarters of our mages during the actual taking of Mal Evol, more than half of the population of Neveyah." Halee was silent and then quickly resumed her lecture.

"Another thirty-six are at various stages of novice training, and three with healing ability will not make journeyman as they don't have the right temperament, being selfish, manipulative, and sadistic in small ways. They are not acceptable to Aeos. We will train them enough to use farm magic and send them back home with permanent inhibitions so they can no longer abuse others with their empathy. All they will know is their gift wasn't strong enough.

"There is another reason we search for mage-gifted children. The ones who go wrong are more dangerous than anyone can imagine. Father Rall and your grandfather, Wynn, fought against the last of the great rogue-mages. In fact, until your father came along, this was mostly what your family was involved in: protecting the people of Neveyah from rogue-mages who preyed on the general populace. This is the purpose of the Assassin's Guild within the Temple, searching out the ones who have chosen to disobey Aeos and removing them permanently."

Shocked, Edwin said, "Do you mean you kill them? Simply because they aren't in the Temple?"

"Edwin, I know it sounds harsh. The bargain Aeos has with Tauron is this: any mage who uses his talents to cause harm to another person is Tauron's property. The first time they use their gifts to harm another, he claims them, and he never lets go. They always work his will, trying to bring Aeos down. The damage rogue-mages do to the people of Neveyah is terrible. It ranges from simply using their abilities to commit petty crimes, to murder, and everything in between. We don't tolerate any abuse of the gifts, and those who will not be bound by the vows must be blocked permanently. Murderers are executed. This, by the way, is a Temple secret. It is done for the protection of Neveyah."

Edwin nodded, saying, "I understand...now. I'll never speak of this outside of the Temple. I promise." Saddened, he said, "I hope I'm never called upon to make such a choice."

"We all hope so, Edwin. It is not something we do lightly." Halee's face was grave. "But let's not dwell on these unhappy things. Today is a day for rejoicing because you have returned to us. I was there the day you were born, did you know? We celebrated with your parents and your grandfather. We were your family then, and we still are."

"I didn't know," Edwin replied, feeling happiness at the thought. "I guess family is as much love as it is blood."

"You're right. Love is what family is all about." Inadvertently echoing Father Rall, Halee said, "You are far too old to be a novice. You know as many spells as a first-year journeyman does, you can call your magic when needed, and you have reliable shields and barriers. Most importantly, you have demonstrated enough maturity to handle the responsibilities." She read him the vows and explained what they signified. "Do you understand you will forever be magically bound to giving your life to the service of Aeos and Neveyah?"

"Yes, ma'am, I do. My father often spoke about the importance of duty." He unconsciously smiled the frank, charming smile that made him look so much like his father. "I'm honored to be considered worthy to serve the Goddess and Neveyah."

Halee was stunned by how much he resembled his father as a young man, though his demeanor seemed much more like his mother, Andia's. Edwin was deep and appeared to think carefully about his decisions, unlike his father at his age. She smiled in response to his charismatic honesty, struck with the wry thought he wouldn't be nearly as much fun to travel with as John had been. Calling her mind to order, she continued explaining what she would do in administering the vow. This was the setting of a geas that bound the mage to a strict protocol of behavior in regard to the use of his gift.

Edwin did nothing lightly. As he spoke the vows, a feeling of warmth settled over him, and the honor of being chosen by Aeos to serve her deeply moved him. He was now a healer, a battle-mage, and a priest of the Temple. As she pinned a journeyman's pin on his shirt, Abbess Halee said, "For now, we'll just let it be known you are a healer, which will be simpler and cause less confusion in the Temple at large. Goodness only knows what the magic will choose when you get your augmentations. Fortunately, there are a few battle-mages like Father Rall and myself who have some small healing abilities, so perhaps you won't stand out too much. I'm only good with minor healings, which was a big help when we were questing. I'm a bit better than your father and Father Rall are, but not anywhere near strong enough to work in the infirmary except as a volunteer. All battle-mages who have stars like me are fully trained as field medics.

"You, on the other hand, will need to have private lessons each day in the basic skills and fundamental knowledge of healing, and you must work in the infirmary. Also, you will be writing essays for me on your studies in every area of both elemental magic and healing, so I can gauge your understanding. You will have to do in the next two to four months what the children spend four to six years learning. Then you will need to spend at least two more months learning what your true battle-magic abilities are." Halee smiled at Edwin and added, "I believe you'll be able to do it."

"I would prefer to get going on the actual quest, but I think I understand the reason behind the delay." He firmly pushed his frustration back down, but for a moment, he looked remarkably like his father. "I would choose to work as a healer if it were left up to me," Edwin told her, speaking candidly. "But I enjoy using the battle-magic too and learning from Friedr all the weaponry skills. It's a hard decision to make because I can see so many possibilities for these talents. But healing is my personal choice."

The Abbess spent some time explaining the way the Temple worked. She told him how Aeos spoke directly to the priesthood through what were called prophecies and they were all witnessed by more than one person and written down word for word. "You will know you are hearing a true prophecy, trust me," she said wryly. "You will hear Aeos's Bell. If you don't hear it, it's not a true prophecy, although it may be an omen. True-dreams are more open to interpretation and are often filled with omens and portents." She reassured him, saying, "No one sworn to Aeos can lie and say the Goddess has spoken when she has not. The vows keep us honest as to our service to the Goddess, and so you can be sure you are hearing her words.

"On the seventh day of the week, every person employed by the Temple donates a day of labor on various tasks to supply the Temple stores." She handed him a list. "Here is the sign-up sheet for the crews you might want to report to on Sunnaday. Father Rall dries and preserves food, Friedr usually cuts firewood, and Christoph sews clothing. Aeolyn and I do quilting."

There were a lot of different tasks, and none looked too arduous for Edwin. He immediately chose the firewood-cutting crew. "I like to cut and split firewood," he told Halee. "I've done a bit of it over the years."

As a journeyman, Edwin would receive a stipend of two gold pieces per month. Halee handed him a packet with two golds in it. One was his salary for the time he had been in Neveyah, and the other was for him to use to purchase books and other things he might need for his new home that he couldn't get from the Temple stores.

Edwin had a purse full of silvers and coppers and several golds, his share of what they'd found on the dead rat-people. The Temple provided his housing, food, and clothing, so he couldn't imagine what he would spend his money on. When he mentioned this to Abbess Halee, she replied, "Edwin, you have learned as much about the craft of magic over these last two weeks as even the brightest of students does in two years. You are fighting to protect Neveyah and the Goddess Aeos, as are your companions, and you earned your share of the loot found on those poor feral rats. You must be on equal footing when you leave on your quest. You've earned your money, and believe me, you will continue to earn it."

Edwin suddenly remembered his father had sent her his greetings, and when he told her, she smiled. "Your father was the fourth member of the quest I went on as a newly minted journeyman earth-mage. We shared a lot of good times, John, Garran, Pauli, and I." Her mind seemed far away as she spoke of their adventures. The person she described, however, was a young, brash, and headstrong boy Edwin didn't recognize.

Laughing, she told a little tale of John diverting a stream and creating a romantic waterfall in an effort to impress Andia, Edwin's mother, on the day he met her, showing off with his water-magic. "Your father dove into life with a zest that made everyone who met him want to be his companion."

"It's hard for me to picture my dad young, especially as the person you describe. I would have told you he's never done a reckless thing in his life, if you'd asked me. But now I realize I don't really know him." Edwin's open face was troubled as he wondered how he could have lived with his father all his life and never actually known him.

"You know your father. You know the man he became, not the boy he was. John was an idealist. He fervently believed good would always triumph. To this day, he has never accepted that sometimes evil wins." She sighed. "He suffered terribly when Pauli was killed, you know. We all did. The guilt nearly crushed us. You'll hear the sad tale soon enough. I can't really talk about it." Halee's eyes turned to the window, a pensive look crossing her smooth features. "And then, after all we went through, for John to lose Andia so young, well, it must have hurt him deeply." Her eyes, as she gazed out the window, were full of compassion for his father. "I don't know how well I would handle such a loss, and I've shared more than twenty good years with my husband."

She turned back to him, a smile firmly back in place. "But enough reminiscing. Here is a note for you to give to the seneschal. You must have your own rooms so you can study, but I have asked him to see to it you are near Christoph. Sadly, we have far too many empty quarters than would be optimal and more coming empty all the time, but we must work with what we have. Having you is almost like getting two mages—you are a healer, which we desperately need, and a battle-mage, also desperately needed. When I was a young journeyman, we lived two to an apartment and thought ourselves lucky, but the war with D'Mal has taken its toll on us. Still, we're rebuilding the clergy, and doing our best to ensure people can live well despite the depredations of Tauron's creatures."

Halee looked at Edwin closely and said, "You're doing well at following Christoph's instructions for bleeding off the excess chi. I don't sense any excessive buildup now, but I imagine you were uncomfortable."

"I had to become good at it. It was becoming difficult before he showed me what was wrong and how to keep it away from myself. He helps me too, or I wouldn't be doing as well, I'm sure. I thought I was going mad before we met up with him." Edwin's honesty about his problem charmed Halee.

"You're doing well. I think you will make your father proud, Edwin. Don't worry. You have the self-control to handle it. Both Aeolyn and Christoph told me so." Then the Abbess handed him the note for the seneschal and directed him to the proper door.

Lyell, the seneschal, was tall and thin, with a harried manner, but he was kind and repeatedly told Edwin he only had to ask if there was anything he wanted or needed. "The housekeepers will bring you anything you need from the Temple storerooms. Leave a note for them on the worktable in your sitting room in the morning. If you need to have meals in your rooms or need to send a message, just ask the messenger assigned to your building."

They walked to the door at the end of the large

four-story building. The desk this time was occupied by a bored novice water-mage, a girl of about twelve years of age. The plaque on her little desk stated her name was Kiri, and she was writing an essay of some sort. The seneschal introduced him and handed him off to the startled girl.

She greeted him with some surprise, perhaps because she'd never seen him before in their small community. "Oh. I saw the housekeepers going in there earlier, and I couldn't imagine who was being made journeyman. There's no one old enough right now."

When they entered his rooms, only two doors down from Christoph's and exactly the same in layout, Edwin found them airy, with good views of the Temple herb and kitchen gardens through the large windows. Attractive, well-executed oil paintings of diverse landscapes were hung in various places, and the gently-used furnishings made the rooms look like a home.

A small guest room completed his apartment. "It's for your family to stay in when they come to visit," Kiri said as she showed him his quarters. "I heard when the Abbess was young, everyone was two to an apartment, but now we have more empty ones than full."

"A guest room is nice," Edwin politely agreed, but privately he thought, *I don't think my dad will come here even for a visit. He's made clear his wish to have nothing to do with Neveyah by never mentioning it.* Still, he nodded and smiled as she showed him his new home. If Edwin wanted to, he could heat water on the hob in his fireplace. The teakettle sat to one side, and a teapot and two mugs rested on the mantel, along with a canister of tea and small pot of honey. The apartment was perfect for the journeyman mage who spent a lot of time studying, with no time to cook or clean. From the sounds of it, he would be busy while he was preparing for the quest.

"Um...." Kiri obviously wanted to ask Edwin something. He nodded his head in encouragement and waited. "Where are your augmentations, if I may ask? I don't see any on your face. I know it was rude of me." She blushed a deep scarlet.

"Don't worry, Kiri, I know it's confusing. I'll be augmented tomorrow, and since I'm from far away, I haven't received them yet." Edwin tried to send her as much assurance as he could. "I'm from the world of Ariend, from a little town called Markett."

"Oh. Ariend is the world protected by the Almighty Father. John Farmer was from there," she answered, smiling as her confusion cleared. "We studied about him. He came here as a novice, though."

"He's my father, and where we live, there is no magic, so we don't need augmentations until we come here." He held his hand out to her saying, "My name is Edwin Farmer, and you're the first friend I've made other than my teachers."

"I love it here," Kiri told him fervently, shaking his hand. "Well, I have to go back to my station, but if you need anything, please tell me. It gets boring when no one has anything for me to do. I'm glad to have met you, Edwin." She skipped off to her desk as merrily as any twelve-year old might anywhere in either world.

On entering his bedroom to unpack his kit, he was glad to find the closet already stocked with several pairs of loose linen trousers and white shirts, the basic clothes everyone wore. Underclothes and socks filled a basket, and a note from Aeolyn reminding him to requisition new boots from the Temple stores sat on top. An empty basket for soiled clothing sat in the corner.

Immediately, Edwin changed into the loose trousers and a clean shirt. He folded up his brown leathers and rolled up his armor to take with him when he worked out with Friedr.

A wave of homesickness washed over Edwin when he saw the quilt that covered his bed. The pattern was exactly the same as his at home, the last quilt his mother made before her death. He sat at his table, consumed with thoughts of home and his parents.

Christoph's knock jarred him out of his temporary bout of self-pity. "Are you ready?" His eyes took in Edwin's change of attire. "Good. I see you understand completely. I borrowed one of Dane's shirts for you to wear today, if you don't mind changing quickly." He was dressed in a simple shirt of moss green and loose trousers. "I'll dye two of yours while you're working out with Friedr this afternoon so you'll have green to wear in the infirmary. Battle-mages wear white shirts for working, and if you wear white, your patients won't realize you're a healer. They'll think you're training as a field medic and won't pay any attention to you."

They went to the infirmary where Christoph introduced Edwin and showed him around. Many of the healers were surprised to see Chris there and with a private student in tow. "We thought you lost to us for all but the most serious of cases," a sweet, white-haired healer named Beryl exclaimed as she hugged Christoph joyfully.

Turning to Edwin, she smiled and said, "I healed your father many a time, often from his own foolishness. Goodness, he loved a fight. I'm glad to see his son has some sense." She winked at him, adding, "Even if you do swing a sword, you naughty man. Halee told me about you and your dual abilities. I don't envy the path you are now set on, though I've often wondered what it would be like to cast fire or lightning."

After he and Christoph finished at the infirmary, Edwin went to the weapons barn and geared up. Just as Edwin expected, Friedr succeeded in beating him black and blue in his effort to teach him some skills.

Later as they washed up in the men's dressing room, Edwin asked Friedr how he knew who could—or couldn't—use battle-magic.

"You can feel it too if you open up like you do when a rat-mage is casting magic and you need to put up shields," replied Friedr. "A battle-mage has an aura that pushes against that of other people. I can feel your strength, like a blazing fire several feet away. I'm told all mages have an energy field, but neither Aeolyn nor I have any healing magic, so we can't sense it. This is why Aeolyn didn't know you were also a healer. But I've heard that with your healing sight you can see the energy fields that surround battle-mages. Open your senses and see if you have the ability." Friedr smiled. "Now, I'm going to surprise Aeolyn by arriving home on time, and with a bouquet of flowers. See you for dinner tonight."

Smiling, Edwin looked at Friedr's departing back with the healing sight and saw he did indeed have a faintly golden aura. *Is this the warmth I feel around Friedr and Aeolyn?* He analyzed how he felt around Christoph and realized his friend's presence was soothing and restful. He'd noticed, when he looked, a faint green-golden aura around his friend.

As Edwin walked the corridors, he practiced looking at the mages. After a while, he found he could tell the type of magic each person he met had and how strong they were. He could even see when they had little or no chi.

Temporarily at loose ends, he decided to walk to the shops and find a gift for Aeolyn and Friedr's new home. He found a set of six wine glasses with red stems that cost two silvers, feeling daring for spending so much money. The glassmaker's wife wrapped them in tissue for him and placed them in a basket that she gave to him simply because of his smile, refusing to accept even a copper for it.

Later when Christoph arrived, he presented Edwin with a new feast-day shirt, embroidered with small green and blue geometric designs around the edges. The leather laces at the cuffs and throat were dyed green. "You need a nice shirt to wear for special occasions, and this qualifies. We'll be the first guests in their new home."

"This is the fanciest shirt I have ever owned," Edwin said as he put it on. "My feast-day shirt at home isn't nearly this nice." Christoph wore one he'd dyed a moss green and decorated with tiny embroideries that mimicked his tattoos. "How did you do this so quickly?"

"Embellishing clothing is my hobby. This is a simple, basic design and easy to do quickly. After my interview with Abbess Halee, I was free all morning before we went to the infirmary, so I had plenty of time." Christoph's sunny mood was infectious. "I usually work on something like this in the evening when I'm alone. It calms me, and I can think as I do it. I'll make you another one after you've received your augmentations and I know the main element of your battle-magic."

Christoph approved of Edwin's gift for Friedr and Aeolyn's new home. He too carried a basket, a set of embroidered napkins and a matching tablecloth inside. "I finished these last week before we left to meet you," he told Edwin.

Together they walked down the narrow cobbled street, and Christoph pointed out various places in the Mage's Quarter of the Temple district that Edwin might need to know. As they approached the neat little row-house their friends lived in, Edwin was surprised by the little vegetable gardens lining the walks to each home and said as much.

"We use every space for growing food here in the city, even the gardens of the empty houses. There are a lot of people to feed, not only here in Aeoven, but all over Neveyah," Christoph replied. "In the back gardens you'll find a small cobblestone area for the summer kitchen and picnic table, and the rest will be a vegetable garden and a place for a few chickens. We dry and preserve everything that doesn't get used fresh, and all the surplus food goes to the Temples all over Aeoven for distribution to the local people. Father Rall instituted this ten years ago when he was elected to the Holy Seat. We do keep a certain amount in the storehouses in case there is a famine year, but we make sure no one goes hungry."

"It must solve many problems," said Edwin, thinking such a program would have saved Christoph's family from suffering.

Friedr answered the door, wearing a red shirt with yellow flowers neatly embroidered around the cuffs and collar and the same sort of dark blue, loose linen trousers all mages wore. He was bursting with pride, hosting them in his pleasant home.

Edwin was once again struck by Aeolyn's deceptively fragile beauty. She smiled warmly and greeted them with hugs. Bright flowers were braided into the coronet of her dark hair. She was clad in a white shirt embroidered with red roses up the sleeves in a design that matched her augmentations, over a narrow ankle-length skirt of dark blue linen, also embroidered with roses. She wore a simple white apron over them.

It was a bit disorienting for Edwin to see everyone in something besides battle leathers, but he liked it. He told Friedr, "It feels like a feast-day, being all dressed up like this."

Friedr laughed and said, "She cooked enough food for a feast day. You're in for a treat."

They were surprised and touched at the gifts Edwin and Christoph brought for them, and Friedr immediately poured the wine. "This will taste much better in these glasses than in our tea mugs, nice mugs though they are."

Aeolyn marveled as she examined the table linens from Christoph, who blushed at her assessment of his skills. "Chris, it is amazing how the back of everything you embroider is as nice as the front. If it weren't for the seams, you wouldn't know the difference."

Friedr admired Edwin's new shirt as he led them to the warm and cheerful kitchen. "I see you received one of Chris's creations, too. He's famous for them."

A bouquet of colorful flowers in a hand-painted vase stood in the center of the round table in the alcove. Edwin admired the vase, eliciting a pleased response from Christoph. "My friend Dane's young cousin Zander made it for them as a wedding present," he said, coloring slightly. "You will meet Dane soon. Zan is eleven and a novice lightning-mage. Dane raised him, since their parents are dead." His face broke into a smile. "If you remember, I told you my first patient with traumatic injuries was a young boy—Zan was the boy. He was injured in a house fire and was healed physically, but his uncle died saving him, and Zan witnessed his death. I worked with him for two years so he could live like a normal child. He suffered from night terrors so badly he couldn't be away from Dane, but he's doing well now and loving every minute of his life as a novice. His scars are healed on the inside as well as they are on the outside."

Edwin could tell by the faint blush that Dane and his cousin were important to Christoph. Perhaps Dane was the mysterious boyfriend Rila had mentioned. "He's talented," offered Edwin. "I like the way he painted the vase. You would never know a child had done it."

"He is good, isn't he?" Chris's proud smile confirmed Edwin's guess. "Lightning-mages are often the best artists. Most of the paintings that hang in the bachelor quarters are their work over the years. Father Rall's wife, Feia, is one of the finest artists in Aeoven."

Everywhere in their home were the signs of Aeolyn's handiwork, from their clothing to the curtains and the cheerful tea towels hung neatly by the sink. Edwin was pleased and somehow unsurprised to see this side of her. "She always cooked wonderfully when we were camping, if I could call the fire without her help, that is." he told Friedr. "You're a lucky man."

Friedr agreed, smiling in his domestic bliss. "I always knew she was the only one for me."

Chapter 8

The next morning, promptly at eight, Edwin visited the colorist, a priestess named Janae, who was to give him his special tattoos. She seemed familiar, although he couldn't place her. Her strength of magic was lightning, as Christoph had told him. Three tiny stars above her collar bone indicated some small, healing talent.

While her journeyman assistant prepared things for the ritual, Janae explained the tattoos would be created magically to enable Edwin to store excess chi for later use in the working of spells that might require large amounts of it. "Young battle-mages of around nine years of age usually receive one small augmentation, a lightning bolt in front of the ear, so they can get used to the extra chi stored in their system and learn how to access it. Young healers usually receive three stars on their brow," she said, with a comforting smile. "Color is determined by the type of magic the mage has the most affinity for and will be using regularly."

Edwin was the first ever to receive a tattoo for healing magic *and* one for battle-magic on what they referred to as the day of first coloring. His augmentations would also be much larger, as he was older and deemed able to deal with the sensations of the stored chi. The seers all foresaw he would need unusually large augmentations to complete the quest.

Soon, Edwin was reclining stark naked on the colorist's table. Fortunately for him, he wasn't body-shy. The magic chose where the augmentations would be placed, and that was never fully known until the ritual was complete. He understood that due to the nature of her work, Janae and her assistant, Elner, saw each and every member of the clergy on her table, so his lack of clothing didn't upset him the way it might have bothered someone else.

Over the course of an hour, the magic gave him a leafy green vine twining his right forearm and wrist and trailing down the back of his hand for healing chi. A spiral of barbed vines with the four elemental colors equally represented circled his left bicep twice from his elbow and crossed his shoulder to just above his collar. His left thigh now sported the same barbed vines climbing in a close spiral from knee to hip. A crescent moon on his left temple with three small stars of green trailing over his right eye and a blue lightning bolt outlined in red on the cheek in front of his left ear completed his new augmentations.

"It's funny," Edwin told Janae as he stared at his new tattoos in her mirror. A strange heat was slowly rising in his veins, and some part of him knew he had to learn how to channel it or be consumed. "I used to nag my dad to let me get a tattoo, and he always told me to wait. He said when the time was right, a tattoo would choose me. I thought he was putting me off." His voice sounded odd, as if he were speaking down a tunnel. "Dad would never talk about his tattoos. He always said he got them when he was too young to know better. Now I'm here, I know he was a battle-mage. But he never told me anything about it. I wonder why he didn't want me know."

The priestess looked at him and then spoke hesitantly, as if against her better judgment. "Your father was a great hero, but in the end, even he couldn't save the land of Mal Evol when the Bull God sent his children to take the valley. What your father did was an amazing feat, a miracle. He built the shield that protects Neveyah from the mind-magic of Stefyn D'Mal, the High Priest of the Bull God. You will learn of this in your studies. Your father is a humble man. He honestly doesn't believe his accomplishment is out of the ordinary. Nevertheless, it remains to this day the most extraordinary work of magic ever created. John conceived and implemented it when no one else would have even thought of it. And John was desperate enough to use his minimal healing empathy to link with Halee and Garran to build it, though how they did so, no one knows.

"John was the High Commander of the Temple army. He fought harder than anyone and lived through battles no one should have survived. John personally led the Temple forces and drove the children of the Bull God back to their new domain in Mal Evol, and in the battle of Ronan's Vineyard, the bloodiest battle we ever fought, he faced terrible odds with only four hundred warriors and still bought enough time for the Temple to consolidate our forces around Braden. And with his magic-shield, he stopped them from entering our land.

"Still, our land of Neveyah is whittled away each year. What D'Mal didn't win in the taking of Mal Evol, he is winning piecemeal, a hectare a year, with his thorns and the poor demented rat people. Now the garden city of Braden lies threatened. John Farmer left the task unfinished, as you must also do. Will you be ready to do the same when the time comes?" Edwin looked at her and numbly nodded his assent. "John didn't like to leave the job half done, but Neveyah is a land where the finishing of a task may take generations. And the man I knew wouldn't speak about it as he was unhappy with the way things went. It's his way."

"You know my dad?" Edwin knew he shouldn't be surprised, but he was now feeling somewhat disassociated from his thoughts. The heat was rising in his veins, and a faint roaring sounded in his ears.

"I do. I trained with him when he first came to Neveyah. He quested with my sister, Halee. Andia, your mother, was my very dear friend." She smiled kindly at Edwin. "We were roommates as journeymen. Now you must put on this robe and meet Christoph in the garden through this door." She bled the excess chi off, which helped momentarily, and checked his tattoos one last time. "I'll have to add to this in small increments while you remain here. If you depart Aeoven by Holy Day and winter solstice, when you arrive in Braden, you must stop in to the Temple and have their colorist, Jamson, add more to each," she told Edwin. "You're going to need it. Within three months, these won't store enough chi to keep up with your abilities, even with what I'll be adding between now and your date of departure. Now go rest and try to get used to the feeling. You'll learn how to store and access the chi soon enough."

Edwin's senses reeled. He fought the urge to let the magic run wild, feeling nearly overwhelmed by the way his senses were magnified. Christoph waited for him in the specially shielded garden off the colorist's study. He shunted the excess chi away and they immediately began walking in circles, working on channeling his chi and damping the sensations as it built up in his body.

Edwin's vision was improved, so much so that the

normally dim corridors now seemed well lit to him, and now he understood how Aeolyn could see so well in the dark. As he and Christoph paced in the garden, Edwin began to shake and sweat with the effort of not letting his magic run wild. Christoph bled off his chi as he'd done when they first met and began the task of getting him used to it.

Edwin's augmentations were much larger than normal, being the magnitude of the first, second, and third colorings of a normal mage in each of the disciplines. He had gone straight to the level of both a journeyman healer and a journeyman battle-mage.

Because of this, he was suffering from a condition known as augmentation reaction. The temporary volatility caused by the buildup of focused chi was extremely dangerous and was the reason they were usually done in small increments. The mage had to learn to control it and smooth the flows, bleeding the excess off harmlessly. There were reports in the archives of mages going mad and laying waste to their surrounding area, which was why Christoph was there to help him.

Edwin wouldn't be working out with Friedr until his augmentations were fully healed. With Christoph's help, it would be a matter of two days at the most.

As the day progressed, Edwin passed through several stages, beginning with shaking, sweating, and severe disorientation, which moved on to extreme euphoria and silliness, and then to a strong need to sleep. Each phase he passed through signified his recovery. There was some pain in the actual augmentations, but it wasn't too bad with the application of soothing ointments and healing spells.

During the night, Edwin dreamed he stood on the walls of a large, overgrown rose garden at the base of a dark tower. He saw a thin, pale girl wearing a full-skirted dress like the women of Markett wore, whose hair fell in a long, thick braid to her knees. Doggedly, she weeded and clipped one tiny corner of the garden, trying to bring order to the chaos. *Marya...,* he thought groggily, as he turned over and fell into a deeper, dreamless sleep.

*** *** ***

By working diligently at handling his chi-flows, Edwin was able to go back to work in the infirmary the next day, although he was somewhat distracted and had to force himself to concentrate. He was pleased to find he had all the chi necessary to cast his healing spells effectively.

However, his patients were a little confused by the new lightning bolt on his cheek. A few of the patients he and Christoph had as patients were retired and semi-retired battle-mages, and they understood well what his augmentations signified.

"But healers can't cast fire or use water as a weapon, which is what this lightning bolt clearly says you can do. Green, red, and blue in equal measure on one mage—I've never seen such a thing before, and I've seen everything, or so I thought." Jules Brendsson, who'd known Edwin's grandfather quite well, was a fire-mage suffering from a crippling joint ailment. His voice was filled with incredulity as he went on, "It seems all wrong. I can heal a few minor wounds like cuts and scrapes, but I only gained my star when I was augmented twenty years ago during the invasion. Of course, if a healer was also going to be a battle-mage, it would be a member of your family who would be the lucky one." He smiled paternally as he patted Edwin's shoulder and looked at his augmentations sympathetically. Edwin and Christoph together worked on Jules, who forgot about Edwin's strange augmentations as his pain was eased and he was able to walk more easily.

As the day progressed, Edwin found that, with his hair down, the lightning bolt didn't draw much attention.

As they left the infirmary, Christoph remarked to Edwin, "I'm afraid Jules will have to retire to a less stressful job within the temple soon—he can't swing a sword anymore. He's managed to hold it off longer than most, but his case is typical of older fire-mages. Something about the use of their magic is debilitating over time."

Edwin was fascinated to discover that fire-mages often suffered from arthritis and gout, and lightning-mages frequently developed various cancers. Kidney failure was most common in water-mages, and earth-mages tended toward congestive heart failure and lung troubles. Most intriguingly, healers who possessed the ability to call water did not seem to suffer from kidney failure. He felt sure there was a reason for it somewhere but didn't know what to look for yet. He told Christoph, "It must be some small thing intrinsic to healers that protects them, but what could it be?"

Chris had no answer for that. The problem interested Edwin, and he found himself thinking about it at odd times. He checked out many texts on the subject from the college library. "There must be some way for battle-mages to avoid these diseases," Edwin later told Christoph. "I wonder what causes them."

"It's the long-term results of the elemental magic working on the body." Christoph shrugged. "It's the curse of being a successful battle-mage, which healers who can call water are not. Healers have been dealing with this problem since the college was first started. But you're the first to also be a battle-mage, so you may be able to discover something we haven't."

"I'm interested in working in this field if I have the opportunity," Edwin said. "I'd like to find ways to help them. I need more experience, and then I'll have a better idea of how to go about it."

"Well, I'm sure there would be no problem with you making it your area of emphasis. I don't believe anyone ever has," Christoph replied. "Once we're on the road, we will be healing at each farm and village we pass between here and Arlen. Since we'll be going on this quest, they've decided you'll also be making your required away-posting. Once we get back from Mal Evol, you'll be an upper-level journeyman, and you can declare your area of healing."

In this way, the next few days passed quickly. Though it was strange at first, Edwin eventually became used to looking in the mirror when shaving and seeing his colorful self. He immersed himself in his studies, and they occupied him completely. At times, it seemed almost as if he was driven to learn.

He was obsessed by the fact he knew they would be leaving Aeoven and he wouldn't have access to the Temple library to answer his questions. Edwin had so many that he kept a notebook nearby at all times to write them down, crossing them off as he found the answers.

For the evening meal, he often dined at Christoph's
with his many friends, cheerfully helping to carry the
trays to and from the huge Temple kitchen. Friedr and
Aeolyn regularly dined with them, helping Edwin with
his studies. Their friends accepted him as an equal and
enjoyed his company as much as he did theirs. For the
first time as an adult, Edwin was in a social group that
included women who didn't stalk him like a hunted
deer.

Dane Bransson was the healer selected to instruct
Edwin in healer's barriers—the mental shields that
protected them from picking up the random thought of
others. He was in love with Christoph and, as Edwin
had wondered, was in fact the mysterious boyfriend
mentioned in Wister. As far as Edwin could see, Chris
reciprocated, but something held him back from
committing. He was admittedly not attracted to women
and was seeing Dane only, but it wasn't a formal
bonding, and they hadn't moved in together.

Dane was the sole guardian of his young cousin,
Zander, the talented young novice lightning-mage
whose art graced Friedr and Aeolyn's table. Until
Christoph came into his life, Dane's whole existence
revolved around the raising of his only surviving family
member. But with Zander in the novice quarters and his
own career advancing well, Dane now had time for his
personal life, though his travels often limited it.

It was apparent Christoph wasn't ready to settle
down. He loved Zander, feeling like a parent in many
ways. The problem was he knew he was too young and
felt the boy deserved a real father. Zander didn't care.
His heart was set on the three of them being a family.
However, Christoph's past inability to be a faithful

partner caused some drama for them at times. The last thing he wanted to do was upset Zan again, and ever since their last drama had unfolded, Christoph made every effort to be honest.

Fortunately, Dane wasn't the type of person to mope and feel miserable. "I try not to have expectations," he told Edwin privately. "Sometimes we don't get what we want, and we have to learn to live with it. Chris isn't a monogamous man by nature, and he never pretended to be. And truthfully, I've a hard time trusting him because he is easily seduced by any new fancy that captures his imagination. Although he's been constant lately, that could change. I love the man, but I'm under no illusions about him. It's bad for Zan though, and when things fall apart as they always do, I know I should just walk away. It would be better, but I can't let go of him, and Zan wants Christoph as his father more than anything. Being so young, he doesn't understand what the problem is."

Edwin learned a great deal from Dane about healer's barriers. There were many things about barriers that Christoph had been unable to teach him, though he had some rudimentary skills with them. "Christoph has shaky barriers. This is why he doesn't heal in the infirmary regularly. But the Abbess knows about his problem, and I'm constantly working with him trying to improve them. I'm worried he won't be able to cope once you leave the soil of Neveyah."

One afternoon in Edwin's sitting room, as they sat working on raising healer's barriers and talking about the quest, Dane said, "I know it has to be Christoph to help Marya when you do rescue her, especially if she has been raped. Even if she hasn't been abused in such a way, we know she'll have suffered great trauma. D'Mal's madness affects anyone with the tiniest shred of sensitivity, and as you know, healers are empaths. All who have been recovered alive were unable to heal ever again. Their gifts were as dead as if they were burned out, and we know we'll have to deal with this in regard to Marya. Christoph really is the *only* healer for this situation. I only hope you can help him with his barriers as you are able, though he is stubborn and sensitive about this problem. Yours are already stronger and more reliable than his." Dane's voice conveyed his concern.

"I don't know what I can do to help him if he won't accept it," Edwin answered. "I'll try to find a way to shield him if I can't get him to pay attention to his barriers. Once I know more about how they can be used, I might be able to think of something."

"You battle-mages will need to maintain an earth shield against the soil in Mal Evol." Dane's serious tone had Edwin's attention. "The earth itself is under a spell there, and the priest Stefyn D'Mal is the one who has set it. The soil is poisoned, perhaps by his madness or some other power. Either way, it is being forced to become a mirror to Serende, the true world of Tauron, the Bull God." He paused, thinking about the situation, and then said, "Christoph can't even make a water-shield well. His water-magic is minimal, and I don't think he works with it much since he usually takes the easy way with things. I don't know how you can help him and still keep yourself safe."

"I'll figure something out," Edwin promised. "If nothing else, I'll make him help me with my barriers constantly, so he'll be paying attention to his own.

When he's teaching, he's good with them. He forgets to maintain them when he isn't, though."

***

Daily Edwin went to the infirmary and worked with Christoph. He learned quickly and rarely had to be shown a technique more than twice. Beryl tested him regularly and was pleased with both his progress and judgment. She was certain he would be able to follow in Christoph's footsteps as a healer of emotional traumas because of the way he handled assisting with several difficult cases and working through their fear and panic. "Your ability to remain calm under stress, when the patient is most terrified, is what we need," she told him after they left the home of a particularly troubled family on one of the farms outside of Aeoven.

"I simply hold their fear away from me," Edwin explained. "Then it doesn't seem like they are my emotions, and I don't feel it the way the patient does. I learned to do this when we saw the boy who was injured in the fire in Wister. When we first began treating him, I nearly panicked too, and I did the first thing I could think of to separate my emotional self from him. Once I did, I realized this is what I would have to do if I didn't want to lose myself every time I saw a patient."

Chapter 9

Edwin's days were full, and he often read long into the night, trying to get as much studying done as he could. Even though he was regularly up late, he still found himself awake at dawn. His dreams were usually of warm, brown eyes and honey-gold hair. She was the same girl he'd dreamed of since the age of about sixteen when he left his childhood behind. The difference was, before he left home, the dream wasn't frequent, but often enough he believed she was the girl he would bond with. Now he saw her each night. Usually he stood on a wall and watched her cutting roses in a great overgrown garden. He was sure the dream meant something, but he didn't know who he could talk to about it. Still, she had become clearer to him, and he was now convinced he was dreaming of Marya, the girl they were to rescue. Why he dreamt of her so often he didn't know, and he was too embarrassed to speak of it to his friends. He felt strange for being obsessed about a girl he'd never met.

As the weeks passed, Edwin was promoted to mid-level journeyman and began having his own patients, people with minor injuries and illnesses. His disappointment at the delay of the quest was lessened by the realization of how much he needed to learn before he could battle a mage as strong and capable as Stefyn D'Mal was reputed to be. Still, many nights he felt as if he were a caged animal, pacing back and forth in frustration.

Despite his elevation within the healers, Edwin felt he wasn't advancing as rapidly on the battle-magic side of his education. Father Rall insisted he unlearn his habit of weaving the magic, and Aeolyn worked him hard at doing so. Once Edwin understood it was all about visualization, he began to make huge strides. Things that made no sense to him rapidly became completely comprehensible. At first, he tucked his hands into his pockets so he wouldn't forget and begin waving them about, but he quickly developed the skill to call the elements with a strength that impressed his teachers.

He worked each day calling battle-magic with Aeolyn, and also practiced building shields up at the first sign of an attack. She would throw a spell at him, he identified what she was casting before it left her hand by the feel of the element building, and then he raised a shield before it hit him. The process seemed cumbersome, but Edwin didn't know enough yet to explain why it felt wrong to him.

Healer's shields, called barriers, were still in some ways a mystery to him. They had to be constantly built and maintained, or they would fade, and the patient could overwhelm a healer while he was trying to help them. Being a healer meant Edwin was possessed of empathic abilities, and his gifts were considered unusually strong within the craft. Being in crowds made him uncomfortable, as did being around someone angry, and he noticed that Christoph always cast calm as he entered a crowded room. Several other healers did too, but Edwin felt it wasn't the answer.

Edwin's barriers were strong, and he rapidly became one of the best at raising them. Still, he was sure there was a better way to build them. On Dane's advice, he began maintaining barriers at all times when he was around people to avoid picking up their moods and being affected by them, but he had to keep sustaining them and found it annoying. Carrying the healer's barrier and the elemental shield at the same time was awkward, and he began looking for ways to hold them together without having to constantly monitor them. He was the only mage to ever have the problem, so no one could give him guidance when trying to merge his dual abilities.

The elderly fire-mage, Jules Brendsson, always found the time to talk to Edwin about magic and the situation he found himself in. Though he was unable to provide any help about merging his barriers with his shields, Jules often offered good advice. The old mage, who'd been a close friend of his grandfather, would often tap on Edwin's door first thing in the morning and chat with him for a few minutes on his way to the dining hall. The feisty man used two canes because of his joint ailment, but insisted on walking everywhere and moved quickly for a man as infirm as he was. Edwin learned a lot about his own family by talking to him. Jules was a fountain of knowledge about everything and everyone in the Temple.

Edwin still had no idea what magic he was strongest in, although he'd been augmented three times since his first coloring. Abbess Halee told him, "Often when a mage is well-balanced in the elements, it is a later augmentation when the magic chooses you. After you have gotten used to the next one, they will test you again, and more will be disclosed as to your true abilities. Most likely, this will happen in Braden, so Garran will have the pleasure of evaluating you."

Father Rall occasionally assessed him in all aspects

of his battle-mage training, even sparring with him and correcting his sword techniques. Afterwards, he would talk to Edwin. "You look a lot like your grandfather did at your age except for the healer's stars, but you're quite different from him in every other way. Wynn was the quintessential lightning-mage—brilliant, flashy, and a true genius in many ways. He was likely to say anything that popped into his mind. His happy streak used to drive his father and son mad, both of them being water-mages. Even I found him hard to take in the morning after a long night in the common room around the ale keg." Rall laughed. "Wynn was always blurting out the truth, which was occasionally a riot, but that sometimes got me, Jules Brendsson, and Devyn D'Mal into trouble in strange towns. Also, he always answered rhetorical questions and casual sarcastic remarks seriously. It was a habit that drove your father mad as a teenager. John often felt like he was being raised by the village idiot, which was completely unfair, but natural given the circumstances."

"I can see Dad would have trouble dealing with that, as he does have a sarcastic streak," laughed Edwin. "I still can't imagine him young though."

"Oh he was, I guarantee you. And he was as wild with the girls as his father was until he met your mother. Your father was also brilliant, but even as a journeyman, he was more of a craftsman with his magic than Wynn was. John's understanding of the many nuances of water-magic and shielding is, to this day, unparalleled. He never relied on luck for anything. Instead, he planned every move completely and knew exactly what he could count on every step of the way. He was strong and confident, and inspired his companions to achieve more than they ever thought they could." Father Rall smiled kindly at Edwin. "Your father's great failing was the belief he was solely responsible for the massacre of the royal family of Mal Evol." Rall's eyes twinkled as he added, "He wasn't, of course. The events were destined to happen, and nothing he could have done would have changed anything, but he can't accept it."

"No, Dad doesn't believe in omens or fate. At least, so he says," replied Edwin. "But he must, because he was here and everything revolves around the prophecies, as I am finding out in my studies."

"Your father believes. He simply has a hard time accepting it. When he duels with fate it beats him every time." Rall laughed. "The interesting thing about your grandfather, Wynn, was he was never beaten in a mage-duel, and he never lost a battle. He is accounted as one of the finest warriors in the history of the Temple. But he never thought of himself as such. In his own mind, he was an armor-smith.

"Before leaving Neveyah, he made your father a special sword. Wynn believed his last sword was his finest masterpiece as a smith, and I assure you, he created many marvelous weapons and wonderful armor. He told me John's sword was something special, but wouldn't say why. Only Wynn himself knew what the sword was really capable of, and it was the only secret the man ever kept. I suspect many things in regard to his masterpiece, but John has neatly avoided discussing it whenever I have brought it up.

"Somehow, Wynn always knew your father would be a water-mage. He handed the sword to his son on the morning John was called to come here. He didn't appreciate it until he became an adult, but Wynn knew he would eventually see it for what it was."

Edwin was stunned. "I've never seen my dad's sword, if he still has it. He's hidden that from me too."

"He has it. He is bound to it with a geas. Only John can unleash the magic that resides in Riverbinder." Rall looked closely at him and then asked, "How will you handle disappointment? Will you turn failure into success as Wynn always managed to do, or will you let it kill your joy as your great-grandfather, Liam, did and as your own father has done? It will be interesting, seeing how you deal with your trials and sorrows." Father Rall clasped Edwin's shoulder companionably. "It is a sad fact of life you will face both on your current quest and in any quest yet to come."

Edwin enjoyed their talks immensely, feeling somehow closer to both his father and his grandfather because of them.

Edwin was at last outfitted with new leathers and the Temple armor made especially for him. The armorers created it in a trance similar to the one the colorist entered when she did the augmentations, lacquering it with a deep, midnight-blue finish, embossed with green leaves outlined in gold, along with tiny, golden suns, water drops, and lightning bolts placed at seemingly random points, although Edwin knew nothing was ever random in Neveyah. His new armor was bespelled specifically for him, to protect him in the areas of magic where he was most vulnerable. No other battle-mage had armor like it. The green signified and enabled his healing magic. The armorers were amazed when they gave him the finished armor.

"I knew when I saw your augmentations this would

be the most unusual armor I have ever made," the master-smith told Edwin, winking at Friedr as he made the final adjustments. "They're keeping you a secret, aren't they? I hear you'll be giving the young barbarian a run for his money soon enough."

Friedr looked at the smith with the flat look he'd perfected and said, "You have let your sword languish for too long, Ralf. Why don't we spar this evening?"

"You can't trick me into becoming one of your victims, barbarian. You boys from the North are crazy. Besides, I have to make the weapons you want to beat me up with, and it takes all my time," replied Ralf seriously. "We're so shorthanded here. You can't imagine what we're up against. The army is taking all of my mages. I pulled Feia out of retirement to help with the special armor. She facilitated the finish on this, Edwin. You've been given a masterpiece." Feia was Father Rall's wife. She was a brilliant, but often unstable, lightning-mage known for both her ethereal landscapes done in oils and for frequently making Rall's home life somewhat less than peaceful.

Every day Friedr worked Edwin as hard as he could, and Edwin loved every minute of it. His sword skills were improving at a rate that pleased his instructor. "You know, I didn't like killing things when we were on the road, but I love sparring with the swords," he told Friedr as they walked home one evening. "It's a great hobby for me."

"Weaponry isn't a hobby. It's to save your life," Friedr replied with an affronted look. "You're good at it, and it is a shame you have no appreciation for it. But don't worry, you'll have plenty of practice once we leave Aeoven. Anyway, you're doing much better than most of the idiots I've worked with lately. Half of them can barely keep from cutting themselves, and they have been at it for far too long to be this dismal in their abilities."

For the first time, Edwin realized he would spend Holy Month and winter solstice away from home. He missed his father more than he ever thought possible, but was able to send a long letter and a new leather belt with a silver buckle inset with a turquoise water drop crossed with lightning as a Holy Day gift via Abbess Halee. She too was sending a letter detailing Edwin's progress and asked if he had anything he would like to send. "My husband, Bryson, and Kalen, Father Rall's son, will take the package to the portal. They're your father's oldest friends and will stay one night before they return with his replies. You will hear back from him before you leave on your quest. I promise."

"But I've met them before in Markett. So they are from Aeoven." Edwin now knew his father was in frequent contact with Neveyah. "They let me believe they were from Kingston and were old army friends of my father's."

"And so they are, Edwin. Bryson and Kalen both served with John and me during the war," she replied, the twinkle in her eye fading. "Many who served with us died doing their duty. It is the task of all of us eventually."

"I will do whatever I must. I know it won't always be easy. I've read the histories and know about some of what you faced," replied Edwin, as seriously as Halee. "I'd rather die myself than lose a friend, but we don't always have the choice."

Edwin experienced many changes in the months after his arrival in Aeoven, more than he realized. He'd become a well-respected journeyman healer and was on his way to becoming one of the better battle-mages, though no one other than his close friends and instructors was aware of it. No trace remained of the bored, unfinished young man he was on the day he left home. In his place was a quiet man with a purpose and a calm strength that would have pleased his father if he'd been able to see Edwin as he was now.

***

On a rainy day in the last week of the year, the four questers were summoned to Father Rall's study. Abbess Halee was there, and so were several other members of the higher clergy.

"The omens are right for you to leave on your quest at the end of next week," Father Rall told them. "It will be a new quest in the new year, always a good omen. Have you had the chance to get used to your new armor, Edwin?" He nodded, and Rall continued, saying "The good people in the Temple storehouses have at last been able to outfit you four with the rest of the necessary items for a quest of an undetermined length of time. If you find you need anything between here and Braden, you may draw on Temple funds to pay for it, and you may also requisition items from Braden Temple."

After dinner, the clergy assembled in the Temple chapel where the Holy Father planned to announce their imminent departure, along with other business that marked the end of the year. The chapel wasn't a place of splendor or lavish displays of wealth. Instead, the simple walls were covered with the same lustrous wood paneling one might find in many homes in Neveyah. A large, round, hammered-copper font was centered on a simple stone altar, and a blue flame burned there, with no apparent source of fuel, like no flame Edwin had ever seen. *It feels holy,* he decided with awe when he saw it for the first time. The roof over the altar was open to the sky, and a sense of peace and serenity pervaded the sanctuary.

Father Rall took his place before the altar. He calmed and centered himself and then turned to face the assembled clergy. As he did so, a bell resonated, ringing through the heads and hearts of all who were there to hear it. It was the most beautiful sound Edwin had ever heard, although it wasn't audible but instead rang through every fiber of his being. The Temple seemed to darken as Father Rall fell into a trance. The congregation inhaled as one, holding their breath expectantly. A single ray of light that appeared to emanate from above him through the open roof suddenly illuminated the Holy Father. His voice became deeper and resounded through the sanctuary.

The words were heavy with great portent. *"The storm rises in the lands of Neveyah, though it does not bring its wrath fully for yet awhile...when falls the Beloved Hero into darkness, then will the storm's wrath fall upon Neveyah. The children of the Bull-God answer the call that rides on the wind. The light of truth remains shrouded beneath the Throne of Stone and Bone. The cradle of the rightful heir lies obscured by the truth. Let the Hero go to the Shadow Castle to seek the hand of she whom darkness has claimed. The moon is dark—in stealth seeks the Hero for the window to the Tower of Roses, in stealth he unbars the door to the forbidden room. Four heroes depart and five return, yet the battle is not won, but only the first skirmish. The Beloved must fall to darkness ere the light of truth is restored to the Shadow Castle. Blood and tears reign in the Shadow Castle until the Hero Foretold comes to restore the scion to the throne."*

The Temple brightened, and whispering filled the chamber as people discussed what they were privileged to witness. The scribes hurried to write it down exactly as it was spoken before they could forget the words, so transcripts could be sent to each Temple in Neveyah.

Father Rall appeared momentarily shaken. The striking, silver-haired woman who was his wife, Feia, took his arm and led him to one side, where she saw to it he sipped some water and collected himself. Nodding brusquely, she stepped back to sit by their son, Kalen, and his wife.

The Holy Father spoke again, and this time his voice was the normal, kindly baritone Edwin knew. "The quest laid upon us is to begin in earnest. Tomorrow we will finalize the plans and make the preparations for our questers' imminent departure. We pray the Goddess will guide and protect them."

* * *

The next morning, Edwin and the others gathered again in the study of the Holy Father. He sat quietly while Abbess Halee reminded them the quest was simply to steal the girl back and get her away from D'Mal, thus removing his leverage against the Temple. "This is not the time to take him head-on. The omens are all wrong. If you follow the Goddess' instructions exactly, you have a chance. 'In stealth seek the forbidden room,'" she paraphrased. "Do this and Marya has a chance. The foretelling is clear—to go beyond it will bring failure, and she will be lost to us."

Father Rall said, "There is another part to this quest you do not yet know about, but which you must also accomplish. You must somehow count how many legions are now in Mal Evol and poised to fall on Neveyah. We know they are there. We simply need to know how many and where they are gathering so we can counter their strike. That Mal Evol is poised to strike isn't known outside of this room." The group solemnly laid their right hands on their heart, a common ritual signifying it was a secret that would never leave their lips.

As they walked back to Christoph's apartment for a farewell party Aeolyn asked, "Will you share the Holy Day feast with Friedr and me, Edwin? Chris will be there, as will Dane and young Zan."

"Of course." Edwin suddenly realized his father would be spending the holiday alone. "I...." He stopped walking, unable to speak any further, his sad, blue eyes meeting her dark compassionate ones.

"You're thinking of your father." Aeolyn was full of concern for him. "He will likely celebrate with the neighbors, am I right? The ones with the funny name whose lands march alongside yours? You've told me a lot about them. They've been good friends to you both since your mother died."

Edwin looked at her, grateful for her common sense. "You're right. Of course, Mr. Legg and his son, Josiah, will have invited Dad to share their table, and I was able to send him a letter and a Holy Day gift." His face broke into his charismatic smile, and he added, "I will enjoy the better feast, though. When I last enjoyed her efforts Josiah's new wife wasn't as talented a cook as you are, though I am sure she's improved."

She smiled, and her husband squeezed her hand. "No one cooks like my Aeolyn." Friedr beamed with pride.

With a smile, Edwin agreed. A stray thought crossed his mind, causing him to smile even more widely. *Christoph is right when he calls Friedr cute whenever he raves about his bride's virtues.*

Chapter 10

Edwin said goodbye to his rooms. He felt a sense of pain, even more than when he found himself walking away from the portal and everything he had ever known. Leaving his books behind was hard and he agonized over how many to bring with him, knowing he would have to carry whatever he brought. "I'll come back soon, and I'll be able to study more. This is my home now," he promised himself as he finished packing his kit, preparing once again to depart in the dark hour before dawn.

Since Edwin was also making his required healing journey on this trip, the team led two heavily laden pack ponies carrying desperately needed medicines to the city of Arlen. The route was indirect. Taking the northern trade road would add two weeks to the journey, and they would be healing as they traveled to Arlen. From there to Braden, they would stay on the trade road since healers were more plentiful in the big towns of the South. Arlen, a mountain town, was in need of aid as it had been experiencing an influx of refugees from the abandoned farms and villages of southern Mal Evol for the last five years.

The group was in high spirits as they started out. Edwin's training had progressed much faster than they thought it would. Friedr felt the hard work Edwin had done on the farm made his transition easier for him physically because he was used to working long days when he came to Neveyah.

As they walked out of the city through the western gate, the companions talked quietly of their quest to rescue the girl they held dear. She was someone Edwin had never met, but nonetheless felt as if he somehow knew and loved her. *Why do I feel so sure she is the one I dreamed of again only last night? Why do I see her so often? She might not even like me when we meet. I have to be prepared for such a thing.* But he said nothing, feeling peculiar for becoming so preoccupied with someone he'd never met. And Edwin *was* completely obsessed with her and embarrassed about it. He had done some amazingly strange things because of his obsession, at least in his own opinion.

While still in Aeoven, he'd visited Dane's rooms, and noticed a portrait of Marya on the mantle over his fireplace, along with sketches of his other loved ones. She was beautiful, with green and blue augmentations of stars and butterflies. Honey-brown hair and mischievous brown eyes completed the picture.

The girl looked so familiar to him and Edwin was unable to get her picture out of his mind. He was so smitten that he had copied it while sitting unnoticed in the corner of Dane's sitting room during a party. *She's the one I'm looking for. I know it in my heart. But what if I'm just an infatuated freak, imagining she's the only girl for me? Friedr would knock me in the head—and then Chris would fix it.*

Edwin was a fairly good sketch artist, and his copy was nearly perfect. He'd found himself packing his secret portrait of her, layered in the pages of the manual on general healing techniques, the book that he finally settled on. *I'm an idiot. They'll mock me forever if they find out.*

Even though they were covering what was to them, old ground, he listened avidly as they quietly discussed the situation. Of course, he knew the basics, but he wanted to hear what they had to say about it, so he asked a few questions, thinking he would distract them from seeing how fixated he was.

Marya had been kidnapped while walking from the city of Braden to her next destination and was imprisoned in the Keep of Mal Evol, now known as the Shadow Castle. The goddess apparently sent Father Rall a vision the moment the squad of minotaurs took her captive.

The Shadow Castle was haunted by the shades of those who lost their lives in the dungeon beneath the once beautiful citadel. It had been occupied for the last twenty-two years by the Baron Stefyn D'Mal, who still refused to assume the title of king, insisting he was only a caretaker for his dark god.

Though her status was in doubt at first, the visions led the Temple's seers to agree that Marya was deeply unhappy, but well enough cared for despite her captivity. Edwin's own dreams showed her in pleasant rooms, but they could be wishful thinking on his part.

The army D'Mal controlled was completely made up of minotaurs—males who committed their lives to fighting for the Bull God and who willingly underwent the terrible, physical alteration that separated them from the rest of their society. They were fierce warriors who'd taken control of Mal Evol. They now held all of the eastern high plains and the northern half of the immense crater valley.

John Farmer's shield slowed the poisoning of the lands in the southern quarter of the valley southwest of Mal Evol City, which fell twenty two years before. The smoking ruins of the city that was once the pinnacle of civilization in Neveyah were hastily rebuilt in a style apparently reminiscent of Serende. That city and most of the valley was now completely under Stefyn D'Mal's dominion. The western and southern areas were now nothing but league upon league of abandoned farms and vineyards, bearing huge crops of thorns and scorpions instead of the fine wine grapes that once made the valley famous.

Mal Evol was actually an immense crater valley surrounded by impassable cliffs and sheer mountains, open at the southern end to the rest of Neveyah at the Braden Gap. Now, even the valley's southwestern vineyards and the villages of the Braden Gap were gradually failing and dying due to the slow poisoning of the land. The vineyards east of the River Fleet, long the pride of Mal Evol, were no more. Each year more farms failed. Their people either fled to Braden and the southern areas of Neveyah or they fell under D'Mal's control.

D'Mal held the Throne of Stone and Bone, which was directly bound to the land itself. When he was seated on the throne, he knew every creature that lived and walked in the valley of Mal Evol—every mind was open to him, and they were blind to all but his will. The fact that he controlled the Throne of Stone and Bone seriously complicated things. Edwin and his companions were to rescue her as quietly as possible without drawing his attention until they were far away from his reach. That was going to be the trick, since the moment he sat on the throne, he would know the mind and intent of each living thing that walked on the soil of Mal Evol, although Edwin didn't understand how that worked.

He was reduced to listening to any scrap of gossip he could about both his father and Marya. As his friends talked among themselves, he did hear some things he hadn't known before and found himself hanging on their words.

As they settled into their first camp, Edwin sat quietly, sorting out the things he'd heard about the man everyone feared and hated so much.

He'd learned Marya spent two years as a journeyman, traveling and living among the people of southeastern Neveyah, whose lands were sometimes inside Mal Evol. Some were desperately poor and most were unable to pay for potions from the herb doctors. She dedicated her life to caring for them, often feeding and providing for them from her own stipend. This was why she had been singled out to be kidnapped.

Stefyn D'Mal maintained he possessed evidence she was using her skills to stir up resentment of his god's "benevolent" rule. He alleged the Temple used her as an unwitting tool to undermine him, and so he took her prisoner, intending at first to ransom her in exchange for his complete domination of the entire valley of Mal Evol, all the way to the city of Braden.

The action of kidnapping Marya for what Stefyn D'Mal claimed were purely political reasons soon turned into a living nightmare for her. The baron believed holding so revered a healer hostage would force the Temple to kneel and give him the city of Braden in return for her safety. Thus, he would gain a foot in the door in his bid for control of all of Neveyah, but the baron fell in love and now would not part with her, ever. His intention was clear, and the Temple would not negotiate with him, refusing his overtures.

Edwin listened closely as his companions discussed everything they knew or feared regarding her captivity, but no one actually knew much about her situation. As he lay looking up at the starry sky, he wondered how she was faring and if she was holding up well. He found himself saying a prayer to Aeos just before he dozed off.

***

Only Marya knew the true nature of her peril, and she was definitely in dreadful danger.

Daily, D'Mal attempted to convince her to bond with him of her free will, misusing his immense, twisted, empathic abilities to coerce her. The baron terrified her. She was fully aware of the depth and scope of his madness, enough so she treated him carefully, praying for help. She didn't know if any was on the way, but still she hoped. Marya wasn't sure how long she would be able to hold out against Stefyn's overwhelming desire to possess her.

Fear threatened to crush her each time he came near. He'd punished her once before, locking her in his dungeon—she didn't know how long—and the experience had broken her. She had no idea what the actual date was because she was not allowed a calendar. She didn't dare try to make one, because the terror that he would punish her again now ruled her life. What was most disgusting was how he knew and savored that aspect of their relationship. The thrill he felt in forcing her to enjoy his companionship was indescribable.

Stefyn was by no means an ugly man. On the contrary, his dark eyes were mesmerizing. Long, curling, chestnut hair framed a face that was striking, but his perfect beauty shrouded the insanity lurking beneath the surface. Charming, witty, and handsome, he was extremely compelling. Even without his magic, no one would ever discount or fail to heed him. He was fascinating when he chose, but the poison of his madness was clear to Marya's healing sight, when she'd still possessed the ability to use it.

The truth was he both captivated and horrified her, inspiring deep and complex emotions she didn't care to examine too closely. She loathed and liked him, enjoyed and feared him. His sexual charisma was extremely powerful, and he blatantly used his empathic powers to enhance it. He abused every rule ever taught at the Temple about the most powerful of the gifts of Aeos—empathy.

It was the most strictly regulated and carefully monitored of all the mage gifts because empaths were granted the power to take over and control the minds of others. Healers were never admitted if they were not caring, and above all, committed to serving Aeos. The unacceptable were quickly weeded out and rendered harmless and then sent home with permanent inhibitions against injuring others. The vows bound the accepted completely and enabled the absolute faith the people of Neveyah had, faith the healer would die before willingly harming anyone.

Unfortunately, the mad priest was her only living companion other than her minotaur guards or the two human servants, and they didn't ever speak to her. Stefyn forbade it.

At one moment, he was an amusing and pleasant companion and the next a brutal, tyrannical child. His devotion to the Bull God and flagrant use of strange, dark magic to bind his servants were disturbing. He was lavish in his use of it, drawing chi through the Throne of Stone and Bone from the legions of minotaurs, the people of Mal Evol, and the ghosts that haunted the keep. He even drew chi directly from the Bull God himself to perform his greater works.

Exactly what his magic was, though, was completely foreign to Marya. She had never seen or heard of anyone who used it the way he did. It was not merely elemental, nor was it only empathic. It seemed a mix of both, with the addition of something more. The magic of Stefyn D'Mal was a terrible, dark thing, and he used it as casually as he did anything else.

Massive amounts of unfocused chi swirled around him, and when he sat next to her, she often found the hairs on her arms rising as if from a nearby lightning discharge. No mage in Neveyah could live with the amount he bore in his body. They would go mad.

Stefyn told her all his dreams and ambitions, as if she was the first person he'd ever confided in. She knew she wasn't, but it was one of his charming characteristics and one that made her most wary. He would often sit beside her and tell the most intimate of secrets as innocently as a child, and then again, he would talk about his grand plans as any man might. On the same night Edwin made his prayer to Aeos, Marya once again sat listening to Stefyn's mad ramblings.

"I was born to rule this land. The injustice that robbed me of my birthright simply because my mother was not the queen has been rectified. Because he was born of the right mother, Max ruled in my stead." His laughter held an edge that frightened Marya. "The one good thing our father did was to hide me in the monastery and offer my life to the priesthood of

Tauron. His fear I would embarrass him by my very existence saved me. He stupidly secreted me away in the one place that gave me the opportunity to claim my inheritance. In concealing me from Aeos, he gave me to Tauron. There is no taint of illegitimacy in his world. I'm the eldest son and the strongest. Therefore I am the true earthly ruler of Mal Evol. Tauron himself guided me, and I did as my god willed me to."

It was difficult for Marya to listen to him, as Stefyn's voice often broke, and he began trembling as he spoke of his brother, making her feel the need to comfort him. He always told the truth, and it was terribly hard to hear. "I loved Maxon, loved him dearly, but he usurped my rightful place. Max had to be taught manners, but he refused to learn. It could only be punished by death. The dread god came, showed me the way, and gave me the strength to do what was required, despite my weakness in loving my errant brother." Tears would fill his eyes and flow down his cheeks, but he never noticed them.

"Maxon's mother, Queen Irena, was good to me. Perhaps she even loved me. But Tauron required a sacrifice, and so of course, I obeyed him. I had to suffer to truly know his love. Only through pain, Marya, only through pain." Whenever Stefyn spoke of the queen, he would usually break down, sobbing heartbrokenly. The first time it happened, Marya didn't know what to do, it happened so suddenly. Now, she sat with tears streaming down her face as he wept over the murders of his family, murders he committed because his god demanded it.

Purged of his sorrow, his conversation now concerned his great task. "I will bring all of the lands to kneel before the Bull God. The goddess has not the strength to defeat him, nor will she defend against him forever. She has lost Mal Evol, and it is only a matter of time until I hold the heart of Neveyah. You will soon rule beside me as their high priestess, my dear, as Aeos will rule beside the true god as his wife. That is the way it is meant to be."

Despite his edict no one should speak to her but him, Marya actually did have other companions, though they were rather disconcerting by their nature. They came to her as friends when she was in the dungeon, a place she couldn't bear to think about now. Her luxurious rooms were at the top of what long ago was known as the Rose Tower, directly above the prison. The guilty knowledge she lived in comfort high above the horror that lurked below was hard to accept. The shadows comforted her when she was held there and now kept her company as her lonely days passed. They spoke with her as she went through the motions of performing the daily tasks she was allowed to enjoy, telling her what they remembered of their lives. The children were so sweet she couldn't help but love them.

Of course, the guards, who couldn't see them, thought she was mad.

Marya's secret friends were the shades of the departed who roamed the corridors of the castle. At first, they were quite troubling, as she had never believed in ghosts before. Stefyn couldn't see them and thought she was as mad as he knew himself to be. "I am sorry, dear lady, but it happens around me. Are you sure you are not losing your mind? Your barriers are fragile, you know. A mere breeze could shatter them."

That Stefyn could not see the ghosts surprised her.

He fed on them whether he knew it or not, drawing chi through the Throne. They were his family, his loved ones, and now they were empty husks tied to D'Mal and the Throne of Stone and Bone through the perverted magic that ruled Mal Evol. The shadows grew in number with the death of each guest in the dungeon. Their bones formed the base upon which his power rested, and their life force was the power upon which his god fed.

"A pretty circle, my dear. I'm told I'm as mad as any man could possibly be, and yet you are seeing things that are not there and conversing with rosebushes," he would say when her conversations with her ghostly friends were reported to him. "Yes, it makes a pretty circle, don't you think? A mad wife for a mad man! What could be more perfect?" A wave of coercion would roll over her, buckling her frail barriers, but not quite crushing them, though he could easily have done so if only he didn't delight in the game and the sweetness of her fragile resistance. "We were meant for each other. Why else are you here?"

Marya believed Stefyn had never wooed a woman before, though at first she found it hard to understand, given his purported age. His notion of courting her seemed drawn from a badly crafted romance novel and followed a rigid and prescribed etiquette that didn't vary in any way from day to day.

She spent the morning and early afternoon resting and enjoying appropriate feminine hobbies, in other words, activities he chose for her. High tea was served promptly at four o'clock and a formal dinner punctually at seven-thirty, followed by polite conversation or perhaps a stroll about the conservatory and galleries.

Sometimes they played genteel parlor games such as cards or chess until midnight.

He was fond of taking her arm to escort her about the keep in a companionable sort of way. She cringed from his touch, though he never attempted to kiss more than her reluctant hand. His courtliness was one of his many insidious forms of intimidation. He made it clear she was allowed to resist him for only as long as he chose to savor it. He was certain she would give in and bond with him.

It was a thought that nearly stopped her heart.

"I am nothing if not patient," he would often tell her, with his most charming and enigmatic smile. "I always win in the end. Always! You are a prize worth waiting for. I will have you, you will come to me of your own free will, and when you do, the true god will have Aeos as his wife."

Marya wondered how she would survive when he decided to force her to become his wife. He would not be patient forever. His desire to possess her, body and soul, was a never-ending thirst he would one day choose to quench, with or without her consent. The power of his yearning nearly crushed her will. *How long,* she wondered daily, *how long before I crumble and nothing of me remains except a shadow roaming the halls, crying for release? Will he be able to see me when I am nothing?*

Stefyn's moods swung violently, and Marya constantly worked to gauge what it was each moment. However, she was afraid to sleep and was often numb. If her response to a comment or joke should be wrong, she suffered the consequences, although he always apologized most sincerely afterward, weeping and healing her bruises. "Forgive me, my dear. God help me. I'm mad, you know. It's the price I must pay to remain in this land."

All who slept in the Shadow Castle knew the power of Stefyn D'Mal's dreams. He was regularly tormented with nightmares of his dead family when he did sleep naturally, which was seldom. Even worse, his rare "good" dreams were a horrific morass of lust and degradation in the most vile and unspeakable terms.

Still, though he too feared to sleep, he would often tell her, "You must be willing to give up everything to achieve true power, or you do not deserve it. Tauron required a sacrifice, and I gave him the only thing of any value to me. I gave him my brother, my family." Sobs would wrack him and Marya frequently despised herself for feeling pity for the monster he was. But she did feel pity for the lonely child he once had been, in spite of her knowledge of his guilt and depravity.

He set no barriers to contain his empathic sendings. Anyone with a shred of sensitivity who slept under his roof was drawn into his dreams. Marya slept as seldom as possible and tried to wake herself the moment she slipped too deep, for fear she would be caught up in whatever perversion surfaced in the sick, violent maelstrom that was Stefyn D'Mal's subconscious mind. If his dreams had only involved sex, she could have understood it, though it would have been imposition enough.

Marya now knew she was indeed the only woman he'd ever courted, though he'd had many lovers. She didn't care that men filled his dreams far more often than she did. If his dreams weren't so horrific, it would have been humorous. She was the only woman he had ever wanted sexually, and it appeared almost as if his desire for her was forced upon him.

During the time she was held in his dungeon, she learned the perversion of sex was a central facet of worship in some of the more arcane and secret rituals Tauron demanded of his high priest. How she escaped his altar she didn't know. The power he and his god obtained in those rites was staggering.

Marya was trapped. If she didn't get away from him, she would surely end her days as mad as he believed her to be.

The mere thought of his touch threatened to send her screaming. His kiss on her hand was nearly unbearable. Deeply depressed, there were long dark times when she contemplated suicide, but hope that the Temple would somehow rescue her stayed her hand.

In her bodice, she kept hidden a long, slender shard of stone she'd found in the high-walled garden below her tower. She was allowed to stroll there each afternoon under the watchful eye of the grim minotaur guards who dogged her footsteps always. The shard was her last refuge, for if no rescue came, she would plunge it into her heart rather than submit to him.

Marya dreamed several times of a young man in Temple armor coming to rescue her. The last time, she fell asleep while reading before the fire and saw him standing outside her window. As soon as she realized she was dreaming, she woke herself up, fearing it was another attempt to drag her into the sewer that was D'Mal's mind.

She knew it was a dream because she didn't recognize the man and she knew every mage around her age. If she'd ever met him, she would never have forgotten his face. He was a golden-haired young man with as strikingly handsome a countenance as the Baron D'Mal, but where Stefyn's masculine beauty was dark and cruel, the young mage's was fair and full of kindness. Sadly, he was only a dream, one that made her feel even more alone, if it were possible.

Long ago, so long it might never have happened, Marya wore the moss-green leathers and armor of a Temple healer. On feast days, she wore a beautifully embroidered shirt and matching skirt, embellished by her own hand, and she had always felt well-dressed.

Now, Marya was dressed in exquisite gowns specially created for her by the most famous dressmakers of Mal Evol City. Each one was uniquely designed and chosen to please the whims of a madman. The slaves of Mal Evol City designed clothing for the females of the nobility of Serende, plying the trade for the wives and daughters of the minotaur elite as they once did for their own nobility. Their finest works now clad her in her every waking moment, from the time she arose until she fell exhausted into her bed after midnight.

All of the style and craftsmanship that was the hallmark of those famed dressmakers now went into her wardrobe, and Marya felt no appreciation, no gratitude for it. She would rather have worn her old green leathers. Though they were dilapidated from her continual journeying and needed replacing, at least they symbolized who she truly was—a healer.

Now, this fundamental part of her life was gone, as if blown away in the wind. She was no longer able to sense her healing empathy. The beautiful clothes were one more symbol of her complete captivity. The emptiness she felt at the loss of her gift was overwhelming in its intensity and seeing herself in a mirror wearing such finery only emphasized her loss and imprisonment.

Stefyn personally chose every item she wore, from her most intimate underclothes to her shawls. All her toiletries from soap to perfume were selected by him, as were the books she "enjoyed" reading, and the hobbies she was allowed to pursue.

She often felt like a favorite doll, dressed and cared for when the whim took him and set back on the shelf when more important things intruded. Thus, she spent hours in the dead queen's garden, wondering each day if she would join the sad queen in the shadows. She wandered with the shades of the royal family and their household, ghosts tied by blood to the lands of Mal Evol and unable to pass on to heaven because a foreign god desired a wife, and a lonely abused boy wanted acknowledgement from his family.

Marya carefully built and tried to maintain barriers against Stefyn's mind-magic, but they were fragile and of little use. Often she was panicked and unable to think coherently, knowing her barriers crumbled and failed little by little with each passing day. She wondered, *If they do send someone to rescue me, will I be sane enough to know them?*

Chapter 11

During their first few days on the road, the companions met only a few beasts, and those were easily dispatched. But the further from Aeoven they traveled, the more trouble they encountered. By the third night, they were taking turns standing watch at night lest they be attacked in their sleep. "It's no wonder there is so little commerce on the roads here," Edwin said to Friedr. "In Ariend, they're full of wagons and people journeying on horseback. Here, the only people who travel must go with armed guards or in large groups. The highways are empty most of the time."

"Horses are expensive," replied Friedr. "Most have at least one, but Aeos has ordained the clergy will use their legs to ensure we stop and get to know everyone we meet on the way. In this way, we can assist them if they need help. I don't mind it. It certainly keeps you healthy. When we must travel quickly, we can ride the mail coach."

Despite the inconvenience of walking, the journey was already proving much easier for Edwin than the one from Markett to Aeoven. The four of them easily dealt with the rat-people and other strange creatures that roamed the trade road looking for easy prey. Edwin's blade skills improved daily. Friedr began training him in dueling, casting spells while swinging a sword. Edwin found it difficult to do both efficiently at the same time, although he had no problem with the individual tasks.

"Don't worry so much. Either you will become

proficient, or you will die an ugly, needless death. It is an easy choice." Friedr's sense of humor was rough but accurate, as far as Edwin could see.

Many opportunities arose for Edwin to practice his healing skills after each skirmish, though he soon discovered he couldn't heal his own wounds. Christoph was surprised Edwin hadn't known, saying, "Can you carry yourself? It's the same thing."

Edwin and Christoph also healed as needed at every farm. Even if there was a traveling healer in the area, Christoph refused to pass if there was someone who was sick or injured. He told Aeolyn, "We owe it to the people of Neveyah to help where we can. Besides, this is Edwin's first away posting as a journeyman, and he must heal as often and as much as he can before we enter Mal Evol. This is the experience he must have in order to truly develop."

Four days into their journey in the late afternoon, they neared a farm, the home of Elles and his wife. As they approached it, both Edwin and Christoph were assailed by an overwhelming sense of pain and fear, causing them to quicken their steps. When they knocked on the door, they found that Aysse, an older woman, was having a difficult birth with her seventh child. Her labor began suddenly, and there was no time for Elles to send for the midwife. His wife was in grave trouble.

Christoph was terribly worried, as he'd never delivered a child. Both the mother and baby were likely to die without some sort of a miracle. They halted there for the night, while Christoph tried to decide what to do. He was unable to leave her and unable to help. Forcibly maintaining his veneer of calm, he frantically wracked his brain for anything he could remember about childbirth. "I was always in training as a mind healer. I never trained with the midwives," he told Edwin. "I have read some texts, but it was long ago."

To everyone's surprise, Edwin stepped in and took control of the difficult situation, declaring he would deliver the baby with Christoph's assistance. He immediately began organizing the household and getting everyone busy and out of his way. "Aeolyn and Friedr, help get this place cleaned up so she has nothing to think about but her child. You take care of the other children and keep them occupied."

Friedr took the little ones out of the house and got them busy tending to the animals in the barn, doing the evening chores for their father, while Aeolyn did the dishes and swept the floors. They were tasks their mother began earlier but was unable to finish. Aeolyn made sure a large quantity of water was boiled so Edwin would have enough available to bathe the baby and mother when the time came. Aeolyn also found the store of baby clothes, diapers, and nightgowns, along with the tiny blankets for swaddling the newborn on arrival, placing them where Edwin could reach. Afterwards, Aeolyn and Friedr took the worried children off for a picnic dinner to keep them busy while Edwin and Christoph took care of their mother.

"I have done this many times. Don't worry. We can do this, though it will be difficult," Edwin confidently assured both his teacher and the frantic father, as his healing senses delved Aysse.

Turning to Christoph, he said, "I'll deliver the child. I have enough chi to maintain the trance for as long as it will take, but not enough to sustain the pain relief spells too. You'll supply the strength as if we were performing a surgery, but it'll be as much about skill as magic. Between the two of us, we'll get her through this." He sensed Christoph's apprehension. "Don't worry. I'll tell you what's needed." He turned to his patient, soothing and calming her.

Edwin then turned to her husband. "You must sit here and hold your wife's hand and give her all your love and support, as she will need it desperately. Do not allow fear to overcome you. You will do as I tell you, helping to raise her to a sitting position and supporting her shoulders or pressing on her belly." Elles quailed, trying to back away.

Edwin spoke to him sharply, saying, "You were eager enough in doing your part in conceiving this child. Now you will help as I ask you to or they will both surely die!" There was steel in his voice and determination in his eye. Turning to Aysse, he continued soothing her, his calm assurance more effective than any magic. He then cast a dampening field over her and laced the pain-relieving spells into it. Linking with him, Christoph took up the spells, maintaining them. When he felt Christoph's surge of self-doubt, he said, "Think of this as assisting at a surgery. Together, we have more than enough chi to do this."

Christoph was impressed with Edwin's leadership. Unable to argue with Edwin's logic, Elles did as asked.

Two problems complicated the birth—Aysse wasn't built to have children, and the baby was breech. It required much effort to help deliver the child, but with Christoph casting pain-inhibiting spells and strengthening her when she could no longer push and the father helping, Edwin was able to ease the baby boy into the world. He then used every trick he ever knew to keep the mother from bleeding to death, sealing her torn flesh using the healing magic he'd been taught for performing surgeries.

The sun's first light shone through the window as Aysse, weary but happy, suckled her newborn son. In the quiet hours of the dawn, she drifted into an exhausted sleep while Christoph and Edwin rested and cared for the baby. Worn out, but relieved and proud, Elles slept with the older children, who all needed the comfort of his presence.

Christoph was overwhelmed with emotion, cradling the baby with as much joy as if he were the father, while Aysse slept. "I forgot babies came into the world so very tiny," he murmured softly to Edwin. "I haven't seen a newborn since before I left home." As he gazed at the tiny infant's perfect features, Christoph was suddenly overcome with the awareness he would most likely never have a child of his own, and for a moment, the sadness was more than he could bear.

Childless couples often adopted orphans, but there were always more people waiting than children to go to them. Often, bonded males arranged with bonded female couples for the purpose of having children to share between them, but Christoph was deeply aware he could never make such an arrangement with any woman.

For the first time, he felt a sharp pain at the thought. He and Edwin talked quietly in the corner while the rest of the household slept. "I know I'm not ready to settle down, though when I do bond with anyone, it will be Dane," he said as he caressed the baby's fuzzy head. "I'm so wrong for him right now. I won't agree to it until I know I can be completely faithful. I can't swear to this yet. It's completely unfair to him and his young cousin, Zan, who wants me to be his father. But I can't seem to change."

"You're right, my brother," Edwin agreed with him so. "You're not ready to settle down yet. But Dane would like to, and I hope he is willing to wait for you. It may be he will find another before you're ready. How will you handle that?"

"I wouldn't like it, but I'd never blame him. I haven't always treated him well," Christoph admitted with some discomfiture. "You heard Rila in Wister, when she so rudely aired my dirty laundry. But now that I'm holding this tiny miracle, I envy you and Friedr. You'll both have this joy for yourselves someday." To Edwin's surprise, Christoph, who always evinced a frank view of life, appeared somewhat embarrassed. "I simply can't function that way with a woman. I…it was a disaster the one time I tried. I can't tell you how dreadful it was for my self-image." Christoph's words were spoken with a crooked smile.

He looked up at Edwin with an uncomfortable expression on his face. "I should probably tell you what really happened, since I brought it up. Thankfully, Friedr glosses over the uglier aspects of my 'glorious' career as a bard-in-training." His eyes were full of shadows and a wariness that wasn't usual. "You know I choose to work with rape victims. I do this because I know what they've suffered, from a firsthand point of view. I can heal them because I understand the complex emotional injuries they're suffering from, and I know what they often need most.

"You know some of my family history, but Friedr makes it sound better than it was." Christoph drew on every bit of courage and decided to simply get on with telling it. "My mother had too many children to feed, and there was only Granddad to look after us most of the time when she was, er, working, and he wasn't really capable of caring for us in his state of mind. We spent our time on the streets, pretty much raising ourselves. Many people prey on children in such a situation, as I was to discover.

"Mum was relieved when my patron asked to train me, as she didn't have to worry about feeding me any longer. I was glad because I could send her what I earned and she would be able to take care of my younger siblings. Although I was thrown from the frying pan into the fire, the situation was better since I no longer went hungry or lacked for decent clothing.

"I had barely turned nine. As it happened, my patron, Donan, wasn't what anyone would call a nice man, though he was skilled as a bard. However, he was a man with unsavory habits who was no longer welcome in towns such as Aeoven and Wister. Somehow despite his troubles, he retained his master's pin and was still allowed to take apprentices.

"Looking back, I realize he selected me for training only because he recognized in me a boy who would one day be attracted to other boys, and he used me in such a way himself. But for the most part, I was able to get along with him, at least for the first few years, until I began to enter puberty. And I truly loved being a bard. Music was such a panacea for all that was wrong in my life. I loved the applause, finding approval in the eyes of my patron when the audience tipped me well. Also, this was where I learned to make clothing since highly embellished costumes are an integral part of the bard's ability to impress the customers, and I enjoyed the task. Though Donan was an abusive person, he knew the craft and taught me well. We traveled, performing in all the small, rural inns throughout the south of Neveyah, going from town to town, following the trade roads.

"I was then twelve, and once again we returned to Braden. Donan sold me to a hard, cruel-looking merchant for the night, though I begged him not to. I'd seen her watching me with hot, lustful eyes, while I performed, and she frightened me. She was rumored to sell daze-spice and to use her own merchandise to excess.

"My patron sometimes sold me to merchant men, to my shame and sorrow, but this was the first time a woman asked for me. When I protested, he struck me, telling me she had paid as much as I could earn in a week, and I would do whatever she wanted, no matter what it was. Donan beat me, shouting that when my voice changed, I would be worth nothing to him as a singer, and if I had no other use, I would be cast out.

"All I could see was my mother starving and back on the streets, selling her body again for little more than enough to buy bread." His eyes were wide and full of remembered dread.

In an instant of clarity, Edwin realized this was the moment Beryl told him to watch for—Christoph had never completely recovered from his own traumatic experiences, and this could be the moment to perform the healing she asked Edwin to do.

I've regained enough chi for this, and he is distracted by the baby. This is what he would do if our positions were reversed, he thought. *Beryl was right. He won't notice me using his own method on him.* Full of compassion for the dreadfully abused child Christoph had been, Edwin opened his healing sight, casting soothe on him. Carefully, he began prepping Christoph for healing, using the technique he'd assisted with in treating rape victims. Christoph relaxed somewhat, completely unaware of the spells Edwin cast upon him.

Soon though, he tensed again, fully reliving one of the most terrible moments of his life. "The merchant lady…she…I couldn't do what she wanted, at least not in a way that pleased her. She began cursing and mocking me. Desperately, I tried to do what she wanted. I did try! The more I tried, the less I was able to please her, and she became violent." His voice caught, and he had trouble speaking. "I swear I wanted nothing more than to satisfy her and then have her go away and leave me alone."

Christoph's lips trembled, and he was lost in his painful memories. Unobtrusively, Edwin layered his healing spells into a dampening field that settled over Chris unnoticed. As it took effect, his voice lost the panic, and his face visibly relaxed, exactly as intended. "Then from somewhere she pulled a knife. She was shouting and vowing to unman me for making a fool out of her. She cut me again and again, but I managed to avoid being castrated." Edwin continued casting soothing spells to help him get through telling the difficult parts of his ordeal.

"My blood…it was everywhere…for some reason the sight of my own blood…so much of it…." Completely unaware of having been prepped for a major healing, Christoph continued, speaking now as if he were telling someone else's story, a slight feeling of detachment making it much easier for him. "I can remember the hysteria building inside me, and I meant to run, to somehow hide from this violent madwoman, but instead *I* went mad." This was said with only a hint of the confusion Christoph felt at the time. "All I can clearly remember is Donan's belt lashing me again and again and finding myself lying naked on the floor covered with my own blood. The woman lay dead with her knife through her heart, and her hands clutched around it."

"In her drunken effort to castrate me, she tripped and fell on her own weapon. My patron, having heard my screams of terror, came in and saw her. Angry and fearing he would be implicated in her death, he then beat me senseless, drawing the attention of the innkeeper." Christoph paused and then said, "I honestly thought I was facing my own death. I'd never endured such physical pain or such fear. Then I realized I was hearing Donan's every thought and feeling his vile emotions as he beat me with his belt. He wanted nothing more than to kill me. I became hysterical, begging him to leave me alone.

"The innkeeper burst in on us. I clutched his ankles with my bloody hands, begging him to kill me cleanly rather than give me back to Donan."

Christoph was silent for a moment, and Edwin sat quietly, waiting for him to continue, sensing he was sorting things out in his mind. "The innkeeper was horrified such a terrible thing had occurred to a child under his roof, and I sensed his mind was filled with pity. I wondered who he could be thinking of, feeling desperately sorry for that person. I didn't realize he was looking at me as if I was a child, because my own childhood had ended the day Donan became my patron. I couldn't imagine someone being as cruel to a little child as I saw reflected in the innkeeper's mind. I did lapse into unconsciousness then, I think.

"When I awoke, a Temple healer, Beryl, stood guard over me. She healed my injuries enough so I could be taken to the infirmary, and then she covered my nakedness with her own cloak.

"Beryl first truth-read Donan and then me to discern what really happened. The constable ultimately took my patron away, charged with the rape of a child—me. The penalty for such an offense is castration." Christoph's eyes were dark and full of an unreadable emotion. "Goddess forgive me for this uncharitable thought, but I'm glad someone finally stopped Donan from destroying any more children's lives, though I wouldn't have asked for it to happen that way. Having spent a quarter of my life with him, I didn't know anything different, you see." Pain and guilt were starkly written in the lines of his face. "Beryl then took me to the infirmary at the Braden Temple."

For a moment, Christoph was silent. For the first time, because of Edwin's healing intervention, he was able think calmly of the terrible turn his young life had taken through no fault of his own. "Now you know my dirty secret. Now you know why I'm so good at understanding what victims of rape actually go through, from the self-loathing, to the fear of intimacy, things that forever poison their relationships. It can make some people promiscuous, unable to settle down even when a good person comes into their life. We often feel unworthy. Some of us have a secret guilt, feeling it must have been our fault it happened, believing we could have changed it somehow, though when you look at the actual situation, nothing could have altered it."

Edwin sensed anxiety in Christoph, fear he would now be unacceptable to Edwin as a friend. He immediately sent feelings of acceptance and compassion. Christoph's body relaxed, and he unconsciously breathed a sigh of relief as he felt his friend's unconditional love and support.

Continuing with his explanation, he looked earnestly at Edwin, trying to convey the gravity of what he was saying. "Also, there is another thing that is serious." Christoph's expression was solemn. "Some victims grow up to become abusers if they are not removed from the situation and taught differently, especially if they have learned to be predatory in order to survive. It requires patience and support on the part of the healer and a great willingness to be cured on the part of the victim. Fortunately, Beryl took me in hand. She saved me.

"She placed a small forgetting on me, so my experiences were distant in my mind, and I was almost like other children. I'm quite sure she must have placed certain inhibitions in my mind so my responses were appropriate for a child of my age, which is what I've done in similar cases. For the rest of my childhood, she worked with me, and I wouldn't be here today without her dedicating so much time to healing my internal scars. She took me to an environment where no one knew my secrets, a place where I could live without shame. It was heaven to me.

"From the moment Beryl saved me, I never looked

back except to send my mother money." Christoph's face was bleak. At last, he looked tenderly at the sleeping face of the infant they'd worked so hard to bring into the world. The child's mother was still sleeping, exhausted from her ordeal. "It isn't a pretty story to hear on the first morning of your life, is it, little man?"

"You are who you are, Christoph. You will have much happiness in your life. I can foresee this," Edwin told him, his healing sight still wide open. "You may not ever have a child of your own blood, but you will be a father. Somehow I know this. Blood is not the most important thing. Love is."

Edwin's concern and acceptance of him despite his sad experiences soothed Christoph, easing the guilt he felt when he remembered that part of his life.

Edwin also knew he had to do one more thing. Softly, subtly, he cast soothing spells while Christoph was distracted by the tiny baby, placing the healing feedback in his subconscious mind. Now, Christoph wouldn't associate his own normal and natural physical responses with the degraded and dirty feelings Donan created and left behind. His relationships would no longer be tainted by the experiences of his childhood.

Christoph held the baby close, as if protecting him from the cruel world. "You're a kind man, Edwin Farmer." He spoke softly, unaware his own techniques had been used on him. "I'm glad I told you my sad tale. Beryl thinks somehow these experiences combined to make me unable to raise proper barriers. This is the truth, and I know it."

"I'll help you with your barriers, and work with you as much as you want me to, Chris," Edwin told him. "I want to help you if you'll let me."

Christoph mutely nodded his head. "Dane told me I should let you help me. I'll be more responsible." He looked up with a grin, saying, "He told me you have better barriers than just about anyone and I should pay attention to your instruction."

The baby's mother stirred, and they returned to her side. Soon they were involved with tending to her needs. But Christoph didn't forget the compassion Edwin showed to him, nor did he forget the promise he would someday have a child to love, though it wouldn't be his own blood. Healing others helped him to heal himself, but some people never completely recovered, and the victim often didn't know how deep the scars were. Christoph didn't understand how badly damaged he was by his life with Donan and the events of the terrible night with the lady merchant.

Humming cheerfully, he went about the less glamorous tasks of a healer with a merry smile, making Aysse laugh with his silly jokes as he and Edwin changed her bedding, bathing her and making her more comfortable. Soon she was once again nursing her newborn son, with a happy smile on her face that touched Christoph's heart.

He told Edwin, "I should perhaps like to train as a midwife for a while when we return. I'd like feel again the happiness I felt today for Aysse, Elles, and their new son. I know so much about how life gets messed up—it would be good to know something about the joys of new life and hope."

The rest of the family began to stir. Aeolyn showed the oldest daughter how to make porridge and other simple things. The daughter did have some idea of how to cook, having helped her mother, so Aeolyn simply helped her feel more confident, showing her how much wood to add to the fire and other small things she needed to know.

Friedr showed the other children how to care for the home, sweeping and tidying with them. They swore faithfully to keep it as clean as their mother would. Together they did the laundry, hanging it out. The children followed Friedr slavishly, as all children seemed to do, even the toddler.

After their late breakfast, Aeolyn and the oldest daughter left to go get the midwife, who checked the mother and could find no fault with Edwin's work. "You two have done good work. It's what I'd expect, mind you. I think only a Temple healer could have saved them, if you want to know the truth," she said, speaking confidentially. "I was worried something like this would happen. I don't think I could have saved them both."

"I'm afraid she may never conceive another child, and if she does, I feel strongly she will not survive the next birth," Edwin told the midwife, who agreed with his assessment of the mother's health. "She had difficulty with the birth of each child, didn't she?"

She nodded. "You've learned well if you can tell this. But you can see into her with the sight, can't you?" This time Edwin nodded. "You can see she's built wrong, and I've told Elles this before. I have some herbal remedies that will be of help," replied the midwife.

"The Temple can provide things to help prevent conception and avoid a tragedy here," Edwin told her.

The father was so grateful he fully agreed to

anything that would prevent his wife from suffering so again. "Maybe husbands should be required to at least witness the birth of each child," the midwife said. "It certainly has changed his view of the whole thing."

Edwin smiled and nodded, but privately he wondered, *Why would I not want to be there for the birth of my child? These men make no sense to me.*

"Though we have healed her internally using our skills instead of stitches, you must still watch her carefully for childbed fever," Edwin told the midwife. "We've done all we can for her, so such a complication is unlikely. She must not try to do too much too soon. Now your abilities will make all the difference."

Once she assured them she would remain there for several days until the mother was well enough to do light work, they continued on their journey, satisfied the family would be able to take care of their mother and newest sibling.

After they'd gone about a league, Christoph finally asked Edwin the question burning in his mind since the day before, but which he hadn't wanted to ask in front of Elles. "Edwin? Where did you work as a midwife? I thought you'd never worked as a healer before."

"I have never healed people before this. But I've either assisted or delivered by myself at least a hundred difficult births on the farm. Lambs often come into the world in such a way their mother doesn't survive. My father and I lose very few ewes in the birthing process." He saw Christoph's look of shock and asked gently, "Would you have had me let the woman die and the child too? I knew what to do, and I did it. I couldn't have done it without you casting the spells to inhibit her pain and strengthen her, though. This was the worst sort of situation to have to deal with." He smiled at the look of astonishment on Christoph's face. "I couldn't walk by such suffering and not help her." Christoph finally nodded his head, still amazed at Edwin's audacity. He'd formed a new respect for Edwin, as they all had.

When they made camp, the men talked quietly, unable to sleep, although Aeolyn drifted off immediately. As he thought about the woman's agony, Friedr shuddered and swore he'd never put Aeolyn through such an ordeal.

Edwin looked at her as she slept by the fire. He closed his eyes briefly as he delved her with his healing sight and then opened them. "Don't be worried about such things. Aeolyn will have no trouble bearing children. She is healthy and properly built for it." Friedr looked shocked at Edwin's matter-of-fact settling of the issue, opened his mouth to say something, and then closed it.

"Well, you did bring it up," Christoph chided him. His wicked grin gleamed in the firelight. "Edwin seems to have a good understanding about these things."

"But he lacks delicacy," Friedr complained. "Aeolyn is not a sheep to be appraised for her childbearing qualities." His face was red, and he looked rather affronted. "He sounds like the village head-woman, trying to make a good match for her favorite niece."

Now it was Edwin whose face wore a shocked expression. "Friedr! I love and respect Aeolyn as if she were my own sister. I would never treat her in so casual a manner. But I was raised on a farm, in a farming community. Please forgive me if I misunderstood you. I thought you were worried if she would survive bearing a child. Most husbands do worry about it, and I have the ability to tell you one way or another. Where I come from, the whole of life from conception to birth to the grave is widely discussed. Believe me, it isn't taken for granted."

Edwin abruptly yawned widely and apologized. Then he continued, "At the Boar's Head Inn, we talk about everything openly and perhaps too frankly for your taste. In my town, fathers are there for the births of their children. They often discuss it over a pint of ale, and we all know the details. This is why I know how women are coached through the delivery of their children." His smile at Friedr was sardonic as he said, "I was sort of surprised to find it isn't the case here. It continually amazes me. You people all know how to die here, but birth is a complete mystery. Nothing is more interesting to my neighbors than the delivery of their children and their neighbor's children, yet funerals seem to be the important topics of conversation in the common rooms here."

Smiling hugely at Friedr's obvious consternation, Christoph told Edwin to go and get some sleep. "I will wake you when it's your turn to stand watch." *And in the meantime, I will have a talk with Friedr about the facts of life,* he thought to himself, a wide grin splitting his face as he added a log to the fire. *Of course Edwin is matter of fact about it. He's a down-to-earth person, but he's also a healer more than anything—a healer who was raised on a farm, valuing the one thing farmers value and work with every day: life.*

***

Once again the days monotonously passed with the team marching and camping, interspersed with fighting the rat-people and other wild things. As they walked, the snow-capped mountains grew nearer, rising higher and higher until they filled the eastern sky.

Fortunately, they met no major emergencies at any of the farms they passed, though as always, they healed minor illnesses and small injuries. Edwin's training continued, and daily he grew in strength and ability.

A farmer in an out-of-the-way village with no name had a case of blood poisoning, and they were able to cure it easily, Christoph showing Edwin techniques for cleansing the blood of infection.

In the town of Prona, a boy had pneumonia, and at first it was serious, but with proper treatment, he made a complete recovery.

A poor man's cow had an infected udder, and Edwin was able to show Christoph how to take care of it without using his magic. "I can't believe a Temple healer would lower himself to heal my cow," the farmer told Edwin. A wry grin creased his ancient features. "But I'm glad you did, young sir. I've no money to hire the animal healer to come all the way out here from Varden."

"I'm a farm boy myself," laughed Edwin. "I know how hard it is to care for your animals, and I know how expensive it is to have the animal healer come out. Besides, your cow is your source of income. Without her milk, how would you make the fine cheese you just shared with us?"

They left his home with their bellies full of the good soup the old farmer prepared and a wheel of his cheese in their baggage on the pack ponies. As they continued eastward, Edwin wondered what they were walking toward, and his anticipation made him hurry a little. The escarpment of the Mountains of the Moon loomed, the snowcapped wall of peaks taking up a great portion of the morning sky.

Chapter 12

They'd been on the road for three weeks by the time they entered Arlen, marked on the map as the home of the mercenary companies. It was a strange, noisy place, yet there was an air about it that felt secretive.

The garishly painted houses were narrow, often three or four stories tall with steep, slate roofs, shops on the ground floor, and living quarters above. They were jammed together as if there was no room for them, which was indeed the case. The tall buildings lined narrow cobbled streets full of people with an odd accent. "They all sound like my mother when they talk. It's like a foreign country." Edwin stared about in wonder, the noise and chatter overwhelming. "Aeoven is so peaceful compared to here."

Bakers hawked their goods amid the other merchants, all shouting the quality of their wares. Merchant ladies hurried by in dresses far too expensive for any woman in Aeoven and far too elaborate for working in a garden or doing housework.

Edwin was immediately struck by the contrast. As was the custom in Aeoven, the people in the surrounding towns wore simple, Temple-made garments.

But in Arlen, even the poorer women wore ornate, full-skirted dresses reminiscent of the women of Markett. The dressmakers were some of the more prominent merchants along the busy streets, each one with a shapely lady standing in the front window of the shop, wearing the finest examples of her employer's work, demonstrating the style and quality of the clothing made in that particular establishment.

Arlen was the northernmost of the border towns in Neveyah, and was originally constructed hard along the Cascadia escarpment, in the shadow of the mountains. The town was clearly expanding, currently being built into the base of the Mountains of the Moon. The sound of noisy construction on the new city walls filled the air, new walls being built of granite. Immediately behind the line of hills beyond Arlen, the immense escarpment rose in sheer cliffs looking as if cut by a knife, a league or more in height above the verdant plains of western Neveyah.

"Those high mountains are the old world of Cascadia, the world of the god Ariend. This is where the worlds once touched, but now Aeos has the care and keeping of his world, and the veil separating them was swept away." Friedr's calm voice explained the incredible change in the landscape.

It was as if the countryside was patched together in a ragged seam. The worlds adjoined at impossibly different heights. The sun took an extra hour in the morning to clear the mountains that loomed over the town of Arlen.

"I remember reading of the origins of the escarpment, now you mention it," replied Edwin, completely amazed by the sheer size of the immense cliffs that stretched the entire length of the mountain range. "The books don't describe them accurately. They're incredible."

"They're building a fortress here," said Aeolyn with surprise as they walked the narrow streets. "Look at the way the wall is built into the base of the escarpment."

Friedr laughed at Edwin, who stared about himself so much that he stumbled. "Come on, farm boy, this isn't the first big town you've been in. Stop gawking. Pay attention to your feet!"

The Thieves Nest Inn was pleasant, and the barmaids were friendly enough, especially to Edwin, but no one volunteered any real information. As soon as Aeolyn mentioned the Shadow Castle, even that dried up. The innkeeper found two rooms for them, and he personally showed them up, nattering on about the weather and the dangers of travel this time of the year. His speech was heavily accented, reminding Edwin again of his mother.

Edwin came down first and as usual, in the common room packed with men, had the undivided attention of the friendly-girls. He could have done without it, as it was impossible to relax with the ladies fighting each other for the privilege of harassing him. He longed for the peaceful evenings in Christoph's rooms with their friends, lively and spirited discussions that didn't involve his having to hide from the women.

Friedr at last came downstairs, and after shooing the girls back to the bar, he sat drinking with Edwin while Aeolyn went off to soak in the bath. Christoph sat by the fire, polishing their boots.

Edwin truly confused Friedr. *Here is a man who is able to dive right in and deliver a baby without flinching or cringing.* He shuddered at the thought. *He fights the most vicious of beasts with a mad grin on his face, looking like some demented, sword-wielding maniac. Then he heals anyone who needs it and mourns the dead creatures that have come to grief at his hands.*

But invariably, he panics and runs from the liberal charms of the friendly-girls who can't get enough of him. There must be a reason why. I don't know any other man who would let such opportunities pass him by as Edwin so regularly does. But perhaps he doesn't like girls. Maybe I have read him wrong.

At last, he asked Edwin, "Why do you never take what these lovely ladies offer? Is it simply you're not interested in girls? Some fellows aren't. It isn't too unusual. Do you prefer boys? I know some fine, un-partnered men of that persuasion if you're lonely."

Edwin choked on his ale and sputtered, before finally getting his breath back. "As do I, Friedr, as do I. But...ah, no, I much prefer girls. At least I would if they weren't so pushy. I actually like them a lot, far too much for my own comfort sometimes," he replied, casting a quick glance at the women who lined the bar looking at him with longing. "Tonight, more than ever, I wish I didn't have this vision in my head, but I do." He looked away as he admitted his problem, knowing his face was bright red.

Out the corner of his eye, he saw Christoph near the fire, almost bursting with trying not to laugh. Edwin couldn't help it—he started to laugh himself. "I've always known who I'll bond with, and I don't want to have to do a lot of explaining when I do meet her. I admit that it's difficult at times. I'll know her when I see her."

"And you respect her. You won't take advantage of what's offered by women who only want you as their pleasure-boy," said Friedr. "Well, if you wish, we can protect your pretty face from the unasked-for kisses of ardent barmaids." He clasped Edwin's shoulder in a comradely fashion.

Turning on his bench, Friedr shouted toward the fireplace, "Christoph! Stop eavesdropping and come help me protect our friend's virginity." Edwin choked again, and Chris howled with laughter.

The evening passed companionably. As they sat laughing and joking with each other, two armed men wearing the chain-mail of mercenaries entered the common room. They looked around, noting everything and everyone, and stationed themselves, one at the foot of the stairs and one by the door. A thin man with lank, dark hair, clad in well-worn armor similar to that of the Temple, entered, followed by another who also remained at the door. The man smiled at the bartender as he crossed over to their table. The guards at the door were obviously his personal protectors, signifying his importance in this town. The demeanor of the staff and regular patrons highlighted he was the town's leader.

He introduced himself as Jaxon Sellsword. He was young to be so revered, perhaps Edwin's age, though his eyes seemed much older, as if he'd seen far too much and was surprised by nothing. His bearing indicated he was a man who'd fought all his life and was at ease with it. "I understand you seek information about Mal Evol and the Shadow Castle."

"We do," replied Friedr, beckoning to the bartender. Ale was brought, and he gave an extra copper to the barmaid who lingered by Edwin's shoulder, twining her fingers in his golden hair. Friedr shooed her away. "Have you information to sell?"

"Not to sell." Jaxon's eyes twinkled, though his low voice was sober. Staring after the barmaid, he said, "That's quite a problem your friend has. I don't think

I've ever seen it so bad." He turned to Edwin. "You look deceptively handsome. You have the feel of a Temple assassin, though you bear none of the signs, and the crescent moon says it's impossible."

Edwin shrugged and looked Jaxon full in the eye, smiling lazily, saying nothing. "Healer's crescent on your brow, and flowering vines trail across the back of your right hand. Lightning on your cheek, and warrior's vines peep above your collar. This is a remarkable thing. I don't like strange things in my town. I always feel compelled to sort them out and assuage my curiosity."

Edwin smiled even more broadly and settled back, loosening his sword in its scabbard, fully prepared to fight if necessary.

"It's interesting that the son of your father should feel like an assassin to me, though as I say, you bear none of the signs." Jaxon's voice was low, but his words carried to those around the table. "I believe you may be a very dangerous man to cross, Edwin Farmer." Edwin still said nothing, although he now looked interested.

"He is. More so than you imagine," Christoph replied calmly, and Jaxon nodded as if he expected to hear it confirmed. "He is a healer adept who is a full battle-mage and an adept with the sword. That combination is dangerous, in my opinion, but not to you, my lord."

Friedr glared at Christoph, who shrugged. "How is it you know his name?" Friedr stared at Jaxon with the deadly, flat look he sometimes got when killing some particularly nasty thing. "You looked deceptively intelligent until you spoke of a subject that is none of your business." His low tones were as cold as ice.

Laughing at the discomfort he'd managed to instill into the gathering, Jaxon replied, "Yes, Sir Fire-mage, it is as you say—I'm an idiot. Nonetheless, I make it my business to know this very handsome man who is sitting in my common room in my town, refusing to consort with the most eager and generous of ladies. This reminds me of a tale I once heard of a man who often passed through here, long ago in my infancy. He was also much remarked upon. This man, it turned out, was bonded to my cousin several times removed." He smiled disarmingly back at Edwin. "I have much reason to be grateful to your father. Edwin Farmer, you're all I have left of family."

Edwin sat stunned. "I'm glad to meet you, more than you can possibly know. I'd thought myself alone in this world," replied Edwin, clasping hands with his cousin. His charismatic smile charmed even the jaded Jaxon Sellsword. "I was told I might have a distant relative in this town. I'd no idea you would be as alone as I am."

"We'll have our reunion tomorrow, I promise, and we'll talk about everything you and I both wish to know." He looked at Friedr, who sat with a slightly stunned look. "But, in the meantime, about the information. I will tell you what I know for free, but I have a request of you." Jaxon looked around the table. "If, while you are carrying out your task, you should achieve that which we all wish for, remember the *infant child* of Maxon the Unworthy was never officially accounted for, though many declared him dead. Now I will tell you a Temple secret."

He looked at the group, who each solemnly laid his

right hand over his heart. "As I love the Goddess, I swear I am that child."

Edwin felt the surprise of each person at the table.

"We go to the Shadow Castle to retrieve a thing that belongs to the Temple," replied Friedr carefully. "Our instructions are to recover only that which is ours. We have no intention of drawing the unwelcome attention of anyone who currently sits on a stolen throne, you understand. We are unprepared for such an event."

"I know what you seek to reclaim and wholeheartedly wish you success. We here in Arlen value her as much as you do. She refused my offer of a guard, fearing her patients would be frightened of him. Then, my men were not able to get to her in time to effect a rescue, though they did track her captors to the Shadow Castle. They were able to bring the information straight to Braden."

Jaxon looked at Friedr and said, "I would simply ask this: when the time comes, whether now or one hundred years from now, remember that I live, as does my infant son. It is for my sad people I ask this. I have saved a remnant of them, and there's hope more can be freed before the garden city falls to the Lost One and we're locked out of the Valley of Sorrows."

"I've heard the prophecy," replied Friedr. "Surely, we're not nearing the end-times. Surely, there is still time." He spoke the words as if praying, hoping against hope.

"Sadly, Sir Fire-mage, I fear we are nearing the last days. Thus, I've made it my business to save as many children of Aeos as I am able. So long as they remember who they are, I shall spirit them away from the City of the Dead." He sighed heavily, looking at some sad thing in his mind's eye.

Abruptly, Jaxon shook himself and said, "But here, I haven't told you the information—my childhood nurse, a woman with, shall we say, an 'earthy' past, long ago told me of a small, secret gate hidden in the garden wall beneath the Rose Tower, that some now call the Tower of Bones." Edwin was startled, hearing the tower that figured so prominently in his dreams named. "It's a very dark garden when there is no moon, and once this gate was quite useful for private trysts.

"Consider this: if a maid's clandestine lover could find the gate useful, why, then a thief could easily enter or leave, should he wish—but only on a moon-dark night. You will see why when you get there." He looked over at a table full of traveling merchants and their guards and then leaned forward as if talking to his closest friends. "I tell this knowing it's safe, and you will carry it either to the grave or to his Holiness, whichever you see first."

Jaxon leaned back and tossed a money pouch to Friedr, who accepted it with some confusion. The huge warrior's face cleared up as he felt the contents, and he tucked it into his shirt with a knowing smile.

"I'll take the horse and thank you for offering it to me," Jaxon said as he stood up, automatically casting a wary eye around the room. "It is good doing business with you. The mercenaries of Arlen stand ready in case of need, at the usual price of course. The Temple has only to call." With that, he flipped a coin to the bartender and walked out into the night, followed by his guards.

"What was that all about?" asked Edwin, speaking

in a whisper, his brow furrowed. "I don't remember us having a horse to sell. We need our pack-ponies."

"Don't be so wool-headed, farm boy," whispered Aeolyn, who only caught the last of the conversation. "There are others, not of Arlen, in this room tonight. It was a cover for what's really in the little money pouch. Come on, Friedr, what is in the bag?"

"I would guess it is a key of some sort," suggested Christoph quietly, smiling faintly. "Perhaps to a gate beneath a certain tower?"

Edwin sat silently for the rest of the evening, pondering what Jaxon told him. *He's my cousin,* thought Edwin, trying to organize his thoughts. He was unsure about Jaxon, who repudiated his own father and claimed the name Sellsword. Did he do this to protect his identity, or was it because the family name D'Mal was now so hated? Perhaps it was for both reasons that he used a mercenary's name rather than his bloodline's. Despite that, he was charming, and Edwin liked him.

Edwin looked forward to the morning. Knowing he wasn't alone in this world was comforting to him. He suspected Jaxon felt as solitary as he did.

***

Once again, Edwin dreamed he was standing in the dark garden. Shadows whispered, leading him to an unlatched window. "Friend.... Come, friend...," they called to him. He levered the window open and climbed through, walking across the dark room to a door that stood ajar. Again, the shadows tugged at him, urging him to open it.

A girl in a white, high-necked nightgown stood before a mirror, slowly brushing her hair. Edwin carried a picture of her, but she was far more beautiful than it showed. A wedding dress hung on her wardrobe door, and tears flowed down her cheeks. He stood shocked at the sight of her. She looked white and drawn, as if she'd been ill. "She wasn't ill, but imprisoned, warrior," spoke the shadows, as they revealed themselves as the shades of the departed. "The bride was held in the dungeon below until only recently. Now she is his captive in the Tower of Bones. We are with her. She will be safe until you come for her, but you must hurry."

"Marya," he whispered.

She turned, recognizing his Temple armor, and said through her tears, "Hurry! He grows impatient."

Edwin turned and found himself outside the garden walls. Long rows of standing stones marched along a lane that appeared to lead from a small, kitchen gate. The stones shielded the view from the castle, as if the sight of carts bringing supplies to their keep might have offended the people inside.

Abruptly, he woke up and was unable to get back to sleep. Slipping into his trousers and shirt, Edwin dressed quietly so as not to disturb Christoph, who snored lightly in his cot. He went down to sit before the low fire in the dark common room.

***

At dawn, Aeolyn found him there, sleeping with his head on his arms, when she and the others came down for breakfast.

Edwin related his dream, and Aeolyn listened solemnly. "It was surely a true-dream," she said. "The Goddess has sent it to show you the way."

"The shadows told me she was imprisoned for a long while. Now she's in rooms that look out on a

152

walled garden. They also referred to the tower she is being held in as The Tower of Bones. I'm almost afraid to find out why they give it this name. I feel sure the only way to approach unnoticed is to use the kitchen lane. The tower garden must be the one Jaxon gave us the key for," Edwin said, thoughtfully. "Marya said we should hurry because *he* grows impatient. Impatient for what, I wonder. There was a wedding dress hanging on the wardrobe. Do you think he would dare? I mean, she's a priestess of the Goddess, not the Bull God. Is it allowed?"

Christoph nodded sadly. "There is no doubt the Baron Stefyn D'Mal has none of the restraints sane men have. Did she look, ah, well?" The healer's eyes were worried. His gaze flickered to Aeolyn and back to Edwin, as if silently asking him something he didn't want to voice.

Suddenly, Edwin understood and felt sick to his stomach. "She was crying, but I don't think he has tried to take her by force—yet. She was afraid, but I didn't sense he has done such a thing."

Aeolyn gasped and pressed her hand to her mouth. Friedr put his arm around her, saying "Our Marya is strong. She knows we are coming."

Christoph's normally smiling face looked grim. "Edwin, you said he hadn't raped her *yet*. You're right, we must hurry."

After their discussion with Jaxon the previous night, it was clear they could no longer travel openly as Temple clergy and needed all speed. They decided to stay in Arlen for two more nights. Aeolyn arranged to disguise their appearance so from a distance, they wouldn't stand out from the local farm folk in any way.

While she made those arrangements, Edwin spent the day in his cousin's company, finding he was a witty and charming man. He also met Jaxon's shy wife, Eleia, and their newborn son, Dex. Edwin soon realized the salvaging of the people and culture of Mal Evol was Jaxon's main priority in life, and his life in Arlen completely reflected that. His mercenaries served much the same purpose as the Temple militia, protecting the merchants when they traveled the dangerous roads. His assistance was freely given to the Temple, and his service was invaluable.

"On the Day of Redemption we'll be ready. Our people will be waiting to take back our land, and it'll be our sons or grandsons, yours and mine, who'll see it." Jaxon's enthusiasm was only slightly dimmed by the knowledge he wouldn't be the one who reclaimed his father's throne.

"I'm not sure I want to fulfill any prophecies," Edwin told him with a wry smile. "I simply want to do what I have to and get on with my life. I'm a healer, not a warrior."

"We seldom have a choice as to our roles when it comes to the plans of the deities," replied Jaxon, clasping his shoulder. "The Mother of All has spelled out our fate in the stars, and we find ourselves walking the paths we have been set upon. That we are here together is a sign the end-times are approaching."

The same evening, Christoph borrowed a harp and regaled the common room with several bardic tales, ending with the epic tale *The Fall of Ariend*, which told the tale of the god being sealed into the haft of a crystal and marble spear by the Bull God, Tauron, in his effort to steal Ariend's wife, the Goddess Aeos.

At the end, Jaxon knelt in front of Christoph and in an extravagant gesture, tearfully kissed his hand amid the cheers and whistles of the packed common room. The song was the central tale of the creation and founding of Mal Evol and was considered a national treasure among the expatriates. "You are welcome here anytime, Christoph Berryman. You will be treated like royalty when you return to Arlen, I promise you."

Jaxon's florid display seemed a little extreme to the companions, but his behavior was repeated over and over as the townsfolk returned to their homes. "It must be their cultural nature," Edwin told Aeolyn, who was amused by their behavior, "though I don't recall my mother being overly dramatic. But she left Mal Evol for the Temple in Aeoven as a young novice healer of eleven years."

Once the medicines they carried had been delivered to the local healer, Aeolyn sold the ponies and bought Friedr and Edwin chainmail. She also arranged for a cart and donkey. She was dressed in a high-necked, grey wool dress of slightly better quality than the farm women's. With Christoph fixing her hair in the local style, hiding her facial augmentations under dark ringlets, she looked the part of a moderately prosperous merchant. Christoph was her brother with his hair combed forward in the local style, hiding his identifying marks. Edwin and Friedr were dressed as mercenary guards with helms. She told Friedr, "No one will believe you are simply a trader, my dear one. You carry yourself like a warrior looking for a battle, and even a merchant of my lesser status will have two guards."

"He walks that way because he's *always* looking

for a fight," Christoph quipped. "Fighting is his hobby."

"But he does keep us entertained with all the healing we get to do on his hairy hide." Edwin laughed. He'd gained a lot of experience in sealing gaping wounds by having to heal Friedr so regularly.

"Humph. I wanted to wear a fancy, purple surcoat." Friedr pretended to sulk. "Chris gets to wear all the pretty clothes."

After a quick consultation with Jaxon, who was pleased to help, Aeolyn arranged for them to take a load of potatoes to the next big town of Widge, hiding their armor in bundles under the cargo.

As they were preparing to leave Arlen, Edwin realized he was beginning to feel out-of-sorts. The buildup of chi would make him a target of the feral rats unless he remembered to bleed it off. He yearned for solitude, something he couldn't have under the circumstances, and struggled with the excess chi. It was a struggle, trying to remain a pleasant companion, though he didn't feel at all like his usual self.

In the livery stable at the inn when they first took ownership of the donkey, Edwin felt a terrible longing for home and the farm in Markett. As he groomed her, he formally named the donkey Sweet Pea, to Friedr's dismay. Edwin immediately took over caring for her, as he'd done for the pack-ponies they had traded in. Grooming Sweet Pea soothed his frayed nerves.

"You shouldn't name an animal you may have to eat," Friedr said. "Besides, we will be leaving her in Braden, and it will be changed again by her next owner."

"Her name is Sweet Pea, and it doesn't matter if people change it. It's hers for now." Edwin finished currying and checked her hooves. "I can't just call her donkey." His voice was sharp despite his desire to remain cheerful, and he immediately apologized to his friend, saying, "We have to get to a Temple with a colorist soon, Friedr. I'm starting to feel out of balance despite my best efforts. I'm sorry."

"I understand," he replied. "We'll arrive there before the mail coach by traveling like this, but I'll have Christoph help you. We can't afford to have you go mad."

On the way out of Arlen, Edwin stopped at a merchant's stall and bought a wide-brimmed straw hat for Sweet Pea, cutting holes for her ears. Aeolyn smiled at the gesture and tied a ribbon around the hat's crown, tucking a few wild flowers into it, saying "Every girl loves flowers."

Friedr slowly shook his head. "Farm boy, you constantly amaze me."

As they rolled south along the base of the escarpment, beneath the Mountains of the Moon, Edwin was uncharacteristically quiet. He wouldn't be healing until they arrived in Braden, where he would work in the infirmary for a few days. All he could do was ride in the wagon, posing as a guard, and worry about his problems.

And Edwin *was* worried. He worried about what waited for them and about his abilities that were growing stronger than he had the chi for. Every time they battled a rat-mage, his first or second casting took all his battle-chi, and even a deep slash began taking half his healing chi. His spells were powerful, though his ability to store chi hadn't kept up. The problem was he dared not cast a truly effective spell for fear he would find himself with nothing left, despite the fact he had been augmented twice since his first time. To keep from fretting about his lack of chi, he quietly began trying to find ways to solve the problem.

At first, Edwin attempted to draw chi from the surrounding area to no avail. He thought he should be able to, since it naturally gathered about him and stored itself in his augmentations. But if there was a way, he didn't find it, and said nothing about his problems to his companions. Instead, he cared for Sweet Pea and often stayed in her company.

As they traveled, Edwin often walked beside Sweet-Pea, enjoying her company and the scent of the farm that clung to her. He needed the comparative solitude, and she was a soothing companion. "I know what's really wrong is only my being out of balance," he told her. She gave him the compassionate look donkeys often had. "I keep thinking about my father. It might do Dad some good to see the way Neveyah is now and how people think of him. He's a hero to them, even if he does believe he's a failure."

During the journey, while he was occupied with trying to comprehend why he couldn't draw chi from the natural world, Edwin found a great many things he *could* do using the natural chi. He discovered how to tie off a ward against midges and other flying pests. Christoph immediately began using and enlarging upon it.

"And the beauty of this new trick of Edwin's is once we tie it off, we don't have to maintain it until the next day," Christoph enthusiastically told Aeolyn. "It uses natural chi, not our personal chi." Making wards was a healing magic, and so she was unable to make them, but Chris and Edwin made sure everyone was protected from the bloodsucking insects that loved them so.

The road followed the Fleet River as it wound its way south along the escarpment, and they made good time. Soon they rolled in to Widge, delivered their potatoes, and arranged to take a load of carrots on to the garden city of Braden. There, in the Fleetside Inn, Christoph ran into an old acquaintance, a young water-mage named Glynn, who was traveling on Temple business. He was aware they were traveling incognito and didn't greet them as fellow mages. However, Glynn prevailed upon the healer to regale the common room with some of his more risqué songs, which he was happy enough to do. Since the three men looked like they were getting a bit deep into the ale, Aeolyn slipped off to bed early.

Christoph finished the evening off with a bawdy tale called *The Tale of Mother Alys and Her Merry Daughters*, a tale of amazing naughtiness that brought down the house, with everyone laughing and singing along with the chorus.

The next morning found the three of them feeling slightly delicate, but rolling out of town at dawn nonetheless. Aeolyn's obscene perkiness left them feeling rather less than jolly, but their temporary ailment cleared up by noon. That was good, as they were harassed by pack after pack of rats and other creatures before they made a wary camp. "It's your chi attracting them again," Aeolyn sighed, as Edwin healed a gash on Christoph's forehead. "You're not storing all you gather, and it radiates, telling all the beasts a meal of great tastiness is waiting for them."

"I'll make a greater effort to bleed it off," Edwin promised, and he redoubled his efforts whenever he started feeling out of sorts. It helped a little, but the beasts were still attracted to them, often attacking Edwin first.

The journey from Widge to Braden was difficult. Edwin healed Sweet-Pea twice, and the cart suffered some abuse from a large, one-horned beast. After three day's hard travel, it was with great relief they entered Braden. The gatekeeper told them the gates were closed at dusk and not opened for any reason until dawn. "There are many things lurking out there that are not welcome in the city."

"I believe we may have met some of them," replied Friedr, looking at their poor cart. "They seem to dislike carrots as much as I do."

Aeolyn snorted her opinion of his view of vegetables.

The mage on gate duty directed them to the market, where they delivered their cargo. The pleasant city was much larger than Aeoven, with lush gardens and flowers in front of every home and window. They then took their cart to the local Temple of Aeos, where they would stay while they prepared to make the last leg of their journey to the Shadow Castle.

For some obscure reason, Edwin was reluctant to leave Sweet Pea behind. The stable master there took one look at Edwin's face and said, "You was raised a farm boy, wasn't you? Don't you worry, young mage. She'll be treated well here." Edwin reluctantly said goodbye to his four-legged friend, feeling rather ridiculous for being so sad.

They were given rooms in the guest lodge at the

Temple. Edwin didn't go down to the local tavern with the others, telling them he was tired. The truth was he simply couldn't face the common room. Edwin was full of worry about his inability to store enough chi and concerned that even with his augmentations, he would soon not be able to cast even one spell without completely draining himself. Despite his worries, he soon fell asleep. It was filled with dreams of a brown-eyed girl.

Chapter 13

The next morning, Edwin met his companions at breakfast. "You have to see the colorist as soon as possible," Aeolyn told him.

Edwin silently but fervently agreed, and she took him to the abbott, a large man named Garran Andreson. Edwin immediately gave his father's greetings and said his father was well and as happy as he could be, since his wife's death.

"I heard Andia was taken in an epidemic. I admit I grieved for John, but especially for you. They loved each other deeply." Abbott Garran was full-bearded and felt a lot like Friedr to Edwin's mage sight, but not the way Father Rall did. Garran wasn't from the North, so he wasn't a barbarian. Edwin finally decided he was a fire-mage and a weapons master, as Friedr was.

Abbott Garran had received a letter from the Holy Father and had been expecting them. "There's a great deal of your father in you, though you seem to have your mother's calm, thoughtful temperament rather than his brash arrogance," he told Edwin, clasping his shoulder in greeting. "John was a brother to me, at one time. We travelled together many years ago. It was our first quest. We trained together."

Edwin looked thoughtful, trying to picture his father as a teenager, and failing.

Garran said, "Before you leave, I'll work with you myself so I can tell your father how well you're really doing. Now that you're back there's no reason he can't return too, and we need him. I've decided to make a trip to visit him."

Edwin nodded. "I hope I don't disappoint you, sir," he replied, with a smile. "I'd like to send him a letter, if I may?"

"Of course," Garran agreed. "He'd like to hear of your adventures since leaving Aeoven. Halee has most likely told him some of what's going on, but not what he really wants to know, because she doesn't want him worrying. I disagree with her in this—I think John needs to know what you're facing and that I think you can handle it." Edwin blushed, not knowing what to say.

"Perhaps you want to know more about your father's part in this drama that has spanned so many generations of your family." Abbott Garran looked at Edwin, marveling at how much he resembled John as a young man, though his augmentations were already different.

"I was a journeyman fire-mage, spoiling to be appointed to a real Temple quest. There were many opportunities as the children of the Bull God had found a way to enter the land of Mal Evol and harass our people there. The senior clergy was disturbed that Tauron's people could enter Neveyah. The only way they could possibly have come through from the world of Serende was if a member of the ruling family granted them entry, but we couldn't discover who had done such a thing. Maxon, the king of Mal Evol, certainly hadn't. His children couldn't have as they were too young, and his only living uncle was the Abbott of the Temple there and sworn to the service of Aeos. It wasn't until much later that we discovered exactly what had happened.

"The Temple's goal was to try to keep the children

of the Bull God, from taking Mal Evol. John was convinced we were going to win and force them back to their true land despite Holy Mother Lera's vision to the contrary. His drive and determination kept us going during the darkest days." Some dark emotion passed through Garran's eyes momentarily.

"Though we tried, we couldn't push Tauron's minotaur legions back across the dead lands. They had a strong, young priest on their side whose like had never been seen. He was a mindbender and a battle-mage combined into one."

"A mindbender?" Edwin had never heard the term.

Garran shrugged, saying, "A mindbender is a mage born with the healing talent, who's never been augmented and who isn't suitable to be bound by the vows to work for the good of Neveyah. The Temple makes every effort to weed them out before they take root and have the chance to become rogue-mages. They're too dangerous to be allowed to wreak their havoc on the populace."

Understanding dawned in Edwin's eyes. "I've read of them. We don't have to worry about them anymore because the Temple finds those with talent when they are children and trains them properly."

"Yes. They're the most dangerous sort of mage you can imagine. They have the power to control the minds of those they come into contact with. In the past, mindbenders always sought out untrained battle-mages, placing them in their thrall and using their skills. The way we usually dealt with that sort of threat was to whittle away the mindbender's thralls, and then kill them."

"I've read of many of those sorts of quests,"

offered Edwin.

A bitter smile crossed Garran's face. "It didn't work with this new threat. This particular one was also a battle-mage in his own right, with the added complication of being a priest of Tauron. He used Tauron's magic as well as Aeos's. And surprise! Not only was he their highest priest, despite the fact he wasn't a minotaur, but he was actually the previously unknown, illegitimate older half-brother of Maxon, the king of Mal Evol. He had the blood connection to the throne. He was a child of Aeos who was stolen by the children of Tauron for the sole purpose of gaining them entry into Neveyah. Stefyn D'Mal was a force we couldn't have predicted." He shook his shaggy head in disgust.

"He possessed powers that were the direct manifestation of their hideous god. One year before John came to Aeoven, Her Holiness, Mother Lera, was sent a disturbing vision from Aeos, mentioning Stefyn D'Mal directly, although at the time, no one knew whom the prophecy was about. It referred to one who was 'the Broken Child.' This child of Aeos would take the Valley of Sorrow for the children of the Bull God. This vision was the first true sign the end days of Neveyah were upon us.

"Soon after that Mother Lera had that vision, a barely fifteen-year old John Farmer appeared at the appointed place, with no idea how he arrived other than he was tracking a lost sheep and found himself in Neveyah. His father, who was often an eccentric man, had behaved strangely that morning, even for him, upon hearing a sheep had strayed. Wynn forced a unique sword-belt on John and said he loved him. Then he shoved him out the door.

"Pauli Oakheart, a fine lightning-mage with adept potential, who was also Marya's uncle, was sent to bring him to Aeoven. Being sent to meet the new, unknown mage was Pauli's first away posting as a journeyman. They were both as green as newborn babes.

"John was strong in all the elements, but his great strength was water-magic. He studied with us for two years in Aeoven, and he soon outstripped all the battle-mages in his ability. Toward the end of his second year as a journeyman, he met and fell in love with Andia. Her family was well known in Mal Evol City. The fact their daughter was a healer was a source of great pride to them. They loved your father, taking him into their hearts and home with great joy when he and Andia were bonded before we left on our first quest. John was overjoyed. At last, he was part of a large family. Your bloodline has always been very much alone, with never more than a single son born at a time."

Edwin nodded. "I've always wanted a large family too. When I'm bonded, I hope to have many children. No child should grow up as alone as I did."

Garran shook his head. Edwin obviously didn't understand what he had just been told, but rather than ruin the young man's hopes, he simply continued his story. "Your father was quite the young brawler in those days. He couldn't walk away from a fight, and before he and Andia met, he couldn't walk away from the friendly-girls. The girls adored him to the extent that at first he and Pauli disliked each other intensely because of the rivalry they developed on their walk to Aeoven from the portal. Water and lightning mages frequently have difficulties in their relationships with each other.

"Nevertheless, Abbott Rall kept assigning them to work with each other. Neither one liked to lose in any competition—and that's exactly what happened whenever they fought each other instead of concentrating on their common goal. John finally realized he needed to cooperate with Pauli, and Pauli didn't know how to stay angry with anyone, although women still kept getting in the way between them.

"Despite their differences, John and Pauli learned to trust each other, and in the end, they were truly closer than brothers. I often think it was because of their history that his final sacrifice affected John more than words could say. He was never the same after Pauli's death."

"What happened? Dad has never once spoken to me about Neveyah."

Garran's attempt at a cheerful expression faded slightly as he replied, "We were pulled out of our normal positions with the army and sent on a secret mission. You might not believe this, but your father is one of most brilliant tacticians in Neveyah. He understands troop movements and battle planning like no one else. But he also possesses other skills—the water-mage on our team had to be him.

"We were tasked with bringing all who could be saved of the royal family of Mal Evol to safety.

"The Temple in Mal Evol City was seized by the enemy and burned to the ground. Devyn D'Mal, the abbott and the man everyone thought would one day hold the office of the Holy Seat, was the first of the clergy sacrificed on Tauron's unholy altar. We lost more than half of the Temple clergy in the taking of Mal Evol City alone.

"That black day—and Pauli calling 'thunder walking' on the enemy's legions until he lost consciousness and they overran him—is etched into my memory. Where he pulled the chi from, I can't imagine. Perhaps in moments of desperation, we can accomplish more than we think we can. The legions kept coming and dying—there seemed to be no end to them.

"We ran, dodging the battles and desperately looking for a way to the keep. Pauli's sacrifice allowed us to escape into the Grand Canal that flowed past the western gate. On the second night after leaving the burning city, we were camped far to the southwest, unable to go north to the keep as we wanted to.

"John had a trick that was his specialty, and he used it to search for a hidden creek. But what he found was a way to the keep of Mal Evol along an underground river. Apparently, no one told him it was an impossible use of magic. I don't know anyone else who could sense water like John. If there was water anywhere, he would find it.

"Using her earth-magic, Halee made an entrance we could walk through, disguising it so it was undetectable unless you knew what to look for. We crept through the dark, beneath the raging battles, and made the journey in six days, with little rest and without much food. Water we had plenty of, and for light, we relied on the luminescent fungus growing in patches along the way. We carried a lantern, but oil was in short supply. John put the fungus in the lantern, and we walked by the ghostly green light it produced.

"Halee smoothed the road and made it passable,

making decent spots for us to camp. We lacked fire, for there was nothing to burn, and food was terribly scarce.

"We emerged into a cave at the base of the cliffs beneath the keep, and once again, Halee made a cunningly disguised exit for us, as the natural one would have required us to crawl on our bellies to get out. We entered the keep through the wine cellar and stole through the ruin and destruction of the empty, abandoned castle until we came upon a scene of the most unspeakable carnage."

The abbott was silent, his eyes bleak as he recalled one of the days so long ago that changed him and his companions forever. Edwin considered casting ease once more, but Garran forestalled him. "No need to ease my pain again, though I thank you for the thought."

Continuing his story, Garran said, "In the end, we were able to save one child, an infant boy left for dead, lying unnoticed among the bloody, mutilated corpses of his family. Fortunately for us, the legions and their master were occupied in Mal Evol City, and so we were left unmolested. We camped inside the cave while Halee healed us of our small scrapes with her small ability and such potions and ointments as remained. She had kept her wits about her in the cellar, taking a wheel of cheese and many other items of food and medicine she thought we could use, filling her pack and mine.

"It was John who knew how to keep the child alive. The infant was able to eat the cheese if we chewed it first, and we dipped a rag in water for him to suck on to keep him quiet, though he seldom cried. Still, he was far too young to be weaned and spent much time sucking his rag. At last, we ran back through the dark, dank caves to safety and then back here to Braden, with the baby wrapped in my spare shirt for warmth and carried inside John's vest.

"Once we arrived, we left the child with a nurse in the care of the Temple. When he was seven, we brought them to the tiny village of Arlen, where the remnant of his father's guard gathered. They took Jaxon, and in secret, they reared him as their king. He will remain, as will his sons and the sons of his sons, until they one day regain the throne of Mal Evol. This has been foretold."

Edwin leaned back, surprised. "He's also my kinsman. I understand why my father never told me of him. He would be in terrible danger if he was known to the enemy." Edwin nodded, his thoughts skittering across many things.

"You're both in danger solely because of who you are and what you each represent. It's more than enough danger for anyone." Garran sighed and continued his story. "We rested in Braden and made plans to reclaim Mal Evol, but nothing came of our efforts. We threw all our resources into the battle, but we were only successful in keeping Stefyn from taking more than he already had.

"We had a special task at a place called Ronan's Vineyard, to distract the enemy's eyes. It sounds simple, but it wasn't." Edwin sensed Garran's anxiety spiking. "I just can't talk about it, except to say we accomplished it, but were overrun. We made our escape, and in the aftermath, John had a true-dream that showed him a way to shield the midlands of Neveyah from the mad priest's mind-magic. This shield combined the elements of fire and earth with water. We did what John's dream told him.

"By virtue of a miracle, which we were never again able to duplicate, John linked us. Halee believes he pulled the chi from the surrounding area through his sword. Whatever he did, it nearly destroyed our ability to sense and use magic. Wynn Farmer made the sword especially for John when he was still a toddler; it's beautiful and is a masterwork. I believe some unique property of the sword enabled that magic."

"Now I know what's in the old trunk by his bed," Edwin said thoughtfully. "I never felt comfortable asking, and he never told me."

"I suspect there's an old set of leathers and the armor of a water-mage in the trunk as well," Garran replied. His pleasant face grew firm. "He'll have to wear them again one day, no matter how much he claims he won't. I've dreamed it."

Edwin shook his head. If his father had turned his back on Neveyah, he would never come back, unless a miracle happened. Garran thought so too, judging from the look on his face.

The abbott continued his story. "The shield is as strong today as it was twenty years ago and runs the length of the Mountains of the Moon, crosses the Braden Gap, and ends to the far south of Neveyah, beyond the Horn of Misery.

"My belief is that if Pauli had still lived, it would have been a type of physical shield too, but without him, the shield is only half what it should have been. It lacks the element of lightning. I firmly believe if the shield encompassed the four elements, it would have prevented the poison, which currently sucks the life out of the borderlands, from encroaching upon the farms and stealing them for Mal Evol."

Edwin nodded, thinking about what Garran had just told him. He had suspected there were more ways to use shields than he'd been taught, and now he knew it was possible. It would simply require a lot of effort and work to discover them. Abruptly, he realized the abbott was still speaking.

"Only the rocky Cascadia escarpment and the Mountains of the Moon are immune, which is why the poison is taking so long to infect the Southlands. Now it's sweeping around the mountains and through the Braden Gap. It's taken twenty years, but now at last, the poison has spread to the southernmost end of the escarpment, the Horn of the Moon. There's nothing to stop it from sweeping though Braden and turning north to take all of Neveyah.

"Some have said the permanent link with the mind of the Bull God snapped Stefyn D'Mal's tenuous connection with sanity. He's like us, a child of Aeos by birth, not a true child of Tauron. Others believe it is similar to an augmentation reaction on an unprecedented scale. I've heard the legions say his insanity only manifests itself when he is in Mal Evol. This tells me it's the buildup of unfocused chi that causes his madness. And I tell you now, the madness he suffers from is most dangerous. It makes him terribly unpredictable."

Edwin was stunned. "I think you may be right, sir. I've experienced it myself." He then frankly explained to Garran the problems that manifested themselves when he and Aeolyn were delayed for so long in getting to Aeoven and the current need for him to get more augmentations quickly. "The rats must think I'm bait or something." Edwin sheepishly looked at his hands.

"The poor creatures seem to want to die at my hands more than anything. I hate it. Kill or be killed—it's no way to live."

"You sound like your father. He said exactly the same thing. And yes, you'll most certainly be seeing the colorist when you leave my study, Edwin. I was worried you were too long arriving here, although I know your training as a healer had to be taken into consideration.

"And now, about your quest." Abbott Garran sat quietly for a moment, tenting his fingers. "I only know the Goddess has made one thing clear through Father Rall's visions and now your dream. The only way to get Marya back is to go in quietly, in such a way you won't be noticed, and take her out the same way.

"If you try to take Baron D'Mal head on, you will die, or worse. And believe me, Edwin. For you, there *is* a fate worse than death. He has the most powerful empathic ability ever known and is most persuasive and completely unscrupulous. Stefyn D'Mal has the power to subvert a mage.

"If he were to control any of you four, let us simply say Marya will no longer be safe, as he will immediately move to consolidate his position with her in the most brutal of ways.

"But even worse, if he was to subvert *you*, he would first break you and then turn you and your abilities against us. Neveyah would be lost at that moment."

"Sir, I'll follow the Goddess's instructions exactly. I'm fully aware I don't have the skills to face him, and I doubt anyone but the Holy Father does, if I understand what you've told me. No one on our team will attempt to do anything other than rescue Marya and get her out safely," Edwin assured him. "You know how responsible Aeolyn is."

Edwin left his interview with Abbott Garran feeling rather disturbed and emotional about what he'd been told, especially as it related to his father and his own part in the wild quest he was embarking on. He understood why his father felt he'd failed, and he reminded himself that he wasn't even going to meet the Baron D'Mal, that his only task was to rescue Marya.

He accepted that if he tried to do more, he would fail and she would suffer the consequences. Yet though he understood this, a burning desire to blast the mad priest into his dark god's arms raged in his heart. Even so, Edwin wouldn't go against his father's wishes on the matter. Now he understood what John meant when he said, "Just do the right thing. You'll know what it is." Now he understood why his father never spoke about the war in Mal Evol, realizing he was broken by the experience. *He never learned how to grieve,* thought Edwin.

He still found it hard to picture his quiet, reserved father as a brawling, wenching daredevil, though everyone told him stories that pointed it out. Try as he might, he simply couldn't feature his father fighting over friendly-girls or leaping into trouble as he'd been assured over and over he did. However, it did explain why he'd had such sage advice to offer Edwin regarding the friendly-girls.

He was still pensive as he knocked on the door to the colorist's workshop. The colorist, Jamson, was an ebullient lightning-mage who obviously enjoyed life and a glass of ale now and then. "You must be Edwin

Farmer—I've been waiting for you," he said as Edwin entered his study. "Janae sent me a letter detailing the work she facilitated for you. It's always a privilege to be allowed to expand on her work. Father Rall has also sent me a letter explaining that the seers insist you must have as much as you can physically bear today, as you will have need of as much stored chi as you can access once you enter Mal Evol. I will be gentle, but this is an area in which we say 'no pain, no gain.'

"I want you to understand you're receiving today what most mages get over the course of several years or more. You will have some difficulties for a day or two, and I can't predict how they'll manifest themselves. Don't worry, I have asked Christoph to help you manage your chi after we're done. Do you understand the extreme sensations you experienced at your first coloring will be magnified exponentially by today's augmentation? You'll have a much more intense experience with this than you did the last time." Privately, Jamson worried it was too much to give in a single day, but the Holy Father's note was adamant Edwin must be completely augmented before he entered Mal Evol, and Rall felt he had the force of character to handle the side effects, with the help of a healer.

"How do you pick the designs?" Edwin asked. "I keep forgetting to ask Janae."

"The magic itself chooses. We colorists simply open ourselves to the Goddess's will, using the sacred magic, and it guides the augmentation. Your unique strengths and needs are addressed through the will of the Goddess and your part in her plan."

"The tattoo will choose you, my dad said,"

ventured Edwin. "He's going to be pretty amazed when he sees what has chosen me. I'm already more colorful than he is, at least around the face." In the dressing room, Edwin stripped off his clothes in preparation for the ritual, feeling somewhat nervous. He'd suffered a bad reaction after his first augmentation and couldn't imagine how it could be worse. Donning his robe, he returned to the study and frankly confessed to Jamson he was feeling a bit anxious this time, but thought he could handle it with Christoph's help.

Jamson laughed in sympathy and then began the preparations. Two journeyman assistants entered the room and prepared the special table for Edwin to recline on. "Edwin, this will be such a large undertaking I'll need the help of two journeymen, Shanda and Lane. We'll be linked, much the way healers are when they must perform large healings. Calm yourself and clear your mind. Open yourself to the will of the Goddess. We will now begin." Shanda placed her hand over Edwin's eyes, and he felt himself relax into a nearly trancelike state.

***

Christoph waited in the specially shielded colorist's garden. He looked up as Edwin entered, his eyes wild. He held his robe clutched closed with his left hand, and the belt dangled unnoticed in his right. He was obviously trying to cope with the massive amounts of chi swirling in his system.

Sensing the surges Edwin was experiencing from across the garden, Christoph automatically soothed him and shunted most of the chi away to bleed off harmlessly. He could feel Edwin struggling to concentrate and use the skills that had gotten him through the first coloring, but they were ineffective.

"I… help me…. Don't let me do it," he begged Christoph. "It wants to break loose. Don't let it." He was shaking and sweating with the effort of controlling the surging waves of sensations and impulses. "I feel too much. Even the breeze in my hair. It's too much. I feel like the magic will escape…what damage it will do I can't imagine…. How do you handle it?"

Christoph quickly layered a dampening field over him and cast soothe again, continuing to bleed off the excess. "It's different for me. I've received my augmentations over the course of many years, a segment at a time, and I still don't bear as many as you. We'll walk in this shielded garden far away from everyone, and we'll practice letting the chi flow naturally instead of surging as it's doing now. You'll get used to it, I promise, but tonight is going to be uncomfortable, even with my help. We'll get through this together. This will help with the pain." Casting the spell for ease, he layered it into the dampening field.

"The pain kept it in check," replied Edwin, with a grimace that turned into a groan as the effort of not letting the magic run wild was nearly more than he could handle. His entire body shook uncontrollably.

Quickly, Christoph bled more off. "I can help with it, don't worry. Concentrate on me as much as you can." He cast healing and soothing spells, and then they walked about the peaceful garden, bleeding the excess chi off and practicing for the rest of the morning the exercises for controlling the flow.

Later, as he napped on the cushioned lounge chair, Edwin dreamed of Marya. She wore an elaborate, full-skirted, brown dress like the women of Arlen wore, with a fine woolen shawl around her shoulders in shades of grey and rose. She walked through a jungle of wildly overgrown rosebushes, followed closely by a looming minotaur guard. The roses snagged and caught on her skirts, but she didn't seem to notice.

Her head barely reached above the guard's waist, and she looked rather like a child who was too thin to be healthy. He carried a beribboned basket, a trowel, a garden-claw, a pair of clippers, and a pair of gloves tucked neatly in it. It looked tiny in his huge hands, and the blue bows contrasted oddly with his coarse armor, making the dour guard look rather like the butt of some sort of joke.

Marya put her gloves on, looking numb and depressed. She knelt and began working where she'd apparently left off the previous day. As she loosened the soil and pulled weeds, the minotaur guard stood stiffly, holding the tiny basket and towering over her. He was obviously completely bored and didn't notice the shadows gathering around her, bending over as if to confide in her. Nodding and talking to the shadows as if she were conversing with her friends, she clipped and pruned the roses, gradually bringing order to one tiny corner of the huge, wild garden. The dream slowly faded, and Edwin drifted into a more natural sleep.

By the afternoon, he was able to manage the flow of his chi, though he still needed help with the pain and healing. They returned to Edwin's room, Christoph offering to stay for the night on a cot the housekeepers brought up for him.

Later when they met Aeolyn and Friedr at dinner, Edwin was calm and able to handle his chi with very few surges, though Christoph still maintained a heavy dampening field on him.

Afterward, they asked to see his new augmentations. When Edwin gingerly removed his loose shirt, even Friedr's eyes, normally impassive, opened wide at his appearance. Edwin pulled his hair back. Christoph had never seen anyone augmented so extensively in one lifetime, much less one session, but didn't say so. *The Goddess has her reasons, but he is new, both to magic and to the whole idea, poor Edwin. It doesn't seem fair.* Chris kept his thoughts closely shielded.

A crescent moon now crossed the palm of Edwin's right hand. The leafy green vine and tiny blue flowers now twined from the web between his thumb and forefinger, across the back of his right hand, all the way to his shoulder. Tiny runes for empathy and compassion were closely woven into it all along its length. At his shoulder, the vines and blue flowers divided to spread down the right side of both his back and chest.

On his left side, the barbed vines now circled his arm from wrist to shoulder, down his back to his waist, with the addition of many tiny runes for both strength and skill woven in, weaving in and out of the barbed vines from his shoulder. A rune for luck adorned his right cheek under the corner of his eye, the long strokes curving around the eye to his brow, and the small rune for true-sight was centered on his brow. Runes for courage and strength were placed across his shoulders. A rune for stealth rode high on his neck, behind each ear lobe. The mark of the assassin. Christoph couldn't believe a healer was marked in such a way.

Shocked by the magnitude of his transformation, Aeolyn's eyes filled with tears. She touched his right cheek in sympathy, but all she said was, "Now you won't lack for chi when we cross into Mal Evol and you're called upon to do what you're meant to do, whatever it may be. I've never seen a mage marked as you are."

Aeolyn explained what his augmentations signified and why they were so surprised he was given so much in such a short span of time, although Edwin understood why from a first-hand perspective.

"Warriors have vines with thorns or perhaps dragons in the elements they are strongest in. If they're to also be weapons masters, runes for strength and skill will be added. You have these now, and you have the thorn vines in great abundance, more even than Friedr.

"Assassins will have runes for stealth, skill, and luck. You now bear the marks of the Temple assassin. Adept healers have stars, crescent moons, and flowering vines, with runes for true-sight, empathy, compassion, and strength. You bear all of these signs, again more even than Christoph or Dane.

"Healers are *never* augmented with runes of stealth, as it is the *assassin's* rune. It allows him or her to go in secret for the sole purpose of *killing* by stealth. The crescent moon on your palm signifies the Goddess considers you a senior adept healer. No journeyman has a crescent on their palm unless they're at the end of their posting and about to become tenured senior clergy.

"The runes for strength, courage, and luck indicate you are a warrior mage-adept. The runes for stealth indicate Aeos has a special task for you, one that you and *only* you will be able to accomplish in secret. The stealth rune is usually given *after* a mage has become a tenured senior adept. I can only think the runes for empathy, wisdom, courage, strength, luck, and stealth must give you great power and the understanding to use it wisely.

"You've been blessed with the marks of the healer adept, the warrior mage, and the mage assassin in full and equal measure. The Goddess has a plan for you, Edwin Farmer. I'm glad I'm not you." Aeolyn finished her explanation with a sad smile for his plight. She wasn't sure what to think of his transformation, or what it could possibly portend.

Friedr said solemnly, "Those for whom the Goddess has a plan lead complicated lives. Things will become interesting, I fear."

They were all silent, wondering what these strange new augmentations signified for Edwin, who more than anything simply wanted to live a quiet life healing the people of Neveyah.

***

Edwin dreamt he stood in the garden at the foot of the dark Tower. "The Tower of Bones," whispered the shadows. "Our bones." He was wearing his midnight-blue Temple armor. Once again, he entered through the unlocked window and crossed to the door that stood ajar. This time he climbed a circular stair to a closed door at the top. He lifted the bar and opened the door. Inside he saw Marya seated before the fire, her augmentations faded to nearly nothing, though she looked somewhat healthier than when he first saw her. She looked up and said, "Who are you? Why do you haunt my dreams? I don't remember you, and I should, if you're truly from the Temple. Why don't I know you?"

Edwin entered more fully into the room, brushing his hair back from his face, and seeing her fear, he held up his right hand, saying "I'm a friend and new to the Temple. Be brave and be ready."

Her eyes widened in shock as she took in his augmentations. She reached toward him, and he abruptly found himself outside the garden in the shadow of the wall. The standing stones marched like jagged teeth in the light of the moon, and he could clearly see the lane that served the kitchen. A huge, ugly dog prowled along it, its hindquarters clearly visible as it passed between the gaps in the stones, its muzzle not really clear to him. The dog stopped, lifting its nose as it scented something, its head turning away from Edwin. He didn't recognize this breed and strained unsuccessfully to see it more clearly before turning to view the keep, seeing it silhouetted against the starry sky. Minotaur guards paced the parapet atop the garden walls.

Abruptly, Edwin woke. Careful not to disturb Christoph, he went to the small sitting room and lit a lamp. Taking a pen and parchment, he wrote down his dream, every detail—drawing the moonlit garden, the window he'd twice entered through, and sketching the room with the door ajar, the circular stair, and the barred door. Then he drew Marya seated before the fire. Last, the standing stones and the hindquarters of the dog, disappearing between them, sketching the hound as well as he could remember it. Once he finished, he returned to bed and fell into a more restful sleep.

Chapter 14

Marya lay with her eyes open, staring at the sliver of the new moon through her window. She had dreamed of the strange, young man again, and this time he spoke to her. "*I am a friend and new to the Temple. Be brave and be ready,*" he had said.

If indeed it was a true-dream, then help was on the way. But what if it was some new torment devised by Stefyn? Why would he send her a dream of a young warrior mage with a healer's stars and a warrior's luck-rune? She'd never heard of a warrior with a healer's crescent moon. It was something she most definitely would have known of.

Under his hair, she glimpsed a lightning bolt next to his ear in both red *and* blue. On his neck, the tendrils of a healer's flowering vines showed over the collar of his armor on the right side, and on the left side, the barbed vines of the warrior showed. Behind his earlobe, high on his neck, was part of a rune she couldn't fully see but that looked like part of a stealth rune. He was a warrior, clearly, but a healer too—and an assassin? Not a minor healer, but an adept who claimed he was new to the Temple.

He was a mystery.

The Bull God didn't use tattoos to augment the storage of chi in his acolytes. Marya had never personally met any other priest of the Bull God, though they often visited Stefyn for his guidance, but she did know he was the only human. The rest were minotaurs who barely concealed their hatred of him. Stefyn instead drank dark potions from an amethyst goblet to replenish his chi. He bore a massive load of unfocused chi stored in his body that he apparently couldn't fully use, as he had no augmentations to contain and focus it. What he was able to use was negative chi and that was something she didn't want to understand.

At last, Marya decided those strangely mixed-up augmentations must have come from Stefyn's mind as a tease, something to give her hope that he could later snatch away and then punish her for daring to believe in. He wouldn't know the augmentations were all wrong and couldn't possibly exist on one person. They were ludicrous, like two mages glued together. They were definitely the product of Stefyn's imagination and were very clumsy. She picked up on them right away, which meant he was playing a deeper game. Stefyn was never so inept in his torments. He must have hidden something in plain sight. What had she not seen? What was the real game now?

She shivered, and not with cold, watching the moon set and the sky lighten with the dawn. Birds called forlornly in the walled garden. A tear rolled down her cheek, and she thought, *If I were a bird, I would fly as far from here as the winds would take me.*

***

The team remained in Braden for two weeks. During this time, Abbott Garran took Edwin's training in hand personally, thoroughly testing him to find out what his abilities really were. Aeolyn and Friedr were handed over to Garran's assistants, Moran and Piers, two older mages with a great deal of experience in Mal Evol. They spent several days traveling with the two, greatly enjoying themselves.

During the hours Edwin trained, Christoph

immersed himself in the infirmary, working with two rather difficult cases.

After much experimentation and practice, Garran discovered exactly what Edwin's augmentations did for his abilities. Edwin was now an accomplished "far-seer." He could send his healer's senses under the earth to detect what might be happening there. Even more easily, he could send his senses out on the wind, seeing everything in the local environment ahead or behind of him.

Although Garran tested Edwin repeatedly, no one, mage or healer, in Braden Temple could sense him as he rode the wind or followed the currents of the earth. He was able to far-see for up to a league around his physical body and would be able to go much farther with practice. What the limit of this skill would be, Garran couldn't yet predict.

Edwin could sense but not yet grasp other skills, and the abbott was curious to discover what came of this never-before-seen talent. "At the rate you're progressing, the next month will be the time when your talents will fully manifest themselves. I'll expect a detailed report from Christoph on everything you say or think on this expedition. Edwin, you must keep a journal of your thoughts and activities regarding your gifts and abilities, starting today.

"Father Rall has decreed all tenured-adept mages must keep a daily journal. It will not be read by anyone but you, while you're alive, but will be placed into the archives of the Holy Seat upon your death. This is critical, as your knowledge must not die with you. Father Rall is right when he says too many mages have taken their knowledge with them to their graves. Will you keep an honest and faithful accounting as I'm asking of you?" Abbott Garran looked at him expectantly.

"Yes, I'll do it, although I'm not sure I want anyone to know my private thoughts and feelings," replied Edwin slowly, feeling somewhat embarrassed. "I'm really rather a private person, Abbott. It's hard for me to share some information about myself."

"Trust me, it will only be read by the abbacy and the Holy Father or Mother occupying the Holy Seat at the time of your death, and most likely, you won't care at that point anyway." Garran smiled wryly, saying "I'm not happy about sharing so much of myself either, so I do understand. Your knowledge and thoughts must be available to future generations if we're to provide them with the skills they'll need to win the war with Tauron." He looked at Edwin, trying to read his expression. "I write every day, even when I'm out in the field. There are things in my journal I really don't want my son to read, but I write them anyway because it's actually a good way for me to organize my thoughts."

After a moment of thought, Edwin said, "I can see why Father Rall wants us to do this. Everyone has theories and ideas that may be of value to the Temple, but like me, they may be unsure, and so they won't volunteer them unless there's a good reason to. I'm confused about so many things, Abbott. I'd like to think I don't appear as insecure and inept as I feel at times. I will do it, I swear."

"You're not an inept person by any means. Quite the contrary. I wish I could go with you to monitor the rest of your training myself, but the omens are clear on this, and I'll never go against them again." Abbott Garran was firm in saying so, his serious tone belying his wry smile. "Writing down your thoughts and ideas will help you develop your theories into workable practices. You're the first air-mage ever in the Temple, but I feel sure you won't be the last. You must develop every aspect of your gift to the fullest because you'll be teaching those who follow. Aeos is changing the rules of magic, and she has begun with you."

"The last thing my father said to me was that I should do the right thing," Edwin replied. "I will sneak in and try to get Marya out without drawing attention to us, I promise, and I'll keep a diary. I know Aeos is counting on me, and I won't let her down. Why else would she have given me these strange augmentations?"

"It's when you get there the 'right thing' becomes cloudy, Edwin. It's often hard to tell it apart from your deepest desire. I pray you'll have better clarity than we did." Garran's expression was neutral, hiding his turbulent emotions. "John took the responsibility for the failure upon himself, but we were all convinced we were doing the right thing. Remember—there are four of you on the quest, and all bear the responsibility of success or failure, not only one person."

Later when Edwin began writing his journal, there was a lot to try to document, and though it didn't read well to him, he did his best to be honest about his difficulties using his magic as well as his successes. He decided it was better simply to pretend it was his private journal because he couldn't be completely honest if he thought someone would read it.

He did have a problem he thought was rather

unusual. Edwin found when he sailed under the earth, he *felt* the coolness of the water and the fire of the deep. He didn't feel it as pain, but as something nearly sexual. There was an intimacy, frightening in its intensity.

The sensation of riding the wind was something else entirely. He discovered how easy it was to lose his sense of self when he was far-seeing. After an incident when Christoph found him seated, unconscious to the world, he decided to only range out of his body if someone was there to bring him back. The episode scared him, but he tried not to allow it to inhibit him, thinking, *These skills are given to me by the Goddess so we can accomplish this quest and bring Marya out of Mal Evol. I have to learn how to use them safely.* He was unable to talk about it, as he could find no words to express the problem and found it difficult to write about it, but he did try to do so. It was too personal, almost sexual, and though he noted it in his journal, Edwin couldn't bring himself to speak of it to anyone.

In a task that was far more relaxing, he, Friedr, and Aeolyn sparred for two hours daily. They worked out under Garran's keen eye, with him trading off against each of them and stopping and correcting them at various points throughout the workout. He was a demanding weapons-master, pushing them to their limits, except for Friedr, who pushed him. Friedr enjoyed the workouts keenly as there was no one else who made him work to succeed as Garran did.

The abbott was pleased with Edwin's progress toward mastering the sword, telling Friedr privately he might find himself outmatched one day soon. "Before you're done with this quest, he'll be your equal, Friedr. You'll have yourself a regular sparring partner who'll push you. I promise he'll soon be your better."

"I've begun to worry about that myself," Friedr replied, a rueful expression crossing his face. "He learns quickly and rarely repeats his mistakes. He's completely focused when he has his sword in his hand. That sort of intensity is scary, between you and me. Most of my students are lazy. But even though Edwin *loves* training, he hates fighting. He's a terrible foe, quick and decisive, dispatching his enemies with no playing around."

"In this regard, he's like his father, though his style is different. John is a master of finesse and a thing of beauty to watch in a mage-duel. Edwin is much more aggressive and bold. I must say the smile he always seems to wear when fighting is a little unnerving, as are his unusually random moves. You can't gauge what he's going to do next by his last move, so the element of surprise is always on his side. It will make him formidable in a mage-duel. Try to stay one step ahead of him and you'll be fine," Garran advised Friedr. "Intensify the training by adding combos and salvos— bombard him with more than he's comfortable shielding against. He'll struggle at first, but he must learn as much as he can before you enter the soil of Mal Evol, because you will be limited to swords-only there. And Friedr, once you're there, you must not use offensive magic at all, even the most minor, or you'll draw unpleasant attention."

Friedr nodded his head in acknowledgement. "Piers has impressed this upon us. I know we're no match for the mad priest. I'll heed your wisdom in this most strictly."

***

In the evenings they all went to the common room of the local tavern along with several others from the Temple. Garran wasn't surprised to see the effect Edwin had on the women, but he was startled at the restraint he showed. "Your father only showed such moderation after he met Andia. For the first few years I knew him he cut a swath through the friendly-girls. They couldn't get enough of him. You may look like him, but you're completely different. In many ways, you're more like your mother."

"I still can't feature my father acting like a pleasure-boy," Edwin replied. Garran started laughing, as did everyone else. "Well, I can't. He avoids taking up with the friendly-girls as much as I do at the Boar's Head in Markett. But at least now I know why he offered such good advice about them."

Early each morning, Edwin assisted Christoph in the infirmary, healing many injuries and illnesses. Chris had been uncharacteristically quiet since the day they reached Braden, and Edwin was somewhat worried. When they first arrived, Edwin asked if he was going to visit his family.

Startled, Chris rather abruptly said, "No." and then blushing and feeling embarrassed, he said, "I'm not ready to face this town or my family. I may never be able to do so. But I do write to Mum, and I always send her money. It'll have to do until I can get past some of the things that lie between us."

Edwin didn't press him any further, understanding the scars Christoph bore were still raw in some ways.

***

On their last day in Braden, the abbott met with Edwin in Jamson's study to check the augmentations one last time before the companions continued on their quest. Garran was sure the Goddess saw a need for him at this time, or his particular talents wouldn't have emerged. "What that need will be, I can't imagine," he said, shaking his head. Jamson fully agreed with him.

Garran looked forward to visiting John and letting him know his son was well and happy, taking another gift Edwin had found for his father. *Though how anyone who is as heavily augmented as that boy is can be well is beyond me.* Garran's thoughts were mixed as he walked back to his study. John disturbed him, and their friendship had grown strained over the years, but he still cared about him. *John won't be happy about all of this, but oh, well. Maybe this will bring him home at last. He can't sulk forever. He has got to get over whatever it is and just move on. I'll force him, if I have to.*

Their last evening in Braden, they dined with Garran and his plump, cheerful wife, Salya, along with Garran's quiet assistant, Moran, and his bond-mate, Piers. Piers was a lightning-mage of about thirty, and Moran, who was around the same age, had his strength in fire. They had worked extensively with Friedr and Aeolyn, giving the two in-depth training on how to proceed once they entered Mal Evol. The evening passed congenially with good food and excellent company, and they retired early in preparation for their departure the next morning.

***

The group was subdued as they left the city of Braden in the dark hours before dawn, through the long-unused north gate. Though it was seldom opened, the gate was kept oiled, and swung on silent hinges.

The older, somewhat grizzled lightning-mage on duty bid them farewell, her eyes betraying her worry for their safety on their quest. *This is the only town we have passed through with a mage on guard duty at every gate,* Edwin thought as it closed behind them and they started down the rugged road. *This is the only gate they keep closed at all times.*

With a mixture of anticipation and fear for what the future might hold, Edwin began walking the rutted, abandoned road to Mal Evol. The difference in their surroundings was both immediate and surprising. *This road hasn't been used for many years,* he thought. *It feels like we've walked out of civilization and into the wilderness.*

Chapter 15

The companions each carried a heavy kit with enough ration bars to live on for three months if necessary, though Friedr was vocal in his hopes it wouldn't be required. "They're quite nutritious, but it's all that can be said for them. They're like eating bricks. The little soup packets are much better if you can have a fire."

They left behind their regular armor and wore a new set, specially crafted for their quest and sent to Braden to await their arrival, this time black and lacquered in such a way it didn't gleam or shine. It was the armor of the Temple Assassins Guild and absorbed the light. Specially tailored for each, it was also bespelled to both allow the wearer to go in secret and to make the wearer appear uninteresting to casual observers, as well as protecting them in their own areas of elemental weakness.

"Moran and Piers were dressed in black," Edwin remarked to Friedr as they trudged along the rough, rutted road. "But I couldn't see their augmentations. Their hair covered them."

"Moran and Piers are members of a select group of mages who share one particular augmentation with you, the stealth rune. It's not generally known," Friedr replied. "They were surprised to hear a healer is augmented as a warrior, bears a stealth rune, and carries a sword. If we had been there longer, you would have worked with them too. They were thorough in teaching Aeolyn and me many of the skills we must have to do this task and come back alive, while the good Abbott was schooling you in your magic. We've all learned a great deal in the last two weeks."

"I'd prefer to wear my hair down as they do, but I have to tie it back when we're dressed for battle," Edwin commented. "It's like the stealth runes want to hide or something."

"You look like a friendly-girl with it down, farm-boy. You're too pretty for your own good. The augmentations at least make you look a bit manlier," Friedr said slyly, hoping to needle him.

"Why, I never knew you thought so about me, you big, handsome barbarian." Edwin smiled wickedly and batted his eyes. Friedr's face turned red, as he vainly tried to find a witty retort. Edwin then leered lustfully, causing him to retreat in confusion, while Christoph laughed uproariously.

"You did tell him he was pretty," Aeolyn reminded Friedr, enjoying his discomfort immensely. "You asked for it."

"Well, he should grow a beard or something to make himself look a little manlier," he sulked. "I'm only saying the truth! He looks like a flaxen maid." His companions just laughed.

"Well, at least we know what those assassin's runes mean for you now," Aeolyn ventured, once they stopped laughing at Friedr's discomfort. "Nothing is stealthier than this far-seeing trick of yours. I sure can't feel when you're using it. Can you, Christoph?"

"No, I don't feel it, not at all," he replied. "It's amazing and will be extremely useful all too soon, I think." He felt happier with each step they took away from Braden. He began watching the ground as they walked, and soon he was picking up small, round stones as he came across them. After finding three good ones, he began juggling them.

"I have to learn how to do this." Entranced, Edwin's eyes followed the rocks as they made circles in the air. As they walked along, Christoph taught him how to juggle, and soon Edwin decided to find his own round stones, completely enamored with the newfound game.

The others watched with amazement, but didn't want to learn the skill for themselves. Friedr explained, saying "I'll enjoy watching the street jugglers so much more for knowing they can do it far better than I can. Besides, I'm not as in love with self-inflicted pain as Edwin is. Look, he hit himself in the head again." His muffled grunt of pain made Friedr laugh. "This is a fun game after all!"

"It's why stones make such good teaching tools," Christoph replied with a sly smile. "The student must improve or suffer the consequences."

"He's going to knock himself senseless trying to learn this useless skill," Aeolyn ventured, with a sidelong look at Friedr. Christoph recognized her look. She was setting them all up for a "discussion," a conversation that would be an argument to anyone else. She would debate either side until she was blue in the face, her favorite form of entertainment. He pretended not to hear her, as did Edwin. Edwin never rose to her bait.

"Aeolyn, no skill that teaches dexterity is useless," Friedr disagreed, immediately walking into her trap. She smiled happily, and they debated the point off and on for the rest of the day. Edwin improved at his new game, developing enough that he and Christoph began tossing the stones to each other as they walked. Edwin's occasional yelp of pain usually elicited a laugh from Friedr. "Christoph, you needn't beat him senseless. That's my job."

As they crossed a shallow creek carving a path across the old road, Edwin accidentally disturbed a nest of water-sprites. The look on his face when the little queen doused him with icy water was hilarious. He then walked wide of the nest, apologizing to her profusely as she stood chittering at him angrily. "Water-sprites aren't dangerous unless they're with a water-wraith," Christoph told him as they all laughed. "Those are quite rare nowadays, though. I don't know of anyone who's seen a water-wraith in years."

"If they still exist, it'll be in Mal Evol," said Aeolyn, gazing seriously at the eastern horizon as if seeking an answer of some sort. "All sorts of elementals are known to make the valley their home now, fire-sprites and thunder-lizards being among the more difficult to deal with."

"At least water-sprites don't bother you unless you step on them," Friedr said, glancing sardonically at Edwin. "Fire-sprites on the other hand—we kill them when we come across them. They're not native to Neveyah, and you can really be injured by them. They came here from the other worlds of the eleven Gods. Their ancestors couldn't return home when the borders were closed to Tauron, and so we've dealt with them ever since. We also kill water-wraiths and waterdrakes because they prey upon people and livestock."

"What's a thunder-lizard?" Edwin asked curiously. "I've heard about fire-sprites before, and they seem nasty enough to deal with. These thunder-lizards don't sound fun at all."

"They range in size from three feet to twelve feet long and have a tendency to zap you with a powerful lightning spell when they're disturbed or hungry. Once they do so, you can't sense your magic, so you're totally at their mercy. They too will prey upon people and livestock when they're big," replied Friedr. "They can be deadly, so we must kill them."

As the days passed, they put away the stones, having no time for juggling. The rat-people and other beasts made their presence known, and the group was once more skirmishing far too often for comfort. By the evening of the sixth day, the stones were only brought out in camp.

"I thought the creatures would stop stalking us once Edwin received his new augmentations, but he's still attracting them as if he were a fountain of unfocused chi," Aeolyn commented. "For some reason, the beasts like him as much as the women do." She laughed wickedly at Edwin's wince.

"It must be the combination of the two magics," suggested Christoph. "Maybe they can sense it."

"I'll try to work on my shields. Maybe I can find a way to use them so they don't notice my magic," Edwin replied.

"Shields are shields," retorted Aeolyn, in the tone of one who has said it all before and too often. "They only do certain things, and it's all you can do with them. But you should keep your basic shield up at all times, or you'll be in trouble, like with the water-sprite."

"I will, believe me," he assured her with a wry smile. "That was more surprise than I usually like to receive."

Over the next few days, the companions struggled to maintain cheerful attitudes in the face of the ever more sparsely growing landscape they walked through. Each day, the trees grew further apart. One afternoon, Edwin saw a small clump of thorny bushes he'd never come across before.

"You'll see all too many of these soon enough," Christoph told him as he cut them down and poisoned the roots. "That'll stop this one, but the rest are poised to invade us, like an unstoppable army." His usually cheerful face was bleak as he destroyed the plant.

The beasts they came across were different on this side of the Braden Gap, though the rat-people were even more active in the area. In the distance, Edwin spotted some unusually large razor-horned creatures the size of bears. "Thunder-cows," said Friedr. "Whatever you do, don't cast lightning at them. They cast it right back at you, only magnified a hundredfold."

Apparently, thunder-cows didn't really bother anyone. They grazed on the parched, nutrient-poor grass that now spread over the southern end of the Valley of Mal Evol. "They aren't good to eat," Aeolyn added, "but if you see a calf that appears to be alone, you must leave the area immediately or the mother will attack you."

"And sometimes the bulls attack for no reason when the cows are in season," Friedr said. "They can gore you terribly, besides packing their powerful lightning charge."

"These are strange animals. I'd never have thought 'cow' when I saw them," Edwin said, wonderingly. "We don't have any animals with magic in Ariend."

"The elementals are from some of the other worlds and were brought here by a rogue-mage in the old days, in the same way waterdrakes were," Friedr told him. "I hope to see a waterdrake someday, though they may be extinct in Neveyah now. It's sad, but people weren't safe, as they were known to eat our sort in rather large quantities."

Daily, Edwin worked on learning and using his skills, developing rapidly in his abilities against the magic creatures, with his shields up and his sword flashing while he countered any element they might throw at him. The demented rat-mages nearly always threw fire, which was easily countered with earth or water. Water was the weapon of choice against the lightning-enhanced creatures, while lightning worked against the annoying water-sprites that infested the creeks and low-lying areas. A tiny little zap would usually drive them off. Edwin didn't like to hurt them if he didn't have to as they were interesting to watch and didn't go out of their way to bother anyone.

"Well, at least he's willing to kill the beasts he attracts," Friedr remarked as Edwin efficiently dispatched a lone rat-person who leapt out of a bush at him, shrieking madly and slashing with his vicious claws as he went for Edwin's throat. "What I find interesting is he doesn't play with them. He eradicates them as quickly as he can with no fuss and no mess." He turned to Edwin. "Where's the fun in that, farm-boy?"

"I don't like to slay things, barbarian," he replied as he cleaned his blade. "Kill or be killed is no way to live. I do what I have to so they don't kill me, but I don't have to like it."

With each league they traveled, the land became more barren and more desperate. The trees grew more sparsely and were twisted and gnarled. The brush soon became nothing but straggly scrub and thorn as high as, and sometimes higher than, Friedr's head. Strange birds uttered calls like taunts and were answered by even stranger cries. Snakes lurked in shrubbery, but their armor and leg-guards protected them from the bites of the startled reptiles.

The worst problem was the scorpions, as they seemed to have no fear of humans. Every boot, glove, and bedroll needed to be thoroughly checked before they could be used. The stings were painful, but with prompt application of antivenom and healing spells, they managed to keep each other healthy enough to fight the packs of feral rats that wandered about looking for easy prey.

Over their armor, they wore hooded cloaks that covered them from head to foot, made of coarse grey-brown wool, hiding their armor and shadowing their faces. At first glance, they looked like the shabby cloaks most of the poor people in the southern lands wore, and the questors blended into the drab colors of the beaten land they were crossing. When they sat quietly with their hoods up the four mages disappeared into the scenery.

In Aeolyn's pack, a cloak for Marya lay folded as small as she could make it. Each companion carried a part of her personal kit and bedroll. They couldn't bring any spare clothes, and Aeolyn hoped she would still have her armor and boots. They couldn't manage those and their rations too.

Whenever they stopped, Edwin sent his new senses

out, searching for traps and other unnatural dangers. Many wild beasts moved too quickly to be avoided, so despite his scouting ability, the four still skirmished with those who would make a meal of them.

They made plans for what might lie ahead, though no one was sure how they would proceed when they arrived at their destination. "We must find the hidden gate without alerting the guards." Aeolyn tried to make plans as they sat around the small campfire, one of the last they would have on their journey. "If we can do that, the rest will fall into place."

"What we need to do is draw the guards off so Edwin can go in and bring her out," said Christoph.

They looked at him. "No, we all need to go in for her. That's why we're here," replied Friedr. "She doesn't know him."

"No, he's right," asserted Aeolyn. "She'll recognize he's from the Temple. He has the armor and the augmentations to prove who he is. We need to distract the guards while he goes in to get her. Edwin was sent the dreams, so he's been shown the way. It must be him."

"He has the special augmentations for stealth and luck," Christoph added. "Aeos has given him this burden for a reason. He's a healer and thus is not of the right temperament to be an assassin. This must be why."

After a moment, Friedr agreed, adding, "We're going to have to hide ourselves from D'Mal somehow. Once he realizes she's gone, we won't be safe, at least not while we're on the soil of Mal Evol. Somehow, we must delay his discovery for as long as we can."

"Garran told me of a way, an underground

waterway my father and his companions used to save Jaxon as a baby," ventured Edwin. "Halee smoothed it into a passable road with her earth-magic and made it safe to travel on, according to Garran. If we can find where it begins and ends, maybe we could use it."

"Have you tried?" asked Christoph. "Do you also have an affinity for finding water like your father did?"

"I'll try," replied Edwin. "From what I've heard, I'm not as strong in water, but I'll make the effort." He closed his eyes and sent out his senses, searching for what he knew must be there.

"He has more strength than many water-mages," murmured Aeolyn to Christoph as Edwin entered his trance. "He just doesn't realize it."

Sailing under the earth, Edwin felt the very soil telling him of the poison that came from the east, an amethyst poison, suffocating the life out of the vineyards, forests, and farms that once lived in harmony with the earth. After a long search, he found water far to the west, along the base of the Mountains of the Moon.

The others talked quietly so they wouldn't disturb him. "He's much stronger in water than I am," agreed Friedr. "Edwin may find the underground river John Farmer used, but who's to say it's a road we *should* use? I think when he discovers Marya gone, Stefyn D'Mal will sit on the Throne of Stone and Bone. He will know every person, every animal, and every insect that walks and breathes in Mal Evol and turn them against us. All he would have to do is post guards at the place where the road exits, and he'll have us all." Friedr sat back and waited for his companions' response.

"Are you saying he'll be able to know our minds?"

Fear chilled Aeolyn for the first time on this quest. "What's to stop him from knowing this now?"

"He hasn't looked?" Friedr shrugged. "If he were to look, he would see, of that I feel sure."

"You're right, *and* you are wrong," said Christoph slowly. "He can't see us here. But when we enter his land tomorrow or the next day, I think there is a way to hide our minds. We must drink no water and eat no food that is of his part of the valley. It is after we have Marya back we will be in the most danger. She's had no choice but to eat and drink of D'Mal's land and he will see her clearly."

"How can we carry enough water? We have more than enough rations, dry though they are, but we always rely on being able to call water from the local area." Aeolyn looked to Friedr and Christoph for answers. They looked at Edwin, who sat tranced as he searched the earth.

"Perhaps there is a way. But it will be challenging for him." Christoph's face was thoughtful. "He must try to call it from the air. If he can call it before it touches the soil of Mal Evol, it won't betray us to the Throne of Stone and Bone." He looked at Aeolyn's skeptical face. "It's worth a try, anyway. If he doesn't have the ability, we'll have lost nothing. We can't travel for days with no water, not and survive. He must begin trying to develop this ability tomorrow."

Standing, Christoph touched Edwin on the shoulder, bringing him back.

Once again, he had lost himself in the glorious sensations. He forced himself to speak normally, though he felt something akin to anger at being called back to his body. "We've come too far. We missed the entrance by perhaps fifty leagues. We're due east of it," Edwin told them, stretching and yawning, wondering what to do about his secret problem. "The underground river seems to angle from the northeast, where I'm assuming the keep is, to the southwest of the valley, emerging close upon the base of the escarpment, but I couldn't follow it all the way north. My range is still not good enough."

The others looked at him, shock and surprise mirrored on their faces. "Um, tell me again how far to the west you found the entrance?" asked Friedr, his voice sounding odd even to himself. "I should probably make a note of it. Your range is increasing daily." Aeolyn and Chris exchanged meaningful glances, but said nothing.

Edwin complied and then yawned again, saying, "I'm fairly tired, and if I'm going to be alert for my watch, I'd better try to get some sleep." He couldn't look at his friends for fear they would see how disturbed he was, and for some reason it embarrassed him.

"You should get some rest, all of you," said Christoph firmly, and then he took the first watch, while the others slept.

***

Each day, the grimness of the land around them seeped into their spirits a little more, and even Friedr struggled to stay optimistic in the face of the desolation around them. "It's the spell that D'Mal has set on Mal Evol. It's spreading inch by inch into Neveyah. We should carry an earth shield under us now. Dane told me this would happen." Edwin's comment surprised them, but they could all see the sense of it. "I'll shield

Christoph." They immediately felt better once they set them, and Aeolyn was impressed Edwin could carry one that covered someone else too.

"It must be one of your new abilities, to stretch your shield over a group. I've never tried to do this. It could be useful." She always looked for an advantage in any skill.

On the evening of the eighth day out of Braden, they crossed into Tauron's Mal Evol. The change was felt most strongly by Christoph and Edwin, but even Friedr and Aeolyn could feel the ominous silence of the land.

"This is the place where John Farmer set the shield after the Battle of Ronan's Vineyard, with the help of Garran Andreson and Halee Randsdottir. It holds, but is being pushed back daily. One day, it will be anchored on the walls of Braden." Christoph's matter-of-fact statement belied his unease. *Will it stop at Braden, or will it continue to retreat until it is nothing more than a ring around Aeoven?* His thought was reflected in his eyes, but went unvoiced.

Christoph was terribly affected by the sorry state of the land he grew up in. His parents' farm was long abandoned, but his heart ached for the place he once knew and loved.

Edwin sent his spirit out, examining the shield set so long ago on a desperate day, hoping to find some sense of his father in it. Perhaps it was his imagination, but he sensed a familiar vibration. It was a water shield and ran hundreds of leagues along the entire border, with no gaps. *It works because it's flexible and doesn't break. Instead, it simply adjusts to a new position. Abbott Garran told me it's tied to and powered by the natural chi of the water under the land. But I can sense it's also somehow tied to the earth.* Once again, his father amazed him, and his respect for Abbess Halee and Abbott Garran increased. *Three vibrations. It took them all to set it. I can see why they had nothing left afterward.* The way his father set the shield gave Edwin some ideas, but he was too tired to think about them right then. He wondered how it was tied off so well, but he couldn't see. *The ties on a personal shield never hold. They always fade, and then the shield disappears unless you maintain it at all times. If I could figure out how to do this....*

Coming back to his body, he told the others what he saw. "There were only three of them when they set the shield. They'd lost Pauli on the first quest and couldn't find another to take his place because Mal Evol City was massacred. Fully half of the clergy of Aeos was killed or taken to the altars. I suppose that by the time they came to this place, no lightning-mages were available to round out their team." He looked at his friends, suddenly realizing he could lose one of them. "It must have been hell. I can't imagine what it took for them to keep going after losing him. And to add even more gloom to their quest, I think this is where they lost an entire squad of Temple soldiers who gave their lives protecting them."

"Your father never got over it. He carries remorse and grief in his soul. That's why he took you away from Neveyah. He wanted you to have peace," Christoph's voice was full of compassion for both Edwin, as he struggled to know his father, and for John Farmer, who wished for his failings to remain unknown by his son.

"At least now I understand why he fought so

desperately to save Neveyah." Edwin's voice was full of grim certainty. "If it falls, Markett will be next. We have no magic there, and the king's army isn't made up of the sort of men who can deal with this nasty, tragic way of life. It's comprised completely of the pampered sons of the rich who could afford to buy their way in. The Bull God would simply roll right over them with no effort whatsoever." In the back of his mind was the question, *Is this the reason for the bargain the Almighty Father has made with his daughter Aeos? Is this why I was born? To protect the world of Ariend?*

The realization the fates of two worlds could be so intertwined, with the survival of both hanging on his family's dual heritage, was staggering. Edwin was quiet and introspective for the rest of the evening, quietly doing all his tasks but volunteering little conversation.

***

The next day was like every other. The cold dry air was clear, and the sky was blue with the morning mists hovering over the land. At times, high clouds appeared, but they never brought rain. The land itself was bleak; life here was hard and grim. After some experimentation, Edwin found a way to call water from the mist and to shape it with his newfound air-magic, but it was time-consuming and difficult, requiring intense concentration

"The land itself is suffering," Christoph told Edwin in a low voice as they moved from cover to cover. "It cries out, but no one hears it." His sorrow and pain were intense as they traveled through the desecrated place he once called home. Edwin cast soothe on him, which brought a small smile from his friend. "Healing the healer?" The sardonic smile looked out of place on his elfin face, underscoring Christoph's grim state of mind.

Edwin smiled and clasped his shoulder. "I will as often as is needed, my brother."

They camped, silent and subdued, in a hollow, protected by thorn bushes, without even a low fire for the first time since setting out on their quest, and they talked quietly as they prepared for the night. Christoph solemnly spoke to Edwin. "It's heartbreaking to see the fertile vineyards and vast woodlands that once covered Mal Evol reduced to this."

Edwin listened as Christoph told of how the land was once covered with the most verdant forests in Neveyah. "My grandfather's farm was a beautiful, green place, with rich soil that would grow and nourish the most delicate and rare fruits." Christoph's eyes shone as he remembered his early childhood. "My granddad always told me how our strawberries were so big, so juicy and sweet that for generations, the lords of Mal Evol would have only ours for their table. Someday I'll return and bring back the beauty and grace that was Mal Evol before the Bull God came to destroy my family."

"I pray you have the opportunity," replied Edwin, looking though the dark, thorny branches to the sky and the stars shining forlornly. "This is sad beyond belief. My mother's family lived in Mal Evol City. They died when it fell to Stefyn D'Mal, so I have no family but my father and Jaxon."

Christoph fell silent, lost in his hopes and dreams for the future. Edwin opened his sight, and as he did so his senses expanded to take in all the land beneath him, reaching even to the hidden corners, tasting the soil and breathing in the possibilities. He felt the earth yearning to burst free. Springtime lay waiting to be called forth by the one who was yet to come.

A bell rang, echoing though Edwin, ringing sweet and pure. The tolling vibrated in his every fiber, sweet almost to the point of pain. He *knew* the bell and it knew him. A voice, as if from a great distance, spoke of what he saw. "The verdant springtime lies coiled beneath the surface of the shattered lands, waiting for the call of the Beloved to set it free. The Beloved Hero falls to darkness; he sows the poisoned seed across the shadowed land, yet will he rise up to set free the land of Mal Evol on the day the land takes him home. All will see the fruiting of the land of the Living Shades. This will be the sign; the day of redemption is at hand."

Abruptly he returned to the present and saw his friends staring at him. "Edwin, do you know what just happened? You were sent a vision, a message from the Goddess." Aeolyn looked at him with awe, as did the others. "I must write it down, word for word. Friedr, help me find my pen and ink. Quickly, find a parchment!" They scrambled to get the words down while they were fresh in their memories.

Edwin sat looking at Christoph. Surely his prodigious healing magic would benefit this poor land if the poison spell set by the Baron Stefyn D'Mal could be removed. His compassion for the land and the hidden people was growing with each day that passed, as was Edwin's. *If anyone could heal this land, it would be Christoph,* thought Edwin loyally. *But it's a grim prophecy, what with the falling into darkness and all. It didn't say how long before it would come to pass.*

Suddenly, an unreasonable fear took hold of him as

he looked at Christoph, fear for his friend's safety. *I must somehow save him, but from what?* Edwin slowly shook his head. *I must tell Aeolyn, but how do I tell her without alerting the others?* He saw Aeolyn and Friedr struggling to write down the prophecy word for word by the light of the waning moon. It would have to wait until an opportune moment.

Christoph, however, was silent, staring into the darkness. When Edwin asked if he was feeling well, he simply said he was tired. At last, they bedded down for the night, and Chris took the first watch. When the morning came, he was his normal cheerful self, buoying up the flagging spirits of his companions.

Chapter 16

The four mages would have no fires while they were in Mal Evol, in some part because of the danger of wildfire in the thorn brush, but also to avoid being noticed. Their meals would be cold rations, and they would have no light at night. Still, they sat in a ring facing each other, quietly talking in low whispers and sharing the comfort of friendship. When the first birds were calling raucously in the grey hour before dawn, the companions were already moving silently toward Marya and the Shadow Castle, careful to leave no trail for anything, beast or soldier, to follow.

The morning mists held water in a form Edwin could use to fill their jugs and though he worked hard to concentrate and form it, it was a slow process. Each day his ability improved, and he used slightly less chi.

As they traveled, they developed a feel for the land and the creatures that made their homes there. They came to recognize the strange and amazing varieties of birds, some that blended into and hid in the thorn bushes, scorpions, snakes, and, of course, the feral rats who mindlessly stalked prey. "Where do these rat-people come from anyway?" asked Edwin as he cleaned his sword after having killed another one. "Why do they keep attacking us when we don't seek them out?"

"They're not native to Neveyah," Aeolyn told him. "They started appearing in Mal Evol about twenty years before the fall." The sound of her stone on her blade punctuated the silence of the morning. "Some have said the rats are the lost children of the god Ariend, whom Tauron murdered. I don't know what they are myself, other than a plague. But I've never seen a female of their species, and the males I've seen are all completely mad."

"Stefyn D'Mal created them, I've heard folks say. I don't know if he's of such an inclination or ability, but either he or his god is certainly responsible for them overrunning Neveyah." Friedr paused in cleaning his sword and wiped his brow with a sleeve. "He can't break through the barrier with his mental magic, and so he sends them to soften us up, to harry the countryside, and to make it harder for the rural people to live. They're attracted to high concentrations of chi, but they're vicious and consumed with hunger. They'll eat anything."

"Well, his plan is working," Aeolyn said. "There are farmers in the outlying villages who've been overrun and have resorted to setting bounties on them. The Temple armsmen stay busy with the hunt, and yet they don't seem diminished in any way."

"The feral rats were only the first wave of his war on Mal Evol," Christoph replied quietly as he mended Friedr's vest sleeve. "I read somewhere that Tauron set a curse on them, sending the males mad before they ever see their children. The women must drive them out for everyone's safety. Their villages are in the highest mountains, where we can't breathe well. For them to be down here is part of the curse. The air is too thick here for them, and they're drowning. It's why they're so bluish." Christoph shrugged. "Tauron tried to destroy them in his hatred of Ariend, but Aeos and the Almighty Father did what they could to prevent such a terrible thing, though they couldn't completely undo his handiwork. The rats began appearing here in the lowlands when Father Rall was a young man on his first quest, and the thorn bushes, scorpions, and snakes followed. D'Mal has turned Mal Evol into a replica of Serende. It's the most beautiful landscape he can imagine. The mad priest believes he has done the land a favor."

"And these weapons are taking Neveyah for him, one thorn bush and one innocent traveler at a time," mused Edwin. "It's a good plan and takes no effort on his part. All he needs to do is to introduce these things and then sit back and watch them do their work. He apparently has all the time in the world, so it doesn't matter how long it takes. He'll still be there, a winner at the end." The realization made him want to scream, but he restrained himself. "Everything we do is a futile effort to hold him back." Edwin's frustration came across in his tone of voice, startling his companions. They were unused to him voicing any thought or feeling in less than a calm, dispassionate manner. "There must be a weakness here, something we can exploit!"

Later the same night, Friedr stood the first watch. The waning moon lit the landscape, emphasizing the stark shadows. The hours passed, and he thought about Edwin's comments and the girl who waited for them to rescue her, wondering if she were holding up well. *Aeolyn frets about how slowly we travel, but we can't go faster. We don't even have a plan to get Marya out of there yet. I have no idea how we can accomplish such a thing without drawing attention.* Though he considered the problem through his watch, he came to no good conclusion. At last, Friedr roused Christoph, burying his turmoil under the stoic exterior he usually portrayed.

Christoph, too, was unable to sleep because his thoughts kept him awake. "Much lies below the surface of Edwin Farmer," he spoke in low whispers as he took his place. "I've been thinking about what he said this evening. He usually never allows his zeal for anything to show on his face, but it's there, lurking below the surface. He's passionate, perhaps more so than most. He simply keeps a tight rein on his emotions."

Friedr looked sharply at him, eyes narrowing but he said nothing, simply nodding his head and going off to his blankets, leaving Christoph to stand the second watch.

***

On the third day in Mal Evol, they passed a village, once the main stop on the trade road, now completely empty and long abandoned. "Was this your village?" Edwin wondered aloud to Christoph. Most of the buildings had no windows, and dust and sand filled them to varying degrees.

Chris replied, "It could be the ruins of Bryton. I don't know for sure, but yes, it could be." He looked around, clearly wondering if he would find any part of his early life in the wreckage of the town. "Yes, this was it. There's the sign. You can still read it, almost."

Edwin spoke softly as he looked around. "My mother's family lived in Mal Evol City, but they were all killed when the legions first ravaged the country. Father Rall and Abbott Garran told me some of it, but I know little about her or her family, although I now know I at least have one living relative. We're all we have left of Mal Evol, and neither of us ever lived there." Christoph sensed his sadness and cast soothe, eliciting a wry smile from him. "Don't waste your chi on me, my brother. Friedr is going to need it soon enough. He's bleeding again and so is Aeolyn."

Christoph was now assuming most healing duties since Edwin was searching on the wind to scout for them and calling water from the mist. Those tasks required equal amounts of both healing and battle chi, and though he possessed huge reserves to draw upon, Christoph knew it took a lot to perform those tasks. Still, he was fortunate his chi reserves rapidly replenished themselves, far faster than the others did.

Friedr and Aeolyn had been scouting ahead and skirmished with one of the stranger beasts, one they hadn't seen before. Both sported gashes requiring healing, and both were tired. They weren't using magic if they could avoid it, so as to not draw the unwelcome attention of anyone, creature or mage who could sense the use of it.

They stayed the night in one of the three deserted houses whose windows were still intact and that were relatively sand-free inside, having a meal of dehydrated soup, then heating water to bathe in. As soon as they were done cooking, they extinguished the fire so as to draw no attention, knowing in Mal Evol, any attention would be unfriendly.

Edwin was able to call water from the high, wispy clouds, but it was much more difficult for him. Fortunately, there was always mist in the mornings, which he found much easier to call from than the scant clouds that brought no rain to the parched valley. He spent the time to get all the water Aeolyn needed for bathing that night and did so again in the morning.

They departed before dawn as usual, feeling like

intruders in the overgrown, weed-infested streets.

Occasionally, the wind carried the faint scent of small fires, but they saw no smoke. If anyone lived in the dead lands, they were as determined to remain unseen as the companions were.

As they traveled now, they frequently crept around the camps of D'Mal's minotaur legions, giving them a wide berth. "Why are there so many legions here? This land is already conquered. They must be planning an assault on Neveyah, but what's holding them back?" Aeolyn worried over the problem incessantly. "Father Rall is right. Something bad is building here." She and Friedr faithfully noted all the encampments and counted the troops as they made their way north, using their little spyglasses and Edwin's scouting abilities.

"When we pass, both Edwin and I can feel the conflict simmering like a festering wound," Christoph told Friedr. "They were promised plunder and women for the taking. They don't understand why they're being held back."

Christoph scouted ahead when Edwin tired of far-seeing. He was silent and quick, simply reappearing in the underbrush next to them on his return.

"He was the best scout the Temple had before you came along," Friedr told Edwin as they sat in a circle, huddling together for warmth. "He never leaves a trail or makes a sound. If he weren't a healer, maybe we could have made an assassin of him too." He winked and turned a bland face to Chris, who, of course, rose to the bait.

"I'd never have been an assassin," Christoph replied in the tones of one who'd heard it all before. "I have no battle-magic. I have only minimal water-magic.

I can barely call water when I stand by the well with a bucket. Assassins have to be strong in lightning and fire-magic and be able to use them in great quantities."

Friedr agreed. "He can't even kill in self-defense. It's a bad trait in an assassin." They laughed again, quietly, but Aeolyn glared at them.

Edwin's eyes sparkled. "Somehow, I can't picture our Christoph sneaking around killing people with the occasional cat-zapper or hot-shot, but I *can* picture him singing them to death with the *Tragicke Tale of Elynne and Rande.*" His goofy expression and crazy grin made even Aeolyn smile.

"Edwin—you're so funny sometimes," she murmured, stifling a giggle.

"Ooh." Friedr winced and rolled his eyes at the mention of the melodramatic saga of star-crossed love so popular with the elderly female audience. "Christoph Berryman, the Singing Assassin—no villain is safe."

"Oh, Goddess. That old chestnut would bore anyone to death. It wouldn't be a challenge. I've seen entire rooms full of people begging for a swift end to the agony on hearing the entire travesty done with 'true passion.'" Christoph pretended to be offended. "I wouldn't be caught dead singing that depressing old thing." His eyes got the wicked look that meant he'd thought of a smart comeback. "I'd prefer to sing them *The Tale of Mother Alys and Her Merry Daughters.* They'd die laughing!"

Friedr and Edwin both burst out laughing at the mention of the bawdy tale. "Oh yes. I almost *did* die when you sang the whole thing our last night in Widge." Friedr's chuckle subsided as he noticed Aeolyn glaring at him. "Well, it was hysterical. The whole common room was rolling on the floor! You shouldn't have gone to bed so early, wife." His attempt to stop giggling failed under her scrutiny, and his suppressed chuckles set Edwin off again.

"You might as well announce we're here," she whispered crossly as she brushed her long, dark hair. Red-faced and grinning hugely, the boys exchanged guilty looks. "Why don't you have a party while you're at it?"

They tried manfully to smother their laughter at the look on her face, but it burst out anyway. "Stupid men," she muttered. "Stupid, stupid men." Her hair hid her smile.

Slyly, Christoph sang the refrain, "She stood them on their heads, their heads…and bounced them on their beds, their beds…. Her sisters dear said 'that's not fair…. Mother says you have to share….'"

Edwin and Friedr completely fell apart, laughing uproariously, making no attempt to smother it. Even Aeolyn had to stifle her giggles.

"…She kicked so high she grazed the sky and cried 'Let's have his bro-ther!'"

***

At dusk on the evening of the seventh day inside the Valley of Mal Evol, they reached a low crescent of hills sparsely forested with sickly pines and covered with the ever-present thorn bushes. Traps dotted the landscape, cunningly hidden. The moldy bones of the unfortunate decorated many of them, and the companions were quiet, moving slowly and silently through the scrub. They stayed far away from the grim city, as strangers would be immediately noticed in the dark and gritty town, traveling instead far to the west along the base of the forbidding mountains.

"Someday I'll go there and see where my mother was born," Edwin told Christoph. "At least I will once the land has been cleansed." He wondered briefly if he would live to see that day.

"Edwin, I'm sorry, but Mal Evol City was completely burned to the ground, even as your father and his companions were making their escape," Christoph told him sadly. "Now I hear it's little more than a poor copy of any lowly village in Serende. It's no longer the gracious, bustling city your family lived in. The Temple of Aeos was leveled, and a new one to Tauron was built on her hallowed ground. There are no shops or commerce such as we would find in the towns or villages in Neveyah. It's a garrison town for the legions when they're forced to languish in Mal Evol. When we were in Arlen, you were closer in spirit to how your grandparents lived. The children of Aeos who live in Mal Evol City now serve the minotaurs and are under heavy compulsions. Those who could escape have long since done so. The rest are not like us anymore except in looks. They've all been forced to kneel before Tauron. That evil rite takes everything that made them children of Aeos and twists them until they belong utterly to the Bull God. Do you understand what I'm telling you?"

"I don't really understand, but I believe you're telling me the truth," Edwin replied, as a feeling of loss settled in his spirit. "I hoped.... I don't really know what I hoped. Oh well. At least we'll bring Marya out of his keep, and it'll be a victory for us."

Later that evening, Christoph returned from scouting as they settled in to a cold, dark camp. He told them they would reach their goal the next day. "It's not far now to the keep of Mal Evol, over this ridge in the center of the half circle formed by low hills, that on the map are called Ariend's Moon, though I don't know why, other than they appear shaped like a crescent, with the keep tucked up hard against them. We must now go even more carefully."

"If we can avoid fights, it'll be good, but this is a harsh land," replied Aeolyn. "It's always some wretched thing's day to die at the end of our swords. We'll try to keep our skirmishing as quiet as possible. I think our scuffles will be passed over as simply another creature finding an unwilling meal."

"In two days, the moon will be dark, and we'll have to move then or wait for a month," ventured Edwin. He rarely volunteered any suggestions, feeling the others were more able to discern what was best for them. However, if there was one thing a person who farmed the land watched, it was the phases of the moon, and in this area, he was more knowledgeable. "Will she be safe if we must wait another month?"

"Have you had any more dreams?" asked Aeolyn. She'd begun to look attentive when he did offer a comment, perhaps because he didn't speak unless he was sure of what he was about to say.

"No, none like the ones you already know about," replied Edwin. "My dreams are not so pleasant in this place." A shadow crossed Christoph's eyes briefly, so fleeting Edwin wasn't sure he'd even seen it. "It's the soil, I think. During the day, we're shielded, but I can't figure out how to build a shield that'll stay up when I'm sleeping."

"Nor are my dreams pleasant," agreed Aeolyn

soberly. "If you do find a way to keep the shields up while we sleep, it would be a good thing to know. Are we close enough for you to ride the winds tonight as far as the Rose Tower and the walled garden? Then you could at least find the hidden gate."

"Perhaps. My range is increasing daily. I'll try." Edwin was reluctant, but wanted nothing more than to see the garden and maybe glimpse the prisoner in the tower. He didn't know if she would sense his presence, but felt sure he couldn't let her see him again until the moment they freed her. Stefyn D'Mal would certainly see the hope in her mind and decide to discover the cause of it.

His reluctance stemmed from the changes occurring in him. Each time he rode the wind or sailed under the earth, he risked abandoning his body forever, and each time the desire to do such a thing was more intense. Edwin now struggled with this craving with every fiber of his being, but he couldn't stop using his gift. It was all that saved them from stumbling into many of the deadly mantraps over the previous two days, traps he was not surprised to find. And he wouldn't stop using it even if he could. He dreamt of it now, as often as of Marya.

Edwin sent his senses out riding the wind. There was a candle burning in the high window of the tower, but he didn't look in despite being sorely tempted to do so. *Marya is sensitive. She might know if someone is watching her,* he told himself firmly. Instead, he moved lightly, a gentle breeze among the vines and roses covering the stone walls surrounding the garden.

After disturbing a sleeping thrush in its nest, Edwin found what they were looking for. *The bird felt the breeze as I moved with the air. She thought her nest was more protected than that.* Silently, he laughed as he rode the wind. The gate was located at the northern corner of the garden where the wall met the tower. It was made to blend into the wall and was completely hidden under a heavy cover of vines that moved and rustled gently in the wind. If he hadn't been familiar with how stone walls were built, he'd never have found it. Edwin, however, had helped his father repair many on their farm. He found the telltale keyhole and then searched out the miniscule cracks where there was only the appearance of mortar. He smiled mentally as he found what he was looking for. It was completely hidden beneath the overgrown shrubbery and vines, and no guard was posted anywhere near it inside the garden. The head-high thorn forest marched right to the walls of the keep.

Three pairs of guards were posted atop the walls. They paced along the parapet of the garden at varying intervals. Another guard was posted inside the garden beside a door he hadn't seen in his dreams.

The window he saw so often was on the same side of the tower as the secret gate and completely out of view of the guard at the door. *This is why I've been shown the window and not the door,* thought Edwin as he returned to examine the gate more closely. *We'll need to get some oil for both the hinges and the lock. Where would we find oil?*

He moved along the wall, feeling the silkiness of the air caressing him with the sweetness he had no words for. He knew he was tired and should return to his body. Reluctantly leaving, he ghosted back to the hill where they were camped, passing through a small bank of clouds as he did so.

Edwin was already tired when he began, and so perhaps it was because of his exhaustion that the feeling of the clouds distracted him. The intensity of the experience was indescribable, and it consumed his awareness. The satin of the water in the clouds mixed with the air filled him with the desire to go farther and farther, to abandon himself to the sheer ecstasy, and he no longer had the strength to resist its lure.

How long he was lost in the clouds he didn't know.

Feeling someone nudging his shoulder, Edwin came back to his body. For a moment, he was disoriented, wondering where he was. Then as his awareness returned, he stretched and attempted to stand up. He reeled, and the world spun while Christoph steadied him, holding him up, his face full of worry.

He knows what almost happened. Edwin's thoughts skittered around, not wanting to think about it and not willing to talk, holding onto Chris until he could stand on his own. He was completely done in. Far-seeing equally used healing and battle chi and he'd already used both for most of the day. Now he'd gone and lost himself for who knew how long. He shivered at the thought that he could easily die and never know it.

Edwin suffered a strange sense of embarrassment to think he could so easily give himself up to the nearly physical pleasure of the experience. Fear, cold and pure, gripped him. He had to use his gifts, that was a given, but he didn't know how to solve the problem.

Aeolyn was immediately alert. "What did you find?"

Edwin's voice was thick, and he had trouble forming the words. "I found the secret gate, but there's a problem. We're going to need oil for the hinges and lock. They're badly rusted. And there are guards, as we knew there would be." He rubbed his eyes. "Tomorrow I'll look for oil. I'm sure D'Mal's servants keep the door hinges well-oiled inside the keep. Maybe a tool shed will be found somewhere near the kitchen."

He sat down to rest for a moment and immediately drifted into a deep sleep. Christoph smiled as his spell took hold.

"Why can't you look now?" asked Aeolyn. "Edwin? Oh, my. His battle-chi is completely depleted."

"He's exhausted all his chi," replied Christoph, laying his hand on Edwin's forehead. "He spent all day far-seeing so we could avoid D'Mal's pleasant little traps. He just used the last of it finding the gate, plus he's been maintaining an earth shield on me all day. He needs to sleep, or he won't be able to call water in the morning." He looked up at Friedr. "Help me get him into a better position, or he won't be able to rest well enough."

Privately, Christoph was afraid he knew why Edwin was completely depleted, but he avoided talking about it. All Chris could do was watch him carefully and bring him back when it looked as if he was getting lost in the magic. *I should have brought him back sooner. I should have been watching his chi levels more carefully. I have to monitor him more closely.*

After making Edwin more comfortable, they decided to divide the watch into three, sharing his equally. With him settled, they quietly planned their next moves. Friedr said, "We must decide how we're going to distract D'Mal for several days while we get

Marya to the Temple at Braden. If we can't focus his attention elsewhere, we may as well give up now."

"He uses the legions of minotaurs as his guards. Nothing distracts them," replied Aeolyn. "But maybe we can focus his attention on a problem that concerns them. Maybe a barracks fire?"

"No, I'm sure he'd demand that Marya heal any of his men who were wounded, and he would discover her absence immediately," countered Christoph. "What we need to do is stir up a little rebellion in his forces, something he'll have to personally attend to."

"It's a good idea, but how are we to do this?" Friedr looked expectant. "We don't have a lot of time, if Edwin's correct."

"They're visitors here. The minotaur soldiers are from Serende, the land of the Bull God. The actual border lies as far from Mal Evol City as Ariend lies from Aeoven. It's a two week's march from here, even for them, because they must travel in squads and carry all of their supplies. But there must be something we can do to get them stirred up and focused toward their homeland," Christoph mused. "They fight among themselves under normal conditions, and even more so now they're frustrated at not having been allowed to rape, pillage and plunder in the city of Braden. These men have been through the ritual that changed them into minotaurs—they're Tauron's most elite warriors. They don't understand why they're being held back from what they were created for, and frankly neither do I."

Chris paused for a moment as an idea struck him. "Unless D'Mal is feeding off them in some way. In fact, it's the only reason I can see for him holding them back. He must be drawing chi from the legions. Their unrest is simmering, not quite boiling over, but kept just on the edge. It would create a lot of natural chi just waiting to be gathered, if you have the ability to do so." Christoph's mind spun as he considered the possibilities.

Aeolyn shifted, stretching. "They're going to be used against us, and soon. I keep thinking about the prophecy. What was it exactly? 'The children of the Bull God answer the call that rides on the wind.' Edwin rides the wind. Could he...could he whisper rumors of trouble in the homeland to them using his air-magic? It might get them moving east." She was quiet for a moment, thinking. Then she said, "Does he have this sort of ability? He's the only mage ever to have this skill. It must mean something important."

"No one knows what his limits are," replied Friedr. "There's never been anyone with this ability to far-see and call water from the air. And even if he could do that, would he be able to get them moving fast enough?"

"We'll speak to him in the morning," Christoph replied. His gaze lingered on Edwin's fatigued face as he cast a healing spell on him once again, somewhat easing his exhaustion and allowing him to fall into a more restful sleep. "But even if he *can* do such a thing, it may take us the whole month until the next dark moon to accomplish it. We simply can't allow him to burn out in this fashion every day. He won't be able to do what he must in order to rescue Marya if he doesn't get more rest." He adjusted the cloak around Edwin.

Friedr and Aeolyn looked at each other, wondering about Christoph's fretfulness, both suspecting he was hiding something. They'd been his closest friends since he came to the Temple and knew him well.

"And then there's the problem of getting D'Mal's attention focused on his homeland," said Aeolyn, turning back to the problem at hand. "The legions are fairly stupid, even their generals. He is anything but. We must never underestimate him. Even though he's completely mad, everything he does has a reason behind it, and he isn't easily distracted."

"That's the critical element in this plan," agreed Friedr. "If he's distracted by this enough to leave Mal Evol, we have a chance."

"What if he takes Marya with him?" asked Christoph. "What's to stop him?"

"Well, perhaps if he thinks it's a war, he'll leave her behind for her safety." Aeolyn took a deep breath and let it out slowly, saying, "Surely he wouldn't take her into a battle. We must see to it that he hears about armed rebellion in the outer provinces of Serende, many days away to the east. Something on his borders, far enough that he must travel in person and yet near enough to threaten his rule here."

"He must have to do a certain amount of traveling anyway," suggested Friedr. "There's no way the legions we've passed are capable of controlling themselves as they have been without his firm and continuous guidance. They seem to be loosely affiliated gangs, and their war chiefs are more like tribal leaders than military generals. They're champing at the bit to get into Neveyah and pillage a village or two. It'd be impossible for D'Mal to sit on the Throne of Stone and Bone all the time to guide them."

"I agree they don't seem to have any military

training." Aeolyn found herself looking at Edwin's sleeping face, wondering why Christoph kept glancing over at him. He was sleeping deeply, but normally. "The legions are dangerous because they fight without restraint. They don't care about tactics. If a plan goes wrong, they just sacrifice a squad of warriors to achieve their goal by sheer strength of numbers."

Christoph yawned. "I think the only time D'Mal has to travel physically is when he has to deal with something so far away that it can't governed by the Throne of Stone and Bone. He can communicate directly with each of his commanders, so he can control them. Their god has told them to obey his chosen priest, and they're obedient to Tauron." He yawned again. "And now, I must go to bed, or I'll be falling asleep on my watch."

He checked on Edwin one last time and then crawled into his bedroll after making sure no scorpions were hidden away in it. He fell asleep immediately, leaving the others to work out the details of the new plan.

Friedr looked at Aeolyn with a serious look on his face, speaking low. "I think we're going to have trouble with Christoph. It's the same old problem, I think. But does Edwin know?"

"I don't think he's encouraging it, but he's an empath. I'm sure he does know. He calls him 'brother' two times a day at least. But you know how Edwin is. He accepts people for what they are and knows Chris is famous for his crushes, so he's simply ignoring it. He won't do anything to hurt Dane." Aeolyn pursed her lips. "The prophecy states 'Let the Hero go to the Shadow Castle to seek the hand of she whom darkness has claimed.' In the prophecies, Edwin's family is only ever referred to as either 'the Hero' or 'the Hero Foretold.' He'll meet Marya, and when he does, he'll find the girl he has waited for, and she will fall in love with him. The Goddess has decreed it. We'll wait and see what happens." She shrugged, saying, "Christoph is a smart man."

"I'll speak to him the next time it comes up if I can do so without causing trouble," Friedr decided. "What worries me about Edwin's recent prophecy, since we're speaking about such, is the bit about the Beloved falling to darkness. I'm sure it refers to Marya. She's the only one in D'Mal's clutches, and she's empathic. You remember your novice classes on healers—D'Mal is a mind-bender. He can subvert her. That's why this delay is bad."

Aeolyn shook her head, eyes dark with worry. "The prophecy says '*He* shall sow the poisoned seed.' I can't worry about this now. She has to remain strong. This is Marya we're talking about. Surely Aeos is watching over her—after all, she intends for her to be Edwin's wife."

Friedr nodded, unwilling to dash her hopes. With the dark turn of their conversation, his mind was filled with shadowy thoughts. Most of all, he worried about Marya's safety and her sanity. *Who can possibly predict what a mad servant of a mad god will do or not do? Aeos, Goddess, watch over Marya and keep her safe.*

Friedr held his wife close, taking as much comfort as he could in the familiar scent of her hair.

Chapter 17

Early the next morning, they began creeping through the thorn bushes and scrub to the line of hills rising in the shape of a crescent, half a league from the keep. Aeolyn decided they would make their base high up there, where they could observe the Shadow Castle from far enough away to remain unobserved, yet close enough to see who approached and departed from any direction. From that vantage point, they would also have a view of the road serving the kitchen entrance, as it skirted the base of the hills on its way from the city to the keep.

Many man-traps dotted the landscape, cunningly concealed. As usual, some were decorated with the grisly remains of the unwary rat-people who frequently stumbled into them. Christoph only allowed Edwin to far-see briefly, barely long enough to get them safely from point to point so he would retain enough chi to search for oil when they halted for the evening. He himself scouted for roaming squads of legions and found none. This close to the keep, he suspected, D'Mal had nothing to worry about. The traps did their jobs, and he was crazy enough to enjoy the challenge of taking care of any who succeeded in gaining entry.

In the late afternoon, they arrived at a rocky ledge where they could see well. There was plenty of shelter, allowing them to watch the keep and remain unseen.

As the red sun set, they sat silently, waiting for night to fall. At last the stars came out, and the sound of insects calling emanated from the thorn bushes all around them. They sat with their hoods up for warmth, as Edwin rode the wind. Aeolyn kept her small spyglass trained on the kitchen gate, and Friedr watched the stark landscape surrounding the keep, while Christoph surveyed the garden wall. Their spyglasses were coated in the same light-absorbing black as their armor. No errant, reflected ray would give them away under even the brightest winter sun.

Once he returned to his body they discussed their plan with Edwin, and while he chafed at the delay, he came to believe it was their only chance to get in and out of the keep undetected. "If I do have the ability to whisper on the wind, it'd be helpful, but I can't imagine how to do such a thing," he replied to Aeolyn when she presented the plan to him. "I'll think about this and try to figure it out. If nothing else, we can write rumors on scraps of paper and leave them in the camps. There're some who seem to read manuals of some sort, I've noticed. It'll be dangerous though, sneaking into their camps."

Aeolyn agreed, saying, "It's a good idea. We'll do what we must. I think if we can get the legions to leave, we'll have achieved more than simply a distraction," she told Edwin, with a light in her eyes. "We'll have given D'Mal a personal setback he'll have trouble recovering from. Think about it—all these legions are lounging about here doing nothing. Why? They're to attack Braden, once D'Mal has drawn all the chi he can from them. I'm sure of it. There's no other reason for them to be here, in the mood they seem to be in. They're spoiling to go to war. But if they leave, he'll have to go through all the trouble of getting them back. They won't want to return, and once they're off the soil of Mal Evol, he's lost control over them. He'll have to start all over again, and it could take him years to regain what he's lost. Who knows how long he's been planning and assembling this attack force."

Edwin searched for the legions, and Aeolyn mapped them, noting the groups who had moved since the previous day. Christoph and Friedr scouted the area for a place for them to camp and found one for the evening. "It's good, but it's still not the best we can do. I'll find a better one tomorrow," Aeolyn said critically when they were all gathered. "We'll need a permanent place, and I'll know it when I see it."

Now they were camped, Edwin searched for a toolshed at the keep. Submerged in the velvety depths of the air, his spirit flowed around the back of the kitchen, past the midden to the small shed he knew would have to be there somewhere. The cool, clear water filling the old well called seductively, enticing him to dive in and follow it to its source beneath the earth. But he had a task to accomplish and reluctantly focused his attention on the outbuilding he thought could be the storage shed.

It was a lean-to, attached to the wall on one side, with a sturdy door and a six-paned window facing away from the kitchen toward the garden. Edwin ghosted over, noticing the winter-dormant plants and hardy, aromatic herbs. They were alive despite rather indifferent care and were waiting for spring. No one had placed mulch around them, as a good gardener would have done, and large clumps of weeds also lay sleeping. *Where there's a garden, there may also be a root cellar and a way into the keep.* If there was, though, he didn't find it.

Unseen as the breeze, he peered into the kitchen

where he saw a bent, old woman, thin as a rake. She was scrubbing the pots in which, judging from the cooling leftovers, she must have cooked a fine dinner. Stacked next to the dishpan he saw the carefully washed and dried china that had served a dinner for two. Two crystal goblets rested on a tray with a decanter of wine, obviously waiting to go up to D'Mal and Marya.

Edwin felt an intense stab of jealousy on seeing the two wineglasses, even though he was wrapped in the velvet embrace of the air. He was assailed by a nearly overwhelming urge to charge in and take her back by force, which he immediately pushed down. *You don't even know her. You just don't want D'Mal to have her. Don't get sidetracked.*

As he watched, a little old man as bent and thin as the woman entered the kitchen. He left with the tray.

Edwin returned to the shed and peered through the dirty window. A bench leaned against the wall with tools scattered haphazardly on it, and a sagging shelf above. On the shelf was an oilcan, as he had hoped. He prayed it was full.

He allowed his spirit to flow to the door and test the lock. After much examination, he decided it could be easily picked. He would need to make some lock picks, but a pile of scrap metal and wood stood near the gate. Soon he was looking at the jumbled bits, trying to decide the best course of action.

He concentrated on the top piece of metal, a flattened tin can. He tried to grasp it with the wind but failed. After two more attempts, he paused, looking at it for a long moment, and focused once again.

"Visualize what you want to achieve." His father's

words came back to him. All his life, his father had instructed him to do just that, and Edwin found it was a useful way to get many difficult things accomplished. Aeolyn too had stressed it when she was teaching him. Visualization was what made the elemental magic actually work, though he hadn't understood the connection at first.

"What do I want to achieve with this piece of tin?" he asked himself. "I want it lying in the dirt in front of me." He pictured the flattened can lying on the soil in front of his body, trying to visualize it as clearly as he could, mentally preparing to try to lift it using the wind.

Suddenly, the world gave a little hiccup, and he was snapped back into awareness of his body. A terrible pain lanced through his skull, and groaning softly, he leaned over, holding his head in his hands.

"What is it?" Christoph was immediately at his side, soothing the headache. "What's wrong?" He laid his hands on Edwin's head, searching for the injury.

As the pain eased, Edwin's eyes opened, and through the sparkles, he could see the flattened tin can lying on the dirt—exactly as he imagined it. "Ohhh. My head hurts. I think I did something I shouldn't have," Edwin said slowly. "Aaugh, Goddess, my head hurts. Did you feel anything odd?"

His eyes watered from the pain, pulsing like a stabbing knife, though Christoph had eased the incredible sharpness of it.

"No, but you groaned, and I could feel your terrible pain," he replied, somewhat confused. "What did you do? I don't see an injury. Let me help." He cast the spell again, and Edwin sighed as his pain was dramatically eased until it was only a dull throbbing instead of a knifing pain.

"What just happened?" Aeolyn crawled over. "I heard you groaning. Are you ill?"

"He did something that gave him a terrible headache," replied Christoph. "What did you do?"

Mutely, Edwin held up the flattened can. "The tool shed is locked. I need something to make picks out of. I tried to lift it using the wind, but it wouldn't budge. So I thought if I visualized it here, on the dirt, I would be better able to get a grip on it. I was going to try to move it with the wind again, but it moved itself."

For a moment, neither of them knew what to say. "And this gave you such a headache you were incapacitated by it." Aeolyn's voice remained calm despite her shock at the turn of events. "Well, we know one limitation of your talent now anyway."

"When I did it, did you sense anything?" Edwin asked her. "It felt to me like the world hiccupped, and then I had an axe in my head."

"I felt nothing," she replied, worry creeping into her tone.

"You have no battle chi left." Friedr crawled over to them silently. "What have you done?" Edwin held the tin can up, and Friedr rolled his eyes. "Why do you have a flat, dirty can?"

"He has no healing chi left either," stated Christoph, his voice sounding odd even to himself. "He thinks he needs to make lock picks."

"Why do you need them?" Friedr gazed at Edwin with an inscrutable look on his face. "I have a set in my kit."

Edwin's face fell, but he repeated his story for Friedr and Aeolyn and then sat silently while they discussed in detail his intelligence and judgment, or lack thereof. They pointed out in particular every instance of foolhardy risk he'd taken in retrieving the metal.

When they finally stopped, Edwin said nothing in his own defense. Instead, he pulled himself together and crawled over to his bedroll saying simply, "Well then, if you're done kicking my sorry backside, I'm going to get some sleep so I can stand my watch at the usual time." He checked his bed for scorpions thoroughly before getting in, and turning his back on Friedr and Aeolyn, he immediately fell asleep.

After a few minutes, Christoph looked at the others who were still fuming. "What he did was pretty amazing, and you two just treated him as if he were a child. He isn't a child. He won't be easy to work with if you don't somehow regain his trust."

"What do you mean *we* have to regain *his* trust? He had no business doing something so foolhardy," Aeolyn started to launch into her tirade again, but Christoph silenced her.

"Have you ever known a mage who could move an object using mental chi simply because he needed it?" He looked at her expectantly.

"No, but still…," she trailed off. Her dark eyes betrayed her uncertainty.

"And so how would Edwin have known if it was a foolhardy thing to attempt or not? He didn't even intend to move it in such a fashion. He was going to try to use his wind magic. Now he feels like you don't trust his judgment, and he's right. You don't. Why? He's never done anything to let you down. He proved he can do something completely new, even though it took everything he had to do it. Why are you angry with him?"

"Because he didn't tell us he was going to do it," Aeolyn finally said. "And I see what you're getting at. He didn't let us know because he had no plans to move it the way he did."

"Well, I'm still worried that D'Mal could feel him nosing around, even if it is on the wind. And what if he did sense the 'hiccup' Edwin felt?" Friedr was slow to anger and even slower to let it go.

"Well, I felt nothing, and neither did you. We're right on top of him and should have if there was anything to feel. You've been perfectly fine with him riding the winds to scout for traps and find the gate and tool shed, up to now. Are you saying you have a concern you haven't voiced?" Christoph looked at him. "If you've noticed, he never argues with you when you correct him as a teacher. He accepts the discipline and learns from it. He only balks when you push him too far or forget he was an adult when he came into his powers and is only now learning the full extent of what he's meant to do here in our world."

After a moment, Friedr looked away. "You're right. I'm being irrational. It's so easy to forget he's still a student." He looked at the tin can. "He truly is a surprising person. I would never have thought of *making* lock picks. What other useful bits of knowledge lurk behind his pretty face? Although he isn't really too pretty right now." Friedr's wry comment made the others chuckle. Edwin was lying on his back and lightly snoring with his mouth open, an indication of how exhausted he was.

"We'll have to make it up to him tomorrow," said

Aeolyn, glancing at Edwin's deeply slumbering form. "Sometimes I forget how new he is to magic, with all his strange abilities. He's so humble and unassuming, but he can be so strong and sure of himself, like delivering that baby. I mean, think of the way he took over and saved both their lives. He'll be one of the great healers once he has fully come into his powers. I can foresee him becoming the Dean of Healers at some point in his future. And yet he is so simple and down to earth, like with the donkey, Sweet-Pea. He knows so many things, and he isn't afraid to learn new ones. It's difficult having a student with abilities we've never seen, and with strength far greater than ours. We're fortunate he is a good-hearted, hard-working man who is also highly ethical. You're right, I owe him an apology."

"He's sleeping soundly right now, so I think it'll be fine to let him take the last watch, as we originally planned." Christoph cleared the ground, setting wards against the ever-annoying scorpions that now plagued the land of Mal Evol. He'd been experimenting with different anti-vermin wards and finally hit upon one that was effective against all but the most determined scorpions. Edwin's trick of tying wards off made sure they could sleep relatively safely. "Now you must rest while I stand guard. I bid you a good night, and I'll wake you, Aeolyn, when it's your turn to watch."

***

It was the early hours before dawn when Friedr woke Edwin to take his watch. "I owe you an apology. You did something amazing, and I was taken by surprise. I should know you would never do anything to jeopardize the quest. The Goddess has given you this skill, and you must use it, though I don't know how much fun it'll be if it incapacitates you."

"I also owe you all an apology," replied Edwin sheepishly. "I realize now I should have come back first and told you what I wanted to try. And I wasted my chi trying to get something we already have. I didn't have to burn myself out doing it. If I'd asked, I would have known better."

"Ah, but now we know two things we didn't before, and they'll both prove useful." Friedr's eyes gleamed in the dark. "We know you can move things with your magic, and we wouldn't have if you'd found out I have lock picks in my kit. We also know you have the skills to make small tools we might need." Friedr chuckled quietly as he added, "And you never know when a flat tin can will come in handy."

Edwin returned his smile and took his place, watching until dawn. By the time the sun was up, he had regained his chi and self-confidence and was ready to begin the next phase of their plan.

He called the water to fill the bottles, and as he did so, he noticed it took much less chi than the previous day. Edwin wondered if using his magic as he'd done the previous evening somehow strengthened him. He filled the basin so they could clean up in the cold water, thinking wistfully of the hot springs and the men's baths at the inn in Wister. At least they still had the luxury of a quick wash morning and night with a soapy cloth and cold water. When they ran out of soap, things would become unpleasant.

After breaking their fast with a few sips of water and cold trail rations, Christoph and Edwin began working with his ability to move things mentally. They discovered he could relocate a feather with no pain, no feeling of disorientation, and using very little chi. Small pieces of wood could be shifted easily and also caused no pain. Pebbles were difficult and made his head ache behind his eyes. Translocating only a small sliver of the tin can however, left him prostrate with a raging headache and took half of his available chi. He was the only one who felt the disorientation.

Friedr and Aeolyn returned from scouting and sipped water and munched a ration bar for their lunch. Christoph told them what they had discovered, adding, "He picked the one thing hardest for him to move, to test his ability on, and then relocated a huge chunk of it to boot. No wonder he was sick." He glanced over at Edwin, who was stretched out on his bedroll.

"Do you think this is a battle-magic or healing?" Aeolyn looked at Edwin's ashen face. "Goodness, you look awful."

"It appears to take both in equal amounts to do this," replied Christoph. "I think it's a facet of his ability to send his spirit out to ride the wind or search under the earth. I don't see it as offensive, like calling fire or lightning, nor is it passive, like healing. It's somehow the result of the marriage of the two abilities. He's gaining strength in this skill already."

"I think I know what causes the backlash when he moves metal." Friedr's face was hidden in the folds of his hood. "It's the water-magic and lightning-magic reacting to the metal."

Aeolyn looked at him questioningly, as did Christoph. Edwin simply waited to hear his explanation.

"You know I'm more of a fire-mage, though I now

have strength in all of the elements. I once cast lightning at a water-wraith. This was on my first solo trip as a journeyman, and I was having no luck using fire against him. As you know, swords are ineffective. In desperation, I pulled my pathetic lightning ability out and tried it. He was standing on the metal bridge at the old mill in Farmington. The result was spectacular— you'd have thought the world was exploding. It knocked me on my backside, and there were bits of water-wraith everywhere," Friedr smiled fondly at the memory. "They usually hiss and melt when you zap them, but something about the metal bridge made it one of the better days of my life."

Edwin grinned at the thought of him capering about over the remains of a dead water-wraith.

"That experience is why I daily practice calling all the elements, especially the ones I'm weakest in. You never know when your best trick will be ineffective against an enemy, and you must always have a good backup plan." Edwin nodded, and Friedr continued. "But in regard to your ability, I'm sure it's the lightning reacting to the metal giving you the headache." He changed the subject with his usual abruptness. "We have also discovered many other things today."

Aeolyn and Friedr showed the map they'd made of the area from their vantage point. They'd marked the places where the legions regularly camped and begun to note the trails used for troop movements. The two were tired and dirty and sported many twigs in their hair, but their smug smiles said they were feeling good about their morning's accomplishments.

"When you're rested, perhaps you can find out how many squads are in the actual area surrounding the keep, if there are any." Friedr looked at Edwin, who was wrapped in his cloak for warmth, his head pillowed on his breastplate and his folded bandana covering his eyes. "If there are any legions, they may be more closely monitored by D'Mal than the others. But so far, I haven't seen any. I simply want to know if they're there or not."

"I'll be happy to do it, in a while," Edwin's reply was somewhat muffled. "It'll be good to do something useful that doesn't give me a headache."

Chapter 18

Aeolyn lay on her stomach, so still a field mouse was paused directly in front of her, his tiny hands busily stripping the husk off the seed pod of the omnipresent thorn bush. Quickly gobbling his seed, he scurried on his way, oblivious that he'd been under her watching eyes all along. *At least something can benefit from these wretched thorn bushes,* she thought as she watched him hurrying off to his burrow.

The land was covered as far as the eye could see with the forest of often head-high shrubbery covered with three-inch thorns, and was punctuated with the occasional struggling pine tree.

Fir and hemlock once grew there, but with the advent of the Bull God, the thorn bushes took over and starved out the native trees. The pines could have survived well in the dry conditions, but the thorns suffocated them, stealing all the nutrients.

Underneath the thorn canopy, once the companions were only a few yards away from the trail, they could move easily around the trunks and roots of the thorn bushes. Wherever there was light, there was undergrowth, so along the actual trails, the scrub appeared to be a thick jungle of thorns. Once they were inside, however, it was wide open and even Friedr could crawl easily. The interior of the thorn forest was barren of undergrowth and made a perfect place for them to hide. For the most part, their armor protected them, but Christoph and Edwin both spent chi healing several gashes each day.

The legions moved through the underbrush easily

as it was only chest high to the average soldier. Christoph explained that their homeland was covered in the same sort of brush, and the thick skin of the minotaur warrior was resistant to the thorns' attack. Still, they seemed to march only along certain trails without straying off the path.

Aeolyn lay hidden close to several paths and counted the soldiers as they filed past. She'd found a place that lay only several meters away with a view, and she counted the pairs of heavy boots as they passed by.

The legions were not quiet. Their speech was loud and abusive, and their demeanor toward each other was crude. They were oblivious to their surroundings, loudly quarreling and bickering among themselves. There was no doubt they were secure in their position as conquerors in the valley of Mal Evol.

Edwin silently crawled up to lie on his belly next to her. He whispered, "Another squad is approaching from the east, slightly larger, I think."

"Well then," she replied, "we'll hold up here. This is a good opportunity for you to try to contact Friedr. Tell him we'll return to base camp when the legions have passed, around midday."

"All right." Edwin wasn't at all sure how to do that, but Aeolyn and Christoph had decided, unknown to Friedr, he should try to whisper on the wind. Friedr and Christoph were hidden above the kitchen gate, watching the road and counting the carts bringing provisions. By learning what sorts of supplies were entering the keep, they could possibly tell how many people were being fed there. This could give them an idea of how many servants to avoid when they made the attempt to free Marya.

Edwin calmed himself and sent his spirit out to find Friedr. The feeling of the wind was silk on his skin, and it tempted him, as always, to leave his body forever and abandon himself to the pleasure. Earth wasn't quite as seductive, feeling somehow rougher but still sweet, and as difficult to release when it was time to return. Perhaps the roughness was because of the density. Water was as sensual as air to him.

Only the day before, Christoph asked him how it felt to send his spirit out far-seeing and he was unable to explain it, ending up with a lame mumble that made no sense. He seemed to understand it was too difficult to describe and didn't pursue it.

He found Friedr and Christoph in a clump of thorns on the far side of the kitchen road, about five hundred meters above the keep. He formed the thought, visualizing it as a whisper, and tried to float it on a breeze. *Aeolyn says to return to camp at midday.*

Friedr continued watching, having heard nothing.

Edwin tried again, trying to waft the words through Friedr's hair to his ear. There was no way to do it other than to get really close. He'd never noticed how thick his beard was before.

Friedr still showed no sign of having heard anything. This time, Edwin formed the words clearly and visualized pushing them right to Friedr's ear while trying not to touch his sideburns, fearing he would feel it.

"Did you say something?" Friedr asked in a low whisper. Edwin could hear him clearly, something he hadn't tried to do before.

"No," Christoph's low reply sounded clearly as

well.

Edwin tried again, this time pushing the words firmly into Friedr's ear, though he wasn't at all sure how he felt about it.

"...camp at midday," Friedr repeated. "Wait. Did you say Aeolyn wants us to return to camp at midday?"

"No," replied Christoph with a broad smile. "Our Edwin put the thought in your ear. Success!"

"Edwin, if you spoke to Friedr, then give me the sign we agreed on." Christoph wasn't sure Edwin would be able to hear him, as they hadn't tried to have him eavesdrop on anyone before.

A feather wafted to the earth. "Thank you, my friend. Now return to your body and save your chi."

Gladly, Edwin returned, feeling confused. As he opened his eyes, Aeolyn said, "Well?"

"I was able to deliver the message," he replied slowly. "I sent the feather as we agreed when Christoph asked for it." He didn't elaborate and remained quiet as they finished their count. He was as silent all the way back to camp as Aeolyn could have wished for.

Edwin was subdued for the rest of the day, obedient to each task his companions set before him. As a drizzle began to fall, he called as much water as he could to fill all the jugs, the basin, and the long unused cook pot. He was able to get enough for them to wash their undergarments and shirts. Their shelter remained dry, even as the first real rain they'd seen since entering Mal Evol fell. It was a hard, brief rain that was over within an hour, leaving the thorn forest sparkling in the last light of the day. Little moisture touched the parched soil. The thick canopy had stolen it all.

That night, Edwin lay awake, unable to sleep for

the confusion of his mind. Finally, he got up and went over to where Christoph sat watching.

"I noticed you're unable to sleep tonight," he said as Edwin moved up to sit beside him. They faced the Shadow Castle, rising grim and dark from the valley below them. "You've been quieter than usual even for you. What troubles you?"

Edwin was silent. Then he said, "I don't think I can wind-speak to the legions or anyone ever again."

Christoph looked at him and saw the emotional turmoil he'd kept hidden all afternoon stark upon his face. "Why?" he asked.

"I can't say it well," mumbled Edwin at last. He struggled to explain, feeling embarrassed and not knowing why. "I had to—it was like—oh, forget it." He looked at the small window high in the tower so far away and felt absurdly guilty for being reluctant to use this gift the Goddess had given him. "I don't know the words to tell you what the problem is. It was such a peculiar feeling."

"Edwin, may I speak frankly to you?" Christoph also watched the faintly illuminated window.

"I think you'd better." An embarrassed grin briefly lightened his somber features. "I obviously can't."

"You have been unable to explain the sensations you experience when you ride the wind, water, or earth. Is it because it has a sensual feel to it you're not comfortable talking about?"

Edwin looked sharply at him and then back to the castle.

"Yes," was all he said. He stared at the dark towers of the distant keep, unable to look Christoph in the eye.

"Would it help if I told you it isn't your physical

body feeling these sensations, but that they're a manifestation of your chi?"

Edwin looked away from the castle and turned toward him, relief warring with confusion on his face.

Christoph continued. "You are a healer adept. You *feel* your patients' pain and pick up on their emotions. Healing chi is empathic by its nature. We can't isolate ourselves from it. There is no separation between healer and patient, other than the basic dampening fields we call barriers, which allow us to remain detached enough to work. Battle chi is every bit as intimate. It comes out of the very body of the mage.

"Half of your ability to far-see, along with fetching, comes from your healing talent. The other half comes from the elemental magic. So, in you is combined the empathic healing chi and the sensual battle chi. The two together make an extremely volatile combination, as we have seen in your augmentation reactions."

Edwin blushed, glad it was dark.

"Something battle-mages *never* speak about is the sensual side of it. They don't talk about it because it is as personal to them as this is to you. Do you understand?" He saw Edwin's nod. "When a mage first comes into his or her powers fully, there is a deep, intense connection to the expression of the magic, one which is almost physical in its sensations. The fact you are experiencing this tells me you will be fully invested soon. Other students arrive at this place over the course of several years. As with everything else, though, your rate of growth has been increased exponentially.

"We healers know, however, the element a battle-mage is most strong in has intense sensations. This sensual connection is accompanied by strong temptations to let the magic run wild. It is our job to know this." His voice grew grim. "There are occasionally youngsters who die, consumed by the magic they have succumbed to, most usually fire- and lightning-mages. Some are naturally inhibited. They never fully accept it and don't progress beyond the mid-journeyman level, though they don't realize why. They're often attached to the army as battle-mages, and after they have done their duty, they may retire from the clergy as your father did. Often they become great artisans working in glass and as jewelry craftsmen.

"The great ones learn to channel the exhilaration to increase the power of their magic and become adepts. They become the senior clergy and are dedicated to the service of the Goddess for the rest of their lives.

"The Temple takes all the young students under their wing, and these aspects are explained fully so no child has to feel inhibited. Since you're not nine years old as most students are when they go to the Temple, somehow no one thought to tell you about this fundamental part of using your chi." Christoph looked him fully in the eye. "They've never had a student who is as old as you, and it didn't occur to them to have this talk with you. So listen and I will explain why you're so confused."

Edwin listened as Christoph explained what all mages knew and he was only then finding out. As he came to the end of his discussion, Christoph said, "I think we're going to have to work on your blocking and channeling skills so you don't lose yourself. Your ability is our only hope. We can't have you throwing up when you have to whisper dissention in the ear of a minotaur." He smiled encouragingly, waiting to hear Edwin's reaction.

Suddenly, the absurdity of everything struck Edwin as exceedingly humorous. "You know, my dad had a talk like this with me when I was about twelve, only it was about girls and boys and the feelings people have for each other sexually. It didn't mean much to me at the time. I mean, I was raised on a farm, for heaven's sake, so there wasn't a lot I didn't already know in regard to the mechanics of lust." He started to laugh, burying his face in his folded cloak to muffle his howls. Christoph smiled wryly at the comparison. "I was too young to appreciate the emotional aspects of sexual attraction he was trying to explain to me, so not much of what he said made any sense. I think I understand this time. I really am a bumpkin, aren't I?" Once again, Edwin found himself laughing uncontrollably, this time at himself and his own ignorance.

"Christoph, you're a true friend to me," he said, once he'd purged himself of hysteria. "How you put up with my ignorance, I will never know. You're the brother I always wished for, but never had. What I'd do without you, I can't imagine." He didn't see Christoph's face as it went carefully blank.

Later, after Edwin returned to his bedroll and was sleeping soundly, Christoph found himself staring into the dark, feeling an unaccustomed sense of grief mixed with an ache he'd hoped never to suffer again. It was a turmoil he refused to examine too closely, choosing instead to run through his healing exercises. As he practiced the familiar techniques, he was more able to center himself, though he wasn't completely able to raise his barriers. *It must be this land poisoning my spirit,* he thought. *Surely it is the land and not me developing a crush on my student. It isn't going to happen. It is* not *going to happen!*

When he woke Aeolyn to take her turn at watch, he'd regained at least the semblance of his usual serenity.

***

The next morning, Edwin and Friedr began the whispering campaign, and Aeolyn and Christoph searched for a more permanent base since they were now to spend four more weeks there.

"We need a place large enough for us to remove our armor while we're inside the shelter and to completely stretch out at night," he told her. "We're not sleeping well enough right now, and I've been having strange dreams."

Aeolyn looked at him, her brows raised and questioning. "Are they anything I should be worried about?"

"No, if I was having prophetic dreams, I would tell you," Christoph replied. "They're simply weird from not being able to sleep well." He refused to say anymore, and she didn't press him. They were too strange to try to explain, he decided, as they moved from thorn bush to thorn bush, looking for the perfect place to make into their home. He kept having a bizarre dream about the same thing, but it was more like he was looking at someone else's dream. *How can I explain something like this to Aeolyn? She doesn't understand empathy. She'll see it as a weakness. I'm far enough away physically so I'm not being drawn into them. It's more like watching them somehow.*

He thought they must be projected by D'Mal, as

they were certainly perverted enough. They were disgusting, nauseating actually. *I never dream about women, and these are sometimes about Marya. But it's a 'dream' Marya, who isn't at all like the girl I know. The dreams always start out being about men, but it's like the dreamer is being guided to dream about her against his inclination. They're far too nasty for Edwin or Friedr to be radiating.* He had to get his barriers in order. If he was picking up D'Mal's filthy dreams, what else is affecting me?

Trying to remember what Dane had attempted to teach him, he firmed up his barriers and made a conscious effort to maintain them, noticing immediately that the background buzz in his head was cut off. *I must not let my guard down,* he counseled himself. His headache was gone too, giving him an impetus to work even harder. *At least Edwin has the strongest barriers of anyone. He never lets them down except when sleeping.*

Christoph suddenly thought about another empath, one under the same roof as the mad priest. *Oh, no, no! Poor Marya. What she must be subjected to every time she falls to sleep. I'm sure she has her barriers up all the time, though she can only raise them when awake. She was always as good as Dane. I hope she's able to keep them up, though what I've heard regarding D'Mal's effect on healers is disturbing.* He tried to convince himself his friend whom he loved like a sister possessed strong enough barriers to withstand the mad projections.

As Christoph and Aeolyn crawled under the thorn canopy, they looked for a place with both an older, taller thorn bush for the main shelter and a view of the keep, shielded from observation by the many guards who walked the parapets on the walls of the Shadow Castle. At last, they came to a sort of shelf, high up in the hills, with a view of both the front and rear of the keep and a good view of Marya's tower and the garden below it. The main thorn bush was shielded from view by several large boulders marking the edge of a small cliff. The entire valley was spread out below.

As they crawled under the main thorn bush, they found an area eight big men could easily sleep and move around in. It was around five feet tall in the middle, and the central thorn bush was old and dense in the canopy. "I can make this into a nice little home away from home," Aeolyn said. "I'll need a lot of reeds though. Can you get me some from the creek without leaving a trail?"

"Easily," Christoph replied. "Do you want me to go now? I'll make sure the legions are nowhere near. How many will you want?"

"You'll need to get them from several different places, because I'm going to need enough to make floor mats, walls, and a ceiling, and it mustn't look like anyone is harvesting reeds. Mats will make it much warmer since we can't use fire. While you get them, I'll find brush to bring here to make the walls. From the outside, it'll appear to be a particularly thick thorn bush, nothing more." Aeolyn was already looking around.

They slept in the new shelter, though Aeolyn hadn't begun weaving the mats yet. Friedr and Edwin approved of it, and over the next few days, Aeolyn added to the interior until it was as comfortable as a den.

Connie J. Jasperson

Chapter 19

Marya knelt in the walled garden, pulling weeds and working the soil around the silent, central fountain. The earth was cold and not responsive to her magic. *I have no gift at all anymore,* she noted dispassionately to herself. During her bath the previous day, she noticed her augmentations were nearly gone. *I can't access my chi. I wonder why?* She felt misery welling up at the thought but pushed it back down firmly.

Still, she loosened and turned the soil, for no reason other than it gave her something to do. Her days were long, empty hours filled with the activities Stefyn deemed appropriate for a lady of her standing while he ruled shattered Mal Evol. *It's like he read a book of rules, and he must utterly enforce them in order to maintain absolute control in his chaotic world. Surely, poor Queen Irena didn't spend her life as bored as I am.*

Stefyn had ordered the servants to give her anything she required for gardening. They provided her with books to read, needlework to do, and paper for drawing. Nothing really interested her. She simply went through the motions.

When she tired of the silent garden, she would return to her rooms and soak in a hot bath. The only living person who ever spoke to her was Stefyn. He decreed only he could converse with her, and neither of the two elderly servants would disobey him. They were his creatures, body and soul.

After her perfumed bath, she would sit by the fire and read a badly written romance novel personally selected for her by Stefyn or work on the needlepoint flowers he'd decided she should enjoy creating. At half past three, Maisy would fix her hair in an "informal" style that was far too elaborate and she would dress Marya in a lace-ruffled, organza afternoon dress. She never wore the same gown more than once, except for her gardening outfit and Stefyn's favorite, an amethyst velvet creation. There were more dresses in her many closets than all the women of Aeoven owned collectively.

And she didn't value them at all.

Promptly at four o'clock, she would share a proper high tea in the family sitting room with him, pouring the tea and handing Stefyn plates of tiny sandwiches and looking for all the world like a proper hostess.

They would make small talk for exactly one hour. All the while, she would be terrified she might inadvertently say something he considered inappropriate. Then Stefyn would adjourn to finish his work, a thing her mind skittered away from. One of the guards would escort her to her rooms to rest until seven o'clock, when she would dress for dinner and go down to the formal dining room promptly at seven-thirty.

She and Stefyn would dine on delicacies brought in from his homeland, served with the finest wines, also from his homeland, though she no longer cared if she ate or starved. Everything tasted like ashes no matter how carefully prepared and beautifully served.

At nine-thirty Stefyn would stand up, signifying the meal was over. Then they would stroll arm in arm, the picture of companionship. Their path would take them through the galleries he had restored to beyond their former magnificence. They would stop before various exquisite works of art, with his explaining in detail the history of each piece.

Then they would share a glass of wine, and Stefyn would confide in her his dreams and ambitions. He would tell her how well the occupation was going and how the Temple was completely impotent in the face of her abduction. As he spoke, he might make occasional mention of various notables he may have been required to "instruct," and with each mention, she could taste the bile rising. Marya had overheard him giving instruction while she was imprisoned in his dungeon. It haunted her nightmares.

They might play chess or a game of cards, at either of which he might or might not choose to let her win. If she should win by accident, he'd been known to knock her to the floor, though he always apologized most eloquently. Marya made it her business to genteelly lose at any game Stefyn expressed a desire to play.

At midnight, he would escort her back to her apartments, kiss her hand, and bid her a good night. If she was really unfortunate, he would once again gently push her to set a date for their wedding.

She didn't remember agreeing to bond with him, but the perception of their betrothal calmed him somewhat.

Marya had been his captive for at least one full season, and most likely much longer. Stefyn allowed no calendars in Mal Evol, and especially not at the Shadow Castle. He didn't allow any reference to the passage of time other than that of the clock. Each day was the only one he ever lived, and the schedule was never allowed to be disrupted.

She thought he must be at least fifty years old,

though he looked like a man of perhaps twenty-five. She knew he was much older than he appeared because her father's brother, Pauli, quested against him before she was born.

Her uncle died on that quest.

Marya was so desperately lonely she was almost looking forward to high tea, despite the fact he would pressure her to set a date for their wedding. She was terrified she would blurt one out and terrified that if she did *not,* he would decide she needed to learn another lesson in manners. The last one nearly destroyed her.

Regardless of her anxious desire to follow his rules, the thought of giving herself to the madman who lurked beneath the beautiful face brought her close to hysteria.

Stefyn sensed her fear and revulsion, and also the physical attraction she felt for him but fought and hated herself for. It pleased him no end. He used his empathic abilities mercilessly to enhance those feelings, manipulating her mind as if it were his favorite plaything. Of course, he knew she was aware of his abuse of her, and he enjoyed the knowledge of that too.

Each day, he wore her down a little more, taking great pleasure in the process, savoring each small victory. Every time, she broke a little more, and she sensed his anticipation of her complete capitulation was sweet indeed.

When Marya was first kidnapped and brought to the keep, she rebelled, stubbornly wearing her moss-green healer's leathers and refusing to dress in the fine clothes Stefyn brought her. She persisted in trying to speak to the servants. She wouldn't eat, rejected any book Stefyn brought for her, and snubbed his overtures of polite conversation.

The final confrontation ended with her tossing wine in his face. The veneer of civility cracked, and madness looked out of his eyes. She tried to back away, but he left her no exit.

His eyes glittered as he explained in silky tones that her bad behavior left him no alternative. Then he casually knocked her to the floor, bruising her left cheek. As she tried to stand up, he seized her by her hair, and dragging her all the way, he locked her in his dungeon.

She was kept there in complete solitude until she at last agreed to accept his hospitality in a "polite and civilized" manner. The cell was filthy, too small for her to stretch out fully, and not high enough to stand up in. A tiny grate near the straw-covered floor let in light and some air but not enough of either. There was only a hole for personal needs. She was fortunate to have been given the cell nearest the entrance on the lower tier. It was reserved for members of his household as a punishment for minor infractions, to insure discipline was maintained.

Stefyn had stood on the other side of her jail door, and in the most reasonable of tones, he chided her for being rude. "You have not been gracious to me at all, my dear. I *will* teach you manners, and you *will* be fit to be my queen. This lesson will be comparatively easy on you." His voice was so calm, so gentle, so hurt, in stark contrast to the madness raging in his eyes at his inability to control her. "The next lesson you will not enjoy at all, dear lady. Please do not make me treat you harshly. It would grieve me if you were to die."

Hunger and thirst soon became her companions.

Lying in the fetid straw with her face pressed to the tiny grate, she watched the lightening and darkening of the distant sky. At odd times, the slot in the door was pushed aside, and a tray with a tin cup of water and a piece of stale bread was shoved in. No one ever spoke to her. The loneliness was unbearable, and the terrible solitude was what finally broke her. How long she was locked down there, she didn't know. She was kidnapped at the end of summer, and it was late harvest or early winter when she was finally allowed to be a "gracious guest."

The agonized, muffled sounds of the other prisoners were more terrifying than anything she'd ever known. The combined weight of their horror and suffering crushed her barriers as if they never existed. Because of her strong empathic ability, their dread and pain affected her terribly, and while she was down in the dungeon, her barriers completely failed her. Hearing and fully sharing their ordeals and being unable to soothe or ease them in any way was an indescribable nightmare for the healer whose gift was once considered one of the strongest in the clergy. Her mind hung aghast for immeasurable lengths of time, experiencing the unspeakable atrocities, unable to look away or hide from Stefyn's work. He *required* her observation, and so she was the unseen spectator, crying and sobbing for those she couldn't help.

But if she thought the horrific sounds, crushing fear and pain of their daily ritualized ordeals at Stefyn's hands were unbearable, she was to find much worse in store.

Some length of time after he locked her away, he had cause to make a sacrifice to his dread god, and she learned what his true vocation as high priest meant. That was when her living hell truly began.

The altar was centered on a pedestal in the middle of the dungeon, directly beneath the Rose Tower, where she now lived.

She knew exactly what lay below her, and it preyed on her mind.

She stifled a nervous giggle as she thought about the time Stefyn mentioned he'd converted half of the old wine cellar into a proper dungeon, in as offhand a manner as any farmer might remark on having built a new barn. He'd laughed as he said, "What sort of a castle doesn't have a dungeon? Of course, I had to rectify such an omission." It was there he performed the arcane and evil rituals that bound him and the land of Mal Evol to his dark god. They were small, domestic rituals to ensure favor.

However, Stefyn truly was the high priest of Tauron, having been elevated above all others. He was faithful to his god and most fervent in carrying out his duties. He applied himself to his work diligently. He personally handled his own gentle preparation of his offerings. Prisoners received a special treatment designed uniquely for them, educating them to be most pleasing in the event they were called upon to make the ultimate sacrifice. This careful work occupied Stefyn's mornings and involved both intense pain and pleasure for those to be sacrificed, binding them to him and him to them. By the time he was called upon to perform the ritual, it hurt him terribly to give up his gifts because he'd come to love them so much. The surrendering of them was truly a personal sacrifice for Stefyn.

On entering the central area he referred to as his

workroom, Stefyn ritually removed his clothing, always in exactly the same order, and carefully folded it in a precise way. Each item was placed in a covered basket, which was then set on a special shelf for unsanctified things.

He never entered wearing garments because it was a sacred place. As the high priest, he showed his devotion by appearing before his god with nothing to hide. Naked and in a semi-trance, he walked to the altar and, after kissing it, knelt and began praying, asking Tauron's blessing on the sacrifice he now offered up. The actual process of the ritual offering happened in stages and could take two to three mornings, during which time Stefyn would not miss high tea or dinner, and he would comport himself as if nothing sinister was happening in the basement. The stages of the sacrifice were calculated and took time. His god did not appreciate hurried and halfhearted offerings. The longer he lingered over the rites the more satisfied Tauron was.

He then carefully selected a victim from one of the many who languished in the cells ringing the upper level of the dungeon. That particular tier was fitted with special accommodations for those who were to be offered up. Guests lodged there were treated with the most solicitous care, and his personal assistant, a minotaur priest named Brec, made sure they were well cared for and comfortable when he was occupied elsewhere.

After choosing the best one for his purpose, he willed the door to open, and by the simple act of taking over their mind, the chosen one walked to the altar and lay down upon it. Stefyn's magic bound the guest and also gagged him so only whimpers and moans of pain or pleasure could escape. Those sounds were pleasing to Tauron.

Unable to move a muscle, they watched him with adoring eyes as he stood in a special golden font. He began by chanting as he poured holy water over himself in ritual purification. Then he called forth the purple-hued, holy flames for cleansing the knife made of amethyst and stepped up to the altar. His eyes glowed the color of amethyst when the dark god himself invested his body.

Chanting in the strange language sacred to Tauron, Stefyn offered up more than simply the body of his sacrifice. This first stage was composed of everything the victim ever was, all they loved or hated, their secrets, vices, any good they'd ever done, and any evil, so Tauron might know the life now given as a gift. All these things Stefyn drew out of them, and eagerly, they gave him everything that ever made them a unique person. This was the first day of the sacrifice.

Lovingly, he rewarded them. He gave them exquisite pleasure and then prepared them for the next day. He personally saw to it their needs were taken care of, and nourished them with the special potions to prepare them for the next step in their sacred journey. Finally, once again, he purified himself and concluded that stage of the ritual.

The next day began the second stage, during which he shared with them divine and obscene orgasms, offering up their pain and ecstasy for his god's satiation. The energy and power this generated for both Tauron and his high priest were unimaginable. The very air crackled with them. This was the second day of the sacrifice. Once again, the victims were tenderly cared for and given the potions that prepared them for the final step. Again Stefyn purified himself and concluded that stage of the ritual.

By the third day, he had taken every scrap of humanity from them and now began the ritual mutilation in which he devotedly offered up their pain. At the culmination of the ritual, they themselves gave up their lives. The pitiful remains then burned in the amethyst flame that signaled Tauron's acceptance of the sacrifice, and the scent of the smoke was most pleasing to the dark god. This sacred pyre was the conclusion. Only when nothing was left did Stefyn return to the font to once again cleanse his body, washing away the blood and other bodily fluids.

This was the work of Stefyn D'Mal, which Marya could not even think of without sickening and shaking so violently she dared not hold a glass of wine. Whenever he casually mentioned it, she had to set down whatever was in her hand. "This sensitivity is one of the things I adore about you, my darling, but it is a weakness. You must learn to be strong," he told her. "I follow a god of love, and soon you will know the joy of his love as you rule beside me over a Neveyah reborn in glory."

His fond smile would grace his beautiful face as he looked at her, but she was not touched by his physical perfection. What *did* move her was the madness shrouded beneath it.

During her incarceration, she begged and pleaded for him to stop the rituals, pounding on her cell door until her hands bled. She screamed for their release until she had no voice, but no one answered.

She covered her ears to block the sounds, but

nothing could block her healing sight. Her cries of shared pain and fear echoed though the dungeon, the death of those tortured her only relief.

The day came when she was the only living prisoner. From the moment she had been thrown into the dungeon, no one had spoken to her, not even Stefyn. She was alone, utterly and completely. Marya came to believe she was going to die there, and with this realization, she lost her grip on sanity. It became difficult to tell the difference between her hallucinations and reality. How long this lasted she didn't know, but one day, she heard a voice. She thought it was real, and it was next to her, whispering comfort.

That was the day the shadows that haunted the castle began to speak. One in particular took a liking to her, visiting her often and murmuring advice. The shade of the murdered queen urged her to give in, to do his bidding. She promised if Marya went along with his notions, it would buy time until she was rescued. The shadows tried to comfort her, telling her she hadn't been forgotten. The sad queen promised that although it would take a long time, she would have her freedom one day. She swore Aeos had a plan for her, but she also said Marya must be patient. *"You will leave the Tower of Bones,"* the ghost promised her. *"They love you and are coming."*

Once her decision was made to do as Stefyn required, Marya was never the same again.

When Stefyn threw her into the tiny, filthy cell, he gave her a book detailing the proper etiquette for a young lady of society, which she promptly tore to shreds. Before he would allow her out, she was made to memorize and recite every scrap, reading by the light seeping through the small grate that served as a window. She had no idea how many days she spent searching for the pieces, picking through the filth and straw and then holding them to the light. By the time she had learned it all, she had been utterly broken.

At last, crying and begging all the while, she repeated it word for word. Her face pressed to the slot in the door, she promised to follow it to the letter. Stefyn immediately opened the cell, taking her dirty, trembling hands. Tears stood in his eyes as he beseeched her never to force him to punish her again, that he couldn't bear it. Shaking uncontrollably and nearly too distraught to speak, she promised to behave, that she would be a model guest. He then said for this one day she would be allowed to miss high tea to rest, but dinner was served at seven-thirty and he was looking forward to her company that evening.

The silent Maisy half carried her to the apartment she was now to live in, where a steaming, perfumed bath was waiting for her. Marya sobbed, feeling a mixture of intense relief and complete desolation as she bathed the first time. She soaked for a long while, feeling as if the filth would never wash away and knowing her true imprisonment had only begun.

How she made it through the first evening, she had no idea.

***

Now in the winter-barren rose garden, Marya stood, brushing the soil off her not-so-simple brown dress, and placed her gloves and trowel into the tiny basket held by the hulking guard called Girt. Looking at the shadow of the tower looming above, she shivered, thinking, *Stefyn calls this place the Rose Tower, but the shades tell me it is the Tower of Bones...their bones burning on his altar.* Shivering, she went back inside, followed as always by her guard. The winter sun didn't warm the garden. Even in the midday, it was gloomy.

The shadows rose and swirled around her, like wisps of smoke eddying in the breeze. She paused, saying goodbye to the children and Queen Irena, while her guard pretended not to notice her talking to a rosebush again. The guards believed she had slipped into madness, but since she was D'Mal's woman, they feigned ignorance. Of course, the conversation with the shrubbery would be reported—everything she did or said must be—but as long as she was only talking to inanimate objects, she wouldn't be punished.

Goddess Aeos, have you forgotten me? she wondered as she climbed the tower stairs to her apartments. As she walked through the door the bar dropped behind her. With a leaden heart, she prepared for her bath. Certainty she would never again see her home loomed stark in her heart. *Will I die in this tower of horror and bones? Will I never see home again?*

***

In the early morning light, Aeolyn and Friedr spent their time developing more rumors for Edwin to whisper to the legions. From their post behind the boulders, Christoph watched the keep with his spyglass, and Edwin sat beside him, intent on searching the area for the watchdog, riding the wind as lightly as he could.

Before he left his body Edwin sat quietly, spending a few moments trying to combine his healer's barrier into his basic battle-shield. After much experimenting, he happened on a trick of layering water within the spirit barrier as if it was a healing spell in a dampening field, and it worked well. While it took much of the ecstasy out of the experience, he was far more relaxed and able to concentrate on his task. *Now if only I can find a way to tie it off so I can do my work and not have to maintain it all the time. I know there's a way—there has to be. If Dad can do it, I can.*

After much searching, Edwin found the kennel near the quarters that housed the legions who guarded the keep. He found two dogs, obviously a breeding pair. They were huge, easily the height of a man and of a breed he'd never seen before. He examined them both closely and even delved the female with his healing sight. She was clearly pregnant to his well-trained eyes but nowhere near her time, being about four weeks along. Each dog was strangely shaped around the forehead, with two huge, knife-like fangs extending downward the length of a man's hand at the front of the muzzle. Their ears were large and shaped like a fox's, highly sensitive to the smallest of sounds. The dogs' muscular bodies were covered in a short, bristly fur of mottled brown and tan, allowing them to blend into the landscape well. Finding no other dogs anywhere around the keep, he returned to his body and reported what he saw. "I know a breeding animal when I see one," he assured Christoph. "There will be puppies in five weeks or so."

"Those sound like bear-hounds. I've read about them. They're occasionally bred for hunting giant bears in the lands of the Bull God. The dogs have one failing, however." Christoph's smile was grim. "They are not adaptable and are difficult to train. If the handler who raised them from a puppy dies, it's unlikely anyone else will be able to control them. They are only recently bred from the wild. When the handler who is in their eyes the pack leader, dies, the strongest dog will assume the position as leader. When this happens, there are several possibilities.

"Most likely, the pack will turn feral, roaming the neighborhood where they were raised and which they consider their territory." He tucked his little spyglass into its case. "Or they may accept a new handler but are known to suddenly turn on their new trainers, often killing them."

"What do you suggest we do about these dogs? I don't want to have to deal with them while I'm sneaking around the garden." Edwin's memory of those fangs was clear.

"A sleep spell works well on them." Christoph looked unhappy. "But I think we must consider killing them. If they should escape and begin breeding in the wild, nothing and no one will be safe from them. Mal Evol doesn't deserve this."

While Edwin and Christoph were occupied with their tasks, Friedr and Aeolyn were hard at work creating the most convincing rumors they could think of. They leaned over the map they'd all created.

Aeolyn placed a small stone on it to hold it down. "The squad camping at this creek here is from the province of Nuruk. They were at war for generations with Gutuk before D'Mal unified them. So far as I can see, he doesn't dare mix them into the same units. Nuruk is east of Mal Evol, a good seven days march even for the legions. Gutuk is the next province beyond. These two areas are where the rumors must be centered."

Friedr asked, "What about the rest of the legions? They're not all from just these two small provinces. They come from all over the lands of the Bull God."

"The rumors must be threefold. We must whisper that Nuruk has added much of Gutuk to its province, with many new, young warlords rising to prominence, while the best warriors languish here waiting for a war that will never happen. We must inspire the men of Nuruk to hurry to claim the spoils they're currently being denied here. After all, they were promised women, land, and wealth for the taking. There's a great deal of unrest among them. It should be easy to make their greed work for us." Aeolyn paused as she shooed a scorpion off the map, and Friedr killed it. Christoph only maintained the wards against vermin at night so he could conserve his chi for emergency healing.

She continued speaking. "The legions all chafe at being denied the bounty promised to them. Those soldiers from other provinces must be made to see the opportunity that lies there. They should believe that while the warriors of Nuruk are busy pillaging, they have left their own hearths unguarded. We must make them think they can claim the two weakened provinces for their own."

"So first, we must worry the men of Gutuk." Friedr saw her reasoning. "They have to hear of the despoiling of their land. We have to help them with their decision to rush home to fight for their loved ones."

"Yes. They should definitely feel the fear that their women and property have faced the fate they intended to inflict on Braden and southeastern Neveyah," agreed Aeolyn. "They know quite well what prizes the victors will claim in these territorial battles. We have to make them move quickly to defend what is theirs."

"And the third leg of this triangle?" Friedr looked questioningly at his wife.

"We must keep these rumors from D'Mal for as long as we can, until most of his forces have left the soil of Mal Evol. Four days after the last of the legions have departed we can allow him to hear of the civil war and the defection of his legions. He'll move immediately, but will have to go all the way to Gutuk at the least to settle this and try to bring his forces back. To ensure this, Edwin must also whisper the need for the legions to go in secret."

"Will D'Mal not miss them beforehand? He must have some contact with them." Friedr was doubtful this part of the plan could be implemented successfully.

"That is the beauty of this plan. The keep itself is guarded by D'Mal's elite personal forces, bound to him personally. They are his, body and soul." Aeolyn sat back on her heels. "However, the generals in the field are petty warlords, barely under control. To fully control them, he would have to sit on the Throne of Stone and Bone every minute of every day, and even he can't do such a thing. Their strength lies in their autonomy. As long as the generals *wish* to serve him, they do so wholeheartedly."

Friedr nodded his understanding and waited for Aeolyn to continue.

"But they are also children of the Bull God, and their priests resent the power Tauron has invested in Stefyn D'Mal. He has no outward signs of the change the warriors all must go through and which their priests have all undergone. He was never changed into a minotaur because he was groomed from childhood to be slipped into Mal Evol and take the throne by stealth. D'Mal is, therefore, not fully one of them in their eyes, yet he's been placed over them. We must encourage them to hide their dissention from him and sneak off before he realizes they've gone."

"So, the only soldiers who'll be left should be the castle guards. D'Mal will have to leave Mal Evol to deal with the renegades, which will also weaken his hold on them." Friedr removed the stone and rolled up the map, putting it carefully into the case. "That will still leave plenty of guards to frolic with while Edwin goes in to get Marya." He smiled happily, already engrossed in planning his battle. "I'm looking forward to it."

"There will be three of us and seventy or so of them." Aeolyn rolled her eyes at her husband's eagerness. "If we have to fight them, it'll be bad and they might even have the advantage. There must be a better way."

Friedr was already using his stone, sharpening his sword and humming softly to himself. "I need to fight something soon, or I'll lose my mind from the monotony, dear one. Even my sword is bored."

***

As he drifted off to sleep that night, Edwin watched Christoph setting the wards against the scorpions. He suddenly saw the solution to his problem of maintaining his barriers while he was out of his body or even simply sleeping. *It has to be set like a ward,* he thought, as he drifted off to sleep. *It's a ward against me. It is a barrier against my body feeling those sensations and betraying me to an early but pleasant grave, and now I know how to tie it off.* He rebuilt his barriers, expanding them to cover everyone who slept in the shelter, and tied them off, feeling a sense of peace as the new barrier/shield settled and remained firm. *It'll stay up and won't go away while I am sleeping.*

Edwin's feeling of exultation was diminished by his exhaustion. He decided to tell Christoph as soon as he returned but soon fell asleep instead. Nonetheless, his companions were pleased at his new skill, noticing it immediately when they entered the shelter. "No one else I know can shield an entire group of people. I thought it amazing he could protect Chris," Aeolyn told Friedr as she prepared to take her place at watch. "I wonder how he makes them stay up."

I'll sleep well for the first time in days, thought Christoph with relief as he climbed into his blankets. *D'Mal's dreams won't bleed over into mine. But what about Marya? There'll be no relief for her.* Troubled, he eventually fell asleep, hoping against hope she possessed the barriers to survive sleeping in the madman's domain.

Chapter 20

On the morning of their seventh day of watching the keep, Edwin rode the winds farther than he'd ever ventured, following a particular messenger, sent by a minotaur warlord to his brother. For three days, Edwin had been spreading rumors, and they had taken off like a fire raging through the land. When he began his task he had no idea of how ready the legions were for a real war, how much they resented being held back from the rewards they were promised. One by one, whole squads of the legions of D'Mal packed up and vanished into the east, as if they never existed.

The squad of minotaurs he now observed was camped in a hollow on the western border of Mal Evol. The tent that housed the general was surrounded by those of his lieutenants, who camped in twos. They were in turn surrounded by the foot soldiers, who slept in groups of four.

The camp was in turmoil, and the general was compelled to exert his authority most strongly to keep his men from simply abandoning their posts. He confronted the messenger and demanded the news the messenger had announced be repeated.

"Gutuk Province has fallen to the rabid dogs of Nuruk. Nuruk has taken advantage of this waste of time we must endure. They have abandoned this lost cause for a more lucrative war, and slaughtered all who stood in their way. Even now they feast on the spoils. The warriors of Nuruk are far from home, and their hearths are untended. Your brother, Nanchek, bids you to come with him to help hold the lands of Nuruk while their men are away from home." The messenger smiled. "He bids you to consider the mines that are now abandoned while their owners seek easy gold in Gutuk."

As the general looked around him, his men were breaking camp, preparing to leave with or without him. The wind seemed to whisper, "Gold! Gold for the taking." He snorted as he made up his mind.

"Tell Nanchek we'll join him. Anything is better than slowly rotting in this place. We've been lied to! There is no gold or glory here and no reason to remain."

Immediately after the messenger departed, the general re-exerted his authority, forcing the men to heed his words. "We go to Nuruk Province!" His men cheered, holding their fists in the air. "We must go quietly and quickly, or there will be naught left for us. Leave everything that will slow us down. Take only the food you can carry. There will be gold enough for us all!"

Within an hour, the camp was deserted, and the legions were leagues away, heading east more rapidly than Edwin would have believed if he hadn't seen it so many times over the previous three days.

Each time Edwin rode the winds, he was sorely tempted to peer into the window at the top of the tower, the rooms his dreams showed him were Marya's. Twice he glimpsed her in the garden, working the soil and tending the winter-dormant roses, surrounded by the wispy shadows she often spoke to. He didn't linger either time as he didn't know if she was sensitive to his observations or not. He couldn't get her out of his mind, constantly chiding himself for becoming obsessed with the girl he'd never actually met.

He began the return to his body to tell Aeolyn how

well things progressed, scouting for other squads moving toward the east as he went.

***

The days passed slowly. While they waited for the rumors to filter up the chain of command to D'Mal, they consolidated their position, making a comfortable base camp under the thorn canopy. They now rested much easier because they didn't have to sleep in their armor, being instead able to lay it out ready to put on at a moment's notice.

They were able to pull the door, a large tumbleweed, closed on their shelter at night, making it a home where the four of them could live comfortably. When they were inside, their body heat made it a cozy home. Edwin's shield now effectively protected them from the poison of the soil while they slept.

There was nothing to distinguish their den from any other thorn bush in the forest. Even the boulders marking the edge of the small cliff were ordinary. Many of greater size and visibility littered the hillsides, forming a crescent around the Shadow Castle. Edwin determined that it was completely invisible both from the air and the valley below. From this base camp, they had a view of the entire area and could clearly see the road leading from the keep to Mal Evol City. They mounted a constant watch, and though they occasionally saw messengers on the road, they hadn't seen anything to indicate D'Mal had heard any rumors of troubles in his homeland.

The four developed the habit of speaking in voices barely above a whisper, and for some reason, this drew them closer. At night, they listened to Chris telling many fabulous stories he'd learned when being trained as a bard. Sometimes they talked about their families and the people they missed back in Aeoven.

They often played a game with small stones, one interesting to Edwin as it was much like checkers. He, Christoph, and Friedr played it nearly all the time when they were not observing the castle, the third person watching and keeping score and then taking the place of the loser. Edwin was good at it, better than even Aeolyn. She disdained the game though, preferring instead to do small domestic tasks such as mending torn leathers and trying to keep the team as clean as possible, washing their clothes in the creek. She used a different place each time so she didn't create a visible trail to indicate anyone was frequenting the banks.

No one liked how stiff their leathers were when they dried, but it was better than stinking. They owned only one set of spare clothes, rolled up tightly in the bottom of their kit, so it was important to stay clean.

They stayed busy, and days turned into weeks as they waited for the defection of the legions to filter up to D'Mal.

***

On the afternoon of the twenty-fifth day, the four questers were still holed up outside the Shadow Castle. They had fallen into a routine, with Edwin and Aeolyn harrying the legions and Friedr and Christoph, for lack of a better word, skulking about, spying on the tool shed. They found a perfect watching place above and across the road from the kitchen gate, high enough to afford them a view of the guards atop the garden walls as well.

The weather had taken a sudden turn for the worse. At midday, the temperature began dropping, and fog was rising. It gradually thickened all day, and they all felt the cold. The mists periodically obscured their view, but for the most part, they were able to see the road. Only one wagon rumbled down the kitchen lane, the special supplies from Mal Evol City. Keeping a lookout in the cold, damp mist would be a trial for the watchers, but each would sit their turn regardless.

Friedr and Christoph watched from their hiding place above the kitchen gate as a messenger approached the guards. They abruptly left their posts and followed him to the barracks on the other side of the castle. None returned to take their place.

"We must take this chance to get the oil for the gate hinges," Friedr urged Christoph. "We have the lock picks, and now we have the opportunity." He'd been carrying the picks with him, waiting for the occasion to break in and steal the oil.

"It's too easy," Christoph replied, eyeing the empty parapet nervously. "Why have they left their posts? They never abandon them for any reason."

"I don't know, but it's too good an opportunity to pass up." Friedr was already on the move, crawling under the brush toward the kitchen lane. "We mustn't waste it."

"I hate this," Christoph muttered. "It feels like a trap."

They drifted from thorn brake to thorn brake, two silent shadows in the fog. Pausing for a moment, they hid behind the standing stones and then flitted to the overgrown brambles shrouding the stone walls, using the unusual mists to veil their movements. There was no sign they were seen.

Hidden from the kitchen window by the shed itself,

Friedr quietly unlocked the door. He quickly took the oilcan and after relocking the shed, they returned to their base as slowly and painstakingly as they had come. As they sat, nervously wondering if they'd been noticed, they saw the guards returning. They watched as they argued with each other briefly, which was extremely unusual. After they'd finished their quarrel, the guards each resumed the established routine that hadn't varied until that day, behaving as if nothing had changed.

"What do you make of it?" Friedr asked. "I don't think they liked what they heard, wherever they went."

Christoph shrugged, a look of worry on his face. "It can't be good, whatever it is."

***

While Friedr and Christoph watched the kitchen gate, Edwin took the time to search the earth beneath Mal Evol, looking for the underground river his father once used as an escape route. He found it at last, but was puzzled. It appeared too easy, much easier than Abbott Garran described.

It began in a well-hidden cave near the base of the keep and wound through the earth to the western border, where it emerged several days' walk north of Braden. *If you don't know exactly what you're looking for, you'll never see this.*

There was no sign of the door to the wine cellar Abbott Garran told him of. However, after much searching, Edwin found a place at the base of the butte that looked like it once held a large pair of double doors. They would have opened wide enough for a cart to pass through but looked as if they had been bricked up for many years, perhaps since D'Mal took the keep.

He entered the large, dry, sandy-floored cave. After much examining, he found a narrow tunnel hidden at the rear of it. He entered and followed the path carefully. It was easy, a gentle incline with good footing. Then he came to a sharp corner, followed by a narrow chasm he would have had to leap across. It could be done but would have been difficult to manage while carrying a baby.

He soon discovered that once a person was committed to this trail, things began to change for the worse. There were many blind corners and narrow ledges where a group would have to slide along single file, pressed against the wall for long, dangerous stretches. The uneven path was slick with damp moss and mud. It would be impossible to hurry in this place, and yet he knew his father, Halee, and Garran had been forced to run much of the way with Jaxon.

After only a short time, Edwin realized the hidden path had been discovered. Parts of it were pulled down and rearranged to force the escapee down the route D'Mal created especially for them. Half a league down to the underground river, fugitives were required to scale a fifteen-foot drop with only some handholds to help them down. It would be terribly difficult to return quickly. To use this road now would be a fatal error.

His fears were confirmed when after many leagues he came to a cavern. At the end of the narrow, tortuous path was the den of a water-drake. There was a tiny exit, but a person would have to get past the creature and then crawl on his belly through the tunnel. The area was littered with bones and rags. A minotaur's scratched and dented breastplate lay in the mud near the river.

You have a neat solution to your problem, D'Mal, Edwin thought sardonically. *Leave your escapees just enough hope so they put themselves completely in a no-win situation.* Edwin couldn't wait to leave the depressing place. *It's like the thorns and the feral rat-people. You don't even have to feed your pet—it takes care of itself.*

He returned to his body and opened his eyes. Aeolyn looked at him expectantly. "Well?"

"There's no way out. It's a death trap." Edwin yawned, surprising himself and, snapping his mouth shut, apologized for his rudeness. Aeolyn smothered a laugh at the look on his face. Recovering, he explained what was done to the subterranean river. She nodded and said they would have to leave the way they came.

"You need to rest now. Christoph will dismember me if he returns to find you looking like you do." Aeolyn pushed him to his bedroll.

"Yes little mother," he replied with a mischievous grin, borrowing the pet name Christoph always used. She smiled and gave him a little shove.

***

Seven-thirty was fast approaching, and Marya's hands shook as she checked her appearance in the mirror. Maisy had dressed her hair perfectly as usual, and she wore Stefyn's favorite gown, a trailing dress created of deep amethyst velvet that at one time she would have been thrilled to wear. The bodice was cut so low she was forced to leave her stone shard in her room, tucked safely under her mattress. Her nails were clean and buffed to a shine. She hadn't gone outside because a fog, thick and chill, covered the land. It was the first time she'd seen mist like that since she'd arrived. The temperature dropped as the day progressed, and she'd fed the fire in her room all afternoon.

She was now bedecked in the jewelry Stefyn insisted on giving her, though she despised it. Earrings, necklace, bracelets, and rings—the beautiful amethysts set with diamonds in white gold marked her as belonging to him as surely as if they were collars on a dog. Everything looked perfect, but she was almost too apprehensive to go down to dinner. However, she would go despite her trepidation. The consequence of disobedience was too much to contemplate.

That afternoon, Stefyn hadn't appeared for high tea. He never missed it. Whatever could have kept him away, she couldn't imagine. Marya was frightened some new torment had been arranged for her. He never altered his routine unless he had a reason, and those reasons terrified her.

Only the day before, Stefyn had been so charming all through the afternoon tea. But afterward, he suddenly decided to escort her back to her apartment himself instead of having the guard do it, which meant he would be behind schedule in his work. Once they arrived at her door, he casually mentioned he'd sent her Temple armor to be broken up and melted down as she had no use for it any longer. It broke her heart, but she didn't show any emotion, simply nodding her head and suffering him to kiss her hand—a lingering, caressing kiss that disturbed her more than words could express.

When she'd looked in her closet, all her possessions were gone—her armor, boots, and even the filthy leathers she'd worn in the dungeon for that long, terrible time. *I should have washed them and hidden them somewhere. But I'm not allowed to go into the bath chamber without Maisy. He fears I'll drown myself, and so I would, if I could.* Somehow, she made it through dinner the previous evening, numbly answering and politely laughing at all the right places while Stefyn behaved as if nothing had happened.

Of course, she supposed, to him nothing *had* happened. He'd manipulated her into the corner he wanted her in, and now he was systematically removing all her ties to the Temple and Neveyah. It was just another day to him.

But then last night, his dreams caught her by surprise again, and she was completely unprepared for what his mind was occupied with.

No amount of soap could wash the filth out of my mind. I'll kill myself. I will! Her thoughts ran in circles like a rat in a trap.

Promptly at seven twenty-five, the bar on her door was lifted and it swung open. This time it was the massive guard called Wint, who stood there, ready to take her down to the dining room. He'd gotten off lucky today, not having to carry her tools in the pathetic little basket that made him look so silly when he followed her around the garden.

And now she had to go down to dinner, not knowing what Stefyn planned for her or what her role would be. Marya followed her hulking guard in as docile a manner as Stefyn could wish for, her knees as weak as water. As she entered the dining room, she was completely surprised but didn't show it. The table was set for one, and a note stood propped against her wine glass.

My Darling,

I have been called away to settle a dispute beyond the borders to the east. Know I am ever careful of your welfare and have ensured you are most secure. I would never leave you unprotected. After your meal this evening, you will remain in your quarters until I return. Maisy will see to your needs. Brec will release the dogs once you have returned to your rooms. We will be bonded immediately upon my return.

Only the promise of our wedding consoles me as I depart on this detestable journey. Whoever began this farce will pay dearly for it. I wait most impatiently for our bonding night, my dear, dear Marya. It gratifies me to know how often your mind will be occupied with thoughts of our mutual bliss. What we have shared in our dreams is only the merest shadow of what is still to come. The physical side of our life will be most satisfying, I am sure.

Until my return, I remain yours devotedly,
Stefyn

She was to be locked in her rooms, for how long she didn't know. And then she was to be bonded to him after all.

The guards stared at her as she attempted to eat her meal, and she saw their hatred. She'd never seen it before, so why now? *Perhaps it was always there, but they never dared to show it in Stefyn's presence. Strange, I can see it, but I don't feel it. What has happened? My magic is gone, and I don't feel anyone anymore.* Still, she didn't speak to them. She knew better.

Her guards escorted her back to her room, and she heard the bar drop, locking her in, locking her away from the sun until Stefyn returned to make her his bride. *His bride....* Marya's lips trembled, and tears rolled down her cheeks.

As she lay down in her bed, her hand automatically slid under her mattress for the stone shard she'd kept for so long, only to find it gone, replaced with a note.

This was not polite, my dear. Do not worry. I will be as gentle and loving as you deserve. It is your choice. You must deserve it.

She lay staring at nothing until long after the candle guttered out.

Chapter 21

Aeolyn stood the first watch of the evening, her spyglass trained on the valley below. As she observed the dark castle, the moon emerged from behind the clouds. A fine, black carriage left the main gate, making its way down the road to the east.

It was the first time a carriage had been seen to enter or leave the keep.

Jumping up, Aeolyn hurried to wake Edwin, dragging him out of his blankets, wearing only his shirt and underclothes, barefoot and barelegged.

"You must see who's in the carriage." She pulled him to the rocks. "Pray to the Goddess that Marya isn't in it."

He was highly agitated at the thought. Forcibly raising his barriers and calming himself, Edwin sent his spirit out. He floated lightly on the wind and slowly approached the carriage, a gentle breeze drifting down the road.

Ice formed on the thorn forest wherever the mist stood, wrapping it in crystal. Thick fog hugged the valley, and rising high, both the waning crescent of the moon and the myriad stars shone brilliantly in the cold sky, brightly illuminating the crystalline landscape.

As Edwin drew near to the carriage, he could hear the horses breathing hard and the crack of the whip as the driver urged them forward. The lanterns swayed in the darkness. *The horses won't last long at the rate he's pushing them. He must have extras stationed along the road.* The driver and a footman rode atop the fast-moving coach. Both were swathed in heavy cloaks and scarves against the cold. *There's no lady's maid. It's a good sign.*

Edwin was afraid to get too close. No one knew the extent of the abilities the mad priest possessed, nor did they understand how the magic of the Bull God was expressed. The only thing he knew about Stefyn D'Mal was he was known to be capricious, cruel, and volatile, with immense chi to draw upon. The companions had discussed this, and all agreed Edwin must be extremely cautious where D'Mal was concerned.

Ghosting to the luggage rack, he looked at the baggage, counting the trunks and satchels. The baron was traveling in style, but it appeared only one important person was inside. Edwin wasn't sure if he should try to peer in but knew he must in order to satisfy his own anxiety. What he would do if Marya was in there he didn't know. *I could stop the horses' hearts if I had to. It would give me some time to plan a rescue.*

After hesitating for a long while, he finally dared to look. As lightly as he could, he peered inside the carriage. The curtains were drawn but not quite all the way, and a lantern was lit. A handsome, dark-haired man who appeared to be about Edwin's age sat alone reading something that made him angry. His eyes were savage as he read and reread the letter. A massive quantity of unfocused chi fairly crackled and wildly surged around him. With his healing sight, Edwin could see a reddish-purple aura radiating from him. This man could only be Stefyn, Baron D'Mal. Edwin had never seen anyone like him.

He immediately ghosted away after the one brief glimpse and drifted back, looking over the walls of the keep. No one was there except the guards, and he wondered where the dogs were.

He searched for them a while longer before returning to his cold body. As Edwin returned to consciousness, the shock was overwhelming. He could hardly breathe and couldn't move well.

Aeolyn saw he was back and in distress.

"It's my fault," she muttered as she dragged him bodily through the entrance of the shelter. "Quickly, Friedr. Get his cloak! He's chilled to the bone. What was I thinking? I'm an idiot."

Friedr and Christoph looked at each other and as one, they placed Edwin between them. Wrapping their arms around him, they attempted to warm him with their own body heat. Aeolyn wrapped them all together with a blanket, rubbing Edwin's feet with her hands.

It was a long while before he could make any sense when he spoke. After they got him thawed and into his bedroll, Edwin kept apologizing for not gearing up before he went out, thanking them for once again saving his sorry arse from his own folly. "I was so afraid he had her with him. I couldn't think beyond that."

Aeolyn was unusually quiet and volunteered little, returning to her post as soon as she could, sitting a bleak, solitary watch.

The hood of her cape was pulled forward, as close around her as possible, and her bandanna, tucked into the neck of her cape, covered her cheeks and mouth. Even in her gloves, Aeolyn's fingers were cold. She didn't notice.

When Friedr emerged to take his place as sentry, he put his hand on her shoulder and asked her what she was thinking about.

After a moment, she said, "I made a bad decision tonight and didn't make sure my team member was equipped for the weather. He could have died."

"And how is what happened tonight only your fault? He knows to gear up," Friedr replied. "What's really bothering you?"

"I dragged him out of his blankets and gave him no choice." Aeolyn still refused to look at him. "It was a bad decision. Father Rall...he has too much faith in me. I just demonstrated I don't have the ability to lead."

"That's crap. You know it and I know it." Friedr's voice was rough, and his barbarian accent grew more pronounced. "Father Rall is never wrong about his *visions*. But in other areas...well, look how poorly he chose when he bonded."

Aeolyn didn't know how to reply. It was true the Holy Father's bonding was known to be difficult at best. "Affairs of the heart are not what we're discussing. No one *leads* as well as he does. I'm afraid I will fail our people. I failed Edwin tonight."

"Yes, you rushed him out to take advantage of an opportunity. Yes, it did put him in danger, but again, I will say Edwin knows to gear up before going out. It was laid out, ready for him, and yet he didn't put it on, though it would have taken only a few minutes. He also was in too much of a hurry." Friedr held her close, saying, "You always do this. Stop second guessing yourself. No one is perfect." He kissed her forehead. "How hard it would be to live with you if you were."

They sat the watch together, his cloak sheltering them both.

Inside the shelter, Christoph and Edwin talked

quietly, unable to sleep from the excitement. Christoph had healed Edwin, and he'd taken no harm from his chill.

"We're almost at the end of this part of the quest, aren't we?" Edwin stared at the rough ceiling. "We have two more nights until the next dark of the moon, and we still don't know anything about the inside of the keep."

"Don't worry," Christoph replied. He rolled onto his side, supporting his head on one hand as he looked through the darkness at Edwin's shadowy form. "Now D'Mal has departed, you can freely search. We need to know the layout of the interior. You'll be fine. You will scout it tomorrow."

Edwin's mind couldn't stop spinning. He rolled over and faced Christoph. "What if Friedr can't take care of the dogs? They must be inside the castle since they aren't in the kennel or out patrolling the neighborhood with that huge trainer of theirs."

"It seems likely they're inside," agreed Christoph. "But, you know Friedr will have no trouble with them. He's chafing at not having any really good foes to fight. We'll be going through the castle and systematically removing the guards with sleep spells. The ones on the parapet all stay within tight boundaries and never go beyond them. It must be one of D'Mal's special rules because the children of the Bull God are not usually so disciplined."

"They fear him," said Edwin. "They seem to hate him, but their fear completely overpowers them. They don't even mention him by name. They refer to him as 'he.' No whispers of mine will encourage them to disobey him in any way, though I have spread the rumors to them. When I scout the walls, all I ever see are the guards reporting to each other and following the most rigid rules in discharging their duties."

"I've studied all that's known of him, because no one understands the nature of his magic. Stefyn D'Mal leaves nothing to chance unless there is no other option," Christoph replied. "The guards at the keep are under the strongest of compulsions. I feel sure those coercions will hold until his return. These soldiers won't leave their posts, at least not alive."

"What if Marya won't leave? She doesn't know me and has no reason to trust anyone at this point." Edwin turned back to staring at the rough ceiling. All he could think about was the girl he'd seen only in his dreams. The power of his sudden fear that she might be gone caused him to examine his feelings more deeply.

"I can't imagine she won't know you're from the Temple," Christoph said dryly. "You have more augmentations than two mages glued together. Even without them, the armor should tell her who you are." Finally, he surreptitiously cast a low-level sleep spell on Edwin, fearing that as excited as he was, he wouldn't be able to stand his watch.

Edwin was quiet for a moment. "Do you believe in love at first sight?" His voice sounded sleepy.

Christoph lay silent. Feelings he kept buried surged, and it took everything he had to hide them and calm himself. "Yes," was all he said. He didn't want to continue the conversation, fearing where it would go and not wanting to hear what he already knew was true.

"I think I do, too. When I thought she might be gone, I forgot everything you taught me. I couldn't let her be gone. I couldn't lose her." Edwin drifted into a light doze that soon deepened into a restful, dreamless sleep.

Christoph stared across at the man who loved him like a brother, tears burning in his eyes. Resolutely, he ran through his calming exercises, but they weren't effective. *I'm such an idiot. If anyone knew, they would call me up before the conclave and demote me back to journeyman.*

At last, he rose and dressed quietly, intending to relieve Friedr and Aeolyn early.

As he moved up beside them, they could see the turmoil on their friend's normally cheerful face. They looked at each other, and a moment of understanding passed between them. "I'll share your watch a while if you don't mind," offered Friedr. "I'm unable to sleep just yet."

"I, however, am quite tired, so I will leave you two to watch without me." Squeezing Friedr's hand one last time, Aeolyn disappeared into the shelter.

Friedr and Christoph knelt behind the rock outcropping, speaking in low whispers and surveying the valley. The thorn forest below them was completely covered in a coat of ice crystals, lending the desolate valley a fairy-tale quality. The ice-encased forest shone in the light of the rising crescent of the moon, reflecting it many times, dispelling all shadows. It was eerie and unearthly beautiful but allowed no place to hide near the walls of the keep.

"D'Mal has wrought this to make sure no unwelcome guests can sneak in while he's away." Friedr's words were quiet but certain. "The mist freezing to the very bushes, reflecting light until the night is as bright as day—it's clever. It's nearly springtime. I wonder how he does it."

"He can use the Throne of Stone and Bone to bind the weather to his will, though it won't last long after he departs the soil of Mal Evol. But we knew there had to be a reason the omens all tell us we must wait for a moon-dark night," replied Christoph with a lopsided smile.

They looked down on the gloomy castle, seeing the small glow of a lone candle in one high window of the dark tower.

After a while, Friedr gently asked, "What's troubling you tonight?"

Christoph felt an unreasonable surge of anger and quashed it firmly. He managed to speak calmly. "It's not something I wish to burden you with and is nothing important. It's only the inability to fall asleep after all our excitement tonight." He turned to find Friedr giving him a look he knew all too well.

"There is a problem. It's one you find difficult to accept, and this makes it important. It can affect the stability of this team, and I won't allow it." Friedr's voice was quiet. "You've fallen in love with Edwin."

Pain, desolation, and embarrassment raged in Christoph's eyes. "You can't fix this," he told Friedr. "I have to learn to live with it."

"Yes, you *do* have to. He's not as you are. You told me so yourself when we first saw him in Wister." Friedr probed the soreness the way a surgeon lanced a boil. "You're too involved. You do this every time. You *must* practice disassociating yourself better. You start out fine, but you forget to practice what you teach. Then we have to have this conversation." He looked back at the shelter, but all was quiet. "My brother, you would have been a great bard if it hadn't been for the Temple and your healing talent. You romanticize everything, but then you get hurt. You've had a passion for every man you meet at one time or another, including me. You always get over it. This is no different."

"But Friedr, I like men. Who is manlier than you?" Christoph's weak attempt at humor fell flat. "Most men Edwin's age are bonded and awaiting their first child."

Christoph watched the valley as the moon rose higher. All was serene, the stars sparkling above and ice shimmering below. "He's old and wise, and yet young and guileless as a babe. He was never meant for me. I know this, no one better." His bleak smile made his face somehow sadder. "The Goddess has a plan for him. Her plan involves his children and his children's children. He will rescue his dream girl in the tower, and they will live happily ever after, and from them will come the Hero Foretold. Uncle Friedr can't mend this for me."

"It's true he's bound to the prophecies. He has no say in this. Look at what the Goddess has already asked of him, how he has been turned into this far-seer." Friedr watched Christoph's profile. "She gave him these skills because the only way to do this is to cheat, and Edwin is our secret ace-up-the-sleeve. But he's also here for another reason, and *nothing* will interfere with that aspect of the Goddess's plan for him." He sighed heavily, remembering a conversation with Edwin regarding the women who couldn't leave him alone. "She placed a vision of Marya in his heart long before he came here, I think. There will be no one for him but her—ever. Aeos nightly sends him dreams. It has ever been the fate of his family. The Goddess rewards them for their service to her, blessing them with true, faithful love, but in return, she demands their children. It is her will and her plan."

"I know this, really I do! You know I was there and heard the prophecy. That's why this is so upsetting to me. I don't *want* to feel this way. I know better, but this stupid part of me always wants what I can't have," Christoph replied sadly. "He asked me tonight if I believe in love at first sight. I told him I do. I didn't tell him I feel it every week and desperately wish I didn't." His eyes were focused on the tower window. The dim, flickering light faded, as if the sole candle had guttered out. "It would be so much easier if I'd been made differently. What I would change about myself, if I could, is this inability to control my impulses. I want to settle down with Dane and be a family. I want it so badly, but I'm afraid to commit because of this very thing. I'm terrified I will do the unforgivable in a moment of weakness. What would happen to Zan if I broke up our family over some stupid thing like this? Children need security. Zan deserves security."

"You're absolutely right about how bad it would be for the boy. He so badly wants you three to be a real family. It's all he can talk about. What are you going to do now?" Friedr felt tiredness beginning to seep into him.

"I'm going to be the brother Edwin considers me to be and be grateful for that. I'm going to compose sad songs of unrequited love until I feel better. And I will learn to live in my own skin, thanks to Uncle Friedr, who always manages to fix things for me," Christoph replied, with a real smile. Friedr could see the resignation turning to peace in his eyes. "Now you must go to your blankets, and I will practice my basic exercises. I'll be fine tomorrow. You'll see."

"And perhaps you will be more patient with Dane when you next see him." Friedr's voice was kind, and full of compassion.

Christoph could only nod, and his eyes filled with tears of remorse. "I have never wanted to be cruel to him. Never. Oh, Goddess, I love him. But Friedr, I am so wrong for him. Dane deserves someone who wants to make him the center of his universe. I'm not that way. I can't seem to be faithful, though I always mean to be. I always vow I will, and then I keep hurting him, with affairs that mean nothing to me. But I can't let him go either." He sighed, hating himself. "It will kill me when he finds someone who is truly worthy of him. But you and I both know it will happen unless I can commit to him. I'm just so wrong for him."

"Well, we all agree with you on that score. And we all hope for your sake it doesn't come to such an event. But the heart is a strange and willful thing. We never know what's around the corner, do we?" Friedr's voice was beginning to sound tired, but he remained by Christoph's side. "I never thought I would have a chance with Aeolyn when we were students, but the Goddess looked on me kindly, and now she's my wife."

"She can still kick your backside all over the practice yard whenever you try to best her." Christoph's laugh was low. "Like when we were novices. She uses her brains to beat the heck out of your brawn."

"Yes, she certainly can!" Friedr's answering chuckle was wry. "Oh yes, she is one crafty woman but well worth the effort."

"Somehow, Uncle Friedr always makes me see things better." Christoph looked up at his friend. "Thank you. You really are my brother."

They both watched the valley for a while, and then Friedr turned, and after laying his huge hand on Christoph's shoulder sympathetically, he went off to bed. Neither Aeolyn nor Edwin stirred as he removed his gear and crawled into his bedroll.

Chapter 22

Edwin sat watching the fog-shrouded valley as the sun rose. The thick mist hugged the frozen ground, coating the thorn forest in ice. The land was silent. Even the birds voiced no calls, and he wondered if it was because of the unaccustomed cold or something else.

He waited to send his spirit out to ride the wind or sail under the earth until the others were awake. Christoph was still afraid he would get lost, and while once a possibility, it no longer was an issue for Edwin. He was practicing layering a buffer of water into his healer's barrier and was now automatically able to separate himself from the lure of the magic with no effort at all. He maintained it with ease, but as the junior member of the team, he followed their wishes and learned as much as he could from them in the process.

The fog wasn't natural. Neither was the cold, though he couldn't imagine how D'Mal managed the strange weather. *He must have used the throne. I will definitely want to get a look at the fabled Throne of Stone and Bone when I do take a look around in there.* He wore his cloak pulled closely around him, with his hood up and his bandanna covering the lower half of his face to keep his cheeks warm.

The first rays of light shone over the valley, creating an ethereal, beautiful landscape. Silent, the sun rose and the wisps of fog that hugged the vale below glowed softly pink and golden, turning the haunted keep into a veiled, fairytale castle. The mist-enshrouded

Shadow Castle stood in the center of the crystal-encased thorn forest shining like a sea of diamonds.

It was a vision Edwin would never forget. The power and mystery of the view spread before him weren't dimmed in any way by the purpose driving him. He knew with certainty he was poised on the edge of the most important event in his life. The ethereal beauty of the sunrise over the misty valley underscored the awesome wonder of the moment, forever etched in his memory. Edwin's eyes were full of indescribable emotions as he gazed on the sight.

Friedr wordlessly moved up to sit next to him, and they watched the sunrise together in comfortable silence.

The day brightened, and the crystalline coating of ice on the thorn forest gradually began melting wherever the sun's rays touched it. Edwin moved to the front of their shelter and called the water for the day, letting it fill his palms and spill into the basin. He'd developed a way to fill the bottles without touching the water by forming it with his air-magic and funneling it, pleasing Aeolyn. "I'd like to learn this skill," she said when she first saw him do it. "This is much better than the other way, though the other way is better than dying of thirst."

Friedr trained his spyglass on the walls of the Shadow Castle, watching the guards changing, noticing the conversations that happened as the next group came on duty. "It isn't normal," he muttered. "Not normal at all."

"I wonder what they're chatting about." Christoph knelt beside Friedr, his spyglass trained on the castle guards. "There were exchanges yesterday when they returned from their meeting." The two mages spoke in low whispers, their cloaks blending into the landscape making them indistinguishable from their surroundings.

"We need to eavesdrop on them, so when Edwin has finished with the water, let's have him follow them for a while," Aeolyn said from over Friedr's shoulder. "Sound carries too well in this cold. I don't want to risk having them hear us skulking around." She knelt between them, training her own glass on the road leading to the main entry of the keep. "I wish we understood Edwin's trick of calling water from the mist so we could share the task between us. No matter how I try, I can't seem to do it."

"I believe it has to do with his growing affinity with this strange air-magic he's developed. It seems to me he's now coming into his full powers. He has developed a fine touch when he heals. I noticed he used very little chi, less than I would have even, when he took care of the gash you got yesterday, and you won't have a scar," Christoph replied. "This tells me he's truly coming into his powers as a healer adept. If you agree that he is at full strength, you should test him for his battle-magics when we get to where we can do so without drawing attention to ourselves, to see what his strongest element is. I have a theory, but I want to wait and see how he does before I show my true ignorance." He laughed at himself.

"Now you sound like Abbess Halee. You will rewrite the theory of magic one day, I'm sure," teased Aeolyn. "She never offers an opinion until she has complete and total proof she is right. You two and your study of the workings of magic—once you get talking about it, no one can stop you. So what's your theory?"

"I've been fortunate to be her assistant." Christoph's smile lit up his face. "I never lose an argument as long as I remember her wisdom. It's when I forget the distinctions between theory and fact that I get into trouble. But since you asked, I think he is equally strong in each element, that his battle strength is equally balanced with his healing gift."

"I hate to change the subject, but look down there," Friedr nudged Christoph. They all trained their spyglasses on the kitchen gate, where the lane serving the rear of the castle entered the kitchen courtyard. Two guards carried a bundle out. They weren't in a hurry and were arguing about something. They stopped and one gestured toward the keep, and then they moved on.

"I can't make out what they're doing, can you?" Aeolyn strained to see. "What were they carrying?"

"I can't tell, but they left it by the scrap heap instead of the midden heap," replied Friedr. "We should go down and see what it is." He pulled his cloak closer. "Edwin can't do everything all by himself."

"No, you don't have to go in person," Edwin quietly came up behind them and also trained his little glass on the kitchen courtyard. "I've a feeling it would be bad. Sound travels too clearly in this cold now that the mist has risen. That's why D'Mal has created this bit of weather, I'm sure. He wants no one to be able to sneak up while he's away. I've filled all the jugs and the basin. I will refill it for each of us to have as good a bath with cold water as we can in this weather. After we eat, I can go have a look on the wind. I'll also shadow the guards and listen to what they're saying when they meet on their rounds. I need to eat first." He looked apologetically at Aeolyn as he spoke.

They all turned to look at him. "You haven't used much chi to get the water today. That's good. You're really getting better at that. And you should eat, we all should." Aeolyn's smile was rueful. "I often forget."

"It's easy to skip meals. We have a lot to occupy us, and the rations don't seem to be as tasty as they once were," Friedr commented. "They're better than starving though and better than leaving ourselves open to the mad priest."

***

Edwin drifted over the valley slowly. Where the sun's rays touched, the ice was mostly melted, but in the shadows, the canopy remained encased. Many birds were frozen to death in the unusual cold snap, but on the positive side, so were many of the scorpions. Despite the partial thaw, the moisture didn't drop to the forest floor. Instead, the thirsty canopy absorbed much of it before the cold, dry air evaporated the rest.

Slowly, Edwin ghosted toward the scrap pile at the rear of the courtyard, and what he saw there pleased him. It was clearly Temple armor, and while it had been broken apart, it could easily be mended, and a bundle of rags also lay there. He quickly snapped back to his body. He was seated in the center of his friends, as they had decided his body didn't generate enough warmth for the cold weather when he was out of it.

Edwin's eyes opened, and immediately, Aeolyn lowered her spyglass to hear what he had to say. "I've found Marya's armor. At least, I think it's hers. It's for a small woman, about your height, Aeolyn, green-lacquered and embossed with blue morning glories and gold butterflies."

"Yes! It's her armor." Her voice was low but

exultant. "I was worried about how she could travel through all these thorns without it."

"It's broken up, but I can fix it, or you can. They didn't do too thorough a job of it." He took a sip of water and a bite of his morning ration bar. "The first trick will be retrieving it, and the second, repairing it. There was a bundle of rags and leather that may have been her clothes. Hopefully, her boots are there. "

"If they aren't, we can make something from some of the things the legions abandoned," replied Aeolyn. "I've been planning ways to use it to give her some protection for the journey home."

"I can make her a pair of bootlets such as we use in my village in the summer," replied Friedr. "There's enough leather abandoned in the nearest camp to do it. It would be better, though, if we didn't have to take the time to do this once we have gotten her out of the tower."

"If her boots aren't there when you go down to steal back her armor, you will have to make a pair to fit me, and they'll do nicely for her. We're nearly the same size," replied Aeolyn. "We must have everything ready for her the moment we have her out of there."

"I'll eavesdrop on the guards now." Edwin calmed himself and sent his spirit out, seeking the conversations that occurred each time the guards met on their rounds since the departure of their master.

Friedr and Christoph quietly discussed how they could set about retrieving the armor without tipping off the guards.

"If we simply take it off the pile, they'll miss it when they go out with the next bunch of scrap," Aeolyn reminded them. "What we want to do is leave enough behind so they don't notice the important pieces are gone."

"Every piece is important," Friedr disagreed. "We've been gashed, bitten, and attacked every day on this little trip. There isn't one piece of my armor that hasn't been useful in protecting me."

"That's true, but what do you suggest we do to hide our theft?" Aeolyn looked at him hopefully. "We can't let them know we're out here."

"I don't have an answer, not yet. I'll think about it, and by tonight, if no other opportunity turns up, we'll have to sneak in under cover of such darkness as we may have and steal it then," Friedr promised. "I know you don't like to leave anything to chance, but let's see what else happens down there today."

"You are hereby in charge of the armor retrieval issue," she replied, her eyes twinkling. "I'll concentrate on watching the roads to see who comes and goes."

Christoph listened to this little exchange with a teasing grin on his face. "You've taken well to Father Rall's instruction to 'delegate'!"

She rolled her eyes.

While his companions talked in low whispers, Edwin drifted near the parapet atop the wall and stopped at a place where two of the guards would meet and turn around to retrace their steps.

The surly minotaurs approached each other, glaring, and turned away to their appointed rounds without speaking. Edwin tried another pair, with the same results. He noticed the guards seethed with anger and resentment, piquing his curiosity. He decided to linger at one place and wait to hear whatever he could.

Two hulking soldiers approached the place where

they met, and this time they stopped for a moment and spoke, picking up the conversation where they'd apparently left off earlier.

"You should be glad we didn't run off with Narg and his boys," the first guard's voice grated. "I don't want to wake up and find my bloody skin hanging on the wall in the barracks."

"But we don't have a choice, right?" Guard Two was clearly upset. "We has to stay here. We don't have the choice Narg had. I cain't stop walking the watch, though I would if'n I could. My feet do it without me." And he turned, walking away to the other end of his clearly defined area.

"We does our jobs like we're told," replied Guard One, as he too turned. "I don't want to end my days like Narg, but you will if'n you don't shut yer gob. You know *he* don't want us yammering on duty."

"You mean we does it like we is bespelled to do," the voice of Guard Two floated back. "It's no choice. It's dark magic. *He* didn't have to flay Narg. It's bad for morale." He shuddered as he said that.

Edwin drifted around for most of the morning in an effort to hear more of what they were so disturbed about. When he visited the barracks, he soon discovered the source of their discontent. Then he checked the kennel, still finding no dogs. As he drifted, following the guards and eavesdropping, he pieced together the events of the day before that culminated in D'Mal departing in the dark, fuming and consumed by a murderous rage.

Returning to his body, Edwin stretched, aware of everyone's questioning glances. "I know what happened yesterday," he said. "But I need to rest for a while. I'm sorry," he yawned, feeling guilty for needing to recharge his chi.

"You go in. We'll follow in a few minutes," Christoph told him, casting ease so Edwin would rest better. "Get yourself situated and we'll be right in."

Friedr watched something down the hill from their post. Aeolyn looked to see if it threatened them and then resumed putting her spyglass into its case and stowing away.

"We should hear what he found out before we go about retrieving Marya's armor," Christoph said as he, too, looked to see what Friedr was staring at. A vulture now dined on the corpse of a bird who hadn't survived the night.

"It won't be the last, I fear. None of the birds here were ready for the deep cold," Friedr said, shrugging gloomily. "At least the scorpions aren't as bad a problem as they were."

Soon they were all gathered inside the shelter, sipping water and eating a small lunch. Edwin began the tale he was able to piece together.

"Yesterday morning, a messenger arrived from Nuruk informing D'Mal the border had suddenly erupted in unprecedented violence. The legions have completely abandoned Mal Evol and invaded Nuruk and Gutuk. Apparently, we have begun something that is now completely out of hand. It has spread so rapidly the neighboring province of Mektec is now burning, and Khelen, the province of their holy city, is inundated with refugees and is under siege. There is rampant starvation and disease. No place in Serende is unaffected."

"I can live with that." Friedr's wry comment

elicited smiles all around. "Abbess Halee and Abbot Garran will be happy to hear of this misfortune in the lands of the Bull God. Perhaps we have prevented the same thing happening in Braden and eastern Neveyah." Aeolyn nodded her agreement.

"So this is what happened yesterday. They were called to witness the disciplining of one of their own, as one squad of deserters wasn't quick enough getting out of the area. D'Mal's personal aide, a huge warrior named Brec, brought the stragglers back in chains right after D'Mal received the bad news from the provinces. Needless to say, he was beyond enraged.

"He apparently summoned everyone to the mess hall at the barracks to make an example of the deserters. He stood the unfortunate squad leader, a fellow named Narg, in the center of the room. Somehow, D'Mal used his magic to strip the poor fellow of his skin, which now hangs on the wall. He did this before the legions' eyes. The process apparently took several, extremely uncomfortable minutes. What's left is still in the middle of the floor."

"Unfortunate for Narg, indeed." Friedr's dry comment was echoed by everyone. They looked at each other in shocked disbelief.

"The rest of the deserters were also punished publicly, so severely two died during the night. He used some sort of spell that broke their bones as they stood there." Edwin looked ill as he explained what he'd seen. "They're recovering in the dungeon, not that I'm surprised to hear D'Mal has one. Some may survive their injuries but will surely be crippled. You know how minotaurs treat their cripples. They're likely to be killed before they make it home, if they somehow survive the dungeon. The guards are divided as to their opinion of the punishment that was meted out. Some are saying it went too far and has destroyed morale. But the guards are still under the compulsions D'Mal has woven. They can't physically leave no matter what they consciously want."

"What of this Brec? What do you hear of him?" Aeolyn still looked slightly pale, thinking of the cruelty.

"Oh, he is apparently a wonderful fellow. Brec is the dogs' trainer and completely under D'Mal's spell," replied Edwin. "He terrifies the guards only slightly less than the mad priest himself. What he lacks in magic he makes up for in brutality. No one will disobey him. But this is the interesting part—they believe D'Mal sees through Brec's eyes and hears through his ears."

Friedr looked questioningly at Aeolyn, and she shrugged, as did Christoph.

"Yet, some are grumbling, you say. Is it enough to stir up sedition in the barracks?" Christoph's question was asked with a calm voice, but the thought of using healing empathy to torture even the minotaur warriors nauseated him.

"No. No one will risk D'Mal's wrath." Edwin was sure of the truth of his assessment. "And, Chris, don't let this affect you too badly. I have learned a great deal about them this last month. The children of Tauron are a harsh people. Their daily life is filled with instances of casual brutality. This is most prevalent among the men who have willingly undergone the change and become Tauron's elite minotaur warriors. We observed this casual cruelty firsthand while we were spreading rumors. They don't see the world the way we do. They only value strength, and only the strong survive in their society. Narg and his boys got caught. To most of them, this means they were weak and best weeded out of the population. The guards all admit Stefyn D'Mal is much stronger than they are, so they follow him despite the fact he is fully human in appearance, and a small one compared to them at that. Yesterday was just another day for most of them, albeit a day they would prefer not to repeat."

Chris shook his head slowly, saying, "I understand what you're trying to tell me, but I don't like it."

Edwin agreed with him, saying, "No reasonable person would. You're right. I don't like it either. It's a perversion of the gift, but that's how it is."

"Well, we'll have to deal with the guards somehow when we go to get Marya, but we've always known we would. What we did *not* know about is this Brec. Now we do." Aeolyn pursed her lips, as she thought for a moment. "Is it possible for D'Mal to see and hear through him?"

Christoph snorted. "Who knows what's possible? He has powers we have no understanding of. Look at his control of the weather. I would say it's likely he could when he chooses to, but it must take incredible amounts of chi to do so."

Friedr was silent, thinking about what Edwin said and now he spoke quietly. "We must assume he *can* use this Brec in such a fashion. This makes him dangerous. We need to eliminate him immediately, and in such a way D'Mal doesn't realize it." He looked at Christoph. "A sleep spell or perhaps a potion liberally applied in his wine should do it, agreed?"

"Which is the way I intended to help, since I have

no stomach for killing." Christoph's smile was bleak. "I don't have the ingredients available in this wretched wilderness to mix an effective sleeping potion, but I'll spend my chi carefully, on select victims."

They began to build their plans for the actual rescue of Marya. Edwin tried to listen but soon drifted into a light sleep. He knew exactly what he needed to do. The Goddess had shown him many times.

When Aeolyn left the shelter to resume watching the castle while Friedr and Christoph again tackled the problem of retrieving Marya's armor, she found the valley was once more shrouded in freezing mist.

Chapter 23

Marya lounged in her rooms, wearing her nightgown and robe because they were the only comfortable items she owned other than the elaborate underclothes the lady of quality in D'Mal's perfect world wore under her everyday dresses and petticoats. Maisy would have had a heart attack if she were to find Marya lounging around in her underclothes, despite the fact she was confined to her rooms and would have no guests or reason to dress up. Her guards were not allowed to visit her while Stefyn was absent. Still, she knew one of them was most likely standing next to the door to the garden, daydreaming about his next foray into town or whatever they did for fun on their leave.

Bored and lonely, she'd fallen asleep before the fire.

She heard a sound behind her and turning, she saw a heavily cloaked figure entering her room. Marya's heart stopped. "No. Please, Stefyn. Please don't do this!" Her voice was breathless with fear, and her eyes filled with tears. "I'm begging you!"

The man pulled back his cloak. He was the same blonde, blue-eyed young man she'd dreamt of before. His long hair was pulled back in a warrior's braid this time, and she could see many tattoos in the style of the Temple on his face. He held up his right hand, palm out, and she saw the crescent moon. But why did a healer-adept have a lightning bolt, a luck rune, and stealth runes?

"Marya, be brave. Your nightmare will end soon, I promise." Despite his strange combination of augmentations, his face was kind. Even his voice was kind. "Don't be afraid. We're coming for you. Be ready to go in the dark of the moon." His frank smile made her heart skip a beat, despite her fear.

"Who are you?" His augmentations mystified her. A healer, a battle-mage, and definitely a mage-assassin. It made no sense to her at all.

"Edwin. My name is Edwin." Still smiling, he suddenly turned, glancing over his shoulder at the door as if he heard something, and vanished as if he'd never been there.

The door opened, waking Marya. Maisy entered the room with her afternoon tea. She looked disapprovingly at Marya's attire and her hair, hanging loose about her shoulders and long enough to sit on. She set the tray down on the small table and stood near the window while Marya tried to eat a small sandwich and drink a cup of tea. When she finished, Maisy took the tray and left, giving her one more look of dissatisfaction.

Did I have a true-dream? She'd heard of them but never considered she would have one. *Oh, Goddess, I pray it was and not another crazy dream sent by Stefyn to torment me.* Since he'd left the keep, she hadn't been bothered by them, perhaps because he was too far away. But he'd let her have several nights of peace before.

He'd done it to trick her into relaxing enough to actually fall deeply asleep. Because she'd finally been unable to keep awake, Stefyn rewarded her in the most depraved ways imaginable. He was simply waiting for her to let her guard down, and before she could struggle, her mind was seized and she was drawn into his hallucinogenic dreams of seduction. Those dreams were a maelstrom of the most repulsive perversions that would disgust even the most cynical of the body-sellers in Braden.

To Marya, the most degrading part was the next day at afternoon tea when Stefyn mentioned how her participation and obvious enjoyment of the purely physical pleasures of the dream greatly enhanced his own gratification. "Dreams are like windows into the soul, are they not? It is amazing what you see if you only look. I love looking at yours, my dear. You're such a passionate woman. Why do you resist? What harm can befall you in a dream?"

It was surely a trick. No one would really have those augmentations. I must not sleep deeply. Please, Goddess, don't let him dream about me. Don't let him send me his filthy dreams.

***

Christoph and Friedr took advantage of the late afternoon mists and returned to their watch over the kitchen gate. They'd been unable to make a plan for getting Marya's armor off the scrap heap without being seen by the ever-industrious man and woman who appeared to be servants, and so they were planning to take it under cover of dark.

As they arrived in their usual place, a cart rumbled into the courtyard. It was empty but had writing on its side: "G'Pette Scrap Removal – Mal Evol City." The driver tied the mule up behind the garden shed, unhitched him, and wheeled the cart to the scrap heap. Then he turned and went to knock on the kitchen door. The bent old man let him in.

"What do you think we should do?" Friedr asked.

"I think the man intends to take away Marya's armor."

"Well, I don't know about you, but I'm going to go down there and get it." Christoph was already moving. "We have to retrieve it, or she won't be able to travel quickly through the thorns." He disappeared through the underbrush.

"Wait up, Chris." Friedr scrambled after him, trying to go quickly but without noise. "And you're always telling me *I'm* mad!"

Silently, they moved to the thorn brake opposite the gate. They hid there watching as the scrap man and the bent old man emerged from the keep and walked to the scrap heap. They listened as the servant told him what to take and then walked back to the kitchen.

The man began loading the cart. Finding the bundle of rags and leather, he tossed it into the ditch directly in front of Friedr and Christoph. They looked at each other, surprised.

The two listened as he talked to himself, working all the while. "Cain't melt down rags and bits o' leather. Save 'em fer the rag-and-bone man they ought, but there's no accountin' fer some folks' notions." He muttered while he sorted the scrap by size and weight. "This'll take some work, strippin' the steel from the leather. This'll hafta wait 'til I git back ter town." He put the breastplate aside to make a pile, adding the rest of the armor as he came across it.

Then he systematically loaded his wagon, making sure everything was sitting well. By this time, it was beginning to get dark. Christoph and Friedr couldn't see the walls because the fog was so thick. When he finished, the scrap man went to the kitchen. As he scraped his boots, they could hear the woman telling him she had a bite set aside for him to eat, to keep him going until he got back to the city.

As one, Christoph and Friedr moved to the cart, looking like nothing more than two shadows in the fog. As they worked, the thickening mists swirled about them, hiding them from the kitchen window. Taking every piece of armor they could find, they hurried back to their thorn brake. The shadowy mists surged, concealing them from view, and Christoph quickly grabbed the bundle that had been tossed into the ditch. Together they returned to their hiding place, and carefully, silently, they worked their way back to the den.

***

While Friedr and Christoph were out watching the kitchen gate and the scrap pile, Aeolyn stayed with Edwin as he scouted the interior of the keep, kneeling next to him, with both of their cloaks wrapping them together. She shared her warmth with him as the temperature once again dropped well below freezing. Their hoods were up, and bandannas covered the lower half of their faces.

All the windows of the keep were well chinked against the winter. No stray drafts could enter the kitchen. The door fit well into the jamb, with no cracks to be found. He tried to enter through the keyhole, but the key rested in the lock and blocked his path, so he sent his spirit out under the earth, looking for the well. Finding it, he followed the piped water to the kitchen, where the old woman was preparing to wash a few dishes.

It appeared she had served tea with tiny little sandwiches to someone. Several of them were left on the plate, and the sight temporarily distracted him. *How I miss good food,* he thought, as he resolutely ignored them.

He drifted through the open door of the kitchen into a vestibule of sorts. Three doors led out of there; all stood open. Edwin looked into the room to the left. It led to a spiral staircase, which he decided not to go up, feeling strongly it might lead to D'Mal's personal rooms. He decided to return there later. Instead, he looked through the door to the right that went to a room with the window facing the secret gate, a room at the base of the tower. Returning to the vestibule, he took the third door. This exited onto a long hallway that obviously led to the main public rooms.

Edwin drifted through a gallery hung with fine works of art. It led to a glass-walled conservatory filled with strange and exotic plants. The conservatory faced the front of the keep, with sweeping views of the main drive up to the Shadow Castle. This room opened to a large, formal reception room. To the right, through double doors, was the dining room. He returned the way he came, but the kitchen was empty as he passed through it.

He regained his body and described for Aeolyn what he'd seen, while she mapped it out. Their breath steamed in the freezing air as she checked with him to see if it was correct. Then they settled back, wrapped under her cloak again. Once again, Edwin sent out his spirit. This time he went directly to the conservatory through the water that fed the fountain. A small door in the rear corner, where the stone wall of the keep met the glass, caught his attention. It was hidden behind many lush and exotic plants.

Through a large crack under the door, he entered a passage leading downward to a corridor. Halfway down the corridor to the left was a large wine cellar, but it was nowhere near as large as Garran had described; it had definitely been divided. Two thirds was now a dungeon, walled away from the still capacious, newer wine cellar by a thick partition of bricks. Edwin realized that the passageway that led from the conservatory was actually D'Mal's personal entrance. The newly built hallway led past the wine cellar and ended at the heavy door to the dungeon.

Once inside the thick, iron-bound door, Edwin found D'Mal's workroom. When he passed under the door, his shields were assailed by the pain and suffering of many people. Buffering his barrier/shield combination, he looked around and was sickened by what he saw. *Goddess Aeos! This really is a tower of bones...and Marya must endure living directly above this carnage.*

Two tiers of doors now ringed the walls around the center of the dungeon, where an altar made of bones and stone stood. That dreadful altar now held the pitiful remains of a man, deliberately and artfully mutilated. D'Mal apparently had been interrupted in the middle of what he was doing. To Edwin's horror, the man still lived, though how, he didn't know, given the extreme nature of the mad priest's work on him. After giving it some thought, he delved into him, and what he discovered made him nauseous, despite his buffer and barriers.

With no further thought, Edwin calmly stopped his heart. *It was the only kindness this man could have appreciated at this point. With the potions in his system, he might have lived another day, but who would want to, in the agony he was in?* Edwin made a deliberate decision not to tell Christoph what he'd done, as he wouldn't understand it. *This room must be marked on the map so no one stumbles into this place by accident.*

He looked at the cells, and what he saw was vile. None of the men or minotaurs that were in those cells would leave there alive. Most would be dead by morning. Even as he lingered, wondering if there was something he could do, one of them at last slipped the bonds of suffering and passed away. Unable to do anything for the others that would be helpful, he stopped the hearts of two of the most critically injured minotaurs and then left the dungeon, sick in his soul at what he'd seen and done. *They wouldn't have lasted more than an hour or two,* Edwin thought. *Perhaps I should have left them, but I couldn't do it, not in good conscience.*

Edwin returned to the vestibule near the kitchen, and turning to the right, he drifted up the stairs to the rooms he suspected were D'Mal's. He found they were and discovered why he chose to live in those rooms instead of the Rose Tower where Marya resided.

D'Mal's rooms were located directly above the Throne of Stone and Bone. This was the wing housing the fabled seat of power that controlled the land and people of Mal Evol and clearly was the oldest part of the keep.

The throne itself was in a room accessed through a small door hidden under the winding stairs leading to D'Mal's apartments. The door was cunningly disguised, nearly blending into the wood paneling of the walls. A long winding passage led downward to another ornately carved, gilded door, far below the castle.

The throne room had never been meant for the kings of Mal Evol to hold audiences in. It was built for the sole purpose of protecting the throne. Edwin soon realized the entire keep was constructed around it. The butte, which the keep sat on, wasn't a natural hill. The entire rise was created and built around the throne, with the castle over the top of it all.

The sheer scale of such an undertaking boggled his mind.

Edwin sensed the Goddess had her hand in the creation of the butte. The earth whispered the truth: generations of good kings and queens of the bloodline of D'Mal had sat on the throne to protect and nurture the land and the people. *The throne is unhappy in the use it has been turned to.*

The throne itself was carved from an immense spire of marble laced with amethyst crystal jutting out of the floor and reaching down to the bedrock. The gigantic crystal spire was formed in the shape of an immense spear, thrust deep and piercing into the heart of the earth. *Surely this isn't natural,* Edwin thought as he looked it over carefully, following it to the root.

It truly is a spear. The earth is torn asunder, and though it has been there for a thousand years or more, the earth remembers the pain. It must have been set here by a god or goddess, but it doesn't have the feel of Aeos. Nor does it feel like the work of the Almighty Father. Returning to the room, he looked carefully at the throne itself. *Father Rall will need to know of this, if he doesn't already. I'm sure he already knows all about this room and what lies hidden within.*

The throne sat atop the haft of the spear and was

intricately carved. From the long stairway leading up to the seat, arms, and back, he could see that many masters had given their lifetimes to the carving of it—or the Goddess had enabled the masterwork. The entire thing was carved in a perfect replica of an ancient oak tree and taller than any he'd ever seen. Indeed, the whole, giant throne appeared to be a tree when viewed from the foot of the stairway that rose steeply to the seat of the kings of Mal Evol.

Embedded in the haft below the crystal seat was an entire skeleton, standing erect and facing upwards through the seat as if looking to heaven. The man was easily head-and-shoulders taller than Friedr, taller even than the children of Tauron. The earth spoke, and Edwin knew the man in the throne was somehow bound with magic unlike any he was acquainted with, empowering the kings of Mal Evol to watch over the health and wellbeing of their land.

The earth also told him the crystal was poisoned, turned to amethyst with the advent of the dark god. *Once this crystal was as clear as a diamond,* Edwin realized as he ghosted over the throne, examining it closely. *The amethyst poisons the throne, which in turn poisons the land.*

Suddenly, Edwin realized he'd heard the story of a spear and the man within it. *Christoph told the tale in Arlen. This is the God Ariend, the husband of Aeos, the man whom Tauron sealed into the haft of a spear in an effort to steal his wife. I'm looking at a god.* Awed, Edwin spent as much time as he dared examining the throne, trying to see what poisoned it. *I would set you free if I could only figure out how to do so,* Edwin thought. *One day you will be free.* He imagined the god was grateful he cared.

Realizing he'd lingered there long enough, Edwin reluctantly left the hidden room and made a last tour of the main floor of the keep, paying particular attention to the routines of the servants and the minotaurs.

No guards were allowed inside the Rose Tower except to escort Marya to and from her rooms, perhaps because D'Mal didn't trust them. In the rest of the keep, guards patrolled specific areas and didn't overlap. One watched at the locked door from the keep into the garden but didn't leave his post at all and didn't enter the tower. It appeared as if the guard posted at the door was really more to keep someone inside than to keep intruders out. Both the minotaur and his door were completely hidden from the secret gate and the window by both the square shape of the tower and the overgrown shrubbery.

Apparently, the guards patrolling the top of the garden wall were deemed to be defense enough. Edwin listened as they complained to each other, as soldiers often did. They were all pleased at having D'Mal out of the keep, as they didn't have to escort the lady when she gardened. It was a task they found excruciatingly boring since they were instructed never to speak to her on pain of death.

The lady was apparently locked in her rooms for her own safety, though each stoutly averred he would never touch D'Mal's woman. They didn't even mention what the punishment for such would be.

"A puny, scrawny thing she is too." The guards all agreed she was far too small, which they found distasteful. "It'd be like molesting a child." Edwin gathered, for the most part, they liked their women big, healthy, and full of spirit.

"I ain't seen any women in so long, even one of these sorts would be a nice change if'n she was a mite more healthy-looking," a big guard named Wint remarked. "In a good raid, once you get their skirts over their head, they look just like any other woman, leastways the ones in Mal Evol City do. They're too delicate-looking with 'em down. They look sickly and underfed."

Another said, "The trouble is they got no fight. They jus' faint soon as they see you've been through the remaking and you're a real warrior of Tauron. That ain't no fun. I miss the women back home in Mektec. Fight like fiends they do and then break yer bones with loving you. That's proper women for you."

The other guards agreed with him as they turned to walk their proscribed paths, and Edwin returned to his body.

As the late afternoon passed, Edwin returned to the keep several times. In between trips, he rested while Aeolyn carefully noted everything, with him making corrections as necessary. Soon it became dark, and they stopped, but they'd mapped the keep in its entirety. They now knew what rooms were guarded and the regular range of each soldier. Edwin had also discovered the dogs were indeed loose inside but with a large guard who appeared to be in control of them.

Aeolyn agreed he must be Brec. He was now behaving as if he were the lord of the manor. Certainly, the old woman and man waited on him as if he were. And, if D'Mal could take his body over at any time, they were right to treat him so. "I get the impression he is some sort of priest," Edwin told her. "The guards fear him as much as they do D'Mal.'"

Aeolyn agreed that if he was acting as D'Mal's assistant, he must be a priest with some rank in their hierarchy.

The mists hung low, and the stars began to come out, lighting the basin with a fairy-tale quality almost magical to look at. Later, the last waning sliver of the moon would rise, and there would be no place in the valley of ice crystal that was not well lit. Friedr and Christoph had still not returned from their afternoon of watching the scrap heap.

"Where are they?" Aeolyn's whisper was full of worry. They had never been so late in returning before.

"Should I far-see for them? I have more than enough chi," Edwin's whisper was low but intense. He feared something had happened.

"You two make too much noise." Christoph's whispered voice was right behind Aeolyn, who jumped and glared at him.

She smacked his armored shoulder with the heel of her hand, hissing, "Don't scare me like that! Where have you been?"

He opened his mouth to reply, when Friedr appeared behind Christoph and whacked his backside. "What part of 'slow down' did you not hear?"

Chris looked surprised and confused. "All of it?"

Edwin stifled a laugh, and Friedr glared at him. "What are you laughing about, farm boy?"

"Oh, nothing, Father. It's just that I'm usually the one getting smacked. It's nice to see someone else having fun for a change!" Edwin started laughing again, and soon they were all smothering their hysteria in their cloaks. The hilarity relieved much of the tension they were under.

Still trying not to laugh, Christoph laid out all the pieces of armor under the starlight he'd been able to find. Friedr also laid his out, and they carefully went over each piece, noting where it was compromised and deciding what they could do to repair it.

As they labored, the starlight reflected off the ice-covered branches and illuminated their work. Friedr told Aeolyn and Edwin how the opportunity to retrieve the armor was suddenly placed before them. "And then off Christoph went before I could say 'what if it's a trap, bonehead.'" He grinned and Chris shrugged. "Before I knew it, we were haring off down to the ditch by the road."

"Friedr was enthusiastic about picking through the wagon," Christoph added. "He didn't want to leave anything behind. And he was right. She'll need each piece, broken or not."

Aeolyn and Edwin arranged the armor in order, matching the pieces to their sundered mates, while Friedr and Christoph ate. Everything was there, which was a great relief.

Marya's armor was made to be worn over the same long-sleeved, leather vest as theirs with the same tight-fitting trousers. Edwin thought they would be loose on her now, as she seemed thin. They were relieved to find that, even though it was cut apart in oddly sized sections, the armor would be salvageable. Her linen shirt was either missing or part of the bundle of rags.

Normally, Temple armor was bespelled to protect the wearer in the areas they were weakest in, and to strengthen their magic. Friedr felt sure the spells were broken during the breaking of her armor. "It should work almost as well as general purpose armor," he told Aeolyn. "But it won't help her any when it comes to working her magic."

"I don't think she can use her gifts anymore," Edwin commented as he peered at the place where the shoulder met the breastplate. The leather was sliced apart, and using the awl that was part of his Temple knife, he began to make holes to lace the separated pieces together. "Her augmentations are even more faded than my father's." He reassembled both shoulders using strips of leather sliced from the bottom of his own vest. This shortened it only a small amount. "Marya is in an unbelievably terrible place for a healer to be. I think she's shut down part of herself in order to cope with it."

Christoph worked at reassembling the leg guards, while Friedr took care of the lower body of the breastplate where it came down over the thighs. Chris stopped and looked at Edwin with concern. "This is a rare condition you're describing. It can only happen when there is severe trauma. Yet you're sure she hasn't been raped?"

"I'm not completely sure, but she doesn't have that shattered quality. She's as nervous as a cat and seems to jump at the slightest thing, but it could be from the situation she's in," Edwin replied, looking at Chris. "If she's been raped, she's handling it in a way I haven't seen in my capacity as a healer, though my experience is limited to only the victims I've assisted you with." He thought for a moment about the way she reacted when he entered her rooms. "With my hood up, she must have thought I was D'Mal. She begged him not to 'do this' as if whatever she fears hasn't happened yet but hangs over her head. I sensed she lives daily in fear of it happening."

Edwin then thought about the tower that stood directly over the dungeon and the ghosts who named it the Tower of Bones. "But there are other, more terrible aspects of life with D'Mal that could cause her to shut down her empathic self. These things would break any healer, even you, my brother." Edwin's voice conveyed his certainty, and Friedr nodded his understanding as did Aeolyn. "Especially you, Christoph, because your barriers are not as strong as they could be. There *is* a dungeon there, and it's a terrible place."

Christoph looked sharply at him and then shrugged, saying, "I know, and I've been working at my barriers. I do thank you for the shield you maintain under me and over our little home." Then he asked, "But if Marya *has* been raped, what are you going to do? How are you going to handle such an event?"

"I'll do as I've been instructed and nothing more," Edwin replied firmly. "I'll bring her out, and we'll help her then. I won't go against the advice of my father. I promised Abbott Garran I would do the right thing. I want to rescue her, not lose her forever."

Aeolyn listened to them as she reassembled the back-plate, connecting it to the lower half. From the bottom of her own vest, she cut the strips of leather to lace Marya's armor together. *Edwin is a strong man. Friedr would tear down the keep, regardless of the consequences,* she thought as she worked. A sharp stab of fear for Marya shot through her, causing her to pause in her work. *Oh, Goddess. I hope he's right and she hasn't had such an ordeal on top of everything else.*

After a long evening of effort, they finished

repairing the armor to the best of their ability. Marya's leather trousers were more difficult, as was the vest. Whoever broke up the armor made a poor job of it, but they were more thorough with her vest and trousers. Besides being sliced to pieces, they were also remarkably filthy.

The companions shortened her vest to make the laces that united the pieces of her trousers. Her clothes would be an interesting patchwork of leather but would suffice until they could get to Braden. Her shirt wasn't salvageable, but they would figure something out.

"She'll be wearing something, and we can make it work. If nothing else, she can wear my other shirt, though it'll be too short in the arms. I can't imagine who did this to her clothes," Aeolyn said, wrinkling her nose at the smell. "Yeesh—I hope they enjoyed doing it. Anyway, I'll clean her leathers tomorrow if you can get me enough water, Edwin. I've enough soap, but I don't think I should try to sneak down to the creek in this weather. The sound carries too well once the mists lift."

Edwin assured her he would get the water in the morning and would get enough for them each to have somewhat of a bath, cold though it would be. "In these mists, I can easily call as much as we need to fill the basin and the cook pot as many times as you want. It draws little chi."

At last, they finished mending all of Marya's leathers as best as they could. Her vest would be shorter than was optimal, as their own would be, but her armor and leathers were usable.

And wonder of wonders, her boots were undamaged, though they were grimy and the tops and sides were extremely worn, moreso than the soles. Christoph sat on his heels, looking at Marya's boots and leathers for a long while. He picked them up and examined them closely, even smelling them. Laying each piece back down in the order they were worn, he regarded them and frowned, obviously thinking of something unpleasant.

Finally, he ventured an opinion. "I think she wore these for at least a month or more, day and night, without taking them off, in some sort of a dungeon. We don't know exactly when she was kidnapped, but we received word she was being held here in the first week of Scorpius. We've been sent dreams and visions to guide us, but no one has actually seen or heard from her since she left Braden Temple with supplies in early Libre."

Edwin's stomach lurched on hearing the word "dungeon." "In my true-dreams, she looks thin and tired, but D'Mal seems to have her in some nice apartments." Edwin picked up Marya's right boot. "I see what you mean. This is seriously scuffed, and so is the other one. The dirt is ground in, but on the left only, like she was forced to lie on her side for a long period of time. " His expression was grim as he added, "As I told you, there is a dungeon there, Christoph. Believe me when I tell you, it's no place for a healer to be for any length of time. It's worse than anything I could ever have imagined. The shadows that haunt the keep refer to the Rose Tower as the Tower of Bones because it sits directly above the dungeon. I've clearly marked it on the map so you don't stumble into it by accident."

"The seat of her trousers is worn the same way." Engrossed, Christoph turned them over, examining them. "Also, both legs are severely worn on the left side, and dirt is ground into the leather. It's like she couldn't fully stretch out." They looked up, meeting each other's eyes, seeing the anger and helplessness they both felt reflected there. "I know we're not to face the monster down, and we couldn't kill him even if we were to have the advantage of surprise. Magically, he is much too strong for us. But I know how to weaken him." His voice was rough with emotion. "If his power over the soil of Mal Evol was somehow broken, it would weaken him considerably."

Since entering Mal Evol, Christoph had felt the hand of the Goddess urging him to return to cleanse the invading plant and animal life from the broken land. Finally, his anger turned to resolve, and he raised his right hand palm out in the tradition of the Temple. Solemnly, he made the sacred oath. "I vow to you as my witnesses, as I love the Goddess, I will return to Mal Evol." Christoph's low voice was full of emotion and intensity. "I will heal the land, and through the cleansed soil, I will heal the people. My staff to defend them, my magic to serve them. As I love the Goddess, I will see this task done. This I will do or die in the doing."

Something beyond his control drove him. Edwin raised his right hand, placing his palm flat against Christoph's and spoke the sacred vow binding him to the quest. "I solemnly swear I will return with you to make this happen. My sword to protect you, my magic to serve you. As I love the Goddess, I will return with you to see this task done. This I will do or die in the doing."

Friedr and Aeolyn watched this exchange, and an

understanding passed between them. The hand that moved Edwin also touched Friedr's heart, moving him. He looked at her pleadingly, and with a resigned look, she nodded her head. He solemnly placed both his hands over theirs and swore, "As I love the Goddess, we will return to this land and make it bloom. My sword to protect you, my magic to serve you. We will free the soil from the tyranny of the Bull God. This we will do, or die in the doing."

Aeolyn completed the time-honored ritual, serving as the witness. "I have heard and witnessed these vows before the Goddess. Her will shall be done in the fullness of time, under the light of her love." She wrote down the oaths as they were spoken, dating the note. She would give it to the abbess in Aeoven and the Temple seers would begin casting auguries once they returned.

Aeolyn was not moved to swear to the new quest, feeling sure the goddess had a different plan for her.

Chapter 24

The next morning in the light of the cold, overcast sky, Edwin sat in front of their shelter with his palm full of oil, having decided to attempt oiling the hinges of the gate using his air-magic. If he failed, Christoph would sneak in and do it the hard way, though they hoped to keep their presence a secret as long as possible. Friedr sat with Edwin, his cloak wrapped about the two of them, keeping Edwin's body warm in the freezing, gray morning while he was away.

Sending his spirit out to the hidden gate, Edwin visualized the oil penetrating the rust, loosening the hinge. As he concentrated, the oil slowly disappeared from his palm. Seeing it appear in the right place, he focused harder, working it well into the old hinges. He ended up transporting two palms-full before they were satisfactorily lubricated. Then he turned to the lock.

While Edwin worked on his project, Aeolyn and Christoph cleaned Marya's trousers, vest, and boots as best they could.

"It's a good thing we're leaving this place tonight," Aeolyn said, as she scrubbed the boot she was holding. "We're running low on soap and rations. We won't have enough to get us back to Braden, with an extra mouth to feed." She sat back and looked at Chris. "Another thing I've been thinking is once in the keep, we must not kill anyone unless we're forced to, because dead people draw attention. We need to sneak in and out."

"The food will stretch. We might make it to the border of Neveyah before we have to live off the land,"

Christoph replied. "If we go as quickly as we can, it won't matter." He carefully oiled the boot he held, working it in until the leather was once again supple and waterproof. He would do the same with Marya's vest and her trousers once they were dried.

"The problems will begin when D'Mal hears she's gone. We must find Brec and put a sleep spell on him, one that will hold for as long as you can make it." Aeolyn dried the other boot with a rag and handed it to Christoph, who began oiling. "Friedr was looking forward to a good fight, you know. He'll be disappointed."

Christoph grinned. "He'll have to be satisfied with the dogs. They're dangerous, and trust me, they're hard to kill. The archives are clear about it. We can't leave them alive, and we'll have to dispose of them in such a way their deaths aren't noticed too quickly. I can cast a type of sleep spell that will last thirty-six hours on a human, even if the spell is untended. But I don't know how long it will work on a minotaur. We use it for surgeries. I've never had a minotaur to heal, so I don't know what their metabolism is like. They must be different once they undergo the remaking, because they look completely altered from the torso up. I know the process somehow makes them physically larger than the other children of Tauron, and much stronger." He rubbed the polish in with his boot rag. "I've always wondered how they differ from us, besides the obvious. I'd really like to study with one of their healers if they have such, but it's impossible, given we're at war." He looked up to see Aeolyn staring at him as if he'd gone insane. "Well, I have wondered," Christoph said, feeling slightly defensive.

She smiled back at him. "If we can get even twenty-four hours' running time out of your sleep spell, it would be good." Aeolyn smoothed the leather of the vest she was working on. "I don't know how fast he can travel, but I'm sure he'll be very fast, even for one of his kind. Brec is completely D'Mal's creature and will be compelled to protect his master's interests to the death."

"I'll cast a spell of forgetting combined with deep-sleep, so he'll have no memory of us having been there if he does see us. But once he hears Marya is gone, D'Mal will search *her* mind out and know what's happened. He'll immediately put Brec on our trail since he will know exactly where she is. We have to hope he's too distracted with this rebellion to check in for several days." Christoph sat back on his heels and took a sip from his water bottle. "Without the dogs, Brec won't be able to track us as quickly."

"You're the expert in that area. But I think if we gauged his rate of travel correctly, D'Mal should be arriving in Nuruk today. He'll be busy for several weeks at least and will also have to go on to Gutuk before he can return here." She sat back, stretching her shoulders and rubbing her neck. "But we know he'll be checking in with Brec at some point. If we could be in Neveyah when he does, I'd be happier, but we know that won't happen."

The tumbleweed door was moved aside, and Edwin slowly entered, moving stiffly and heading straight for his bedroll. Friedr followed him, helping him out of his boots and armor. Edwin's face was white, and he looked completely done in, his hands shaking with the effort of undressing himself.

"Lie down and sleep. You'll need your chi tonight," Friedr said, with a fatherly look.

As he finished undressing, Edwin replied, "I don't think I can. I'm too keyed up. We're so close, so close. It's almost time, Friedr." A strange excitement filled his veins and set his mind on fire with the expectation of finally freeing Marya. His body hummed with it. He lay down, his eyes alight with anticipation.

Chris surreptitiously cast sleep, and as he drifted off, Edwin murmured, "Thank you, brother."

Christoph's smile lit up his face as he replied, "Any time, my brother."

Aeolyn looked at Friedr and nodded questioningly across the shelter at Edwin. Friedr said, "He thinks he was able to get the oil worked into the hinges well enough, and the lock is well-oiled now too. He should be able to enter and leave through the gate with no trouble, while we use the kitchen."

"He'll be prepared to cast sleep on the guards if necessary," Christoph assured him. "Fortunately, it uses little chi, so he'll be able to cast it as needed. If he sleeps well enough now, he'll be at full capacity when we go on this mad adventure tonight." He polished Marya's boots so they looked nearly as good as his own.

Aeolyn looked around the shelter at their own dirty leathers. "Well, since I'm washing clothes, let's get ours done too." She cleaned all of their vests while Christoph did their boots, and then they tackled their trousers together.

She looked at her sliver of soap and then at Friedr. "You and I will share your soap on the trip home, Friedr. You don't use enough of it anyway."

His blue eyes reflected his dismay. "Aeolyn! I'm deeply hurt. I bathe daily in the teacup of water I'm allowed."

"You do smell like your armor, dear." She wrinkled her nose and then said wickedly, "But I like the smell of your armor...from a distance." She smiled affectionately at her husband.

"I know, dear one. I know." Friedr grinned at his wife, as he spread their garments out to dry.

Christoph chuckled to himself, taking comfort in their familiar exchange. He too was tired and not as clean as he would have liked. Placing Aeolyn's boots where she would be able to gear up easily, he lay down on his bedroll to get some rest in preparation for the coming evening's work. He ran through his mental relaxation exercises and was soon sleeping soundly.

***

Edwin stood in the garden at the foot of the Tower of Bones. He went to the window and opened it, entering the cold, dark room. Crossing the room to the door that stood ajar, he climbed the dark stairs to the secured door. Unbarring it, he entered the room. This time he knew he was once again dreaming.

Marya looked up from her book. Fear and anger combined with despair in her eyes. "Why do you toy with me, Stefyn? Leave me in peace. You've won. I have lost this game."

The cloaked figure wasn't Stefyn. It was the stranger from her dreams. He was clad in the same nondescript cloak, but this time he wore it over the black leathers and armor of the Temple assassin. His hood was lowered, and his augmentations were clear on his striking face—crescent moon with healer's stars trailing, battle-mage's lightning bolts in both red and blue, and an assassin's luck rune curving over his eye. Stealth runes rode high on his neck, behind his earlobes.

He held out his right hand with the crescent moon that crossed his palm. "Be ready. We're coming for you tonight. We will not leave you in this place. Be ready." His open smile and the honesty in his blue eyes once again took her breath away despite her disbelief.

As she looked at him, he faded.

"But I wasn't sleeping," she said aloud, in wonder. She refused to think about it, deciding if it was real, she would be as ready as she could be without her armor and leathers. Her gardening shoes were nothing more than slightly sturdier court slippers and would be little better than going barefoot. She would be ready but not hopeful.

She bitterly acknowledged the dreams were more likely some new torment Stefyn was sending to keep her in line. *Like the stone shard he put in the garden for me to find. He gives me hope and then takes it away. It's his favorite game.* Tears of anger and desperation welled, burning her eyes.

I won't play this game with him, she swore to herself angrily, knowing she was already planning to do just that. *I won't!*

***

The mist didn't lift all day. Icicles formed and hung from the thorn forest canopy, and the cold was pervasive. As evening fell, the fog thickened and the stars were obscured, making the night dark indeed.

The companions packed their belongings and broke camp, leaving no trace they were ever there. Even the mats were taken apart and buried. Traveling silently, they emerged from the thorn forest opposite the kitchen gate, in the shadow of the standing stones. Leaving their possessions in the brake they prepared to do their jobs.

The group was tense with anticipation with the exception of Edwin, who was calmer and more certain of what he was doing than he'd felt since his arrival in Neveyah. He didn't realize it, but he'd assumed a leadership role. His quiet assurance gave the others confidence they would win Marya back and escape Mal Evol with her.

Edwin located the dogs and the guards within the keep. The sentries were at their usual posts, and the dogs were in the conservatory with the huge minotaur whom they believed to be Brec. The bent old man served him some sort of drink, and the dogs gnawed on bones from a large animal, probably whatever had provided the guards' supper. Edwin had seen the massive carcasses the cooks in the barracks made their meals out of.

The old woman was seated at the table in the kitchen, mending linens by the light of a candle. The castle guards who patrolled atop the walls were stationed exactly as they should be, with no changes in their routine.

In low whispers, the companions went over their plan one last time to be sure they all knew what they were doing. They would still each carry part of Marya's gear, as her health and strength was suspect and she might not be able to carry her own.

Then Edwin parted company with Aeolyn, Friedr, and Christoph. Hiding in the shadows, blending into the fog and moving ever so slowly, he circled through the shrubbery outside the walls to the thorn brake opposite the hidden gate. There he watched the guards and counted their paces, choosing his moment. *This is somewhat like snaring rabbits back home in Markett,* he thought to himself as he waited calmly for the opportunity to make his next small move. *Unless you become one with the landscape, you will never get your prey.*

The others slipped through the mists and shadows to the kitchen door. Peering through the window, Christoph put the old woman to sleep. Friedr picked the lock, and they entered the keep, heading to the conservatory. The startled old man was next to fall to the sleep-spell, this time layered with a forgetting. Now he rested comfortably in the vestibule.

Quietly, taking full advantage of their stealth armor's ability to allow them to remain unnoticed, they crept through the keep, circling wide of the conservatory so as not to alert the dogs. Their armor bore spells for stealth and secrecy woven into the making of it, and unless they made a huge blunder, they should be able to go unnoticed. The guards, of course, remained strictly in their prescribed areas. No one ever entered the main area of the keep who wasn't supposed to be there. Christoph cast his spells several times before they finally doubled back.

Silently, they converged on the conservatory where both Brec and the dogs slept. Brec was slumped in a wingback chair before the fire with a bottle of wine on the table at his elbow, the dogs at his feet. Except for the horns and his strange, bull-like profile, it was almost a homey scene.

Friedr entered the room, and the dogs woke with a growl, lunging at him with a strange, hoarse bark that wasn't at all what he expected. *Damn, they're big* was all he had time to think as his sword slid from its sheath. The male dog immediately went for Friedr's throat and the female for Aeolyn's. Their blades flashed as they back-pedaled, leading the dogs backwards to a hallway area to allow them more room to fight.

The male dog snapped and slashed at Friedr with his knife-like fangs, leaping and knocking him down in an attempt to gore him. Fangs flashed and claws flew at Friedr's face. He blocked with his left arm, and his sword spitted the dog, slowing the attack. Yanking his sword free as he rolled out from underneath the dog, he cut the beast's throat. Still it attacked, ignoring the hacking of Friedr's sword, until finally he was able to pierce the animal's heart, killing it at last.

As the dog dropped, Friedr turned to see Aeolyn yanking her sword from the side of the lunging female, pushing it off with her foot. Bringing her sword up close to her body two-handed she turned and smoothly decapitated it.

As the head hit the floor with a squishy thud, she looked at Friedr and then around at the mess. She shook her head. "I don't ever want to have to fight one of those again." They were both covered with gore and sweat.

"I rather enjoyed playing with the puppies," he replied. His innocent smile was spoiled by the blood all over his face. The look she gave him could have fried an egg, as they both turned toward Christoph.

In the moment they engaged the dogs, Christoph had cast sleep on the startled minotaur. Brec had risen drunkenly from his chair, fumbling for his sword, but the spell took hold and his knees buckled under him. As he fell to the floor, Christoph prudently moved out of the way while Friedr and Aeolyn fought.

While they battled, Christoph stood over Brec and cast an extra layer of sleep combined with a deep forgetting, building a layered spell he hoped would hold for a day or two. Smiling rather grimly, he realized the minotaur was seriously drunk, which would aid the longevity of his spells. He added an extra twist, slowing the rate of the liquor's dissipation from Brec's system. "This will hurt you more than me," he cheerfully told the minotaur as he tied-off the spell, making use of Edwin's new trick and enjoying every minute of it. "I do believe you'll have a headache that will quite amaze you when you finally do wake up." He spent a moment delving Brec's body, satisfying his curiosity. *They're not as different as I thought...larger heart...strangely compressed frontal lobes...must be due to the rearranged skull...larger lungs.* As he worked, he realized he was using far too much chi for what he was doing, and reluctantly he stopped, wondering why.

"We must get the dogs out of here and get him into a more natural position." Aeolyn's whisper sounded tired.

They were bloody, but most of it was the dogs'. Aeolyn's right arm was slashed, but her armguard had deflected the fangs and it didn't look too bad. Christoph healed and bound it, saving his chi to recast sleep on their way out if needed. "I didn't even feel it," she noted when he asked if she was in pain. "I was too busy trying to keep her out of my face."

"I couldn't really see your wound very well,"

Christoph told her. "The longer I'm here in the keep, the less I'm able to sense my gift and the more chi it takes."

They looked closely at the corpses. Both dogs had received wounds during the fight that would have felled any normal beast long before the killing strokes. Sighing, they began cleaning up the mess. Aeolyn tidied the room and took the wine-stained napkin to get the blood off the floor. "We have to leave this as clean as we can so they don't realize what's happened for as long as possible."

It took all three of them to lift Brec into the chair and pose him. Then they turned to the problem of the corpses. They checked the map, seeing Edwin's notes showing a way into the dungeon from the conservatory, marked with a large X. There was also an entrance to the wine cellar and storerooms there. "Very convenient for the man who enjoys mixing his work with pleasure," muttered Friedr. "Well, let's get them down there."

After a great deal of struggle and effort, the huge dogs were safely hidden in the first storeroom off the corridor. After they deposited the decapitated head with the corpses, Friedr and Aeolyn opened the heavy door to take a look around the dungeon.

Stunned, they stared silently around the huge space, seeing horror after horror.

"What are two more corpses among so many?" asked Aeolyn, her shock evident. "What sort of monster are we dealing with?" All of poor Narg's renegades were dead, along with several now-deceased works in progress D'Mal was occupied with before his departure.

She suddenly noticed Christoph was transfixed and

shaking. "Christoph, what's the matter?" He didn't answer. "Chris?"

Unable to speak, his eyes met hers, filled with pain and horror. He'd followed them into the dungeon proper and now stood staring at the mutilated corpse of the man on the altar.

"Blanchard. This is Blanchard, the spice merchant from Braden. We always suspected him of having ties to D'Mal, but no one ever.... Aaugh, Goddess. How does Marya stand it, living under the same roof as this?" His voice was nearly a wail, and he trembled violently.

"Oh, Chris," Aeolyn said sadly. She looked at Friedr. "We have to get him out of here—*now!*"

An unexpected side effect of entering the keep was the crumbling of Christoph's barriers, which he hadn't noticed. Now he was in the dungeon, the few tattered bits that remained shattered under the weight of the pain and suffering from the sheer number of prisoners who were still dying down there. His extreme empathy sent him into shock from what he saw and felt.

Friedr chivvied him along. "We must hurry, Chris. Come on. You're needed upstairs. Come on." He finally took Christoph by the shoulders and forced him into the corridor leading up to the conservatory, closing the heavy door behind them. "Oh dear, it was a bad idea to bring you down there. I'm so sorry."

"How has she stood it?" Christoph asked. "How? So much fear and pain. Now I understand what Edwin tried to tell me." He shook uncontrollably, becoming more confused. "He tried to tell me." Again his voice rose in a wail. "Why didn't I listen?"

Meeting Friedr's eyes, Aeolyn took Christoph's

hand, and they retraced their steps, Friedr pushing and Aeolyn tugging. As they got further from the dungeon, Chris began to regain his composure, his feet beginning to work on their own.

Out of necessity, before they were sent out into the field, battle-mages were trained to know what to do when a healer went into shock from an empathic overload. Sometimes healers were required to go into serious situations to rescue the wounded, and battle-mages needed to know how to bring a healer back when it became too much for them. Aeolyn and Friedr maintained physical contact as Christoph centered himself and forcibly rebuilt his barriers. At last, he nodded he was able to continue, although he was pale and still shaken, refusing to speak.

They finished cleaning up the conservatory, using supplies from the kitchen. Christoph grimly checked each guard as they left and also the old man and woman, casting his combination of sleep and forgetting again as needed. Finally he spoke, and his voice sounded calm. "This should hold the guards for two more hours. They should wake one hour before their shift change. The old woman and man should sleep for longer, maybe a day, but no one will notice because they only serve Brec and Marya, or D'Mal himself. The others won't notice anything since Brec has his duties in the dun...away from them and rarely visits. Brec, I hope, will be out for two days, perhaps three, Goddess willing." Christoph was still pale and fighting the urge to run screaming from the place, but he managed to look and sound as if he were back under control.

Before they left, they took the opportunity to wash the blood and gore off themselves, their leathers, and armor in the kitchen, leaving it as tidy as they found it. Christoph thoroughly cleaned and re-bound Aeolyn's wound, casting heal and ease. It ached and throbbed in a peculiar way, but his ability to use his healing senses had been badly affected by the dungeon, and he couldn't see what was wrong with her. Friedr locked the door behind them as they left, leaving everything like it should be.

They arrived back in the thorn brake opposite the ditch where they waited. All three were still horrified by what they'd seen and weren't handling it well. They tried to nibble on ration bars, but until Edwin returned with Marya they wouldn't be able to relax enough to eat much. Friedr and Aeolyn concentrated on helping Christoph regain his seriously depleted chi, forcing him to eat and drink some water.

"It took all of your chi to cast the spells you used in there, and it shouldn't have," worried Aeolyn. "I hope Edwin doesn't have to use his magic for much. We'll sorely need it when we leave here later tonight, if you can't regain yours quickly enough."

Friedr rubbed Christoph's shoulders, trying to help him relax, while Aeolyn gently massaged his temples, aiding the flow of chi. They both desperately tried to recall the upper-level novice classes they'd received shortly before gaining their journeyman's pins. Gerde, a white-haired, energetic, senior lightning-mage taught the class, and they'd been somewhat bored as novices often were and not really paying attention.

At last, Christoph broke the silence. "Thank you, my friends. I wouldn't have made it out of there without you." He stopped, unable to speak for a moment, and then continued. "I...I believe I can bring myself to kill the man responsible for such horror." His whisper was empty of emotion, his eyes bleak. "It would be the simple amputation of a poisoned limb—unpleasant to do, but necessary for the preservation of life."

Friedr and Aeolyn were shocked into silence, both terribly sad their friend, the most gentle of healers, was driven to contemplate such a thing, both feeling as if something was irrevocably changed. His grim face brought tears to Aeolyn's eyes. A chill of foreboding washed over her as she watched him, and she shivered, leaning against Friedr for comfort, her arms around Christoph. He leaned his head against her shoulder, resting his cheek against hers, desperately needing the closeness of his dearest friends. Friedr's arms sheltered them both.

The three sat huddled in the dark with their arms about each other, comforting Christoph and praying to Aeos that Edwin and Marya would make it out of the haunted keep.

Chapter 25

From his hiding place in the scrub surrounding the walls of the keep, Edwin watched as the guards paced their rounds atop the wall exactly as they always did. It took him nearly an hour to get from where he left his companions to the hidden gate. Biding his time, he waited until they paced out of sight and then made his move. At last, he arrived in the thorns by the gate. Silent as a shadow in the dark, Edwin slipped under the concealing vegetation against the wall. The vines made only the slightest of sounds, as if a breeze stirred them.

Remaining perfectly still, Edwin waited until the guards once again passed out of range before placing the key in the lock and turning it ever so slowly. The lock was stiff, and he willed it to turn quietly.

He opened the gate just wide enough to slip through. It opened without noise, for which he was grateful. The vines barely made a sound as he slipped under them, closing the gate. The guards returned, and Edwin crouched in the shadows, waiting for them to pace back in the other direction. *I hope this window truly is unlocked,* he thought as he waited. He looked up, seeing the window he knew was Marya's with the faint light of a single candle illuminating it, and then back to the window opposite him. *We're in trouble if this one is locked. It'll take me forever to work my way back to the kitchen door. But the Goddess shows me, and* only *me, going in this way. It must be true. It must be.*

The guards passed out of the line of sight, and he stepped over to the window. Sliding it open, he entered the room he'd seen in his dreams, turning and lowering it quickly.

Silently crossing the room, he climbed the dark stair. At the top, he paused in the shadows, listening for sounds of fighting in the keep below. Hearing none, he unbarred the door and pushed it open.

Marya was seated before the fire. She wore her brown gardening dress and the heaviest shoes she could find, worn for gardening. Her knit shawl was ready to put on in case this madness was true. A tiny, tightly-rolled bundle containing two sets of the lacy, all-concealing underclothes, which could easily be worn as outer garments once she was away from the keep, was hidden under her pillow, although she didn't know why she believed her dream. Her greatest fear was she would end up back in the dungeon.

She fully expected Stefyn to open the door and drag her away for another lesson in manners. Still, she wanted to believe, although she knew she was playing into his hands.

When the door opened, she forced herself not to scream, holding both hands to her mouth, fear and hope warring in her eyes.

"Marya, do you trust me?" Edwin whispered, lowering his hood. His hair was held back in a braid, and she could clearly see his augmentations. "Are you ready to leave this place?" She glimpsed the leathers and armor of a Temple assassin under his cloak.

"Yes," she said, standing up. Relief colored her voice. "But who are you? Why don't I know you? You must be from the Temple, but I've never heard of anyone augmented as you are. I would remember you."

"Edwin," he said with a rather shy smile that

touched her heart. "Edwin Farmer is my name. I'm a new recruit to the Temple. It's a long story." He handed her the bundled cloak he'd brought, having carried it under the breastplate of his armor. "Put this on over your shawl, and you'll be warm enough until we can meet up with Aeolyn and the others."

Her face lit up with joy on hearing Aeolyn's name.

"Oh! Now I believe you're real," she exclaimed, fighting back tears. "Now I believe. I was so afraid Stefyn was playing one of his games with my sanity." She saw Edwin's face harden briefly as she spoke, as if he actually cared. She wondered why. He didn't even know her, but there was real sympathy in his eyes.

He said quietly, "We've come to take you home, Marya. You'll never have to play his games again." He took the small bundle of clothes she handed him and tucked it behind his breastplate. It took up less space than the cloak had.

As Marya pulled the cloak on over her dress, Edwin said, "We'll go as silently as possible, but we must stay in the shadows. Stay close to me, go when I go and stop when I stop. I promise you will hear my tale once we get away from here." He looked at her attire as if seeing it for the first time. "Please don't be offended when I ask you to tie up your skirts—we've a lot of crawling through brush ahead of us." He felt himself blush. *I'm an idiot,* he thought, blushing again.

She smiled on seeing his face redden. Without a qualm, she tied them up around her waist so her legs were uncovered to the knee where her stockings met her bloomers. *He's rather innocent,* she thought, hiding a nervous smile. *Perhaps he's younger than he looks.*

Before they left her quarters, Edwin made her bed

appear as if she was sleeping. Then, blowing out the candle, they crept out of the room, barring the door behind them. Marya followed Edwin, gripping his hand tightly. She tried to calm herself, but to no avail.

Pausing at the top of the stairwell, Edwin listened, and hearing nothing, they silently slipped down the stairs. Quickly crossing the room, Edwin motioned to her to hide in the shadows next to the window. With his hood up, he sent his spirit out to see where the guards were. Finding them on the part of their rounds that approached the tower window, he returned to his body and pressed further back into the shadows. He felt Marya trembling like a leaf in the wind and forced himself not to put his arms around her. *She doesn't know you, you idiot. You're no better than D'Mal.* He contented himself with squeezing her hand comfortingly.

Marya had seen Edwin standing with his eyes closed and wondered if everything was going as planned. For a moment, she had feared someone was going to catch them, but his eyes opened and he moved back, pressing her further into the shadows. They waited, and she found herself holding her breath. He held her hand, and she clung to it for comfort.

Edwin counted the guard's paces until he once again left the line of sight, and then opened the window. Climbing through first, he then helped Marya. Her bunched up skirts hampered her movements, but swiftly and easily, Edwin lifted her out, and she was able to make it.

Each second she spent trying to climb out she was terrified the guards would hear her. The shadows rose and drifted about them, as if trying to help hide them from any chance observation. "Goodbye," she whispered. "You were right. I'm glad I believed you."

Edwin realized who she was speaking to. He knew, as he'd known in his dreams, that they were more than simply shadows—they were the ghosts of D'Mal's victims. He too whispered a thank you to them.

Marya looked at him, startled. He was the only person she'd met who knew what the shadows really were.

Quickly he closed the window, and they hid in the depths of the garden, the cloaks covering them as they crouched together in the darkness. Again, they waited until the guards disappeared.

Edwin opened the gate, and they squeezed through. He stood completely still under the vines, listening, and then closed the gate, locking it behind them.

They stayed there under the vines, pressed tightly against the wall, as the guard passed above. Then Edwin took Marya's hand and they slipped into the scrub. There were no stars and no moon. Around them, the mists swirled. The darkness was nearly complete, and they were well hidden.

Once again, they waited for the guard to pass, and then Edwin moved. Realizing he was alone, he stopped and turned back. Marya was frozen in place—he sensed her heart was racing and her terror was apparent in her expression.

The sight of the minotaurs through the branches of the thorns as they paced their watches atop the wall petrified her. *No! No! They'll take me back and he'll kill me...after he teaches me manners again! Please, no!* Her thoughts rang as clearly as if she'd spoken.

He returned to her, casting calm and whispering,

"Don't worry, I'm here for you. We can do this, I promise. We're almost there. I'll help you." Edwin looked to see if she heard him. She might have, but he couldn't tell because she was shuddering violently. "We can do this when you're ready." Subtly, he laced the spell he'd cast on her with soothe and added the lightest touch of a strengthening spell so she could continue.

"I'm here with you." He projected calm and strength in his voice, sending her the thought she was safe with him. Gradually, she stopped shaking and the panicked look in her eyes faded. Repeating, "We can do this when you're ready," he laced his spells with an extra layer of calm, buffering her from her own fears. Again, Edwin whispered, "You're strong enough to do this, Marya, and I'm here with you." Unthinking, he moved to put his arm about her shoulders to comfort her, but she shied away.

Marya whispered an apology for doing so, wondering why she felt so skittish. *He isn't trying to hurt me. Why am I being this way?*

Edwin smiled reassuringly, but the raw fear on her face tore at his heart. He reached for her cold hand instead, and she gripped him tightly. *A girl has never been afraid of me before,* he thought, feeling a sense of consternation. *But then, the girls I know have never been in the sort of situation she's found herself in. She has good reason to fear a kindly gesture.*

At last, Marya nodded her head. She suspected he'd cast a soothing spell on her, relieved at the thought Edwin would be able to help steady her nerves. The sight of the guards pacing the walls had transfixed her, like a rabbit staring at a wolf. Now at least she could move, though her terror was nearly overwhelming. His gentleness and kindness were so genuine she let her guard down a little more and, unbeknownst to her, enabled his spells to work better.

Edwin felt her relax and squeezed her hand encouragingly, hoping the weave would last long enough to get to the standing stones. *It's best if she can do this without my help. She'll need it later.* He forced himself to refrain from completely cushioning her emotions, wondering what was wrong with him that he felt so strong a desire to completely mitigate even the smallest feeling of stress and fear. *I'm a fool. I'm too involved! I have to back away and let her have the emotional space she needs.* Immediately, he bolstered his barriers and reasserted his healer's detachment. Once he'd done so, he was better able to cope, allowing Marya to feel her fears, helping only when they threatened to overcome her.

It seemed to take forever, but they finally skirted the walls of the garden and now approached the kitchen lane. The guards passed once more, and they slipped to the deeper shadows of the standing stones, where they waited one last time. Then, shrouded completely by the ghostly shades and mists, they ran to cross the ditch, holding hands tightly. Quickly they crawled under the thorn brake where the rest of the team was waiting.

Trembling and incoherent Marya bit back her sobs, hugging Aeolyn, Friedr, and Christoph as if she would never let them go.

Edwin could see Chris was low on chi. Working as the team they'd become, they cast soothe and calm on her once again, with Edwin unobtrusively carrying the spells. Christoph whispered to Marya, holding and comforting her. Together they eased her distress enough to enable her to continue on the journey they planned for the night, while Edwin healed her scratched legs and one large gash on her arm.

"I...I used to be a healer...before...before...." Marya's whisper was sad as she watched him. Something irreplaceable was lost, leaving her forlorn. Aeolyn hugged her, consoling her. "But I couldn't help them...couldn't help. He wouldn't stop...wouldn't quit. They suffered so much!"

Edwin knew without a doubt what she was referring to, and it made him sick. Kneeling before her and holding her hand between both of his, he said urgently, "It wasn't your fault, Marya. You could have done nothing. Do you understand? They were beyond all our ability to help them, once he began his ritual. You couldn't have helped them. The only kindness they would have appreciated was death." Her brown eyes were full of tears, as she mutely nodded, clearly unable to understand.

Friedr and Aeolyn looked sharply at him, realizing he knew what was in the dungeon, and their eyes met, both full of guilt for having led Christoph down there, when Edwin had marked it clearly on the map for them to avoid. Kneeling as he hunted in his pack for the medical kit, Christoph also nodded his head mutely, unable to express himself any more than Marya could.

With her finger to her lips for silence, Aeolyn led Marya off and quickly helped her into her leathers. Tears streamed down Marya's face as she donned her trousers and vest over the lacy underclothes a proper young lady supposedly wore, feeling grateful to finally have a use for them. Trimmed off at the hips, her delicate shift made an acceptable shirt, and after Aeolyn cut the legs off her bloomers, they were fine.

Edwin had been right—Marya's leathers were too big despite the strange repairs they'd made but would do for the trip home. "At least they're better than nothing," Aeolyn said, eyeing her critically and doing the laces up as tight as they would go. "I don't think they'll fall off."

Marya put her boots on over her stockings and once again bit back sobs. "These are my things! You cleaned them! You fixed them! I thought I would never see my things again. He took them...he took them...took my stone shard...took everything." Her eyes became wild, and she began shuddering again.

Edwin finally layered a dampening field with a stronger soothing spell over her to calm her enough to do what must still be done. Looking at her with his healing sight, he added an earth shield to cut her off from the poison of the land, weaving it in and tying it off so her own chi maintained it all.

Christoph's eyes widened at what Edwin so casually did, with less thought than he would have given to casting a novice-level sleep spell. "Edwin, that was well done," he whispered. Edwin smiled and nodded.

"Shh...shh.... It'll be fine. We're here with you." Aeolyn put her arms around Marya, comforting her. "We must go now." While Marya put her armor on with Christoph's assistance, Aeolyn and Friedr buried the shawl, torn dress, and petticoats, along with the useless, shredded shoes under the thorn bush, using their earth-magic to do it quickly and noiselessly.

Then Edwin turned to healing and soothing the two fire-mages. They weren't quite as distressed as

Christoph but were both upset over something. Aeolyn's arm throbbed, so much so that Edwin could feel it without delving her. "You two managed to find a fight," he whispered dryly.

They simply nodded, but their eyes told him there was much to hear later. "This will leave a scar, I think," he said when he finished healing the dog bite as well as he could. "Chris may have saved your arm by washing it in the kitchen. There's some sort of infection in the dog's saliva, and it's an aggressive poison." He delved her to see if it had spread to her blood, but thanks to Christoph washing the wound out, it hadn't, although he'd have to watch her carefully until it was fully healed. He cast heal and bound it again, packing it with the healing balm they brought for just such an emergency. He then used the pain-relieving spells, and Aeolyn's face lost most of its tension.

"Thank you, Edwin. You're very gentle when you tend to the really painful things." Smiling wryly, she began collecting her pack. "We're lucky to have you."

Edwin grinned. Hearing praise fall from Aeolyn's lips was wonderful. He turned to Christoph, who was in a terrible state, and he suspected he would find out about it later. "Something has upset you. Let me help, my brother." Bolstering his barriers and adding a soothing spell, he wove in an earth shield before tying them off, saying, "We'll talk soon, I promise, but this will help you now."

"Thank you, Edwin," Chris said gratefully, after a moment of pained silence. "I couldn't use my sight or cast healing spells properly there. It worked, but not as well as it should have. I think I know part of what's wrong with Marya, but you're right, we'll talk later.

Right now, we must concentrate on helping her so she can travel tonight. She can't really travel the way she is right now. Something happened to her ability to use magic, and I think I know what the problem is, from a personal point of view."

"I'm glad I'm not imagining things. I can feel her chi, but she can't seem to use her basic skills. If you can sustain the field of spells I've layered over her, I can maintain strength and soothe. She's in poor physical condition and won't be able to travel unless we bolster her. Even so, Friedr and I will have to pretty much carry her most of the way before we can stop and make camp in the morning."

Friedr agreed, and Edwin surreptitiously strengthened Christoph, who simply gave the lopsided smile that seemed to be all he could muster. "Chris, you'll have to catch and maintain all the spells by yourself when I scout on the wind, but each time, I'll return as quickly as I can. This way I can conserve my chi for healing, since I'm the only one who has the full use of my abilities right now."

Marya overheard the last part of this exchange and was confused, but Aeolyn told her, "We'll tell you all about it later. But we must leave this place as quickly as we can."

"Yes! Please, let's leave now," she agreed, overwhelmed by a sense of urgency.

Soon they were moving through the mist, traveling as swiftly as they could, following the empty road. The darkness and the thick, freezing fog concealed them from any who might be awake in the keep. It was nearly midnight. As they ran around the main bend in the road and out of sight, Christoph thought the guards should be waking up, each thinking he was the only one who'd fallen asleep at his post, if everything went according to plan.

The frozen dirt was so hard, their feet left no prints. The mists were thick, forming icicles that hung from the branches of the thorn forest. Periodically, they stopped and Edwin sent his spirit out scouting for any who might be following them, but he found no one stirring other than the guards who still paced the exact same areas they always did. The new shift was completely unaware anything was amiss in the servants' quarters or conservatory.

Dawn found them many leagues to the southwest, well away from the Shadow Castle. As the sky began to lighten, they made camp deep under the thorn forest canopy.

Marya was too exhausted to ask any questions. She fell into her bedroll as if it were the softest bed she'd ever slept in.

For the first time in his life, Edwin didn't trust himself to behave around a girl. Chris grinned at him as they settled into their bedrolls.

"For some reason, you don't fear I'll try to steal your girl. I wonder why," Christoph muttered dryly to a red-faced Edwin. "Is it because you know I prefer men that you trust me so with her?"

"Shut up and go to sleep," he muttered back, grinning widely, "and keep your hands to yourself. *I* am not one of your boyfriends."

Christoph's wicked laugh didn't disturb Marya at all, she slept so deeply. They didn't mount a watch, trusting instead to the thorn forest to protect and conceal them as they all dropped into an exhausted sleep under the shield Edwin raised over them.

***

Sometime late in the afternoon, Edwin was, as usual, awake before anyone else. Sitting in the cold light of day with his cloak thrown back and his shirt-sleeves pushed up, he filled all the water bottles before anyone else even stirred. He sat with his eyes closed and his hands over the basin, calling the water for them to bathe in. It slowly funneled into the bowl, guided by his air-magic. Even in his semi-trance, he couldn't get Marya out of his mind. Now he'd actually met her, she filled his every waking moment. He'd made himself leave the shelter to get away from his wayward need to touch her hair and hold her.

He felt the air gently move and opened his eyes. Marya sat perfectly still next to him, watching. Her face was dirty, and with her fancy shirt and patchwork leathers and her hair coming out of its braids, she looked like a lost waif. Edwin fought down the urge to hold her and shelter her from the world.

"Who *are* you, Edwin Farmer? Where have you come from?" The look on her face made him smile. She looked like a small child who'd asked an impertinent question.

It surprised him. "Um, I'm a farm boy from the village of Markett in the world of Ariend, nothing more. I'm not a great warrior as Friedr is or a powerful battle-mage like Aeolyn. Nor am I as gifted a healer as Christoph is, though I hope to spend my life healing when we're done here. I'm only a farm boy." As he said those words, he realized the truth of them. "I don't think I'll ever go back to the farm. My path has changed. It'll always be a part of me, but I intend to be a healer. I also have to use my battle-magic somehow, to keep my chi balanced, so I'll have to figure out a way to do both. I'm also going to return with Christoph and Friedr to make the land of Mal Evol bloom again, and when we do, we *will* stop D'Mal's encroachment of Neveyah, Goddess willing. Never doubt it."

She didn't know what to say. She could see he'd sworn before Aeos to return on what seemed to her a hopeless quest. Instead, she said, "I was a healer long ago, but no more. Perhaps he took that from me too, something else I will never get back."

This time Edwin didn't know how to reply.

Marya asked another question. "I can see you're calling water, but it's a slow process, as if it's from far away." She closed her eyes. "There's water nearby, but this isn't from there. How is this possible?" The blue of her tattoos was brighter. The chi was returning to her augmentations, but they were changing. The green of the healer was diminishing. What remained was taking on a darker, brownish tint, the color of the plant-healers and herbalists at the college in Aeoven.

"I call it from the mist and clouds so we don't drink the water of Mal Evol. In this way, D'Mal can't see our minds and read our intent." He waited for her next question.

Marya looked at Edwin's augmentations, seeing them fully for the first time, and she was clearly mystified. Touching his right hand, she asked, "How is it you're marked so? These are the flowering vines, crescent moon, and stars of the healer adept. I've seen your work with Aeolyn's dog bite, and you truly are an adept. You've more strength than you realize, and more skill." Edwin's gratified smile warmed her heart with its frankness. *He isn't used to receiving compliments,* she thought. "All the right runes are there for one who will rise high within the healers. Wisdom, empathy, and skill, and they're represented in greater numbers than is usual."

She patted the back of his left hand. "Here you have the barbed vines of the battle-mage, with equal ability in all the elements, closely woven with the strength runes of the warrior and the stealth and luck runes of the assassin. Again, there are many more than are usual on one mage. Your face bears the lightning bolt but in two colors. Then there is the crescent moon and stars trailing over your eye. As if that weren't strange enough, there is the luck rune balancing the healers signs, and behind your ears, the assassin's stealth rune. How is it you're marked so? You must be near my age."

"Christoph believes the Goddess created my talents for the sole purpose of stealing you back from D'Mal," he replied. "Also, I'm new to the Temple, having only been in Neveyah since harvest, five months ago." Edwin saw the question on her lips and answered before she could ask. "I'm the son of John Farmer, whom some here know of."

"I know of your father. My uncle quested with him," she replied with wonder. "Many good things have been said of him, but no one knew where he went when he took his wife and child and left Aeoven."

They sat and talked, and Edwin told her how he came to Neveyah. She seemed to enjoy hearing his story, diverting her mind from her troubles.

It took Edwin's breath away when she unconsciously reached for his hand as he was telling her about the journey to Aeoven and how little he knew of life beyond the confines of his father's farm when he came there.

Soon Christoph was up and about and talking to Marya about his first meeting with Edwin. "And there he was, surrounded by a bevy of buxom wenches, each with plans for furthering his education. He was having none of it—he simply wanted to eat his soup in peace." His low laugh was unforced and happy, as if the trauma of the previous night had never happened. "Of course, I rescued him. Friedr and I knew he was something special right then, before he was even tested, but we didn't know *how* special. He has proven to be much more than a pretty face."

Edwin was suspicious of Christoph's jolly mood, but he went along with it. *He could be putting on a brave face to keep Marya in a good frame of mind. Or he could be avoiding something upsetting to him. It's probably both.*

"Chris, remember when you and I first came to the Temple?" Her voice was low and full of emotion.

"Yes. You were my first friend," Christoph smiled at the memory and squeezed her hand. "I was completely lost and confused. You showed me where everything was and sat with me when mealtime came. You introduced me to Friedr and Aeolyn. I was so lucky to have met you."

"*I'm* lost now," she replied sadly. "I can't *feel* you or Edwin or anyone. My abilities are gone." The sense of emptiness in her simple statement was overwhelming. "I can sense water though, so maybe I'll still have that. Maybe. It would be something at least." Tears rolled down her cheeks.

Edwin reached for her hand in sympathy, and she let him hold it, while Christoph held her other hand. They all sat silently, absorbing the loss she felt so deeply. They had agreed as long as she was able to function and it didn't interfere with the journey, they wouldn't buffer her emotions, because she would have to deal with them sometime, and it would be better to let them out naturally.

Finally, Christoph spoke. "Marya, you still have the ability, but I know why you can't use it." His voice was warm and soothing. "It will take patience and trust. You've suffered serious trauma over the last few months, and you've shut down the part of you that is empathic in order to survive. This is something time might heal, time and trust. Do you trust me?"

"I'm filled with nameless fears," Marya admitted sadly. "They overwhelm me and I panic. I trust you, my dear, dear friend. You know I do. But I know why they sent you on this trip. The abbess, everyone…they're all afraid I've been violated. But he never actually did more than kiss my hand, though he did so at every opportunity." She shuddered. She didn't see the sudden flush of anger that crossed Edwin's face on hearing her words.

"The weight of his desire is overwhelming. The threat is always there—the threat and the knowledge of what he yearns to do to…to me. To anyone, Chris, not only me. What he believes is good and normal…he…he sent me dreams. You can't imagine the depravity." She paled and her lips trembled. Taking a deep breath, she continued her story, saying, "Stefyn stole my magic and took my possessions. He insinuated himself into my dreams if I fell too deeply asleep. It was worse than I could possibly explain." Marya struggled but somehow managed to finish her sentence.

Drawing on all her courage, she told them, "He never violated me despite all of the things he threatened me with, all the unspeakable things I overheard him doing to others, all the disgusting things he forced me to do in my own dreams...." She gave a little hiccup of a sob. "Chris, you can't imagine...he made me...he made me like it...." Her voice ended on a wail. Christoph held her in his arms, delving her and casting spells to help her deal with the shame. Inserting a small forgetting into her short-term memory, he sent her thoughts of support and encouragement.

Edwin lent his support but didn't assist. *You're too involved,* Christoph warned him through the link. *Only lend me your strength.*

After a moment, she was able to continue, not remembering how upset she'd been only a moment before or what she'd admitted. "He didn't rape my body. I know he would have done so sooner or later. His plan was to bond with me immediately on his return. I couldn't have submitted to him willingly with all I know about him." Her voice shook. "It nauseates me to even think of...with him. He takes great joy in knowing my terror and revulsion. He thrives on forcing people to enjoy his attentions." Marya smiled at last, but it was a sad smile. "They always send you to deal with the troubled ones. This time they're wasting your precious skills on one who doesn't require them." She looked at the ground, unable to meet Christoph's eyes.

Edwin's eyes met his over her head, and they silently agreed she was unaware of the magnitude of her emotional injuries. They would have to tread carefully to rebuild her healing abilities, if indeed it could even be done.

"That's only partly why I'm on this trip," Christoph smiled, trying to divert her. "I'm mostly here to teach this ignorant lout healing techniques. You know, Edwin is much older than the other students so he was never enrolled in classes. The poor boy has enjoyed private tutoring. This oaf is seriously in need of a wider social circle. This is his idea of a great party." He gestured at the wilderness around them, rolling his eyes. "In Aeoven, I was forced to pry him out of his books every night so he would eat."

Laughing, Edwin shrugged, and Chris grinned back at him.

"I've been given the best teachers Neveyah has to offer, despite my ignorant loutishness. And I'm quite happy with my social circle now." He smiled at Marya. A warm feeling of contentment at being in her company stole over him, despite the serious conversation. "Christoph lives to have parties." He snickered, adding, "And Dane lives to clean up after them!"

"I'm not so bad, am I?" Christoph pretended to pout. "Besides, you'd never leave your rooms if I didn't have parties."

"It's true," agreed Edwin. "I'm rather a stick-in-the-mud." He couldn't stop grinning.

Marya looked from Christoph to Edwin, her eyes wide, smiling uncertainly. This would have been a dangerous moment with Stefyn. She didn't know if she should smile or not, another sign of her trauma.

Christoph's eyes as they met Edwin's said it all. She was once a merry girl with an easy laugh, but it was long ago. That girl was gone now, perhaps forever.

Chapter 26

Once Friedr and Aeolyn awoke, Edwin excused himself to go and scout. They had discussed among themselves and agreed Marya shouldn't know the full extent of his ability. Aeolyn rightly feared once D'Mal discovered her missing, he would see in her mind how they'd started a bloody revolution in his homeland as a means of getting him out of his own castle. She felt if he were to suspect he'd been manipulated into such a corner, he would immediately rally the children of the Bull God to crush Neveyah in reprisal. Marya could know nothing of what they'd done, because D'Mal could only be allowed to see her retrieval as simply a crime of opportunity.

Crawling away from the group until he was out of sight and pulling his cloak about himself more closely, he centered himself and sent his spirit out on the wind. The distraction of Marya grounded him too well for his own peace of mind, and the wry thought he was completely smitten with her crossed his mind. Despite that, he calmed himself, and in only a moment, he was drifting over the thorn forest where their camp lay hidden.

Soon he found the road and followed it, finding no one traveling in the gray midday. Such emptiness wasn't unusual. During the month they spent watching the Shadow Castle, they had seen few travelers from the west. Two of those lay dead in the dungeon, one on the altar and the other in a cell.

The group had only come about ten leagues. Aeolyn would be disappointed, but they couldn't push

Marya any harder. It was terribly difficult for her, even with Friedr and Edwin half-carrying her most of the way. Tonight would be better. She would be rested because of the barrier/shield Edwin had laid over their shelter. He had sensed that she slept deeply and well, for what must be the first time since her kidnapping.

Drifting over the parapet, he could see the guards walking the walls exactly as they always did. The keep itself was silent, as it usually was. Only the barracks showed any sign of life and this too was completely normal.

He chose to drift on the wind, looking through the windows as it was easier and quicker than following the water into the keep. The more he used the skills of far-seeing and fetching, the less chi he used in performing those tasks.

Peering through the kitchen window, he saw the old woman still sleeping, as was the old man in the vestibule. Drifting around to the conservatory, he looked in and saw Brec still out cold and unlikely to wake anytime soon. Inside, the same guards from the previous evening were returned to their posts and determined to stay awake this time, moving and stretching to keep alert. Each one apparently believed he was the only one to have fallen asleep, and he would certainly say nothing about it.

In the barracks, the men went about their business. All the while, they studiously ignored Narg's flayed hide, which, though it reeked badly, still decorated the wall. Edwin doubted anyone would ever dare to remove it, though they'd finally tossed his remains into the thorn bushes for the carrion birds to pick over.

In short, it was business as usual and nothing to worry about. Ghosting over the thorn forest, he searched out the trails the legions used, finding them to be as empty as the road. Their abandoned camps were forlorn places. The tents and gear too heavy to carry on a forced march were left to rot or be taken over by the thorn forest.

He returned and drew Aeolyn aside, reporting what he'd seen.

After a while, the women went a small distance away to bathe in privacy and talk quietly, while the men did the same. "Aeolyn and Marya were roommates while they were students," Friedr said as he brushed his tangled hair, re-braiding it and combing his beard. "They're as close as sisters. This is why Aeolyn is leading this quest. She couldn't rest until she was granted permission to go on a rescue mission. I'm along solely for my entertainment value."

"We would have those dogs on our trail right now if you two hadn't taken care of them." Christoph chuckled, but his mirth faded as he recalled the events of the night before. "And you're right, Friedr. It was quite an entertaining fight."

"Tell me what happened to you. What affected you so badly?" Edwin looked over his shoulder, but the girls were nowhere near. "I know something bad happened, Chris. You are *way* too cheerful, like when you're hiding something and not handling it well."

Friedr looked sharply at him. *Oh my. He knows Chris well, much better than I thought. He knows all about him and most likely always has.* He kept his thoughts to himself, watching the tension between them as Edwin probed him for information he didn't wish to give.

Christoph's face went blank, and he was obliged to reinforce his barriers before he could speak. "Oh, it was just your usual dungeon."

Edwin immediately knew what they'd found there. Christoph's barriers were as shaky as a one-legged ladder, and now he knew why. "Why were you there? You were to keep to the plan, remember?" Edwin looked from Christoph to Friedr, his whisper sharp. "It was marked on the map so you *wouldn't* stumble into it." His angry blue eyes demanded an answer. "I even told you this!"

After a moment of silence, Friedr confessed. "Well, when we looked on the map and saw the passage to the dungeon, right there where the pooches' corpses were, it seemed like a good idea to put them where they wouldn't be noticed right away." He looked uncomfortable under Edwin's scrutiny. "It was my error. I didn't even think about him being a healer." He sighed, and unable to meet Edwin's eyes, he muttered, "Goddess forgive me—but that place left a mark on my soul too."

As they explained what occurred there, Edwin understood the full force of the pain and confusion that nearly incapacitated Christoph the night before. Simply telling the sordid details left him an emotional wreck. He was unable to do more than barely control his panic, and he refused to admit it, insisting he was fine. Edwin also now saw in Christoph exactly what caused Marya to shut down her empathy. *I've not been affected because of my barrier/shield combination. But they only know how to make barriers, and in that place, those would crumble like a mud fence in a flood. It's how they were taught.*

With his healing sight, he saw Christoph still had no barriers to speak of, resulting in him being compromised by Marya's unstable mental state. Her barely controlled hysteria was subtly affecting him, making him unable to maintain his separation. And he didn't see it was happening, compromising his ability to make logical decisions. Edwin thought, *If I let this continue, he'll spiral out of control and we'll have two victims. We need his ability to heal her mind. He can't heal her if he is broken too.*

Edwin knew what must be done. Snapping his own barrier/shield into place against his friend, he put his hands on Christoph's shoulders and said quietly, "You're having trouble with this. The part that makes you an extraordinary healer is also your greatest weakness. Your barriers are non-existent, and you are being affected by Marya's pain."

Christoph looked at him, surprise and anger flaring in his eyes. "Weakness! *I* am the teacher, Edwin. What do you know of a healer's weakness?" His anger at Edwin's impudence escalated into a flash of rage.

Surprised by Christoph's fury over so small a matter, Friedr sat back, quietly observing the situation. *This is something serious, and Edwin has made a command decision to solve this problem right now. Chris's inability to separate from his healing empathy can compromise us. Edwin isn't stupid.* He watched them through narrowed eyes, knowing Christoph had the power to seriously harm him if Edwin couldn't control him.

"I know a great deal about it, as you know very well. Your experience last night and your deep friendship have made you susceptible to Marya's panic. The empathic connection necessary to perform healing *forces* you to feel it. You know this is true." Edwin spoke calmly, ignoring the barely contained rage flaring more out of control in Christoph's eyes with each word he said. "Even under the best of circumstances, your personal barriers are not as strong as they need to be."

Christoph tried to shake free, but Edwin gripped him by the shoulders, forcing him to pay attention. "Let go of me. This is outrageous!" Hatred flared in Christoph's eyes. "You have no right!" Friedr tensed, prepared to physically break them up, fearful he would have to harm a man he considered his brother in order to save him.

"This is where I get to use the tricks you taught me." Edwin looked solemnly at Christoph, still forcing him to meet his eyes. "I will help you maintain your distance from the memory so you can see it dispassionately. I'm placing a dampening field on your emotions now—do you feel it?"

For a moment, Friedr feared Christoph might lash out at Edwin with his empathic ability. He'd never seen his friend so enraged, but the moment passed. The anger faded from Christoph's eyes, and uncertainty took its place.

Friedr let out the breath he hadn't realized he'd been holding.

Edwin quietly asked, "How often do you cast calm when you enter a room? Is it because you can't take the barrage of emotions? We've talked about this before, my brother."

"You're right," Christoph finally admitted after a long silence. "And no, I don't feel what you did. It's deftly done." His voice had a dry tone to it as he said, "Thank you. You have become good at seeing to the heart of the matter. My anger was—aaugh! I owe you an apology. Goddess forgive me. I wanted to hurt you so badly. Please forgive me." Edwin nodded and clasped his shoulder. Christoph felt deeply contrite as he asked, "And when did you learn the trick of isolating an emotion? It's an advanced technique."

"You did it for the boy in Wister who'd been burned so badly, and Beryl has taught me many useful skills. But mostly, I watch you work." Edwin's smile lit up his face. "You really do understand how to calm and soothe your patients, but it's because you're feeling their fear and pain too keenly. I think the reason you're the best healer for emotional trauma is your ability to get right next to the patient's suffering. You will do anything to cure them because you feel it so clearly. And yet, despite that, you have no fear of being overcome by your patient's emotional state although you *should* fear it." Edwin looked to Friedr for support, who nodded in agreement, his flinty blue eyes holding Christoph's confused dark ones for a moment, as if to emphasize his accord.

"You always dive right in, believing beyond a doubt you can cure them, regardless of the personal cost, and then spend the night rebuilding your barriers and trying to ground and center yourself." Christoph started, his eyes betraying his surprise at hearing Edwin speak of his secret, but Edwin continued as if he hadn't noticed. "I find it embarrassing to have to admit this, but the extreme empathy is the one aspect of healing I am fearful of. It terrifies me. It's the occupational hazard that can break us. But don't worry. I'm here to help you right now." Edwin's earnest smile brought an answering one from Chris. "See? What I'm doing for you now is simply the finest water-shield, layered into your barrier."

After a moment Christoph said, "Thank you, my brother."

"Yes, he *is* getting good, isn't he? Only Edwin would think of raising both barriers and shields. But only he has the ability to do so, though it would be good if you could learn it," agreed Friedr sardonically. *Edwin just said exactly what Abbess Marta is always telling him. Will it really do any good?* He carefully kept his thoughts to himself, but suddenly, he felt an unaccustomed sense of foreboding. *What happens if Edwin isn't there to shield him when he's faced with another dungeon? What happens if he can't maintain his barriers?*

Friedr saw the girls approaching and murmured, "Since we're as clean as we'll get in our allotted drop of water, we need to break camp. Aeolyn will want us to begin traveling as soon as it's dark." He would have much to discuss with his wife when next they stopped to rest.

***

They set the pattern they hoped to follow until Braden. There would be ten hard nights of travel to the southern border if they could keep to the pace they were traveling at. At that point, they would have another seven nights before they reached Braden. Their rations might not last to the southern border, however, and then they would have to decide between going hungry or living off the land, which would open them up to D'Mal's view.

Even after they left the soil of Mal Evol, they would be in danger from the baron's wrath. They were sure once Brec discovered Marya was gone, his master would immediately set him on their trail, searching for them. D'Mal would not take her liberation well at all.

Their plan was to find a place a day or so across the border and make their stand. They hoped to have a chance to rest and develop a strategy for taking Brec down. All of the farms and towns east of Braden were now uninhibited. Any one of them would be a decent place to rest on soil still claimed by Neveyah, although they were in danger of falling to Tauron's poison at any time, which was why they were abandoned.

While they tried to leave no trail, they knew there would be something to follow, Marya's mind. Everything they did and said would be there for D'Mal to see unless they were extremely lucky.

Leaving their little copse, they traveled in the frozen starlight. Laughing often and chatting happily, Aeolyn and Marya spent most of their time walking with each other.

Anytime Marya tripped or stumbled, Edwin was there to catch her, making sure she had her footing before he dropped back. Friedr smiled as he watched the romance unfolding in front of his eyes. Somehow, seeing Edwin behaving like a normal man around a woman made him feel immensely better. "I knew he was meant for her, but I needed to see it to believe it," he muttered to Christoph as Edwin once again jumped forward to catch Marya as she tripped over a root.

"He's even worried she might not like him much," replied Christoph, grinning impishly. "I think he has nothing to worry about."

Marya clung to Edwin's hand a shade longer than really necessary, and Friedr snorted softly, saying, "Oh, she's besotted all right. She's fallen for him like a tree in a windstorm."

"But will he be able to restrain himself until she feels comfortable enough to…you know." Christoph actually blushed. "She's been abused in a way just as bad as a physical rape, Friedr. It could take months for her to come to terms with it."

"You know Edwin better than that. You've seen the sort of self-control he has around the ladies," Friedr chuckled quietly. "He's a healer too, don't forget. You trained him to deal with rape victims. You know as well as I do he's the only man for her in Aeos's eyes."

"You're right as usual," Christoph replied, smiling as Edwin dropped back to walk with them again.

"So, Edwin," said Friedr, with a twinkle in his eye, "I've noticed you're very quick to catch Marya whenever she stumbles. Could it be that *you* are falling?"

Turning red and smiling sheepishly, Edwin met his inquiring gaze. "I've completely fallen, Friedr. I freely admit to it. But Goddess help me," Edwin's voice turned serious, "She isn't ready for any sort of relationship thanks to that bastard." The sudden steel in his voice and the jut of his jaw surprised Friedr. "I don't know if she'll ever get over what he did to her." The look on Edwin's face was bleak. "You can't imagine what he did to her in her dreams, using the sacred gift of empathy to do it. He burned it into her mind, don't you see? He's more than a monster. I don't know what he is."

"She'll get past it, brother, I promise you," Christoph said sympathetically. "I'm working with her daily, and she *is* making progress. Have patience. It will all come right, I swear."

"He's right," said Friedr, sensing Edwin needed a little moral support. "Keep on doing as you are, and she'll see you're not dangerous to her."

"But that's the problem, isn't it?" Edwin smiled wryly. "I feel dangerous where she's concerned."

The three men laughed and began walking a little faster to catch up with Aeolyn and Marya.

They traveled as quickly as possible, often taking the trails the legions used for their own purposes. At varying intervals, they stopped, and Christoph and Edwin went off to scout. In this way, they were able to travel nearly three times as far as the previous night. At dawn, they wearily settled into a hiding place well back from the trail. They were quiet and exhausted. Once again, they trusted Edwin's barrier/shield and the thick thorn forest canopy to hide them.

In the midafternoon sunshine of their third day out of the Shadow Castle, Edwin woke and quietly crawled out to call water for the day. He was still tired and unenthusiastic about spending another night traveling hard, but he knew they must make as much distance as they could before Brec discovered Marya was gone.

Holding the jugs, he looked through the canopy and found only fleeting clouds high above. He would have more difficulty getting the water than on previous days. He reached up and willed the water to fill the jugs. Soon he turned to finding the water for bathing. It was more difficult than it had been, but he was able to get what they needed and still retain a good reserve of chi.

When he opened his eyes, he found Christoph seated next to him. "You used more chi than you have lately," Christoph said. He peered through the thorn canopy to the blue sky above. "It's warmer today, and there's no fog."

"Yes," Edwin replied. "I think the spell D'Mal put on the weather is fading." His voice sounded tired.

"Perhaps you should call the water in the morning before we camp, while the mists are still out. Or do you think you will be too tired?" Christoph surreptitiously gauged Edwin's health. It wasn't as good as he would have liked it to be, causing him to check everyone else. They were all exhausted. In a fight with any of D'Mal's guards, it was doubtful as to what the outcome would be.

"What?" Edwin asked, looking at him out of the corner of his eye. "Do you see something you don't like? You don't look so good yourself, health-wise."

"How did you know I was scanning you? No, don't tell me. Just let me believe I wasn't so clumsy you felt it." Christoph reddened, and Edwin grinned at his discomfort.

"We're getting fairly good at layering healing spells and maintaining them, so perhaps we could work something out using strengthening spells," Edwin suggested. He yawned, stretching hugely, and apologized for doing so. "Why can't we tie them off like we do for wards? It's been working with my shields, and I've been doing it with soothe and calm for Marya. It's really helped."

"I don't know. No one has ever tried, so I never thought of it. But no one has shields like yours. The only problem I can see is if we keep on supporting this forced march magically, we'll pay dearly for it." Christoph's worry was palpable. "We must go at a more reasonable pace and stop sooner."

Friedr came to sit beside them, saying, "I know. There's no help for it. We must do as you wish, but we're in grave danger every day we're in this land."

"I'll go back and have a little look at the keep as quickly as I can, and then we'll know who and what follow us." Edwin felt sure Brec was awake. Whether he knew Marya was gone was another story. If the old woman had given her away, then they would be in trouble.

He centered himself, floated above their hiding place, then drifted toward the Shadow Castle. As he arrived near the walled garden, he saw the guards were not in their usual places. *This isn't good. Where are they?* He ghosted along to the barracks, where a terrified and angry Brec was brutally demanding answers from men who didn't have them.

All of the minotaurs who had been stationed at the tower door to the rose garden had been flogged, and one unfortunate guard was in the process of being kicked nigh unto death as Edwin watched. The dogs' corpses hadn't yet been discovered, and Brec was furious. His tirade indicated his belief they had been allowed to escape.

Apparently, Brec's main worry was the dogs might have killed Marya, and if such a thing had happened he would be treated less kindly than Narg was.

The one positive thing that emerged before Edwin departed was Brec believed Marya escaped on her own and was still somewhere in the vicinity of the castle. *At least he doesn't know we've taken her. He has no idea how far we've traveled.*

Edwin didn't watch the sickening drama as it unfolded. Instead he cast widely to see if anyone was on their trail. As far as he could see, no one was following them. That, he now knew, was about to change.

He returned and found only Friedr sitting beside him. Aeolyn and Christoph were talking to Marya, keeping her occupied while Edwin scouted. "Brec is awake. He knows she's gone. He's disciplining the guards, all of them. They'll be looking for her now if I heard his ranting correctly."

Friedr was silent for a moment, then he said, "Then we must be on our way as soon as we can."

Chapter 27

Friedr immediately began breaking camp, and soon they were ready. Aeolyn decided it would be the last time they used the road except when there was no other choice. After this night, they would have to travel more carefully. They were somewhat closer to the border, and Aeolyn still hoped they could arrive there in eight more days even at the slower rate, though Friedr was doubtful.

That morning they had been stalled for half an hour, trying to work out a compromise with Marya once she found out Brec was awake. She was terrified she was going to be the vector that got them all killed and refused to go any further until they somehow eliminated her as a threat.

Her physical condition was poor. Their pace was more difficult for her to maintain than she would admit, despite the fact Edwin and Friedr alternated supporting her.

The other trouble was her connection to Stefyn D'Mal. Now Brec was awake, he would be open to D'Mal's mind. With one look, he would see she was gone and look for her himself. No one knew how it would play out, but each had concerns they carefully hid from Marya.

She brought it up as they were breaking camp, refusing to leave until they cast a forgetting on her. "I don't know how you know what you know, and I don't *want* to know. Don't tell me anything, please! Don't say anything where I can hear you. He's been in my mind and knows how to single me out," she begged them, shuddering. "He's a master of what he calls mind-to-mind touch. He uses Brec as his eyes and ears when he's not there in person, and believe me, it's not Brec simply seeing for him. He takes over his body, wrenches away Brec's mind. It takes a huge amount of chi, and he can only do it for small lengths of time, less than a day, but he's more powerful than you can imagine. When he does this, he has full use of his own skills plus Brec's. Now he's in Serende, where he can more easily draw chi directly from the dread god he serves, though it burns him out to do so. Please cast a forgetting on me. Please!" Christoph reinforced the calming spells on Marya, but she couldn't relax enough to benefit from them.

Edwin layered a dampening field over her again, weaving the spells Chris cast into it and then lacing one more for ease. The combination calmed her somewhat, lowering her rapid heart rate.

Christoph's eyes widened in amazement at how easily Edwin used the dampening field and the innovative way he'd laced his own spells around the one Christoph had already cast, making it more effective. *He will truly be a master. He uses spells in ways no one has ever thought of. I will definitely use that trick myself. All healers will benefit from it.*

Hiding his awe at Edwin's boldness, Christoph spoke gently. "Marya, what if we did cast a forgetting on you? You would still be open to his mind, and then he would have you, unaware of who and what he is. He would lure you away using magic and lies. At least this way you know what he is. You still have some defenses, or he would have had you long ago." His low voice was urgent. "We will tell you nothing. It is the only thing we can do."

"At least blindfold me," she begged Friedr, clutching at his armor. "Then I won't know where we are, and he won't see through my eyes."

He was taken aback by the near hysteria of her anxiety, forcing himself to think dispassionately. *Settle down, Friedr. She's a healer and suffering from trauma. You know what to do.* His deep voice was unworried as he took her hands and patted them consolingly. "Don't worry. We'll solve this minor problem, I promise you." Trying to think calm thoughts, he looked at Edwin, who immediately forgot himself and put his arm about her shoulders, sending her supportive thoughts.

Fortunately, she was too overwrought to be startled by his gesture. Gradually, the lace of spells layered on her took effect, and Marya began to calm down again, and after giving Edwin a quick hug, she quickly pulled away from him.

"Oh Goddess. I'm an idiot," Edwin muttered to Friedr, with a stricken look on his face. "What was I thinking? She can't bear to be hugged by me. D'Mal instilled a fear of intimacy in her she can't get past, because the trauma is still too raw in her mind. I know this. I'm a healer, and I still had to put my arm around her."

"No, Edwin. She's a traumatized healer. Non-threatening physical contact is exactly what she needed right then," Friedr said firmly. "It was an act of kindness. She wasn't threatened by it, she calmed down immediately, and she even hugged you in appreciation. You did just right. We must *not* let her feel alone. It's the one thing they stress when they teach us about dealing with abused healers." Friedr gripped Edwin's shoulder, commiserating with him, acknowledging the damage Marya suffered. "But you have a long, hard road ahead of you, my brother."

Edwin nodded mutely. He couldn't do anything about that, so he turned to solving the immediate problem of how to protect her and still make their way to safety.

The truth was the main trouble *would* be Marya, both her connection to D'Mal and her poor physical health. Edwin said, "We knew these problems would be a major factor in getting you home safely when we started three months ago. It was this way yesterday and the day before. Nothing has changed. We will get you home one way or another. I promise." His earnest blue eyes completely charmed her, but she remained concerned about the danger she posed to her dear friends.

"Edwin, if he finds out you're the one who came for me, he'll do worse than kill you. A nice boy like you—you can't imagine what he's capable of," she replied.

"I've been in his dungeon, Marya—I know." Edwin's calm statement was news to her. He held her hand gently as his words sank in. "I've seen his handiwork."

Marya's face blanched, but she said firmly, "Then you understand why I don't want to be the one who sends you there as his guest." She began rolling up her bedroll, nervously trying to stay busy.

The four held a quick, whispered discussion and at last agreed to blindfold her, though it would make traveling much more difficult. Aeolyn decided the most effective way to do it, saying, "We will stick to the road tonight. Edwin, you and Christoph guide her, one on each side holding her by the arm and carrying her if needed. Friedr and I will scout. We can alternate if either of you become tired, but she'll need the assistance of you two healers to maintain a calm state of mind. She's so close to hysteria all the time, even Friedr and I are being affected by it, and we're not empathic at all, as far as I know. It may be she has no control, and it simply radiates as if she were untrained. We may be able to do this if we stay to the road, but I don't know how long we have now Brec is awake." Aeolyn's whisper was resigned as they decided how to do the monumental task.

"We'll maintain a better dampening field on her, but with her damaged empathy, it's difficult," Christoph told her. Turning to Edwin, he said, "Once she's blindfolded, we'll have to stay in physical contact with her at all times because she's terrified of being alone. She can't tell me about it yet, but I think it's from when she was in the dungeon. One of us must hold her hand or arm and talk to her at all times. She must not be left for even one moment. She might not be able to endure it even with us to support her, though she volunteered for it."

They all looked over at Marya, who stared at the late afternoon sky with a hopeless look on her face. She tried to sit calmly, although she was as jumpy as a cat. She perked up immediately when Aeolyn approached and agreed to blindfold her. The spells layered over her were still effective, and she remained calm as the companions picked up their kits, and using Friedr's spare bandanna to blindfold her, they set out. Friedr and

Aeolyn scouted while Christoph and Edwin each took an arm and guided her. They set as hard a pace as they could manage and maintained it until their first rest stop long after dark.

"Well, the one positive thing is we've had to go more slowly, so we may be able to regain our health and chi before we have to face a battle," Friedr told Aeolyn privately. "But I fear we'll be facing Brec and his minions long before we get to Braden. We can't possibly make it there before he's on our trail. Most likely, the mad priest will be guiding him, so we'll be facing a battle with both magic and weapons. I've a feeling Brec is good with his weapons."

"You're right, we will have to fight him," she replied, "But I really wanted it to be on the soil of Neveyah where we have more of the advantage." Friedr agreed wholeheartedly.

Being blindfolded while walking over the uneven terrain was disorienting and terrifying, but Marya endured it, constantly reminding herself, *I can't let them be caught. He'll kill them. I have to protect them if I can.* Each time she stumbled, Edwin was there to support her. Her nerves were as taut as harp strings, but she managed to keep her fear under control, unaware she was under a heavy dampening field, layered with soothe and calm.

Sensing her fear and disorientation, Edwin tried to reassure her. "Don't worry, Marya. We won't let you fall."

Christoph echoed his words, as they deftly guided her over the rough trail. "Marya, you guided me when I was new and confused and so terribly alone. Let us guide you now."

"Oh, Chris. You were such a crazy, funny boy. Your jokes were famous for keeping the staff on their toes. No one knew what to expect next from you." Marya's giggle was an echo of the old days. "The string in Friedr's pancakes the first morning you were a kitchen helper was a riot!"

Christoph laughed. "I thought I would choke trying not to laugh as Friedr asked in his usual loud exasperation, 'How does he manage to find pancakes with tendons in them?' Poor old Jyll was horrified that something from his kitchen had been less than tasty."

Aeolyn started snickering, and Friedr's face turned red, but he smiled. "That's right. Pick on the barbarian. I did get you back, if you remember right." With a wide grin, he told Edwin, "I snuck into the laundry one night and starched his underclothes until they were as stiff as boards. The poor boy couldn't get comfortable all week!"

"Yes, I do remember, rather well." Chris laughed gleefully. "I used that trick later on Eljer, though he still doesn't know it was me." Christoph smiled wickedly. "Bullying didn't get him far. Still, to be fair, he is an effective journeyman earth-mage, and he seems to be happy with the army."

"Eljer is a complete prat," snorted Friedr. "I put sand in his every possession, including his bed and boots, when he tried to kiss Aeolyn at the summer solstice festival. He was weeks trying to get rid of it all."

"Friedr, you didn't have to be my bodyguard! I gave him a bloody nose. You were always trying to protect me, and I didn't need it." Aeolyn's eyes flashed, and she tossed her head in irritation. "You always made me so mad."

"It wasn't to protect you. I knew better than that," he calmly told her, eyes assuming the flat look that hid his thoughts. "I did it because he tried to kiss you. No one kisses you but me. No one! Not then and not now."

Their childish quarreling made Edwin, Christoph, and Marya burst out laughing, and seeing the humor, they laughed too.

"You're such a jealous man, Friedr," Christoph told him. "I can't tell you how many bloody faces I healed on account of his jealousy, Edwin. But he did keep us entertained." The night passed merrily as they hurried through the dark toward safety.

Marya enjoyed the sound of Edwin's voice and found his quiet strength comforting. Not being able to see him was a positive thing in one way: it removed the distraction of his handsome face. And he *was* attractive, in an honest and earthy way D'Mal's perfect beauty could never compete with. He made her heart skip, though she tried not to notice, knowing she was far too confused at the moment. He had a friendly, open manner, and daydreaming kept her mind off of the peril they were in. She found herself drawn to Edwin more and more as they struggled to take her out of harm's way.

But then she would have to bring herself sharply back to reality. *I most likely have a crush on the new boy, I'm sure. What if I feel this way toward him because of what Stefyn made me do in my dreams? What if this isn't natural? He wouldn't want me if he knew how Stefyn made me feel. Stefyn ruined me when he took my innocence with his filthy nightmares.* She was afraid to ever be intimate with anyone, much less a man as good and honest as Edwin. She felt so unworthy of him. Those thoughts depressed her, and she resolutely tried to put them out of her mind. But they were always there, lurking, poisoning her enjoyment of Edwin's company.

Despite her self-defeating thoughts, she sometimes allowed herself to daydream. *It's like I've been waiting for him all my life.* He gave her a feeling of peace and serenity, as if that was the way it was meant to be. When he was near, she felt whole, although she chided herself for such fanciful thinking.

At least she was able to talk to Aeolyn and Christoph. Each morning after they stopped to rest for the day, the others set up camp, and Christoph led her away for healing. Sometimes she walked with Aeolyn, who was so matter-of-fact and down to earth, and with Friedr, whose anger and helplessness on her behalf was touching.

Marya began to feel perhaps something could happen between her and Edwin, though she still doubted her own worth. "What right do I have to feel this way about him simply because he saved me? I'm sure it's only a silly school-girl crush on the good-looking hero who rescued me from a fate worse than— well, worse than death," she told Aeolyn when they washed up before falling into their bedrolls. Dawn was breaking on the first morning after she'd insisted on being blindfolded. "Oh Aeolyn, it really was so bad. I was so close to being forced to…but he…." Each time she talked about Stefyn, she began to shake like a leaf in the wind.

"Marya, it's all right. You weren't forced to bond with him. We got you out of there. And listen to me, you have every right to feel this way about Edwin." Aeolyn stopped, putting her arms around her and holding her tightly. "He doesn't have a girlfriend, though women throw themselves at him. You're the first and only girl I've ever seen him show any interest in, and you wouldn't believe how friendly-girls throw themselves at him. If it wasn't so awful for him, it would be funny. I must say, he's very interested. You'll have a hard time shaking him, I think, unless you say you're not interested. If you tell him that, he'll never press you for more than friendship."

Marya nodded, but still trembled all the same.

Aeolyn continued, "But if you want his company, he won't pressure you for more than you feel comfortable sharing with him. He's not that sort of a man. Whatever else he is, Edwin Farmer is a healer first and has more self-control than any man I know, even my Friedr."

Each time they stopped, Edwin looked back to see who followed them, quickly far-seeing as much as he could in a short time. At first, he didn't find any organization to the search, but when he checked at midnight, he found Brec taking over himself, knocking down the guard who was leading and trampling him to death in his rage. He was still searching the area around the keep, but he was doing it systematically, using an older minotaur who appeared to have some tracking skills.

"Each man Brec kills is one we don't have to fight," Friedr commented later when Edwin told him what he saw. "It could be he'll empty the keep to search for her. It's what I would do if I were in his shoes."

By sometimes carrying Marya they managed to

cover a great deal of ground before they stopped to find a place to hide for the day. Actually, they were able to go as far as they would have with her eyes un-blindfolded because they were following the road instead of using the legions' trails.

The last thing Edwin did before allowing himself to sleep was call water for drinking and bathing. Then he raised his barrier/shield over the whole group, tying it off. As he settled into his bedroll, he was completely aware of Marya on the other side of Christoph. Despite his exhaustion, it was a long while before Edwin fell asleep.

Chapter 28

They woke in the afternoon of the fourth day and without delay broke camp, quickly sipping some water and eating a ration bar from their dwindling supplies. Immediately after breaking their fast, they set out, staying off the road and using the trails, taking time to scout for traps. The trails took a more winding route west instead of south toward Braden, but they couldn't risk the road anymore. The skirmishing with the feral beasts escalated once again, but they quickly dispatched the wretched things, leaving their carcasses for the birds. Christoph shielded Marya, who was justifiably frightened during the commotion.

Edwin thought wistfully of the comfort of having a real roof over his head. *You don't realize how much you have until you have nothing.* He thought wryly of his tiny but pleasant rooms in Aeoven. *Someday I'll be able to go home, and I swear I will never leave again.*

It was strange for him to think he once wanted nothing to do with his family's farm. Now it was often on his mind. He hoped his father was happy and in many ways wished his father was there. *Dad would have made everything right. It's the way he is.*

As if she sensed his depression, Marya squeezed his hand, asking what he was thinking about. Edwin felt odd to confess his strange longing for the farm and his father.

"You're homesick," she replied. "I'm homesick too." As they walked, they talked about their homes and the families they left behind. Marya thought it was terribly sad Edwin's mother had died when he was only nine. "She must have loved you very much. It must have been hard for her to leave you."

"She did love me, and I've never blamed her. The sickness that claimed her life took many people in Markett," Edwin told her, sending reassurance. "I had many people to console me and many whom I could console. It was my father who took it badly, but he did his best to be both mother and father to me. I was fortunate."

Soon Christoph returned from scouting ahead, and it was time for them to run again. Edwin and Christoph each took one of Marya's arms, and between them, they kept her moving as fast as possible. Even though they were practically carrying her, it was tiring for her.

Perhaps it was because she was blindfolded and forced to rely on Edwin or maybe it was the situation that pushed them together, but whatever the reason, Marya felt completely safe only when he was with her. As they traveled, they talked, and their lives and thoughts became open books for the other to read.

Christoph, Friedr, and Aeolyn exchanged knowing looks and smiles when Edwin couldn't see them. "We knew this would happen, but it's still amazing to watch the Goddess moving them toward each other," Christoph spoke in low whispers to Friedr. "I'm in awe to think from our two friends will come the Hero Foretold, who will save our world and free Mal Evol once and for all from Tauron's dominion."

"It does make you feel strange to know you're part of a historical event in the making," Friedr replied, a look of wonder on his normally placid face.

The cold weather had taken care of the scorpion problem temporarily, but they returned with the warmth. Also, leaving the main road and taking to the trails made their chances of injury more likely. Christoph spent a lot of chi healing gashes and stings as they struggled to reach the border. Each time he or Edwin healed someone, Marya hid her sense of loss. The knowledge she once could have helped them but could no longer feel the magic cut her deeply.

In this way, the nights passed as they desperately tried to get Marya to the soil of Neveyah before Stefyn D'Mal discovered her gone. With each night of travel, Edwin and Marya became closer, developing a bond that was evident even to her, though she still suffered from her ordeal and wondered if she could ever be healed.

At last, Christoph couldn't stop himself. He slyly told Marya how the friendly-girls all were about Edwin. "You wouldn't believe the abuse he endures from them. And then after all the lengths they go to just to capture his interest, he ignores them or has Friedr run them off." Edwin glared at Christoph, who blithely continued spilling all his secrets. "He doesn't like boys, so it must be he has someone else in mind."

"Oh." Marya's voice was surprised and hurt. "You have a girlfriend."

"No, no! I have no girlfriend. Only you! Chris, why are you doing this?" Edwin spoke in a rush, glaring daggers at him. "Marya, please! I think I'm in love with you."

Christoph settled back with a happy smile. Edwin had done exactly as he wanted him to do.

Edwin now found himself telling Marya about his dreams, how he'd always had a vision of who he would bond with, and how he'd found that girl when he finally entered the room at the top of the tower. "I know you've been through hell, and you're not ready to think about such things. But I want you to know I love you. I felt a bell ring in my heart when I first saw you that night. I understand if you don't feel the same way."

At last, feeling bold, Marya said, "I do love you. I heard a bell when you pushed back your hood too. How odd. But I'm broken, Edwin," she told him, grateful for the blindfold that kept her from seeing his face as she confessed she couldn't even think of being kissed without panicking. "It isn't fair to you, and I won't ask you to wait until I'm healed, because I may never be able to get over this. You must be free to find happiness."

"I have all the time in the world. You're the only girl I've ever felt like this for. I'll wait for you," Edwin promised her, his face lighting up with such joy she could hear it reflected in his voice. "I've been waiting all my life for you. I can wait forever, if need be. When you're truly ready, I'll be there, no matter how long it takes. It must be your decision. For now, I'm content to know you care for me too. It's enough for me." Edwin felt such joy that he radiated it, forgetting to dampen his empathic sendings. Soon the whole group was feeling his euphoria. For a few moments, they were a very jolly group.

Once Edwin realized what was happening, he firmed up his barriers and things calmed down again, but it did serve as a reminder to him. "I can't tell you to maintain your barriers if I'm not watching my own," he confessed to Christoph, his face red with embarrassment.

Christoph laughed, saying he enjoyed seeing Edwin behaving like a normal love-struck farm boy. Friedr loudly agreed wholeheartedly.

As the days passed in her self-imposed darkness, Marya took comfort in the small things such as the warmth and strength of Edwin's hands as he guided her over the rough ground. His unwavering good spirits and unconditional support helped her as nothing else could, other than Christoph's gentle and careful healing.

And true to his word, Edwin gave her no indication whatsoever of the many times he forced himself to not put his arms around her and kiss her, moments when to do so would have been the natural response.

With every day and night, she became completely relaxed in his company, feeling both loved and safe. "Maybe this will work out after all, though I don't see how it can," she told Aeolyn as they made ready to sleep in yet another copse. "I know he does love me, though *why* he loves me I don't know. But it isn't fair to him, the way I am. I can't help it."

"Don't worry," replied Aeolyn, squeezing both her hands in her own. "Edwin isn't a boy. If he says he's willing to wait until you're healed, then he is willing to wait."

***

In the early hours of the morning of their seventh day out of the Shadow Castle, the sun was rising and Christoph and Edwin were guiding Marya along a trail deep in the thorn forest. Aeolyn and Friedr scouted ahead, looking for a place to camp. They hoped to reach the southern border sometime in the next five days, but traveling as slowly as they were it, would most likely take longer.

As they walked along, Marya suddenly cried out. Stumbling to her knees and struggling with her blindfold, she moaned, "No, no, no! I won't!"

Edwin managed to grab her arms, but she tore the blindfold off and stared directly into his face, muttering something only he could hear clearly. He slammed a barrier around Marya, completely shielding Christoph from the waves of uncontrolled madness rolling from her.

Suddenly she began raving. It wasn't Marya speaking but the voice of Stefyn D'Mal. Mad hatred blazed out of eyes that were no longer hers.

"So, she did not run away on her own. She has been stolen from me. Hear me, boy! I am coming for Marya. I am going to break her for daring to think she can leave me, and you will be allowed to watch it happen. She can never leave me! She will crawl to me for forgiveness. You cannot hide her from me. I am coming to take her back!"

A wave of the most violent emotions washed over Edwin's barriers, and he saw exactly what was in D'Mal's mind. It sickened him on an abstract level but didn't touch him.

Suddenly, Edwin felt supremely angry in his own right. This madman considered Marya his possession, a *thing* to provide him with pleasure. "Do you think so? You don't have the balls, you pansy-assed little freak of nature. Come and get her *if* you can! I'm waiting for you. She is not yours!" He laughed at the madman shrieking impotently at him.

"You will be broken too, pretty boy! But I will take my time with you, thief. Oh yes!" The madman's raving was cut off as Christoph quickly got the blindfold back on her. Marya began fighting, screaming that she had to go back or he would kill them all. It wasn't until Edwin layered a deep-sleep spell over her with a dampening field that they were able to get her under control. He also buffered Christoph's barriers.

"He is one *angry* 'freak of nature,' as you so succinctly put it, Edwin. He's going to cause us some grief after all." Christoph's voice was shaken. "I can't believe you laughed at him." He giggled nervously. "Those are some amazing barriers you've been developing. I believe I would like to be your student if you don't mind. I don't know of anyone but Father Rall who has shields that compare to yours, and even he isn't as good as you."

Friedr and Aeolyn returned, having heard the commotion. Without stopping to talk about it, Edwin picked Marya up and started running. Carrying her over his shoulder, he set a punishing pace. Startled, the others immediately followed him.

He took to the hard-packed dirt road again. When he came to the place where the trade road turned to the south, he instead took the abandoned, overgrown, and rutted lane that forked off and went directly west.

Crossing the river at the shallow ford when he came to it and running as hard as he could, Edwin headed straight for the nearest border, abandoning the plan of trying to get to Braden. The others struggled to keep up with him.

Edwin and Friedr alternated carrying Marya while Christoph maintained the deep-sleep spell on her. He traded off spell casting with Edwin to keep up their strength. Edwin cast one after another without breaking stride. They ran until they crossed the border and moved well into what they hoped was Neveyah. The change in the land was so palpable, even Aeolyn could feel it.

"It feels like Neveyah. The soil feels like Neveyah, clean and healthy," said Christoph, breathing hard, when they finally stopped. "It's on the verge of being taken though. It feels fragile."

By then, it was once again late evening, and the stars were shining brightly. In one long day, they had covered the same amount of distance they'd planned for four days, and they had done it without sleep.

After much discussion, they decided they would rest there briefly and continue on to a better place before they finally allowed themselves to sleep.

The thorn thickets were more widely spaced, but they easily found one that was large and made camp, too exhausted to sleep. The strengthening spell had that side effect, which was why it was only rarely used.

"You can run pretty well, farm boy. I'm hard-pressed to keep up with you," Aeolyn finally admitted. "Will you tell us exactly what happened now?"

Edwin wasn't sure how to tell them what he had seen in the mad priest's mind. He looked at Christoph for help.

"We've been discovered," Christoph finally said. "What was she saying when she yanked off the blindfold? I could feel a vast rage using her as a conduit." He shivered, thinking of the madness, how it had rolled over his barriers as if they were made of straw.

"It wasn't Marya talking. It was D'Mal. He's a bit unhappy with me right now." Edwin's voice was tired. "We will have to fight him after all, you know. He's coming for her, and he's using his magic to do it. He'll go through Brec, but it'll be D'Mal we're fighting. And I just found out he has the power, more than enough, to fight us long-distance. It felt like he has unlimited power at his command. But at least he can't send the legions to trap us here in this valley, because they're still rebelling and invading their own neighbors' territories. That frustration was plain to see in his chaotic mind."

"Well, that's nice to hear," Friedr commented. His dry humor had reasserted itself once they were safely out of Tauron's Mal Evol. "What do you think he's going to do?" He too looked exhausted but was honing his blade, preparing for a battle, which would surely happen soon. Edwin absently noticed twigs in his beard, a sign of the speed with which they'd traveled.

"He'll use his magic to strike at us in some way, once Brec locates us. He'll be full of surprises, I'm sure. After Brec is done with us, he'll simply pick Marya up and take her back to the Shadow Castle." Edwin skated over D'Mal's intentions in regard to him and rubbed his eyes with the heels of his hands. "I think Brec has been given special health and stamina to accomplish this task. I caught some of D'Mal's thoughts when he looked at me through her eyes." He shuddered involuntarily. "I saw what he plans for her." *And for me....* He squared his jaw. "It's not going to happen the way he wants. I'm not going to allow it."

Friedr caught Edwin's eyes and nodded. "You're right, my brother. We won't be easy prey for the mad priest."

"Where are we? How far into Neveyah are we?" Aeolyn asked nervously. "Are we far enough away he can't use the Throne of Stone and Bone?"

Christoph reached into his vest and pulled out the map. "Edwin turned and ran directly west, so we crossed the closest border instead of taking the trade road to Braden. This orphaned part of Neveyah is called the Green Valley and juts out into Neveyah by perhaps thirty leagues to the base of the most southern part of the Mountains of the Moon. It's cut off from the rest of Neveyah by the mountains. D'Mal can reach us with his magic only by using Brec or Marya because the poison hasn't taken the valley yet, although it is poised to do so within a few years. He can't yet use the throne to do his work here even if he could get to it quickly, which, fortunately, he's unable to. He has to remain in Serende far to the east since that mess is still a thorn in his side. He'll be forced to use Brec or Marya to strike at us. That's what she was screaming about after we got her blindfolded again. She was panicking at knowing he would use her to kill us."

"How long can you keep her under a deep-sleep spell? We'll have to carry her when we travel." Aeolyn brushed the burrs out of her hair, re-braiding it, and then gently brushed and braided Marya's hair.

Edwin held Marya's sleeping form with her head resting on his chest, cradling her as if he could protect her from the world. *This might be the only chance I ever have to hold her. I'll kill the monster for this as much as for anything else he's done.* The bitter thoughts racing through his mind were clear to Friedr, who was fascinated with the emotions Edwin was exhibiting.

Unaware of the drama playing out in Edwin's mind, Christoph answered Aeolyn's question. "It's dangerous to keep her comatose for too long. We try never to do this for more than a week at the most."

Shaking off his anger, Edwin spoke. "A week will be more than long enough, I think. Chris, we need to keep her between us at all times until we get to a place where I can build better barriers and tie them off. We both have to shield and buffer her so he can't send her dreams or contact her in any way. And we have to maintain the deep-sleep spell. He's strong enough to break it if we let the shield lapse, so we have to watch her all the time. I can still far-see and maintain the barrier if you can handle the sleep and healing spells. I can shield you while I sleep, but you have to be near me until I can figure something out. I've been able to shield us all when we're together like this." He adjusted his arms about Marya, holding her closer and more protectively, causing his friends to smile. Unaware of their observation, he said, "The barrier/shield I set will stay up, and if someone tries to break it, it'll wake me. I found a way to layer air which should sound an alarm."

"You do have the barriers, and you seem to use minimal chi in building and maintaining them," Christoph agreed. "The one you slammed over her when D'Mal possessed her was rock solid. There were no weak spots. It completely cut him out of my mind. Thank you."

"Layers," Edwin replied. "If you layer them, there's always a barrier. When the outer barrier goes down, you put up a new one inside. I learned to do this by accident to keep from losing myself in the magic of wind and water, but it works for every kind of personal barrier or dampening field. I think it'll work for battle-shields, though we don't use spirit to build them." He sat still while Aeolyn brushed and re-braided his hair, sensing she needed something to do.

"Edwin," Friedr spoke directly to him. "I could hear his voice when he spoke to you. What did he say and what did you reply? You said something, but I didn't catch it." He looked as if he knew but wanted to hear it anyway.

For a moment, Edwin debated lying about how ineptly he'd handled D'Mal. Finally, he replied. "Do you want the truth? He wants to kill me slowly, with his usual flair for the dramatic. Then he's going to take Marya and make her suffer for leaving him. He *plans* many things, but he will *not* have her." He flushed with anger and his eyes flashed. The set of his jaw was that of a man spoiling for a fight.

This was a side of him they hadn't seen before, and it mesmerized Friedr, who'd had no idea Edwin was capable of anger in the depth he'd been exhibiting all evening. Friedr probed him again. "What did you say to the nice man, Edwin? Tell Uncle Friedr." His eyes narrowed as he watched Edwin's reactions to his question.

"Ah, look, Friedr. I think I said something stupid. It was nothing important." Edwin refused to look at Friedr. His eyes were hot with emotions he couldn't deal with. His face had turned a deep shade of red from anger and embarrassment, and he knew it. Nevertheless, he couldn't stop the way he felt.

"What did you say?" Friedr pressured him hard. "Tell me now." The look on his face told Edwin he wanted answers and wouldn't accept being put off.

"I...um...I told him he wasn't man enough," Edwin finally admitted sheepishly. "I told him he didn't have the...um...you-know-whats to do it." He blushed an even deeper scarlet, looking at Aeolyn, whose eyes were wide in shock or surprise, he couldn't tell which. Sighing, he finished telling the sordid truth. "Then I sort of called him a pansy and said to come and take her if he could."

Christoph burst out laughing. "Oh, come on, Edwin. Tell him the truth. The best part was when you laughed at him." Christoph smirked at his discomfort. "This was *after* he called him a ball-less, pansy-assed little freak of nature!" He erupted in laughter, this time uncontrollably.

Edwin saw the incredulous look on Friedr's face. "I'm sorry, Friedr, but he made me angry, talking about her like she was his *possession*. She's her own person and he has no right!" He looked as indignant as he felt.

Friedr started laughing. "Oh, I'm proud of you. Fighting over a girl! Christoph—our boy has become a man!"

Aeolyn looked at them and rolled her eyes. "Wonderful. He calls a demented priest of the Bull God, who just happens to have a basement full of corpses, a ball-less freak of nature and tells him to come and get her if he can. Now that I think about it, it actually *is* quite manly. Stupid, but manly!"

Edwin tried to look contrite and failed. Christoph and Friedr looked at each other and fell over laughing. Aeolyn shook her head, but she gave in, giggling with the rest of them.

Chapter 29

After the group rested, Edwin rode the wind, looking for a better place to stay. He found an abandoned farm about fifteen leagues further into the west end of the Green Valley, and they set out for it, going as fast as they could travel. It was not unlike those he'd grown up around, and it made him homesick. They arrived there the next afternoon just as the sun was setting.

The farm was situated on a hill in the high end of the valley at the base of the escarpment in the shadow of the mountains. The house overlooked an orchard that was long overgrown. For some reason, the neglected orchard saddened Edwin.

Aeolyn decided they would make their stand there. They were about thirty-five leagues west of the border and more than a hundred leagues north of Braden. The farmhouse sat on a hill where they would have a view of anyone who approached them, and their attackers would have to come uphill to get to them. It had been abandoned for about a year, not long enough to have fallen into disrepair. They would rest and prepare for the coming battle.

There were jittery, nervous chickens that had gone wild and a wide variety of volunteer vegetables in the overgrown garden. While some of the roots would be hard to dig out and most likely be a bit stringy, they would be a lot tastier to eat than the group's normal fare. Since they were now out of Mal Evol, they would live off the land and save their rations for emergencies.

The farmhouse was small, just two main rooms, a

large kitchen and bedroom. A brass hand-pump held pride of place in the pump room attached to the house. The privy out back was clean and well maintained. There was a large, low-ceilinged attic for storage and sleeping children. The owners had taken most of the household possessions, except for the rough table and benches that were joined at one end to the wall of the kitchen. They'd left the place clean, obviously hoping to return someday.

A worn broom and a bucket with no handle were in the pump room, as was a stone tub for washing clothes. It would work as well for people, though they couldn't quite sit in it. They were thrilled at the prospect of being decently clean again. The pump had been prudently wrapped to keep it from freezing, and Edwin was careful to store the rags where they could reuse them when they left. He suspected the winters were brutal, so close to the mountains.

Some cracked but serviceable bowls at on a shelf, along with many other things that were worn but still useable. Everything was neatly stored and only required a bit of a wash. Aeolyn surveyed the things she would have to work with, feeling a surge of domesticity. "Edwin, the things they left behind will do well for us while we're here. It'll be almost like a real home."

The fireplace was completely set up for cooking, with a nice hob, pothooks, and an oven for baking, though they had no flour for bread. Before they fell into bed, they ate a bowl of soup Aeolyn made from the dried packets they hadn't used since entering Mal Evol. The once bland and unappealing mix was a welcome respite from the ration bars they'd subsisted on for nearly two months. They fell asleep feeling comforted and nourished and strangely at home in the rustic farmhouse.

Aeolyn and Friedr claimed the bedroom for themselves, enjoying the luxury of privacy quite keenly. Edwin and Christoph made their beds with Marya's between them, in the corner of the kitchen where, judging from the marks on the rough floor, a small bed once stood. They would alternate sitting beside her, never leaving her alone, though Edwin would have to resume his long neglected training with Friedr and Aeolyn.

The barriers Edwin layered over Marya had already withstood one assault, and they expected more. D'Mal wasn't going to stop simply because they'd shielded her. Exhausted, they quickly fell to sleep.

The next morning, Friedr killed an old rooster while Edwin searched for eggs for their breakfast. They licked their lips in anticipation of a chicken soup. They'd each missed having good food more than they would admit. Christoph found a great many root vegetables that had wintered over, and the herbs were plentiful. Old and stringy though they were, the simple meal would be a feast indeed.

Aeolyn cooked, slicing vegetables and humming to herself. Edwin sat on his bedroll next to Marya and rode the wind, searching for Brec. He found him seven days to the east traveling much faster than they had. He wasn't following their trail exactly, but he was making progress, and three tough-looking minotaur soldiers were with him.

There was a wildness about Brec that wasn't at all his normal belligerent demeanor. He'd apparently had a discussion with Stefyn D'Mal that had inspired new vigilance in the search. *I would say that is one frantic minotaur.*

Edwin told Aeolyn what he saw. "We have maybe four days, if he doesn't rest for long and if he maintains the pace he's at now. Seven days for anyone else."

They talked about the battle they knew would come. Edwin knew the main fight would be a mage-duel, and he was woefully untutored despite Friedr and Garran having worked with him in Braden. He was adept at using water, earth, and air but hadn't practiced fire or lightning since they entered Mal Evol over a month ago. While he'd been limited to water and earth-magic, he'd developed some ideas he planned to experiment with, using fire and lightning. The old barnyard and corral would be a perfect place for him to practice using all the elements.

"Aeolyn, I need to run through my battle-magic exercises when Christoph comes in to sit with Marya," he told her. "I have an idea I need to work on, which could be useful later, but I need you to cast spells at me while I figure it out. Will you help with me?"

"This is good," she replied, smiling at him. "You're thinking like a warrior. We'll all have to spar with Friedr today and every day until they arrive. During the fight with those dogs, I noticed that I'm losing my touch." Her arm was still sore but healing well, though she would have a puckered scar neither Chris nor Edwin could prevent.

While they waited for Christoph to return from working out with Friedr, Edwin opened his senses, checking Marya, the shields, and the sleep spell layered within the dampening field. He repositioned her, making sure the bedroll she rested on was smooth and comfortable. He and Christoph were able to bring her just far enough awake to get her to swallow a spoonful of water and broth at times, but they had to be careful she didn't choke. Gauging her health, he found she was doing as well as he could expect.

"She hasn't slept well since her kidnapping," Edwin remarked to Aeolyn, as he tried to find some good in the situation. "Perhaps she'll be fully rested when this is over."

While Aeolyn cared for her personal needs, Edwin and Christoph saw to her physical health. He took pride in how well she was being cared for. Using his healing skills and working with Chris had been the most satisfying parts of his life in Neveyah, but caring for Marya was more meaningful. He knew why it was but didn't want to think about it until the battle was over. Still, he found himself imagining them living together in his rooms in Aeoven, seeing the home they could have together if only everything would come out right somehow.

Edwin wondered if she would ever again be the merry, carefree person so famous for her healing skills and sense of joy in her work. He repositioned her again, smoothing any wrinkles from underneath her. He picked up her left hand, holding it gently and looking at her as he once again checked her shields.

Aeolyn would massage her legs and back later. When Christoph took over watching her, he would do the same. She couldn't be allowed to lose muscle tone, one of the dangers of the sleep spell she was under.

Aeolyn watched Edwin out of the corner of her eye. She found his tenderness toward Marya touching. *I wonder if he realizes the significance of the prophecy about the two of them.* Almost immediately, she thought, *No, and it wouldn't matter even if he did.*

Edwin didn't know or care about his own part in any prophecies. He'd not thought about the one he witnessed in the Temple since the day they left Aeoven. Certainly, the one he had been the channel for was long forgotten. All Edwin knew was he couldn't get Marya out of his mind. The hope they would someday be bonded drove him to find ways of using his gifts to win his personal war with Stefyn D'Mal.

***

"So what do you want me to do?" Aeolyn stood opposite Edwin in the empty corral with her sword riding in its sheath. Both were dressed for battle.

"What I want is to have you test my new shields by throwing your best spells at me." Edwin was grinning as if he had a trick up his sleeve. "I want you to start out with the small ones, and if they don't kill me, we can work up."

"Well, it's your hide. I guess Christoph can always heal you if this goes badly," she replied, her eyes alight with curiosity.

"Yes. I'll tell him 'it seemed like a good idea at the time.'" They both laughed. "I'm ready," Edwin said as he raised his new shield. "I hope my idea works."

She cast a low-level fire spell at him. It sheeted over him, and he felt the warmth, but no flames touched him at all. "Maybe if I layer a little water in...do it again, but give it a boost." This time she tossed a stronger spell at him. Again the fire didn't touch him at all. This time he felt no heat whatsoever.

"Now try lightning, but be warned—I have a new sort of shield with water layered in, and I hope it'll reflect the lightning back at you. Do you still want to help me?" he asked, hoping his notion worked. Grinning widely, Aeolyn flung a low-level bolt called a cat-zapper at him and danced back as it did exactly as Edwin expected it would.

"I can't believe you're using water against lightning and it's working." Aeolyn was completely enthralled with Edwin's new idea. "All right, farm boy. Let's get serious. I see what we're doing, and this could be useful," she said as she lined up a series of blindingly fast combination spells. "Now you must be able to attack while maintaining your shields, or it's just a slow way to die. I have my own, you know, so fire away."

His shields withstood the onslaught, and he began firing back, copying her style. Then he tried his idea of taking the magic she tossed at him, concentrating it as if it were water in a container, and throwing it back at her. It worked, much better than he imagined it would. His smile grew wider as he concentrated on sparring with Aeolyn, making sure he didn't hurt her. He now knew he had the abilities he would need once they faced Brec. He only needed to refine those skills so they were most effective.

They worked out until Aeolyn called it quits. She was running low on chi and was tired and dirty. Edwin wasn't. In fact he'd only gotten warmed up.

"You still have most of your chi! How is this possible?" She looked at him closely. "You aren't even sweating." She stood with her arms crossed. "You were holding back and still making me work for it." Her dark eyes were as flat as Friedr's.

Laughing, Edwin explained what he'd done.

She looked at him, not saying anything, mulling over the possibilities. "Where did you come up with this idea?"

"Well, it seemed like an extension of fetching," he replied.

Despite Aeolyn's urge to remain upset, she couldn't stay angry when he flashed that wicked grin. She found herself smiling back at him. "Fetching? With the elements?"

Grinning even wider, Edwin said, "I've been thinking about this for a while now. I realized I've been calling water from the mist for a month and thought if I could gather one element, why not all of them? Air is all around me, so I can easily use it. Water already exists in a form I can use. It simply needs to be shaped, and air is good for that.

"The earth is beneath my feet, so it's always handy and easy to shape with air. But fire and lightning only exist in a reusable form under certain conditions, and those aren't as easy to find as mist or clouds or dirt. Since I can send water into a container or make a dust cloud using my air-magic, why can't I send other elements where I want them to go if someone is so kind as to give them to me first in a form I can use? But we couldn't practice them while we were hiding, so I was unable to give it a try until now."

With an equally mischievous grin and a sparkle in her eyes, Aeolyn turned and called Friedr, explaining what he needed to do without telling him why. "The farm boy needs to practice his battle-magic, and I'm too tired. He's coming along much better than he was, but he needs to work at it, especially fire and lightning. Just throw some of your fancy, hot combos at him and keep putting your shields up. He'll be firing back at you. I'm going to get washed up." She snickered as she walked away. "He claims you can't take him down."

Friedr turned to Edwin and said, "Well, Christoph can always heal you, I guess. Don't hold back, I have the shields to take whatever *you* can throw at me." Edwin nodded, still grinning wickedly.

"Go ahead and smile, farm boy. Hope you don't die, but remember you did ask for it." Friedr's style was different from Aeolyn's, much more aggressive and forceful, where she relied on finesse. He spun spell after spell in dizzying and varying combinations, elegantly making his point about his student's arrogance in even thinking he could best him.

However, he rapidly became confused as his magic sheeted off Edwin's shields, and the return volley invariably matched his own in both strength and variety. Edwin even copied Friedr's signature battle combos, gaining skill and strength with each return. The master also soon found himself struggling against Edwin's sword, working much harder than he'd been prepared to. It suddenly appeared as if *he* were getting the lesson.

Edwin was unaware of Friedr's internal struggle. He was so happy to be able to fully stretch himself, he forgot about the supposed taunting of his teacher. Joy filled him as he threw himself into the battle.

Most annoying to Friedr was the crazy smile that didn't seem to go away no matter what he threw at Edwin. His irritation caused him to be a little more aggressive than he planned on being, and Edwin seemed to love it. It was just wrong.

Finally, right as Edwin was beginning to really

enjoy himself, Friedr stopped the battle, demanding an explanation. Then he looked at Edwin closely and saw he still maintained high levels of chi. "Now this is interesting. So far as I can tell, you don't have the ability to throw that kind of fire or lightning at me, and yet you've been doing it. I've not had the chance to train you in combinations, nor do I ever remember showing you those. And you're not low on chi. *Where* are you getting your chi from?"

"You might want to gauge what I can or can't throw at you when my barriers are down. You may be surprised. But as to where I get my chi—I haven't used much because you've been doing all the work." Edwin explained his theory. "I don't have the great reserves D'Mal has, but I can use what he throws at me to fire right back at him. It's a matter of using my air magic to funnel what I receive back to the sender. But we couldn't work on it before now because we couldn't use overt magic. We could only use passive."

"Well, well. This is something new to think about. What else is up your sleeve?" Friedr stood with his arms crossed, pretending to think, but really trying to catch his breath. "You've obviously been putting that crafty mind of yours to good use in your free time. What's your real plan?"

"I need to be able to work on narrowing the focus of the magic I'm returning so it can be used as a weapon to drill a hole in his shields. But I can't expect you or Aeolyn to stand there and let me try to kill you just so I can figure it out." Edwin's grin was a mixture of anticipation and delight, and something about it troubled Friedr.

"No, I think not. So what.... Wait a minute! Were

you pulling your punches there?" Friedr looked outraged. "You don't have to go easy on me, farm boy. I can take whatever you can bring to the party and still kick your butt."

"No, I didn't go easy on you, exactly." Friedr's eyes bulged at the word "exactly." "I didn't focus the return because I think a truly narrow focus would be like a needle or a drill, and I don't want to kill you. If it works the way I think it will, it'll be *very* effective." Edwin's enthusiasm for his idea lit up his face. "Don't you see? If I can get that one hole in D'Mal's shields, I'll have him! His magic will be unlimited, but he'll be confined to the limit of Brec's physical stamina. What we have to do is kill the three guards he has with him first. Then, when Brec dies, D'Mal's vector for magic will be gone and the battle will be over since he'll be in Serende with no way to communicate here." Edwin's jaw was set in a way Friedr had come to recognize. "What I want is for you to throw your stuff at me, and then I will aim it at something else, trying to practice narrowing the focus. I have some other ideas to try out too."

"We could do it tomorrow," Friedr said with a sly grin. "How's your sword arm, farm boy?"

Edwin's grin intensified, and he picked up his blade.

"Maintain your shields and use your wits. This is what you'll be facing in a real fight against a true battle-mage." Suddenly Friedr rushed at Edwin, sword drawn.

Edwin responded, meeting his attack and pressing his own. They continued this way until Friedr at last called a stop. "We're both tired," he said, with his usual genial candor. "I have to work hard against you. We're both learning now."

"I learn so much each time you put me through this. I'm not going to be able to last long against someone with your sword skills, though," Edwin replied. "What worries me are these minotaurs. They're hardened veterans, and Brec will have abilities that far surpass mine."

"Ah, but you've been improving. All the skirmishing we did on the way to Mal Evol and back has improved your skills. You'll do well enough." Friedr looked at the house. "We need to go in and get cleaned up and see if supper's ready." He was sweating and out of breath, something he wasn't used to being when facing a student. *He thinks I was holding back as a teacher, but he almost beat me. I barely outlasted him. If this is only the learning stage for him to practice his theories, Edwin Farmer is going to be an extremely dangerous man.* He looked back at Edwin, who methodically cleaned his sword with his oil rag. *If I hadn't seen his basement, I could almost feel sorry for D'Mal.*

***

Their meal was every bit as wonderful as they hoped it would be, and their prayer of thanks to the Goddess was fervent and heartfelt. The chicken soup was as tasty to them as the finest feast ever to be set before a king.

They were silent as they savored the first few bites. Edwin ate slowly, lost in the memories of his father's comforting soups. He looked at Aeolyn, a feeling of being part of a family welling in him. "I'm sure this is the best I've ever eaten, and I've eaten many wonderful soups. But everything you cook is so good."

She blushed, saying, "Thank you, Edwin. It is rather good."

"She is the finest of cooks, I'll have you know," added Friedr. "I have to say, my waistline suffers when I'm able to enjoy her meals regularly." He raised a toast to her with his water bottle. Edwin and Christoph raised theirs in homage to her cooking also. It was a merry, homey meal, warmed by the light of the hearth.

After the meal, they sat before the fire, listening to Christoph telling some of his more outrageously funny tales, and playing a game of stones.

Later, in the privacy of their room, Aeolyn and Friedr talked in whispers about the events of the afternoon and of Edwin, who'd gone from being the student to being the teacher, though he seemed unaware of it.

The light from the waxing crescent moon shone through the window as Aeolyn absently toyed with Friedr's curls. She loved looking at him in the moonlight. "He's far better a warrior and battle-mage than I am," she told her husband, letting his curls slide between her fingers and enjoying his unbound hair.

"I know. He has me bested too, but I can't let him know it. I'm going to have to keep changing my spells up and work harder at varying my attacks," Friedr laughed softly. "It'll force me to improve my own skills. I can't keep letting him beat me. Goddess knows I haven't had anyone really good to work out with since Garran left to be the abbott in Braden. Father Rall is always too busy, and he's gone most of the time, to boot."

"I'm not at all tired now, are you?" Aeolyn sat up

and leaned over to kiss her husband deeply, her dark hair falling in a curtain around him.

His arms went about her, and they soon put their student completely out of their minds.

Chapter 30

During the night, Edwin was awakened by a probing attack on his barrier. The alarm sounded as he hoped it would, and the shields withstood the assault. Marya, of course, didn't stir. He sat up and looked across her sleeping form to Christoph, who also sat up, wide-eyed. "I see what you mean about the shields sounding an alarm. You need to show me this twist if you will."

Edwin showed Christoph how he set the barrier up, and then after checking their shields one more time, he sent his spirit out, looking for Brec. He found the group making camp for the night. They were three days away, if they didn't lose the trail. He reported what he found.

Christoph tried to set up a barrier the way Edwin did, and while it was small, only personal-sized, it still made a funny, little squeaking noise that would be enough to wake him up if it was probed while he was sleeping.

After the attack, they couldn't sleep, so Edwin showed Chris how to build a barrier that wouldn't crumble and would stay up with only minimal effort. "It's like an ostrich egg, hard to break into but easy to get out of. You have the ability to call enough water to layer into it." Edwin gauged the strength and stability of Christoph's barrier. "That's right, make the finest layer of water. See? Layering the spirit with water makes it stable. Now we tie it off just so…like you do a ward against midges or scorpions. And the best part is most healers can call some water. You don't have to be able to call a river."

"I can call enough water to drink, but that's about it," Christoph replied, with a self-deprecating smile. "Riding the wind and the earth has forced you to develop these new techniques in order to keep from losing yourself. I don't think anyone would have thought of layering the shields the way you do if you hadn't had those experiences. I think my own are going to be as strong as any, even if you aren't there to save my hide." They were quiet as Edwin tested Christoph's emotional barriers.

Chris didn't even feel Marya's deeply buried emotions, though he sat next to her. He was truly able to see her dispassionately for the first time. A smile of joy lit his face as he realized what he'd never known before—true separation. "All you have to do is remember to set the barriers and check them. You'll be able to face the worst D'Mal can throw at us."

"What do you think he's going to bring to the party, as Friedr so happily puts it?" Christoph would be shielding Marya and staying out of the way as much as possible, but he was curious about what they would be facing.

Edwin spoke with quiet assurance. "One weapon will be a full-blown mental assault, because I sensed he believes they are unstoppable, and he will definitely rely on them. He'll also fling the usual elemental magic at us, but I'm sure it'll be extremely strong. I'm going to be totally outclassed by him, but I have an idea that might work. I'll be a factor in this fight despite my lack of formal training. We know he'll have three minions and Brec's sword arm for the physical assault. We have Friedr and Aeolyn, who are each worth two of anyone else in any battle. The handicap D'Mal has is he's going to have to fight this from a distance, using Brec as his vector. Even so, we'll be at the disadvantage overall, I think."

Edwin was silent for a moment and then looked at Marya, saying, "He's not getting her back, not even if he wins this battle. I'll kill her myself first to prevent him from doing what he plans to do to her. You can't imagine the poison in D'Mal's mind."

Christoph was stunned into silence, shocked at Edwin's words. "What gives you the right to make such a decision for her? We will not do this for any reason!" In his outrage, his voice was loud, but he had been completely taken by surprise. "You have no right to make such a decision."

"I've shocked your sensibilities, haven't I? Are your barriers up?" He knew Chris had dropped them. "Don't keep dropping them, even around me. Keep them up at all times. It takes little chi and saves an enormous amount of time.

"This is what I saw in his mind, for her and for me." He accessed the memory and sent it to Christoph with force. "I know it isn't my right to make that judgment. But I believe if Aeolyn and Friedr could see the disgusting things I saw when I was speaking to him, then perhaps they would come to the same decision. I'm sure this is only the little that radiates off the surface of his consciousness."

Christoph's face paled. "I see. I can see what he has planned, and I should have understood before. I've been in his basement. He is…oh Goddess. His god's perversions are so deeply intertwined in his daily consciousness, he is completely insane. I knew this. I hope it doesn't come to us having to make this choice."

His face was sad. "There is much he must pay for. But Friedr and Aeolyn have no empathic skills. They'll not be receptive to you showing them the way you just did me. However they're reasonable, logical people who love her as much as we do. They'll understand what you're asking of them."

"I promised her he would never have her, no matter what. I promised. I'll never break a promise to her." Tears burned Edwin's eyes as he explained what he wanted to do to insure Marya didn't have to suffer in the event of their death. "I can tie the spells off using my dad's trick, so if we all die, or if one of us is left and is his captive, she won't wake up. Nothing he can do will wake her, so he won't be able to hurt her. It's the only thing I can do." Edwin's voice was rough with emotion.

He looked up as the bedroom door opened and Aeolyn and Friedr entered the room. Friedr's long, red hair was unbound and down over his bare shoulders, reaching past his waist and over his hips. "Don't worry so much, Edwin. I would do it for the woman I love too under the same circumstances, if I had the ability. But it won't come to this. We're not in as weak a position as he would like us to be." Friedr's confidence shone like a beacon. "We've been able to choose the ground upon which we'll fight. We'll be rested and have the chance to plan our attack properly."

"Your alarm is loud," Aeolyn said. Her hair was loose, and her brush was in her hand. "I'd like to try to learn this trick of making shields that stay up when you're sleeping and wake you when you're attacked. I can think of all kinds of useful applications for them."

She changed the subject back to the one that

brought her into the kitchen. "Edwin, let me ask you this. Do you think Marya would want this? I know what *I* think she wants, but do you? And this last-ditch, merciful death you have planned for her…is it really to save her from suffering, or is it a selfish thing to keep the man you hate from having the woman you want?"

Friedr and Christoph stayed back, watching the way Edwin reacted to Aeolyn's goading.

Edwin's eyes widened at her audacity, but he remained calm, sure of himself. "Marya told me several times about a stone shard she was keeping, fully intending to plunge it into her own heart if he tried to take her by force." Edwin spoke of it dispassionately, separated from his anger at her words. "She found it the first day she was allowed to walk in the garden after being freed from the dungeon, and seeing the possibilities, she kept it with her, only hiding it under her mattress when a gown was cut so low she couldn't conceal it. She became distraught when she spoke of it. The revelation that he'd planted it for her to find and then had taken it away in what turned out to be another way of playing with her sanity was too much to bear. The stone shard was her last hope for so many months, and he used it to torment her. I promised her he wouldn't have her, and he won't if I can help it.

"So, yes, Aeolyn. It is for *both* reasons. I saw in his mind what he'll do to her. I've shown it to Chris, and he can tell you the filthy details, if you doubt me." As he spoke, Edwin's raw emotions were written on his face, something he was allowing to happen far too often nowadays for his own comfort, but he was desperate to convince her. "I won't allow her to suffer anymore at his hands. And yes, if it makes you happy to hear this, it *is* a selfishly motivated effort to keep the man I hate from having the woman I love.

"If we win, she has her freedom back. She can find her healing skills again, and maybe she'll bond with me or maybe she won't. But if we lose, she'll face a fate worse than anything you can imagine, Aeolyn. I won't put her through it." Edwin's face was stern. "I'll fight to the death with everything I have, but if we all die, we can't save her. This way, even if he kills us, *he* loses."

His voice was filled with intensity and the absolute belief it was the only choice left to them, should they fail to kill Brec and his minions. "I'll die gladly, knowing no matter what happens he's losing the prize he wants so desperately. What would you have us do to keep him from destroying her piece by piece for the rest of her wretched life? His idea of rape isn't simple, brutal assault, oh no! He'll be *very* creative in this regard, I can assure you. He'll take her mind in the process, in as disgusting and horrific a manner as you can imagine. Then he'll keep doing it until she either dies from his 'gentle love' or finds a way to kill herself. For him, the pleasure is in the terror and horror he inflicts upon his victims. He feeds on it."

Aeolyn's face softened, and her voice was gentle. "Forgive me, my brother. I had to hear you say it, Edwin. I wanted to be sure *you* know why you're fighting this battle and making this decision. It's a serious thing we face. We can't under any circumstances leave her to his tender mercies, and what you're planning is exactly what she wants. She begged me to do this the first day we got her back." The others looked at her in surprise. "I promised her we wouldn't allow him to have her ever again.

"But of course we will prevail," she said confidently, winking at Friedr. "I don't like to lose. It's bad for your reputation."

***

After eating a tasty breakfast of the remains of the previous night's chicken soup, Edwin and Friedr stood in the corral opposite a straw dummy. They decided Aeolyn would try to shield the dummy, while Friedr bombarded Edwin with various battle spells. Edwin would catch the magic and direct it at the dummy in shaped and focused return volleys, trying to penetrate the shields.

Friedr started with fire. He tossed it at Edwin, who caught and deflected it, trying to shape it. He managed to shape it into a spear, but it fell short. Aeolyn was working on applying Edwin's trick of spreading her shield to cover someone else and enjoyed the morning's exercise.

It was slow going, and at first Edwin felt discouraged. Friedr said, "Maybe it's only when you throw it back to the sender that you have the momentum of the spell. I'll toss you another fireball. Try to use my momentum to increase the speed of your return volley." They worked at it all morning until Friedr called it quits. He chose not to deplete his chi completely as he wanted to work with Edwin while sparing in the afternoon.

"I still haven't done what I'm hoping to do," muttered Edwin. "Too bad I can't lend you my chi. Now *that* would be a useful trick to have. We made some headway though."

Friedr agreed. "Yes, we did make progress but you may not have the time to figure it out. We also have to work on your ability to cast spells while swinging your sword in a more graceful manner. You flail about so, your attackers will laugh themselves to death."

Still laughing at Friedr's assessment of his skills, Edwin washed his shirt and then himself in the cold water of the stone washtub in the pump room. He was entering the kitchen when another assault on the barriers layered over Marya was launched. Christoph calmly reinforced the shields, finished brushing her hair, and braided it. He stood up with a graceful, fluid movement and tucked her hairbrush into her kit. He appeared happy and relaxed, almost like his old self.

While Edwin did his laundry, Aeolyn and Friedr went out scouting the borders of the farm, making sure there was no way the attackers could sneak up on them unseen.

"You have really been getting good with the barrier/shield, Chris. You can relax again, can't you?" Edwin spread his shirt to dry by the fire. His hair was damp, and he sat at the table, patiently combing the knots out of it. "I didn't realize how much the taint of the land itself affected you. The soil is contaminated because it's bound to the Throne of Stone and Bone, which D'Mal has somehow poisoned. You have a deep connection to the earth because your family was farmers. They were connected to the land they live and work on. Now this valley is under assault from the toxin too, and soon, maybe in only a few years, it will fall and become part of Mal Evol. Shielding yourself has helped you immensely."

"Edwin, the problem goes deeper. I realize now I never understood what Abbess Marta meant when she was trying to explain to me how thin and fragile my barriers were. She was terribly worried about me. I put a lot of effort into them and studiously maintained them, but I didn't have the sort of barriers I should have. I wasn't their first choice of healers to send into this situation. Dane would have been chosen because he always did have the strongest barriers and is actually a good fighter, being able to kill with his staff when necessary. But you will change the way magic is taught, which is my other specialty, the theory and application of magic.

"I'm not a warrior. I'm a scholar and a physician. I was the only teacher available who possessed the skills necessary to work with your formidable abilities. And when we got to Mal Evol, the barriers I worked so hard on started crumbling the minute I set foot on the soil of the place. Still, I was unable to see, despite your shielding me, they were thinning to the point of nonexistence.

"You, as a student, wouldn't have been able to see how weak they were. Friedr and Aeolyn suspected. They were going by my behavior alone. They know me so well after all these years," Christoph said, "But, I myself couldn't tell until you cornered me the day after we got Marya out of the Shadow Castle. When you shielded yourself from me, I was surprised, not just by the strength of your barriers, but also by how quickly you threw them up. They were there in an instant and rock solid. And the fact you felt it necessary to shield yourself from *me* told me I was out of control.

"Then you did it again on the road when D'Mal caught us. You shielded me and cut Marya off so she couldn't be the vector that radiated his poison to the rest of us. You did it without even thinking.

"This far-seeing and fetching you've been blessed or cursed with have forced you to think in completely different ways than we've always been taught. It's going to change the way we think about barriers and shielding. Your greatest asset is your ability to see the possibilities in how something can be used to greater effect. We've been layering healing spells for generations. It's how we get the most benefit from them in serious cases. But you've layered them, woven them into a lace, and tied them off as if they were wards. No one else has ever thought to invent tie-offs for healing spells. You do this with barriers too. What's next?"

Edwin smiled and replied, "Battle-mages raise a shield out of the elements to protect themselves. It was one of the first things Aeolyn taught me how to do." He tied the leather thong around his braid and moved to sit by Marya, holding her hand, watching her sleeping face. "I'm working on an idea to make the strongest battle shield possible. I just need to be able to test it out on someone."

Christoph sat down opposite him. "I've been assisting Abbess Halee in her research for most of my time as an adept, when I'm not out in the community healing. Her life's work is the study and understanding of the basic workings of magic in Neveyah—not only battle-magic, but *all* magic. I can tell you truthfully that no one, healer or battle-mage, has ever considered how water could be layered into healer's barriers to give them strength and longevity. It never occurred to us to look more closely at it.

"Most healers can call a little water, but not much. The beauty of your layered barrier is that it takes so little to make and maintain them you don't need massive ability. Abbess Marta will be happy about this turn of events. The basic separation of magic is going to have to be reexamined. You and your abilities may have revolutionized the theory of magic." His face was full of excitement about his favorite subject. "Imagine me, a healer, using a battle-magic—which is what water is—to protect myself."

"But Chris, it's the main element that supports life. Water unites both healing and battle-magics. This is why most healers can call it." They continued the lively discussion into the early afternoon as they cared for Marya and shared in the preparation of the day's meal. The kitchen was redolent with the scent of stew. A pair of rabbits had stumbled into Edwin's snares that morning. Friedr skinned them and Edwin cut them up. Now they were stewing in the cook pot with vegetables and herbs.

While dinner cooked, Edwin crossed to the upturned log by the fire he was using as his stool and began working on his little project. While he and Christoph discussed the theory of magic, he carved little wooden spoons for them to use. Finishing those, he worked on making a ladle for Aeolyn.

"My goodness, Edwin. Bowls *and* spoons! How civilized we will be." Aeolyn beamed when he showed her. "I'm impressed with your ingenuity, farm boy."

Edwin and Friedr returned to arms practice while they waited for supper to finish cooking. Laughing and joking, they went out to the old corral to work on building Edwin's ability to cast spells while swinging his sword, leaving Aeolyn and Christoph to tend to small domestic chores.

***

Aeolyn and Christoph looked up as the door opened abruptly and Friedr stormed in, heading straight for the pump room. Edwin followed on his heels, pleading. "Look, I said I'm sorry. I didn't mean to do it—it just happened. I thought your shields were better than that. I did warn you though! You know I did." He listened as Friedr muttered something unintelligible to the others. "I told you to raise your best fire shield. You did have it up! I didn't know it was so weak." The sound of more muttering permeated the kitchen.

Edwin lingered in the doorway to the pump room. "I thought when you said to go ahead and throw fire at you, you meant you wanted me to work on what we did yesterday with the swords and spells." When he turned to go back outside, he saw the others staring at him. Christoph had one eyebrow raised, and Aeolyn had stopped in the middle of stirring the stew. Friedr said something that made Edwin flush with anger, and he turned back. "I know. I'm sorry! I should have held your hand and made sure you had your shields up."

"I said 'fire away,' not 'burn the hair off my face!'" Friedr's voice was muffled, but his outrage was clear, and in his anger, his barbarian accent was thick.

"I sort of singed his beard," Edwin admitted, his face bright red with embarrassment. "I'm sorry, Aeolyn. He told me how much you loved it. Now he's afraid you won't sleep with him until it grows back."

Friedr stood in the doorway glaring at Edwin. "I look ridiculous without a beard." His guttural accent was an audible sign of his distress. He'd been in Aeoven for so long it was rarely noticeable. "Now I'll have to shave off the rest, right before the most important fight of my life!" Most of the right half of his face was beardless and very pink. Blisters were forming. He had the rest lathered up. His sword was in his right hand—he'd decided to shave with it. "My luck was in my beard. This is a disaster!"

"You could use my razor," Edwin offered. "It would be much easier."

"A warrior does not use a razor! A warrior does *not shave* before a crucial battle!" Friedr stabbed the air with his sword as he spoke. "And a warrior whose beard has been *violated* shaves with his sword in order to keep the luck that was in his beard! *Tharahk kahn danhk!*" he cursed violently.

Recognizing Friedr was reduced to shouting barbarian obscenities, Edwin backed off and said, "Fine, fine! I'll quit trying to help you. I'm not apologizing anymore. And you can keep your 'steaming horse turds.' That sort of language gets you nowhere with me." He turned his back and walked outside.

Gaping at Edwin's departing back, Friedr shouted, "What villain respects a warrior who looks like a teenager?" He glared at Aeolyn and Christoph. "What are you two staring at?"

Chris shrugged and went back to mending the sleeve of Aeolyn's vest that was torn during the battle with the dogs.

"Well, *I* am looking at an idiot," replied Aeolyn, glaring right back at him. "You'll cut your throat if you're not careful, you fool of a man." She snickered as she stirred the soup. "I never liked the ratty thing. It tickles when you kiss me. I loved you long before you even had a beard."

"Huh!" Friedr stalked off to finish shaving. They could hear his low, rumbling mutters, interspersed with an occasional "Ow!"

"I *suppose* I can heal a slit throat if I have to," Christoph grumbled irritably. He looked at Aeolyn, and they both burst out laughing. When they were finished, he stood and sighed, saying "Very well, Friedr, let's get those burns healed."

***

Edwin sat on a log outside the door, wondering if he should laugh or cry, while his friend was shaving off the beard he'd worn since he first grew facial hair. At least Christoph would heal the burns. *What if his hair never grows back? He thinks Aeolyn fell in love with him for his beard.* Edwin doubted she was so shallow a person, but it mattered to Friedr. *He also told me he grew it to make himself look better. People teased him a lot before he grew the beard.* Edwin couldn't imagine Friedr without the thick facial hair. *Maybe he has no chin to speak of. Some people don't...think about Jordy Londersson...he looked much better after he grew a beard. I know it isn't a barbarian custom because Father Rall doesn't have one and neither does Bors Leifsson. That must be it. He doesn't have a chin and the beard disguises it. Poor Friedr.*

Sighing, he shrugged it off and decided to check on Brec's progress. He floated over the land, and the unfortunate training accident lost its importance as he looked for the group of warriors racing toward them. He cast around widely, finally finding them far south of where they should have been.

Returning to his body, he went back into the kitchen. Edwin spoke without preamble. "They're too far south. They'll be an extra day and night on the road even if they run all the way. And they still might go astray again."

At the rough table, Aeolyn sat next to a giant, sweet-faced, red-haired boy. Friedr's disgruntlement faded as he leaned forward saying, "Where are they right now?"

Friedr's deep voice sounded the same, but it was simply wrong emanating from such a sweet, cute, babyish face. His eyes were the same piercing blue as always, but the problem was he looked like a fourteen-year-old novice, only much, much bigger. Edwin was silent. *Oh, for goodness sake, get a grip, Edwin. He may be cute, but he's still dangerous.* "Wow Friedr, you look...." Edwin stopped, at a loss for words. "Um, you really look, ah...."

"If you even think the word 'cute,' I'm going to leap over the table and show you 'cute.'" Friedr mumbled. "Just get on with what you found. Spit it out."

"They're well south of the city of Mal Evol but have turned east since the last attack on our shields." Edwin's voice betrayed no laughter, gaining an approving nod from Christoph. He firmed his barriers, separating himself from his tendency to giggle nervously. It worked well enough so only Chris knew what was going on in Edwin's distracted mind. "They think we made for Braden via the trade road."

Aeolyn thought for a moment. "They don't know we only wanted to get to safer ground. Chris, can we wake Marya up without him knowing it, under the barriers you have on her?"

He analyzed the situation and then replied, "We may have to, but I don't think we should if we can avoid it. He was able to pick her out of the group when she was awake. He'll hammer relentlessly at the shields Edwin is carrying over her, and he might be able to break them. Right now, he isn't sure it's her he's hammering at. He's aiming at barriers in general. We've unified our barriers by overlapping them. It's a new trick of Edwin's that's working very well."

Friedr muttered, "Edwin is just full of tricks," making Edwin a bit less badly about burning off his beard.

Christoph sat next to Marya and held her hand in both of his. "If D'Mal gets through to her, it will harm her more than I can explain without sickening you. Trust me, please."

"But should we keep her asleep? What if they get lost again, and it takes even longer?" Edwin knelt next to Christoph.

Friedr thought for a moment, and then with an evil grin, he said, "Maybe you should whisper directions to them." He saw Edwin's look of surprise. "Just to sort of keep them on the right road. We need to get this over with. If we don't kill Brec before we head back to Braden, we'll have to watch our backs all the way, and he will choose the battleground. This is a good place for us, and we can heal up afterward here. We are on high ground and have food and shelter. We must make them come to us, or we'll be completely at the disadvantage."

Aeolyn agreed, saying, "While you're at it, make them hurry a bit faster. This way they'll arrive in worse shape. The minute they get here, we're going to pick a fight with them. We must give them the friendly sort of welcome they would give us."

Edwin looked at the rosy-cheeked, angel-faced boy who wore Friedr's shirt and had his piercing blue eyes.

Suddenly turning red, he excused himself, going back outside. As soon as the door shut, the sounds of his hysterical laughter penetrated to the kitchen. Aeolyn and Christoph looked at each other, and turned away from Friedr's affronted face, finding other things to busy themselves with, hiding their smiles.

Soon the sound of Edwin stacking firewood replaced the maniacal giggles that resounded rather loudly in the kitchen, though he did find himself snickering for quite a while.

Chapter 31

The next morning, Edwin was up early, trying to get one of Brec's men to listen to him. He'd been suggesting the right direction at intervals for nearly half an hour now.

We should head north. The thought kept nagging at Gurt. *The signs all point north.* He slowed down. "Footprints by the river there were, when we filled the water bottles. I was sure there were. There's no sign here. No one has been this way in a dog's age. We shudda gone west at the old road to the river instead of taking the trade road at the fork. Now we oughta double back north and then go west."

"What do you mean, west? They have to be heading to their temple in Braden," Wint replied. "Be stupid for them to head west. There's naught but wasteland there and the haunted mountains. They be needing shelter and such. The nearest temple be in Braden."

"What if they just wanted to leave Mal Evol the quickest they could? They be knowing someone must follow them. *She* knows it'll be Brec who follows, and she knows what such means." Gurt had a hunter's instinct when it came to tracking—he knew he was right. "She'd want to be off the soil as soon as she could. *He* cain't follow her as well there as he can here."

Wint agreed he had a point, but wouldn't risk arguing with Brec. "I ain't telling Brec he be going the wrong way. You can do it."

"No sir, I won't either." Gurt wasn't stupid. "He'll

figure it out soon enough."

***

Edwin returned to his body. He sighed and went inside the house. "I'm having a terrible time with these fellows. They're sure they're going the wrong way, but they're too afraid to tell Brec. He'll have to figure it out on his own. I don't think I should try to whisper to him." Common sense said it would be a bad idea. "I'll keep working on his minions. I think one might be swayed to tell him soon."

"Well, you're most likely right about not trying to influence Brec." Christoph rose with fluid grace. "What we need is an idea. I'll go see what Aeolyn has to offer us."

Edwin sat next to Marya and sent his spirit out again. When he located them, they were kneeling by a creek, drinking deeply.

Gurt was talking to the third armsman of their group, an older minotaur named Bann. "Remember I said the bank of the river was all mucked up, back at the fork where the road turns west or south? Well, I ain't seen no sign of anyone since, have you?"

"Well, I ain't, but it don't mean nuthin'. I ain't along on this trip fer me tracking skills," Bann said. "I jus' do as he says and so should you. He says south, so we go south."

What if he finds out? Gurt looked at Brec, who stood glaring at the road all around them. *What if he finds out we knew and didn't say?* He shuddered at the thought.

All of a sudden, Brec burst out, "This is madness. They've left no trace. Impossible! We've missed something, something that'll tell us where they are. We should have overtaken them by now. She's a sickly thing, and he's only one man. They must be behind us, and we've missed them. We turn north."

Gurt, Wint, and Bann simply nodded and made ready to run back to the fork in the road, though they'd wasted a full two days on the wrong turn.

Going back to his body, Edwin found Friedr standing over him, the vegetable bucket in his hand. "I think they're on the right track now. Brec has decided they're heading the wrong way. They're going back to the place where we turned west."

"Where you turned west and we ran after you, you mean." Friedr looked at him out the corner of his eye. Edwin looked uncomfortable at his words. "It was a good decision. We had to get out of Mal Evol. That's all there is to it. It would have been days if we'd stayed on the road to Braden."

"Well, as fast as we were going, there must be some trail for them to follow. I'll seed some evidence if they get lost again."

Friedr went into the pump room with his bucket of vegetables. Edwin glanced out the window at the sky, sensing spring had come, such as it was. The land was falling to Mal Evol slowly, but surely. Holding Marya's hand in the silent kitchen, Edwin sent his spirit sailing under the earth, tasting the soil, listening to the rocks. The land was fighting a losing battle. It was unable to support a thriving farm anymore, yet it struggled. The volunteer root vegetables—potatoes, carrots, beets, turnips, garlic, and onion showed it was fertile only a year ago. The early young vegetables randomly grew where the harvest winds seeded them in the old, untended garden. The rosemary, sage, lavender, and other hardy herbs still survived and in some cases thrived. But the advent of the thorns in their sparse clumps was the sure sign the land was failing.

Returning to his body, Edwin saw Aeolyn had returned. He said, "The farmers who lived here were right to leave."

"Why do you say this?" Aeolyn sat at the table, braiding a rope from long strands of wild hemp and feeling contented at having a useful task.

"I just realized something. Today is the vernal equinox, the Feast of Aeos," he replied. "But the land is falling to Mal Evol as surely as the sun will rise. When I sail under the earth, it feels constrained, as if it won't be allowed to bloom fully. It may not be this year or even the next. The land struggles against the tide but will surely fail."

"Hmm, the Feast of Aeos," Aeolyn mused. "We must have a little ceremony for the Goddess. I'll find herbs to burn, and you must get flowers to decorate our little home with. Friedr and Chris shall also have a feast-day task."

"There are tiny yellow and white flowers in the meadow near the barn," Edwin replied. "It's covered with them. I'll go and get however many you want. I think maybe I can get us a nice, fat trout or two as well. The pond in the pasture looks promising." His casual offer didn't fool her. His eager expression was a dead giveaway as to the nature of his offer.

Edwin wants an excuse to go fishing. Aeolyn realized it was something she hadn't suspected about him. "Friedr will be distraught if you go without him." Her smile illuminated her face as it always did when she spoke of her husband. "He adores fishing and hasn't had the opportunity to do it lately."

Edwin's own boyish, pleased smile charmed her. "I love to fish," he admitted, the light in his eyes confirming her suspicions. "I could spend hours at it. My dad and I have a pond on the farm back in Markett."

Christoph entered the kitchen, carrying the bucket with newly dug potatoes and other vegetables in it. As he set it down, Aeolyn explained it was the Feast of Aeos, and she wanted him to find the eggs for the ceremony. "You and Edwin can find the unfertilized eggs, wherever the young chickens may have laid them."

A smile lit Christoph's face as he thought about his family and the way his mother prepared things for both the feast and the ceremony of renewal.

"All of us children looked forward to finding the eggs and then boiling them with onion peel, wild greens, and beets that we saved for just such a purpose, to stain them brown, green, and pink when we still lived in Mal Evol." Edwin could tell the years Chris had spent on their farm were golden memories that represented the happiest days of Christoph's life. "One egg was always left uncooked, as it is an important part of the ceremony," he sighed in remembrance. "The best part of the day was the sweets that were handed around after the prayer-meal. My mother made the best sweets in all of Neveyah...." Suddenly he looked at Edwin, his face stricken.

Edwin stood up and, crossing over to where he stood, placed his hand on Christoph's shoulder, casting the final healing spells layered with a small forgetting.

"I probably should visit Mum when we get back to

Braden," Christoph finished lamely, feeling slightly confused. "I don't know why I didn't when we were there before."

Edwin nodded. *Some wounds only heal with time. I was afraid the opportunity would never come up to finish the healing for him.*

"That's how we celebrated the Feast of Aeos at our house too," Aeolyn replied, unaware of the turmoil in Christoph's mind. "It was the most exciting day of the year for us." Happy memories filled her, as she and Christoph talked about the feast-day that heralded spring.

As the morning progressed, they found all the things necessary to have the simple, religious ceremony every home in Neveyah would hold as part of their feast on the day of the spring equinox.

Christoph and Aeolyn tended to the huge mass of flowers Edwin had brought in from the meadow, prepared the eggs, and partially roasted the vegetables to later finish cooking with the hoped-for fish, while Friedr and Edwin cast their simple fishing lines with improvised hooks into the pond.

"I must say, this is an excellent way to spend the morning." Friedr sighed as he leaned his back against a tree.

"Yes, it is. It's almost like having a day off," Edwin agreed.

"Well, don't get too relaxed, farm boy. You have work to do this afternoon, and this time you won't get out of it by setting my beard on fire. I'll be waiting for you, and it's every man for himself," Friedr's look was challenging.

"All right, if that's what you really want," Edwin

replied with a sly look. "I'd like to try penetrating shields with the lightning needle and fire spear, two spells I wasn't able to work on in Mal Evol."

"Be quiet and fish," Friedr replied a trifle sourly. Edwin had accidentally shattered his shields with no effort at all the previous day, and the lout apparently knew it. Now he needed to think of a way to defend against Edwin's new approach to battle-magic. "What if we work on shielding first and then spell casting while sword swinging?"

"Fine with me," Edwin replied. He settled back contentedly and put everything out of his mind except the pleasure of the moment.

After Friedr landed two fat trout and Edwin a nice big catfish, they cleaned them and proudly took them back up to the house. Aeolyn was pleased, saying they would be a delicious part of the meal she was working on. She was hiding a smile, and Chris was bursting with a secret he could barely contain, but Edwin and Friedr didn't press them to talk.

It was really fun having a holiday. Even though Edwin wished his father were there to share it with them, he was content to enjoy the day for what it was.

After checking to make sure the barriers were still strong, he sat next to Marya. Chris had braided flowers into her hair, and Aeolyn had dressed her in her clean shirt. She was lying on her left side, facing Edwin. He smoothed the bedroll under her and adjusted the rolled cloak serving as her pillow.

Aeolyn was in the pump room with Christoph, laughing and doing laundry. A pile of twigs sat on the table, waiting to be woven into a basket for the eggs.

Marya was so beautiful Edwin's eyes burned with

unshed tears, and he found himself touching her cheek. His voice caught in his throat as he spoke in a near-whisper, telling her how pretty the flowers in her hair were and how much he wished she were awake. "We'll have the best Aeos feast in all the land, I'm sure. The only thing that would make it better would be you. But we love you too much to put you in danger, so…." His whisper trailed off.

Holding Marya's hand between his own, Edwin said, "When I was a child, the first Feast of Aeos after my mother died was hard for me and my father. Mother always made it so special. She made honey-nuts and delicate little sweets that were so delicious. I was always so excited I couldn't sleep the night before. We colored our eggs, and she put them in a basket in the center of the table, with her best tablecloth and our best dishes. Father made sure there was a lamb for the feast, and Mr. and Mrs. Legg and their youngest son Josiah, who was a few months older than me, would stop by for dinner. Afterwards, there was music. Dad would play his fiddle, and Josiah and I would make ourselves sick eating sweets. You would have loved it, I'm sure." For a moment, he basked in the warmth of happy childhood days. Then his thoughts moved forward to the darker year, the one just after his mother's sudden death.

"For the first feast after she died, we did everything the way she would have. When Mr. Legg and Josiah came, we all felt sad because so many of our loved ones were gone and it was only the four of us now, what with Mr. Legg's oldest son off in the army. And while we were praying, it felt like Mother and Mrs. Legg were there with us, and we felt better. Now it's only my father, but he'll be fine. Josiah and his wife will have invited him to their house." Edwin was silent, lost in his memories and feeling homesick for a moment.

"I miss my father, but I would never trade this journey for anything, no matter what. Meeting you has changed my life." His voice was low, only for Marya. He laid her hand carefully by her side and started to rise, but as he did so, another attack was launched on the barriers he carefully maintained. While it was stronger than the previous one, it wasn't strong enough to break through. The barriers not only held strong, they appeared to show no effects other than the noise of the alert.

Christoph came into the kitchen, worry in his dark eyes. He knelt next to Marya and sent out his senses, checking her vital signs. Finding nothing to worry about, he relaxed and said, "Let's reposition her. She's been on her side for long enough." Together, they rolled her onto her back, and Edwin arranged her long braids with an unguarded look of tenderness on his face that touched Chris.

It made him happy to see Edwin in love, but he was once again stricken with the intense longing to see Dane and the urgent wish to go home and be with his own love. *Maybe I've grown up some too. I hope Dane is waiting for me. I want to have a home with him if he will still have me. I hope he still wants to bond with me. Please, Aeos! Don't let me have messed it up with my own selfishness.* Christoph closed his eyes and prayed silently, as he went to the table and began weaving a basket from the twigs.

"Thank you for braiding the flowers into her hair." Edwin spoke softly, unaware of Christoph's inner angst. "I need to go and find Friedr. We have to work on something I hope will be a weapon we can use against Brec when he's acting as the conduit for D'Mal."

"Go," Chris replied, "but remember I healed his face only last night. *Do* try not to burn the rest of his pretty red hair off." He sat at the table grinning wickedly and chuckling at Edwin's discomfort.

Edwin looked at him, startled, feeling chagrined. "Um, yeah. I'll temper my return volleys."

He finished gearing up and checked the barriers one more time before heading outside. Friedr was out stacking wood for the fire. He grinned when he saw Edwin. "Ready to get your soft, white backside kicked all over the corral?" Friedr sounded like his old self.

"If that's what the lesson of the day is, then I guess so." Edwin laughed as he helped with the last few branches and logs.

Edwin felt Friedr's basic shield go up the minute they entered the corral and firmed his own barrier/shield combination automatically. Before they even reached the usual practice area, Friedr was tossing spells and rushing him with his sword.

Surprisingly to Friedr, the spells sheeted off Edwin's shields, though he couldn't see or feel them. This went on until he threw a lightning bolt.

Edwin took the lightning and tossed it back in the form of a needle aimed at the base of Friedr's shield, causing him to dance back as the shield went down. "Whoa! What are you doing?"

"Having a lesson on shields, as you requested this morning," Edwin replied. Friedr frowned at his ingenuous grin, but Friedr's disapproval didn't deter Edwin from administering a lesson of his own. "This is what happened yesterday, Friedr, only it was a fire spear. What you need to do is layer the different elements so they create one all-purpose shield instead of throwing them up for each spell. If you maintain it at all times, you'll be a lot less vulnerable to attack." Seeing the look on Friedr's face, Edwin stood warily, wondering what was going to happen next. "Once you get the hang of it, it takes very little chi."

"All right, show me the basic configuration you're talking about, because I can't see how." Friedr dropped his shields.

"Call some water to your hand," Edwin suggested. "See, you have it there, and now you can use it for anything you want, up to the limits of the quantity you have to work with."

Friedr nodded, still not understanding. "I don't get what this has to do with shielding."

"I'll take this water and make it part of your shield. Only a fine mist, see?"

"It's a water shield, like any novice can make. It's the first one we learn," Friedr said, still not seeing Edwin's point. "Any novice can do this. I did notice you were finally able to teach Chris how to make one. That's a feat in itself. Now if he'll only maintain it. But I already know how to make one."

"Ah, but do this to it, and you have something completely different." Edwin added the finest hint of a low-level earth shield over the water. The shield was strong, and Friedr could tell it wouldn't go down under most attacks.

"But this is wrong. We've always known the elements fight each other. They can't work this way." Friedr couldn't believe it was holding together.

"If you try to use the heavy battle-shields you lunatics toss up for each spell thrown at you, then yes, they will *not* work in such heavy density. You must make the lightest, finest layer in each element you can manage, and then they will form a shield I can't accidentally break. Not only do they work, but you can layer each element you have the ability to use, tie them off, and they will maintain themselves with only minimal chi drain. This means you can save your chi and your attention for something important."

"I'm not used to thinking in this radical fashion. This goes against everything we've been taught." Friedr shook his head in disbelief. "Well, let's give it a try. Show me how to add a fire shield, if you will."

By the time they quit working, Friedr had developed the technique to a fine art. They even began working on using the borrowed magic they cast at each other to reduce the drain on their own chi. "It's just like tossing a ball around," Friedr said as he lobbed a ball of fire back at Edwin, using his shield. His beardless, angelic face bore the expression of a very large but happy child playing in the schoolyard.

Don't think cute. Don't think cute! Edwin reminded himself over and over again, and if he occasionally laughed a bit excessively, Friedr was having enough fun himself that he didn't notice.

Friedr was tired and sweaty and looking forward to bathing when he finally called a halt to the exercise.

Despite the fun they'd had, Edwin still couldn't really practice his theory, because if it worked, it would most likely kill his sparring partner. "I don't know how to practice what I want to do," he told Aeolyn as he walked through the kitchen to the pump room. "The dummy we used yesterday morning was close but not good enough. I guess I can't really try my idea out until I have a bad guy to take down."

"Well, how soon will they arrive?" Aeolyn's cooking smelled wonderful, and Edwin's mouth watered.

"I'll take a quick look now and then get cleaned up for dinner." He sat on the upturned log and sent his spirit out looking for Brec and the three minions who followed him as well as they could. He soon found them a day's hard running from the fork. They were breathing hard and looking much worse for wear but were still traveling as fast as ever. Brec had a madness in his eyes that made Edwin think he'd had, or expected to have, some bad discussions with his boss.

He returned to his body and told Aeolyn and the others what he has seen. "They will be here the day after tomorrow if they don't stop to rest. It looks like they may be running on magic, but it isn't our kind. Brec isn't looking too well. He looks like a whipped dog, if you want to know the truth, and now he's looking to do some whipping of his own."

They all laughed, and Edwin went into the pump room to get himself clean again. He washed his dirty shirt and hung it next to Friedr's on the laundry rope that Aeolyn had braided from the local hemp. Putting on his clean shirt, he felt almost festive as he thought about how nice it was to be able to bathe every day and have clean clothes.

When he returned to the kitchen with his hair damp and loose about his shoulders, he found the others waiting for him. They had all braided flowers into their hair. Even Christoph had managed, though he had little to secure them into. Aeolyn helped Edwin with his. "This reminds me of home," he said with a catch in his voice, suddenly homesick. "Dad always had the flowers ready to put in everyone's hair as they came in the front door." He caught himself before he sighed and went to sit next to Marya. She looked so peaceful and beautiful, he had to look away. The others pretended not to notice.

Christoph and Aeolyn had decorated the mantle over the hearth with budding apple branches laced with flowers. Branches and flowers also decorated the windowsills. In the center of the table, surrounded by flowers, was the simple twig-basket Christoph had made, with colored eggs resting in it along with the one uncolored, uncooked egg.

The farmhouse looked so festive, Edwin could hardly believe it. The fish, stuffed with herbs and wrapped in wide berchera leaves, had been roasting along with the root vegetables, and his mouth watered. They sat with their bowls in front of them, waiting, and there was a bowl for Marya, as she was to be included in the ritual.

"Friedr, you are the senior priest of the Goddess here. Will you do the honors?" Aeolyn looked at him expectantly.

"Yes, Friedr, you are our daddy on this trip," Christoph added wickedly. Edwin nodded in agreement, and they smirked at each other like a couple of naughty boys.

Friedr rolled his eyes. "You two behave yourselves." He closed his eyes, centering himself and seeking the peace of the Goddess, as did the others. Friedr had spent some time planning what he would say and how he would conduct the prayers for his and

Aeolyn's first Feast of Aeos as a bonded couple. He wanted to honor Aeos properly and make his new wife proud. When he was ready, he rose and stood at the head of the table near the fireplace.

"Tonight, we celebrate the Feast of Aeos. This is the feast of renewal and thanksgiving. The Goddess has blessed us and brought us through the winter with plenty. Now with the advent of spring, we ask her blessing on all the fields and people of Neveyah. She lights the way with her love, and we who follow will surely prosper, though we must walk the paths of darkness in her service."

He then raised the basket of eggs over his head, saying, "Aeos, these eggs are the symbol of your love, the advent of new life, and the circle of life, death, and rebirth. They represent the hope that lives eternally in each heart in this room—the hope that one day we will see the land of Neveyah flourish again."

Setting the basket back in the center of the table, Friedr took the uncooked egg and kneeling by the fire, he broke it, tossing it shell and all into the fire, saying "Goddess Aeos, this egg, symbol of birth and rebirth, we offer to you as a sign of our faith. You bless the land, making it flower again after the long winter. You bring new life to increase our flocks, herds, and families. You bless us with prosperity. You are the Goddess of Hearth and Home, and we offer up our lives in service to you. "

Then Friedr took the bundle of herbs Aeolyn had prepared for him. Crushing them, he placed them in the fire. "May the smoke from our hearth be pleasing to you, and may the prayers we offer rise to your ears as the scent of these herbs rise. We who walk in the light of your love ask only for your blessing on us in the battle we fight on your behalf. Give us the strength and the will to prevail. Our lives we have pledged to you. When our days on earth have come to an end, take us to your great hearth, and hold us warm until the day we are born again, in the light of your love."

After the traditional prayers at the fireplace, Friedr returned to the table. There he ceremonially served each person fish and vegetables, including a portion for Marya, while the others waited for him to do so. When every bowl was filled, he stood. Then he took the bowl they'd prepared to Marya, still deeply under the layered spell. They knelt around her, holding hands. With her in the center of the circle of their love, they said in unison the ancient words, "Bless the fields that grew this food, bless the pond that nourished this fish, and bless all who shelter in this house, under the light of your love."

Then, with the ceremony over, they returned to the table and began to eat the wonderful meal Aeolyn prepared for them. The fish was baked to perfection. The vegetables that had roasted around it had absorbed the flavors of the herbs, and the meal was the best they could ever remember having. They talked and laughed, each telling the others some of the traditions of their families for their holy day feasts.

At the end, Aeolyn and Christoph brought out the finest treat of all—they'd found a beehive, and there was honeycomb for their sweet. "We only took a small amount. The bees will need some for the coming year," Aeolyn said as she set the wide berchera leaf with the treat piled in the center before them. "Christoph's wards worked well. He was only stung once."

They sat on the floor before the fire, and each one

feeling like a child again, they enjoyed their sweets after the feast. They licked their fingers as they sucked the last drops of honey from the comb. The feeling of peace, however temporary, filled their hearts. The four of them sang and told stories until far into the night.

Later, when they'd gone to bed, Aeolyn whispered to her husband, "I'm glad you don't have a beard anymore, dear one. It takes far too long to get the honey out of it!" She kissed his baby-smooth cheek.

"Woman, you have me there," he replied, laughing. "But it was half the fun!"

Chapter 32

As the early hours of the morning brightened into yet another sunny day, Edwin once again sat on the upturned log outside the door, casting widely to find their would-be attackers. He found them napping on the banks of the river, having finally bedded down. Brec was off by himself, lying on his side and obviously having a nightmare.

No, not a nightmare. He's getting a bit of instruction from D'Mal. Edwin watched in shocked fascination as Brec whimpered through clenched teeth, and then in horror as the minotaur suddenly arched backwards, his heels nearly touching his great horned head and his hands clawing vainly at the dirt. The whimper escalated to muted screams as he was held there rigidly in terrible agony. Blood-red tears leaked from his eyes. Brec moaned, "Please. Please! I'm your faithful servant! I won't fail you!" His body was twisted even more painfully into an impossible position, and his screams became shrieks. After much more begging and groveling, he was gradually let go from the grip of his master, but Edwin could see it was no release. Brec fell into a deep dream, one that was perhaps worse than the torture he'd just endured.

Edwin ghosted back to the others, pondering what he'd witnessed. They too were now in the grip of nightmares. *Not a very restful sleep these poor minotaurs are having.*

As he drifted over the land, the sun rose. Its first rays colored the few high clouds rose-pink and golden, and drops of dew glistened like diamonds. It was the best part of the day for Edwin. He enjoyed being the first one up and about in the peace of the morning. Coming back to his body, Edwin stretched his back and shoulder muscles and then stood up, stretching his legs as he did so. Picking up an armload of firewood, he went back into the kitchen.

Christoph was up and adding the last log from the woodbin to the fire. They sat at the table and shared a breakfast of the remains of last night's feast, leaving plenty for Friedr and Aeolyn.

Edwin was disturbed and finally told Christoph what he'd witnessed. "I never saw anything like it," he finished. "What does he gain by tormenting his own people so they'll be less rested when they arrive here?"

"D'Mal doesn't know they're walking into a battle," Christoph replied. "He thinks it's only the two of you, and they're simply going to kidnap Marya again and either kill or capture you for his pleasure."

"It seems like a shortsighted view of things," Edwin ventured. "I find it strange D'Mal has such vast resources of chi and yet is so narrow in his focus. He does his own dirty work, as we've seen in his dungeon. He doesn't delegate well, as Aeolyn would say." The comment elicited a smile from Chris. "We know he sweeps aside Brec's mind to use his body as an extension of his own consciousness in an effort to maintain personal control of a situation. It's inefficient."

"He's an enigma, it's true. Can you imagine becoming the living embodiment of your god on earth? The vastness of his poisonous mind was startling, to say the least." Christoph stood and took their bowls to the pump room to wash them. Edwin dried them and set them on the mantle.

Then they sat by Marya. Edwin followed Chris with his healing senses as he delved her. "This battle can't come too soon," Chris spoke somberly. "She'll have to be awakened if this goes on for much longer or...." He winced as an assault was launched on their shields, even though they withstood the probing, questing attack.

"That was a different approach from his usual bludgeoning attack. Now he's looking for cracks in the barriers, I think," Edwin said, as the attempt faded. He checked them carefully, finding nothing wrong. He then looked closely at Christoph and saw he had dropped his own barriers, relying solely on the one Edwin was carrying on the house. For a moment, he debated mentioning it and then decided an object lesson was in order.

Friedr entered the kitchen and went on through to the pump room. Returning with a full jug of water, he sat at the table. Edwin served him breakfast, which he ate with his mind far away.

Edwin noticed stubble on the left side of Friedr's face, but none on the right. He colored with the realization but said nothing, feeling discretion would be the best course of action.

Sitting opposite Friedr, with his back to Christoph, Edwin visualized and concentrated the emotion he'd felt from D'Mal when he first found Marya had escaped, layering in the knowledge it was only a reflection and a warning. Once he had it isolated and re-formed, he sent it at Christoph with as much force as he could muster.

All of a sudden, Christoph doubled over, clutching

his head and groaning.

Friedr immediately rose to his feet asking, "What is it? Is it D'Mal?" His confusion was evident as he saw Edwin seated, not worried in the least. "Christoph, what's going on?" He looked from one to the other. "Edwin?"

Edwin looked at Friedr and shook his head. Then he turned around and said, "You dropped your barriers. You can't drop your barriers for any reason. Now rebuild them and tie them off." He waited for a moment while Christoph did as he was told.

Once Christoph had his barriers back up and tied off properly, Edwin said more gently, "I can't always be there to protect you, my brother. D'Mal is doing everything he can to break through, and I will be hard-pressed to fight him and carry the barriers on the house when the battle is brought to our doorstep."

Christoph's face was red, but he simply replied, "I know, and you're right. I won't forget again." After a moment, he asked, "What did you do to me? I knew it was you, but it felt like D'Mal."

Edwin told him. They then became involved in a discussion of ethics and how such a skill could be misused. As they talked, Friedr saw Aeolyn beckoning from the door of the pump room. He went to her, and she asked, "What is going on there?"

"Edwin schooled Chris on his barriers again. Only this time the lesson will probably stick." He rubbed his beardless chin, feeling the stubble on only one side. "He did something I've never seen a healer do. He used his empathy to send a painful reminder to Chris to maintain his barriers." Friedr thought for a moment and then said, "The skills Edwin has have never occurred before, have they…but they will. The Goddess is changing the way magic works in Neveyah. She made him into this so he could teach the new ways. I think she's trying to level the playing field with the Bull God. Edwin is the first, but he won't be the last. We must learn as much as we can from him if we're going to teach in the Temple."

"Father Rall and Abbott Garran are right about him. He'll turn the theory of magic as we know it upside down before he's finished with us." Aeolyn looked at the two in the kitchen discussing empathy and ethics. "This is only the first argument that'll happen in this new world." She sighed and rolled her eyes. "At least Edwin is the most ethical man I know. It may be why the Goddess chose him to be the first to have the new skills. She wants a man with the highest ethics to teach the ones who will follow."

***

Later, having checked on Brec and his men and found them sleeping, Edwin, Friedr, and Aeolyn worked on the same problem as before. The straw dummy, made out of old rags they'd found in the barn and stuffed with straw, was a bit pathetic looking, having been flamed, scorched with lightning, and crushed with great zeal. Unfortunately, Aeolyn's shields were not as strong when she spread them to cover the dummy, so they went down easily. They remade him each time, but he was rather sad looking.

Finally Friedr said, "Why don't I stand on the other side, and we can try to overlap our shields. Then we can each alternate trying to kill Edwin, and he can use what we send him to form this needle. But we need to change it up and make him work for it." He looked at Edwin.

"Is this all right with you?"

"Yes. I think it'll work perfectly. Have you ever tried?" Edwin was curious because it seemed so logical to him to overlap shields for strength. "You've never discussed it."

"No. It isn't something battle-mages have time to do when the stuff is flying at you. But with the better shields, we don't have to worry about that anymore." Friedr's smile was broad as he planned what combos he was going to send. "You gave me the idea for it, with the healer's barriers you and Christoph have overlapped over Marya." Then saying, "I hope you're ready," Friedr fired off a volley of fire followed by earth, while Aeolyn pelted Edwin with lightning.

Fire and earth bounced back toward the dummy in an unfocused form and sheeted off their overlapped shield. The next volleys Edwin focused into tighter forms, and the shields withstood them. Finally after nearly half an hour, he thought he knew what to do.

"Watch out, you two. I'm going to try something different." Edwin twisted the fire Aeolyn threw at him around the lightning Friedr cast, using air to focus it and form a needle. *I hope this works as well as I think it will.*

The lightning-needle pierced the shield, and the dummy exploded. Friedr and Aeolyn dove out of harm's way amid a shower of burning straw and rags.

"Holy...!" Friedr picked himself up and dusted off his leather trousers. "What the heck did you do?"

Aeolyn sat on the ground and waited to hear Edwin's explanation.

As Edwin tried to explain what he'd done, Friedr looked at him with an expression of disbelief. "I don't think anyone else can replicate it because you're the only one I know who can use air to form the elements," he finally said. "But I can do something with reflected magic—I feel sure of it. I need to work harder and then I'll have it."

Friedr walked over to the burning bits of dummy and stamped them out. Then he looked back at Edwin and said, "I guess I'm lucky you only burned my beard off. I could have ended up like this poor fellow." The look on his face was comical but, wisely, Edwin didn't laugh.

Aeolyn stood up, saying, "Let's work on overlapping the shields better. If Edwin can do this, maybe D'Mal can too. After all, he's drawing chi directly from his god."

"One thing I want to do is add my barrier to your shields when the battle is on, even though you aren't highly empathic. He'll be sending mental attacks, and it works on the minotaurs. They're not empathic at all, much less sensitive than you two are. Let's see how it works," Edwin said.

They practiced overlapping their shields with Edwin weaving a spirit barrier into them and after much trial and error finally arrived at a point where they could put up a really strong overlapping barrier/shield almost automatically, one that took little chi to maintain.

"I think this is going to be impossible for any mage to break," Friedr remarked. "If we survive this fight, there won't be a single person who can take any of us in a full-on mage-duel when we get back to the Temple." He smiled grimly. "I'm going to kick some butt."

***

That night, Edwin checked again on Brec and the boys, as he thought of them, and found them crossing the river. They were now on the road west, approaching the shallow ford and following the faint trail Edwin and his companions left in their flight from Mal Evol. Returning to his body, he told Aeolyn they would be there sometime before noon the next day.

"Good. We need to get this over with," she replied. "Now we need to rest and store as much chi as we can for this fight."

Unable to sleep, Edwin checked the shields he'd layered over Marya. After checking every inch, he found them holding well. Christoph's personal barriers were up and firmly tied off. Edwin sighed, relieved he wouldn't have to remind Chris again, whose voice sounded sleepily from the other side of Marya. "Don't worry, Edwin. I'll be scrupulous in maintaining them. Your lesson was harsh but necessary. I'll never let my guard down again," he said, chuckling. "The headache alone was reminder enough."

"I don't want you to end up like Marya or worse," Edwin replied slowly. "I couldn't take losing you. My life would be so boring without you."

"I'd prefer to remain in control of my own mind too, so don't worry," Chris's voice sounded like he was drifting off.

His words stirred a feeling of foreboding in Edwin. A vision flashed into his mind. He saw a man who at first appeared to be Christoph. The man had much longer hair than he'd ever worn it, though, dark and curling past his shoulders. To Edwin's relief, he realized it couldn't possibly be Chris. He walked through a thick, lush jungle Edwin had never seen the like of.

The man had Temple augmentations much like Christoph's. He also had water-magic and earth-magic strongly represented along with the healer's stars and crescent moon. Though his features were very like Christoph's, enough to be his brother, his eyes were dark and empty, and his youthful face had a harsh set to it. He walked with an ornately carved staff, set with a large amethyst crystal in the top.

The vision let him go, and Edwin was silent, staring into the dark. *I'm overtired. I have to stop imagining things. There are so many other things to worry about. He'll be safe. I'm only worried because I've never been in a battle like this. Anyone would be worried.* It was a long while before he fell asleep.

***

By morning, Edwin had forgotten all about his worries. He found Brec and his minions about four leagues away, heading for the farm. He went into the cold farmhouse. "Time to gear up. They'll be here soon."

They planned to make it appear as if Marya was hiding in the woods opposite the meadow where they were going to join the battle. Chris would stay in the house with her. They'd let the fire go out, hoping the house might go unnoticed. He would maintain the barriers as long as he was able. All that was left to do was for Edwin to build them in such a way that if they went down, Marya would sleep deeply…forever.

Kneeling by Marya, Edwin held her hand and whispered, promising to take care of her and promising she would be safe no matter what. Then he and Chris built the sleep spell that would be triggered only if they were all dead or captured.

Christoph geared up but sat in the cold kitchen with his staff balanced across his knees. He shivered thinking of the coming battle, praying they would prevail and fearing they wouldn't.

Chapter 33

Friedr, Aeolyn, and Edwin stood at the top of the lower meadow, watching Brec and his minions as they ran toward them. Aeolyn selected it as the place to make their stand since the attackers wouldn't be able to see the house from there. The four minotaurs had been running all night and were racing uphill into the bright morning sun, but it didn't slow them at all. "So much for having the sun on our side," Aeolyn murmured.

"Weapons up," snapped Friedr. "Lace the shields." They raised and overlapped their shields. "How does it look to you, Edwin?"

"It's tight and tied off," he replied after a quick check. He gripped his sword more tightly. "I have the spirit woven in and anchored to each of us, so if one goes down, it'll stay up. Hopefully, it'll protect us from his mind magic," he said wryly. "This is where I get to test it."

Friedr simply shrugged. "It works or it doesn't."

With a roar, Brec raced toward them, swinging a huge sword, shouting, "Where is she? Bring her to me now." His minions moved to flank them, but Friedr lobbed a fireball at Girt, who went down rolling on the ground, frantically trying to put out the flames. Running, Aeolyn cut his head off with one swift move. "Now we're even," she shouted gleefully, bounding back to Friedr's side.

The other attackers immediately converged on Friedr and Aeolyn, who between them fired volley after volley of spells at Wint and Bann, all the while blocking the minotaurs' wild swings. Edwin moved the earth under Brec and Bann causing them to stumble. He pressed his attack on them, hacking and blocking as he evaded their swords.

Brec's eyes appeared to have trouble focusing, a sure sign he was communicating with D'Mal. Wint and Bann ran interference for him, keeping Friedr's sword busy while Aeolyn and Edwin fired off spell after spell, which were somehow deflected. Edwin examined the shield the minotaurs were under while Aeolyn and Friedr fought off their attack.

Bann hacked and pressed forward toward Friedr, mocking him with his gravelly voice. "This is pathetic. Now we're fighting cute little children with toy swords." His hulking body reeked with sweat and exhaustion, but he still hacked and slashed viciously.

At the word "cute" Friedr's eyes went flat. "I'll show you cute, you ugly bastard." He growled as he pressed his own attack, moving faster than Edwin had ever seen. His sword flashed, and Bann stepped back, struggling to regain the advantage and failing. Desperately, he backpedaled further, his tired body not responding as well as it should.

Finally, Friedr ran him through, yanking the sword out with a practiced, slicing motion. Bann's guts spilled onto his feet, and the shrieking minotaur went to his knees. Friedr moved to decapitate him, but Bann raised his arm and lost a hand instead. The second swing put him out of his misery.

"The bastard was right! It *was* cute!" Friedr merrily launched himself at the two minotaurs who were closing in on Aeolyn and Edwin.

Brec's stance changed. Suddenly, D'Mal was there, in complete possession. "Where is she?" Hatred and madness rolled off the companions' barriers. He cast a beckoning at Aeolyn, but she wasn't affected at all, thanks to Edwin having laced the spirit barrier into their overlapped shield.

As one, Aeolyn, Friedr, and Edwin looked toward the woods and back. "Where is who?" Edwin asked, with a knowing grin.

D'Mal's eyes focused on him, widening. The minotaur slashed at him, but Edwin neatly evaded the flashing blade.

"You. You will suffer, thief!" His voice became even more enraged as he realized Edwin was mocking him.

Wint raced off toward the woods, while D'Mal poured an intense lightning spell on all three defenders. Edwin quickly focused the raw element into a needle he flung at Wint, striking the running minotaur. He was stopped in his tracks, and what was left of his corpse lay smoking in the meadow. The thunderclap was deafening, shaking the house and the forest surrounding the meadow.

The defenders turned on D'Mal, who now stood alone against them.

He roared his rage and immediately raised a shield unlike any they had ever seen. There was no flaw, and Edwin could find no place where it was tied off. It wasn't made of spirit, nor was it elemental, nor was it a mix of the two magics. The shield was something completely foreign to his senses. *There must be a weakness. There is always a weakness,* Edwin thought as he searched, probing frantically.

The enraged creature that was D'Mal shifted the huge sword to his right hand, and raising his left hand, he called Bann's sword, which flew to his other hand. Wielding both swords against Friedr and Aeolyn, he advanced on Edwin with mad hatred in his eyes, raining earth on him in an effort to bury him.

Edwin took the earth and balled it, dropping it on D'Mal's shields, temporarily blocking his vision. Shaking it off, he advanced on them with both swords flashing as if each was controlled by a separate mind. Friedr and Aeolyn converged on the blades, and Edwin found himself returning a ball of fire in the form of a spear, which rebounded and splashed off their own barriers.

"Take this, bastard!" Edwin shouted, and Friedr and Aeolyn danced out of the way as he dropped an advanced spell on the minotaur, a deluge of icy water. Stunned only momentarily, the infuriated creature pressed his attacks, leaving no opening for Friedr or Aeolyn.

Desperately, Edwin isolated the earth under D'Mal, and using the water that lay on the ground, he turned the soil into a morass. The creature slipped. As he struggled to regain his footing, Friedr lopped off his left hand.

With a howl of pain, he staggered, and Aeolyn hamstrung his right leg. The minotaur went down, and his shields faltered but firmed up again. D'Mal once again desperately rained lightning on Edwin, more lightning than Edwin would have ever thought possible.

"Take this." Friedr tossed a ball of fire. Edwin wrapped it around the massive lightning bolt, forming it into a needle. Gathering his will, he drilled it right back with as much force as he could muster. Seeing the spell cast at him, D'Mal abruptly abandoned the minotaur as the needle pierced the shield, and screaming madly, the glowing Brec began expanding. Before their horrified eyes, he exploded, raining bits of blood and gore over the meadow.

The wildly rebounding spell echoed back on Edwin, crushing his own shields.

The world went dark to Edwin.

***

Edwin gradually regained consciousness, hearing voices. He heard one in particular, the smooth, silky voice of Stefyn D'Mal. "I told you I would take you back, and I always do what I promise. You will be required to pay for what you have cost me, in tears, of course. Your actions cost me a good servant and my two favorite dogs. But have no fear. Your lover is locked up here as well. My spells were stronger than his, for all I am constrained by distance." He spoke as if he were discussing the weather.

Edwin watched as Marya looked around in confusion. As she touched her throat, she saw she wore a heavy necklace of white gold set with amethysts and white gems. She held up her hands, seeing bracelets and rings of the same color and style. Glancing down, she saw a low-cut dress made of the richest, deep amethyst velvet. It left her shoulders bare as it fell in graceful folds to the floor and trailed behind her.

"What's happened? Where are we? I don't know this place. Who are you?" Her eyes glowed with a brilliant blue that was almost otherworldly. "Who am I? Why can't I remember?"

Her eyes...Marya's eyes are brown. What is this? Edwin's mind was spinning. *This must be a dream.* His field of vision was very narrow, and everything was dim, everything except her.

"Beloved, what do you mean?" D'Mal's voice was soft and compelling. "This is where you spent the best days of your life. You are in the Rose Tower. I brought you here by virtue of my superior magic. Don't feign ignorance, my dear. It's not polite." Stefyn wore a tight-fitting, black velvet coat over a white shirt with white lace at the wrists and collar. Tight, black trousers were tucked into high-glossed black riding boots. His clothing was designed to show off his physique, and it did exactly that. His dark hair was deliberately tousled and framed the perfection of his face in a way that could only be described as breathtaking. "Surely you don't wish another lesson in manners."

He speaks like the villain in one of Christoph's stories, thought Edwin, wondering what was going on and why he was having such a strange dream. *No one really speaks that way. Well, no one but Jaxon, but he's from Arlen, and they're all refugees from Mal...oh Goddess! D'Mal really is his uncle.*

Marya simply looked at Stefyn and shrugged her bare shoulders. "I'm sure I don't know what you're speaking of, sir." Her brilliantly shining blue eyes were curious, and her voice betrayed no fear.

D'Mal's eyes widened in surprise, and the dark beauty of his face showed some confusion. It was a threat that always sent Marya into near hysteria, yet she wasn't trembling with terror. She didn't appear to even know him. In fact, she seemed to know nothing about whom or where she was.

Edwin couldn't move, nor could he speak, but he could feel his personal healer's barrier, still rock solid. Finally, he sorted out what had happened to him. *The*

*barrier is made of spirit and was tied off, so I have
access to it in the dream. My elemental shield must
have been broken by the spell that rebounded on me.*

"Ah, my new friend has awakened." D'Mal's voice
was as pleasant as if he was greeting his favorite guest.

As well he might be, thought Edwin. His own
emotions appeared to be balled up in a corner of his
mind. There was a unique clarity of thought that was
completely separate from his emotional self. *This will
be the real battle.*

D'Mal crossed over to where Edwin lay. Kneeling
next to his bound form and lightly stroking Edwin's
face, he asked, "Are you comfortable? I do so want you
to enjoy your stay with me." The spell of compelling
was combined with a wave of malice and hatred with
the added fillip of barely controlled lust. It rolled over
Edwin's barriers, though the voice was silky and soft as
satin. Neither the emotions nor the compelling affected
him. "We shall become fast friends and close, close
confidantes, though, of course, I am going to take your
life, one piece at a time in the process." D'Mal rose
and turned back to Marya, who looked at Edwin with
pity in her brilliant, blue eyes.

As his sight fully returned, Edwin discovered he
was bound hand and foot. He lay on his side on the
hearthrug before the fireplace in Marya's rooms in the
Rose Tower. He quietly assessed his situation. Blood
ran down his face, burning his eyes. He blinked as he
wondered absently, *Why am I bleeding?*

"Who is this poor man whom you care so little
for?" Marya looked at the perfection of Stefyn D'Mal.
Despite his beauty, she was drawn to the bloody and
battered man lying bound on the hearth rug. "Shall I

heal him?"

"Wife, do you not know your own lover?" He seemed genuinely surprised. "He is the one who stole you from me, stole everything I ever loved when he took you away." His overwhelming pain at the loss rolled over Edwin's barriers, with no effect. D'Mal's mental agony radiated with the power of his god's grief.

It's not D'Mal who loves Marya, but the Bull God, Edwin realized with awe. *Everything that's happened has been the Bull God himself living through his high priest. No wonder he's mad. He is the personification of his insane god. Tauron's mind is broken, and D'Mal must suffer the consequences of serving him.*

"Why don't I know you or him? I would surely know you if, as you say, we are bonded. I should recognize him if he was my lover, but I don't. Why?" Marya turned tear-filled eyes to Stefyn. "What would cause this? I can't feel the healing magic nor can I feel your mind, sir. Why is your mind closed to me?"

Stefyn said nothing, visibly unsure now how to reply.

She turned to Edwin, saying, "I am so sorry, young man. I can't heal your wounds. In this place, my magic is gone." Her brilliant, blue eyes welled again, and a tear rolled down her cheek. An immense wave of sadness rolled over Edwin's shields, as vast as the madness that filled D'Mal's mind.

She's not simply Marya. Edwin was stunned at the thought. *She's the embodiment of the Goddess Aeos, whom the Bull God loves.*

D'Mal grabbed her shoulders and forced her to turn to him, saying, "Heed me now! You are my wife, and to show your faithfulness to me, you'll kill this beast." He placed a knife in her hand.

"Why should I kill a poor man whom you wish to see dead? I'll never kill anyone, not even for you, if you truly are my husband." She put the knife back into his hand. "I won't do this. It's evil." She looked at him, her eyes clear and unafraid. "Free this man if I am truly your wife."

"What do you know of evil? You're an innocent! *He* stole into our home and kidnapped you and took you far away out of the country. *He* is evil," Stefyn's dark eyes were full of tragedy and overwhelming love. He took her hand, folding her fingers around the knife. "You are my wife. Kill him." He kissed her neck, a lingering kiss, and then kissed her hair, holding her close. "Kill this fool who would destroy our home," he pleaded. "He must never go free. He is too dangerous."

"I've no memory of our bonding. I don't know you. I won't do this." She turned her face away from him, shrugging from his grasp. The knife fell to the floor, and she kicked it under the bed. "Don't ask me to do this," she said, sitting in the chair before the fire, looking at Edwin. "I don't know you, and I don't know him. I *do* know I'm not a person who would do what you're asking of me. Therefore, you can't be my husband."

Suddenly enraged, Stefyn D'Mal held out his hand, and the knife leapt into it. "I *do* know him, and I will kill him myself. His life was over the day he stole you from me."

Falling to his knees, he stabbed Edwin several times. Trying not to scream, Edwin groaned, and though he was terribly wounded, the knife did not kill him. Despite the infinite, excruciating pain, he didn't lose consciousness. "Oh, dear," D'Mal sneered. "You can't die. Your body is not truly here. Even when your body dies, you'll remain here, pretty thief. I'll have my pleasure of you, don't worry."

The knife fell again, lodging in Edwin's heart, and this time it stayed there. The pain was unbearable. Tears of agony rolled down Edwin's face and mingled with his blood. "Now you'll have the privilege of watching me get what I want, despite your dismal efforts to the contrary."

Marya's eyes were no longer the brilliant shining blue of Aeos. The warm, golden brown had returned. She looked in dismay at her bejeweled hands and then at Stefyn D'Mal. "What? How am I here? We were walking...."

"You're my wife. You are mine!" D'Mal stood and pulled the shocked girl from her chair. He kissed her lips passionately, his hands demanding and impatient.

She stared at Edwin, horrified, and then pushed D'Mal away from her. As he fell, she rushed to Edwin, and tears ran down her face. "What has he done? Even if I still had my gift, I couldn't fix this!" Kneeling beside him, she placed her hand on his bleeding forehead. "Edwin, Edwin, I'm so sorry. You didn't deserve this." The coolness of her hand was soothing, and he was able to think more clearly despite the pain. "You only wanted to help me."

"You know his name? And you claim to not know *me*?" Rage poured out of D'Mal, crushing Marya's will. Her dress ripped as he clutched it, and for the first time, panic was raw in her eyes. Forcing her to her knees, he growled, "You will pay dearly for this. False, false woman!" He struck her face. "You lied to me." He struck her again. "That is very bad manners!" Jerking her to her feet by her hair, he twisted her around so he was behind her, holding her arms with one hand and forcing her terrified face to look at Edwin with the other. "See your poor lover! See how he suffers for the love of you! All who love you suffer. You played me false, woman. Now I will seal the bargain, and you will be my wife. You have lost your privileges! A lesson in manners is needed!" Rage and lust contorted his beautiful face. "First, you must respect your husband!"

Edwin could see the wooden handle of the knife sticking out of his chest. From somewhere far away, he knew what he had to do. Concentrating with all his might, he imagined the knife in D'Mal's eye. With every fiber of his being, he willed the knife to leave his chest and lodge itself there.

The handle shivered, and pain once again ripped through Edwin's chest, and despite his desire to be silent, a groan escaped him.

Suddenly vanishing from Edwin's chest, the knife appeared in the right eye of Stefyn D'Mal. With a shriek that shredded Edwin's mind, D'Mal staggered back, clutching his bloody face before disappearing.

The room—and Marya—vanished.

Once again, the world went dark.

Chapter 34

Christoph stood at the window in the cold, dark kitchen trying to see what might be happening, but he had no line of sight on the meadow. He could hear the ringing of sword against sword, and the screams of the wounded and dying were clear, as were the sounds of battle-spells being traded back and forth and hissing through the sunlit morning.

Christoph knelt down by Marya and covered her to keep her warm, hoping the wounded didn't include anyone he loved. He pulled his cloak more closely around himself and checked the barriers. Holding her cool, limp hand to his cheek, he prayed fervently to Aeos, "Aeos, give them the strength to do what they must, and hold them in your heart. Please protect them, and let Edwin live to bond with his dream girl. She needs him so much. They deserve to live happily ever after."

Suddenly, he heard an explosion of thunder that shook the house and rattled the windows. Lying beside Marya, Christoph put his arm about her protectively and monitored her, making sure the spells that kept her in a deep, dreamless sleep were holding strong. Anxiously, he checked the barrier, finding it still stood firm.

Another, more massive explosion rocked the house. The barriers buckled and went down, shattering. Sitting up, he frantically rebuilt them, but it was too late. A wave of exultation mixed with lust-infused greed rolled over his personal barriers, and a mad glee pierced his awareness. Christoph knew without a doubt something unforeseen had happened to Edwin.

Marya's eyes opened, glassy and filled with dreams. A low moan escaped her lips, and Christoph immediately did the only thing he could think of.

He cast a deep forgetting on her and tied it off exactly as he had watched Edwin do. As he finished tying off the spell, the kitchen door flew open and Friedr staggered in, bearing Edwin's limp body over his shoulders, Aeolyn right behind him. They laid him on his bedroll, and she immediately began removing his boots.

"D'Mal has her," Christoph said without preamble. "The explosion somehow buckled the barriers, and he now has her mind. I cast a forgetting on her, but I don't know if it will be any help."

"He has Edwin too," Aeolyn said. All three were covered in gore, and tears ran down her cheeks, leaving clean streaks. Friedr stripped Edwin of his armor, and she got his vest off. "Edwin used the lightning needle, and it pierced D'Mal's shields, but it backfired on him."

Christoph had barely gotten Edwin's shirt cut off and was trying to examine him when suddenly his body convulsed and blood leaked from the corner of his mouth. Blood flowed from his side and chest.

"Where is this coming from? I can find no wounds." Frantically, Christoph checked Edwin's internal organs. They were all whole but failing as if they were severely damaged. "He has no wounds! What madness is this?"

No, Aeos rose unseen from Marya's sleeping form. *It's not supposed to end this way.* Laying her hand on Edwin's forehead, she followed Christoph as his healing sight delved him. *I am so sorry. You don't deserve this. You were only trying to save me.*

Edwin convulsed again and then was still. Blood poured from his chest though there was no wound.

"No," Christoph's voice was rough with tears. "No. No! Don't do this, Edwin!" He poured a massive healing spell into Edwin's still form. When nothing happened, he tried to find some sign of life, but there was none. "How can this be? Where is the wound?" He looked at Friedr, shocked and disbelieving what his healer's senses told him to be true.

"His heart simply stopped," he said slowly, his voice rising to a wail of grief. "It just stopped beating." He poured another massive healing spell into Edwin's body, but still there was no response. Aeolyn and Friedr put their arms around him, trying to comfort him, tears flowing down their faces.

Christoph's muffled, gut-wrenching sobs were the only sounds in the still kitchen.

Beside them lay the bodies of their dearest friends. One was dead, and the other was surely dying.

Aeos lay back down beside Edwin and put Marya's arms around him. Gathering her will, she rested Marya's head on his shoulder and sent her spirit deep into his mind, looking for the spark that must still be there.

***

Edwin lay propped up against the old familiar rock outcropping back home on the farm in Markett. As he watched the clouds, he wondered how he got there, back in the world of Ariend. His body was wracked with pain, and it was difficult to breathe. Blood trickled into his eyes. He knew he was dying, but it didn't really matter that much.

His father knelt beside him, holding his hand. "You did well, son, so much better than anyone expected. But I knew you would do the best you could."

"I love you, Dad," Edwin whispered. "I met a girl there. She was so beautiful. I would have bonded with her and brought her home to you."

"I know, son," the Almighty Father, in the guise of John Farmer, told him. "Rest now and all will be well." Edwin's eyes closed, and the god laid his hand upon his chest.

Aeos knelt beside Marya's form. She looked across the two to her father and said, "He promised to protect her and willingly gave his life for her, for me. He deserves so much more than this." She shimmered and rose, laying her hand on Marya's forehead. "I'm sorry I can't completely undo everything you have suffered, child. But for now, you are free of captivity. Bond with this man, and live happily for the time you have. He loves you so much."

"Yes, he does," the Almighty Father replied as he transformed into a form more radiant than fragile, mortal eyes could bear to look upon. "Take my hand, daughter." Aeos and the Almighty Father both sparkled into infinity, leaving Marya holding the sleeping form of Edwin Farmer, her head on his shoulder.

***

Edwin felt the wind on his face, and he opened his eyes. Marya rested at his side, her head on his shoulder and their arms wrapped around each other. They sat leaning against the rock outcropping, watching the sky. Edwin enjoyed the feeling of completion he felt with Marya in his arms.

"I love you," she said, looking at him, with some

part of her fearing he would hate her for causing the ordeal he had been through. "I don't know what to say. I'm sorry I got you into this mess. You didn't deserve to die."

"I don't think it was your fault," he replied slowly. *It's amazing how clearly you can think when the pain is gone.* "You didn't choose to be his prisoner. He kidnapped you. Did you love him?"

"No," she replied. "A little, I think, but I can't explain it. Sometimes I hate him more for that than anything else." Her voice was hurt, bitter. Then she smiled and said in a happier tone of voice, "But at least he doesn't fill my mind with his poison anymore. I feel clean again."

"Aeos," Edwin told her. "She loves you and felt you had suffered enough. She healed you." He exhaled heavily but said what he knew to be true. "D'Mal loved you so much. A small part of you would have had to respond to him, and that was how the poison took root. But I love you, Marya. I couldn't let him hurt you, and I don't think I want to live without you. I want to be your husband and build a life with you. Is there even a small possibility you would bond with me?"

"Yes," she looked at him and smiled. "I will gladly bond with you, Edwin Farmer. But now, we need to go back. Friedr can perform our bonding ceremony." She placed her hand over Edwin's eyes, and he fell peacefully asleep.

***

Aeolyn and Friedr held Christoph until he got himself under control. Turning back to Marya, they were surprised to see she'd moved and put her arms around Edwin's cooling body, resting her head on his shoulder.

"Oh, Marya," Chris said, stroking her hair. Tears flowed down his cheeks. "Where are you now? Who will protect you, now he is gone? We failed you."

They all jumped as Edwin's eyes opened wide, and he suddenly convulsed again, taking a huge breath and gasping.

"Holy Goddess of Mercy! Bless you, Aeos. Bless you!" Christoph immediately used his healing sight to delve Edwin but still could find no wounds. Casting ease and heal, he muttered, "Oh, thank you, thank you."

Marya opened her eyes, struggling to sit up. "Water.... Please, is there any water to drink?"

Aeolyn immediately took her a bottle and held it, supporting her while she drank thirstily. "Blessed Aeos. You're back with us! I was so sure you were both gone." Aeolyn's face was streaked with tears, as was Friedr's.

"Chris," Edwin's voice was faint.

"What is it?" Chris held him in a sitting position. "What's wrong?" His senses could find no injury and no pain.

"You dropped your barriers again." Edwin fell into a natural sleep, a smile on his bloody face.

Aeolyn and Friedr burst out laughing. Christoph did too, once he thought about it. "It's going to be okay now. He really did beat D'Mal! It's over!" The intensity of that realization nearly brought him to tears again. He looked up and saw tears running down his friends' faces.

"Looks like we're going home after all," said Friedr gruffly.

"As if there was any doubt," sniffed Aeolyn. "But I

think you'll be performing a bonding ceremony before we leave here. Look!"

Marya had settled back beside Edwin with her arms around him. Her head rested on his shoulder, and his arm was around her. Their faces both wore contented smiles as they slept.

Here ends this tale...

Myrddin Publishing

unique electronic & print books

Appendices

Time and Calendar of Neveyah

Each year consists of 365 days and is divided into four seasons - Winter, Spring, Summer, Harvest, and one Holy Month. The year of Edwin Farmer's first quest was 3254.

Each season consists of three months, making twelve months that equal 28 days each, plus a Holy Month. Harvest (Autumn) and Winter are separated by the Holy Month of 29 days. The winter solstice falls on the first day of the month following (on the first day of Caprica). This is a month which is sacred to the Goddess Aeos, Goddess of Harvest, Hearth, and Home. It is a time when people travel to visit family and simply take time off for a small vacation, often taking two weeks to do it. On the day that falls between last day of the Solstice Month and the first day of Caprica (called Holy Day,) each family holds a ritual feast in their home. It is a feast of thanksgiving and prayers for the New Year. Every four years an extra Holy Day is added to the calendar, and the day is a festival day all across Neveyah. Such a year is called a Long Year, though it is really only one day longer.

The months are as follows -
Caprica, Aquas, Piscus, (Winter)
Begins on actual day of Winter Solstice
Arese, Taura, Geminis   (Spring)
Lunne, Leonid, Virga   (Summer)
Libre, Scorpius, Saggitus (Harvest)
Solstice, Holy Month—thirteenth month—stands alone on calendar)
Holy Day, Bridge between old year and new – belongs to no month – a day of celebration

Days of the Week -

1. Sunnaday – Minimal business is conducted. Each family's tasks for the Temple as a whole are completed, such as chopping firewood, quilting, making clothes, and preserving food. The members of the temple clergy assemble in work gangs to accomplish these tasks from which they all benefit.

2. Lunaday

3. Tyrsday

4. Odensday

5. Torsday

6. Frosday

7. Restday – no business is conducted, and only minimal work is done on farms and other places where some work must be done seven days a week. This is a day for people to spend with their families or to pursue their personal interests.

Prominent members of Edwin Farmer's Family Tree

Aelfrid, 'Firesword' founder of College of Warcraft and Magic

Liam Farmer

Wynn Farmer—*Mountains of the Moon*

John Farmer—*The Wayward Son, Valley of Sorrows*

Edwin Farmer – *Tower of Bones, Forbidden Road, Valley of Sorrows*

The Prophecies of Neveyah

Aril, Seeress of Ariend's Children, in a scroll given to the Temple of Aeos, in the year 3209

"The worlds tremble in the starry void. The stolen child yearns for his mother's breast in the foreign land and is succored on despair. Vintages of unsurpassed sweetness will be the wines of the last days. Most faithful scion of the line of Keepers, be not diverted by the burning city of old. Hold fast to the altar when the house of holiness is under siege. Your faith and resolve preserves the blood of the Keepers. A place is prepared for you at my hearth."

***

Abbot Devyn D'Mal to the assembled Clergy at Mal Evol Temple in the year 3215

"Keeper, you must save the remnant of my children, for when the end-times are upon you, you shall be barred from the valley of poison and beauty. The wall shall stretch from Horn to Horn and shall be the sign that none from the Valley of Shadows can enter the golden land. The eternal youth, the Lost One, will take the City of Gloom and those of my children left behind will suffer unto the third generation. He stands on the wall and gazes on the golden land, unable to enter."

***

Mother Lera to the assembled Clergy at Aeoven in the year 3229:

"Hark now! The advent of the Bull God is upon us - he comes to claim his bride. She rejects him, and his mad desire is thwarted. Still he claims the dowry as was promised. The verdant lands shall fall to the Bull God, and shall become a wilderness of thorns. Seek the hero who will hold safe the Heart of Neveyah. Take the Heir down the Forbidden Road, and shroud him with the light of truth. Now comes the Hero from the lands of the Almighty Father; from his line shall come the one who will take back all. From him shall come the Hero Foretold who will triumph on the day of redemption."

***

Father Rall to the assembled clergy at Aeoven in the year 3254:

"The storm rises in the lands of Neveyah, though it does not bring its wrath fully for yet awhile...when falls the Beloved Hero into darkness, then will the storm's wrath fall upon Neveyah. The children of the Bull-God answer the call which rides on the wind! The light of truth remains shrouded beneath the Throne of Stone and Bone. The cradle of the rightful heir lies obscured by the truth. Let the Hero go to the Shadow Castle to seek the hand of she whom darkness has claimed. The moon is dark—in stealth seeks the hero for the window to the Tower of Roses; in stealth he unbars the door to the forbidden room. Four heroes depart and five return; yet the battle is not won, but only the first skirmish. The Beloved must fall to darkness ere the light of truth is restored to the Shadow Castle! Blood and tears reign in the Shadowed Castle until the Hero Foretold comes to restore the scion to the throne."

***

Edwin Farmer to his companions on the Holy Quest in the year 3254:

"The verdant springtime lies coiled beneath the surface of the shattered lands, waiting for the call of the Beloved, to set it free. The Beloved Hero falls to darkness; he sows the poisoned seed across the shadowed land, yet will he rise up to set free the land of Mal Evol on the day the land takes him home. All will see the fruiting of the land of the Living Shades. This will be the sign; the day of redemption is at hand."

Connie J Jasperson, Author

 Connie J Jasperson lives in Olympia, Washington. A vegan, she and her husband share five children, a love of good food and great music. She is active in local writing groups, an editor for Myrddin Publishing Group, and is a writing coach. She is an active member of the both the Northwest Independent Writers Association and Pacific Northwest Writers Association, and is a founding member of Myrddin Publishing Group. Music and food dominate her waking moments. When not writing or blogging she can be found with her Kindle, reading avidly. You can find her blogging on her writing life at:

Life in the Realm of Fantasy

http://conniejjasperson.wordpress.com

MYRDDIN PUBLISHING GROUP
Book List

WWW.MYRDDINPUBLISHING.COM

URBAN FANTASY ~ PARANORMAL ~ ROMANCE

YUM by Nicole Antonia Carson (YA)
Can Jim and his great-granddaughter Emily stop the carnage?

Brawn Stroker's Dragula: The Journal of Dee Flaytable by
Nicole Antonia Carro (Mature Readers)
When the Vampire Queens battle, who will win? Dragula is pure smut.
Enjoy!

HEART SEARCH SERIES by Carlie M.A. Cullen (New Adult)
HEART SEARCH, book one: Lost, HEART SEARCH, book two:
Found
One bite starts it all. . .Fate toys with mortals and immortals alike, as
two hearts torn apart by darkness face ordeals which test them to
their limits.

THE GUARDIAN SERIES by Joan Hazel (New Adult)
Book I THE LAST GUARDIAN, Book II BURDENS OF A
SAINT
Delta Pack is an elite force of shape-shifters charged with
maintaining order in both the shifter and human communities. High
adventure and sizzling romance!

HIRED BY A DEMON by Gypsy Madden (YA)
A simple babysitting position goes terribly awry for Vara…Urban fantasy at its best!

GIRLS CAN'T BE KNIGHTS by Lee French (YA urban paranormal)

~~~

SCIENCE FICTION

LAND OF NOD SERIES by Gary Hoover (Appropriate for all ages)
Book I—The Artifact,
Book II - The Prophet
Jeff Browning has been haunted by terrifying dreams since the mysterious disappearance of his father (a renowned physicist). But when he finds a portal in his father's office, he must overcome his fears in an attempt to find him.

THE DREAM LAND Series BY Stephen Swartz
Book I Long Distance Voyager,
The Dream Land 2 - Dreams of Futures Past,
The Dream Land 3 - Diaspora
An epic of interdimensional intrigue, alien romance, and world domination by a couple of high school nerds mashed with psychological thriller and time travel.

MAZE BESET TRILOGY by Lee French (Superhero science fiction)
Dragons In Pieces
Dragons In Chains
Dragons In Flight
Superheroes in denim.

~~~

STEAMPUNK

THE CROWN PHOENIX SERIES by Alison DeLuca (Teen)
The Night Watchman Express
Devil's Kitchen
The Lamplighter's Special
The South Sea Bubble
A magic typewriter, time-travel, a mysterious train—high adventure written with Edwardian flair!

The Infinity Bridge (The Nu-Knights) by Ross M. Kitson (Teen)
Three teenagers are propelled into an action-packed race against time, involving alternate realities, airships, clockwork killers.... and Merlin.

~~~

LITERARY FICTION

AFTER ILIUM by Stephen Swartz (Mature readers)
Seduction and betrayal on the road to Ilium. An epic of interdimensional intrigue, alien romance, and world domination by a couple of high school nerds mashed with psychological thriller and time travel.

TALES FROM THE DREAMTIME by Connie J. Jasperson
(Literary Fantasy, Mature Readers)

Three grownup Tales from the Dreamtime in one novella....A conversation with Galahad, a prince on a quest and a goddess in mourning, a stolen kingdom and the Fractal Mirror. Three tales of wonder and great deeds, three tales of heroes and villains.

HUW THE BARD by Connie J. Jasperson (Medieval Fantasy, Mature Readers)
Fleeing a burning city, everything he ever loved in ashes behind him, penniless and hunted, no place is safe. Abandoned and alone, Huw the Bard must somehow survive.

~~~

EPIC FANTASY

TOWER OF BONES SERIES by Connie J Jasperson (Epic Fantasy, Mature Readers)
Book I, Tower of Bones
Book II Forbidden Road
The Gods are at war, and Neveyah is the battleground.

DAMSEL IN DISTRESS by Lee French under Tangled Sky Press (Dark fantasy)
Even cut flowers can bloom.

PRISM SERIES by Ross M. Kitson (Epic Fantasy, Mature Readers)

Darkness Rising 1 – Chained

Darkness Rising 2 – Quest

Darkness Rising 3 – Secrets

Darkness Rising 4 – Loss

Darkness Rising 5 - Broken

Bravery is measured in moments. The forces of darkness are rising—and tragedy awaits even the most heroic.

THE GREATEST SIN SERIES by Lee French and Erik Kort under Tangled Sky Press (Epic fantasy)

    The Fallen

    Harbinger

    Moon Shades

Prophecy. Secrets. Lies. It's all an illusion

unique electronic & print books

United States   United Kingdom   Australia